Glass Houses

STELLA CAMERON

Glass Houses

𝓴

KENSINGTON BOOKS

http://www.kensingtonbooks.com

KENSINGTON BOOKS are published by

Kensington Publishing Corp.
850 Third Avenue
New York, NY 10022

Library of Congress Card Catalogue Number: 99-069391
ISBN 1-57566-586-7

First Printing: August, 2000
10 9 8 7 6 5 4 3 2 1

Printed in the United States of America

For Kate Duffy, of course!

ACKNOWLEDGMENTS

Todd F. Heiman, Detective, 17th Detective Squad, NYPD
    For his generous help and for answering even the questions I hadn't thought to ask but should have!
Al Regenhard, Detective Sergeant, Midtown South Precinct Detective Squad, NYPD
    For his sense of humor and willingness to entertain my "what ifs?"
Jerry Cameron
    For walking my walk yet again, and for map, route, and time-zone assistance.
Bryan Phillippe
    For having constructive fun with electronic communication questions.
Kate Duffy
    New York consultant.
Suzanne Simmonds
    Midwest consultant.
Philip and Lynne Lloyd-Worth
    London consultants.
Teresa Salgado
    For photography guidance.

Thank you,
    Stella Cameron

One

The next sucker who told Aiden Flynn, detective NYPD, to get a life was dead meat.

Lightning crazed the night sky over Hell's Kitchen and kept a man praying for thunder . . . and rain, rain, rain. Why didn't it rain, dammit? And why had he agreed to babysit Ryan Hill's orchids? And why didn't he just quit now that Detective Hill had gone AWOL after his upstate vacation with dear ol' Dad? Oh, sure, Dad was too sick to be left alone. Probably needed help in and out of the indoor pool at the mountain estate Ryan liked to brag about.

Ah, hell, the suffocating air, or lack of it, was mangling his nerves. Truth was, curiosity kept him coming upstairs from his own apartment to tend plants belonging to a guy he didn't like. Curiosity and competition. His own orchids would do as well as these if he had the equivalent of a green house rather than a couple of lousy, make-do cabinets he'd rigged himself.

Living on the top floor of the building, where an old but sturdy wall of windows wrapped over several feet of sun-sucking roof space, Ryan D. Hill's (never mention that the D stood for Douglas) oncidiums bloomed, one plant after another. Currently, umber and cream blossoms cascaded from small forests of spikes on two Shari Baby specimens. Aiden's oncidiums hadn't produced one bloom, ever.

His cell phone beeped discreetly. What did it say about a man when he was grateful his phone rang? He flipped the instrument open, jabbed at it with his thumb, and said, "Yeah?"

"Vanni here."

"*Finally*. That heap of electronic junk you put together for me is on the fritz again."

"So?" For a boy from a good Italian family in Brooklyn, Vanni Zanetto tended to be short on the words.

"I've got things to do tonight—"

"Places to go?" Vanni said, dead flat. "People to see? Sure, I know. Enjoy. How's my dog?"

"Boss is just fine. And he's *my* dog. Don't change the subject. That damned computer turns Greek on me. No kidding, not a moment's warning, and everything just translates into Greek. Looks like Greek to me, anyway. I'm spending my time getting out and getting in again."

"Lucky guy. Congratulations. Is she a good looker?"

Vanni could be too quick to live. "Save that," Aiden said. "But make sure your mama doesn't find out what a dirty mind you've got. Just get over here and work your magic, buddy."

A sigh wafted, long and theatrical, across the distance between them. "Mama was askin' about you, Aiden. She's got another nice girl she wants you to meet."

"Have you met her?"

"No, but—"

"Sure, I should trust your mama again. I haven't forgotten Milly the garlic-lover."

"So what's wrong with liking a little garlic?"

"Vanni, the woman had to be using the stuff as body lotion. She might even have been substituting garlic rubs for showers—how the hell would I know?" He felt guilty for knocking Milly. "Hey, she's a nice girl, just not my type of nice girl, okay?"

"But this new one—"

"Will you come fix my computer, partner? It'll take me all night to do it myself."

"You'd never manage it yourself," Vanni said.

"I'll let that pass. I gotta get online if I'm going to get any sleep. You know how cranky I am if I don't get any sleep before I go on duty—and you're the one who'll have to listen to me."

"Hey, Aiden old buddy, why don't you hop in your beloved pink panther and get over here? We could drop in at Sully's and—"

"Pink pony." By accident or design, Vanni couldn't seem to get Aiden's favorite wheels, his mint-condition '67 pink Mustang, right—or any car in his beloved collection. "I'm not going anywhere but online. Thanks, anyway."

"Dammit, Aiden." Vanni's temper wasn't hard to arouse. "When are you goin' to quit foolin' around with people you know you'll never meet, and get out in the world?"

"I'm out there every day. It doesn't have much to recommend it."

"Listen, I'll say this slow and quiet," Vanni told him. "Just see how slow and quiet I can be. That's because I care about you. I worry because you're living some sort of surreal existence with a bunch of virtual pals. You do it because you feel safe with 'em. They'll never ring your bell in the middle of the night and ask if you want company, or expect you to make some sort of move on 'em."

"Vanni—"

"Let me finish. You're lonely, but you're scared shitless of commitment."

Aiden felt his temper begin a burn. "You just stepped way over the line. And where's the woman you've committed yourself to, huh?"

Vanni delivered another world-class sigh. "We're gonna talk. Later. And there's nothing wrong with Italian girls. I'll get there when I can—but only 'cause I want to visit Boss." He broke the connection.

"Nice Italian girls," Aiden muttered, not that he hadn't met wonderful Italian women, but he was allergic to being fixed up by or with anyone.

Ryan D's grow lights were all functioning perfectly, his fans oscillating nicely. Too bad.

On a fancy teak and sleek stainless-steel desk with the curved lines of Scandinavian furniture, sat Ryan's computer monitor with its impressive twenty-one inch screen. Beneath the desk on a conveniently wheeled trolley was his computer tower. Aiden couldn't recall how many gigabytes the miraculous hard drive boasted, nor how much memory Detective Hill repeatedly mentioned. If Aiden didn't know better, he'd wonder about his own memory, but he knew himself too well, and was well aware of the less-than-generous habit he had of forgetting what was either unimportant or annoying.

There was Ryan's machine—undoubtedly in perfect operating condition and faster than anything Aiden got to use, while one floor down the "bargain" beast Vanni had assembled groaned and refused to come to heel.

Aiden approached the big screen in its luminous blue case. Who had ever even seen a luminous blue case on a computer monitor? The keyboard was one of those two-part jobs, one for the left hand and one for the right hand—also blue. Large enough for most people to curl a whole hand around, the mouse occupied its own miniature oriental carpet.

Which led to another question: With all of his money, why did Ryan D need to bother his fetid little brain, and his delicate sensibilities, with the business of being a homicide detective? Maybe, rather than having to look after his now-sick father, Ryan had finally twigged to how unsuited he was to life among the unsavory. Maybe he would never come back at all.

A guy could hope.

Aiden sat in Ryan's soft, gray-leather chair and morosely regarded the dark screen. From time to time an orange light flashed below and he heard a perfect life-form churning softly within the machine.

His own hand was too long on the mouse; he'd probably have to use it with just the tips of his fingers. He tested his theory and jerked his hand away instantly. Too late. A faint snapping sounded, and a list appeared—Ryan's incoming mail. After two weeks that list was likely to be long enough to make an orderly mind cringe.

Vanni would take his own sweet time getting here. Why not check e-mail from this machine? Ryan wouldn't mind—and since he'd never know, it didn't matter anyway.

"Nope, Aiden. You can wait." He got up and scanned the bank of wall switches that controlled Ryan's orchid setup.

The list on the computer screen rolled up. Another post came in, and another.

It couldn't hurt to take a look at his own mail from here.

Lightning cracked again, and he glanced at rooftops briefly illuminated. Thunder followed almost at once, low thunder that rumbled on and on like the sound of boulders gathering speed down a mountainside. The weather had been weird, slightly out of whack, all year. Now winter approached but dragged a sultry trail behind it, a nod of the head to an Indian summer that never was.

"And here comes the rain," he muttered, and breathed long and deep. "Oh, yeah." First the big showy drops that needed space to spatter, but blessedly soon a torrent that clattered on Ryan's coveted overhead glass.

Rain made Aiden's soul open up. He could breathe again.

OliviaFitz@bargain.uk was the first entry he actually read on Ryan's list.

Who'd have thought it? Aiden grinned. The crown prince of the 17th Precinct was a closet bargain shopper. Maybe the Ferragamo dress shoes he wore to work were knock-offs.

There was OliviaFitz again. And again. At first he read the names of the people writing to Ryan idly. Soon enough he leaned forward to examine the times on Ms. Olivia's posts. They had arrived from half an hour to an hour apart. Why would someone need to write a series of messages rather than one long one?

None of his damn business.

A siren soared and Aiden smiled. The sound of his city at night. New York being New York. He liked everything about the place.

Thunder roared again, shaking the old building.

Ryan's miraculous machine and its view panel didn't even flicker.

The top post on the e-mail list was highlighted. Aiden tapped the mouse and watched OliviaFitz's message unfold on the screen.

One of the blessings about being a cop was that it took a lot to make you feel guilty. Hey, maybe there was something here that Ryan needed to know about—now.

Rain fell even harder. The lights over Ryan's orchids spread an eerie blue glow that cast reflections of the plants on the windows. Behind the orchids Aiden could see himself at a distance, and the door behind him. He shifted uneasily, then felt stupid.

Ryan Hill wasn't buying phony Ferragamos online.

"Good to hear from you again, Sam. You're so logical and I do appreciate your advice."

Sam?

"I will think about accepting the kill fee for the London Style *layout, but it's awfully strange for the magazine to change its mind. Even if I didn't need the money for this commission, I could really use the credit. Cheerio, Olivia."*

Nothing Ryan needed to know there. She must have the wrong address for her Sam. But what, he wondered, was a kill fee? He might consider it a foreign term for a hit contract, but the context didn't fit.

Maybe it would be kind to take a look at another post from her and see if he ought to let her know Sam wasn't reading what she wrote. Evidently she was a Brit. Wouldn't hurt to do his bit for international relations.

"It still amazes me to think about the way we stumbled on each other. Imagine you writing to me by mistake, just trying to remember an address and getting me. Life is so odd. How can we only have met a couple of weeks ago? It feels as if we've known each other forever."

And Vanni thought his partner was lonely? The way Olivia wrote to her Sam made Aiden pity her. He might even feel sad if he could remember how.

"Having a dog yourself, you'll understand how I felt about Wilbur. He was just in too much pain to go on. I stayed with him at the end. We'd been

pals for 11 years, since I was 15. Felt like forever. Even though it's more than two years later, there's still a hole where he used to be. Forgive me for going on about it. You've been so understanding. This is strange, but I can feel how kind you are.

"Your Boswell sounds a dear. How perfectly awful that those bad men hit his mouth with a baseball bat. I'm sure it was very expensive to have some of his teeth capped with metal, but you're the kind of person who wouldn't spare any expense to help a beloved animal."

Aiden's eyes glazed. Well, hell. That was it. Ryan Hill was Sam, had to be since he'd evidently claimed ownership of Aiden's Boswell, Boss to people he didn't hate. Very few called the dog Boss. *Bad men? Baseball bat?* Wait till Vanni got a load of this. Ryan Hill, alias Sam, and a dog-hater trying to impress some Brit female with his generosity to animals. And lying about Aiden's Boss, an ornery retired police dog who had earned his titanium mashers by keeping his teeth embedded in a rapist's arm while the crazy bastard slammed away at the animal's mouth with the butt of an empty gun.

And Olivia could feel how kind Ryan was?

"*Anyway,*" she continued, "*thank you for writing back so quickly. How do you stand the unpredictable weather in New York? I melt when the temperature gets close to 80, and freeze at anything below 40. I must admit that you make Hell's Kitchen sound intriguing . . .*"

Dear Ryan was definitely Dear Sam. So the stud who boasted that he had a woman for every night of the week and some to spare, still went looking for extra jollies among what Vanni called "virtual pals." Who'd have thought it?

"*Are you sure you have an extra room I could use? Oh, what am I saying? I know I won't come, but it is awfully sweet of you to offer. Toodles, Olivia.*"

The message had been sent about two hours ago.

He ought to check his mail and get out of here.

Slowly, he clicked on Olivia's next post and felt an unfamiliar rush of remorse. He was snooping out of idle curiosity—and boredom.

"*Sam: Thank you for saying you do mean it about the room. As I already wrote, I really appreciate the offer.*"

Aiden fell back in the chair and stared. Obviously Ryan had read and responded to the first post Aiden had read. Ryan was communicating with Olivia from wherever he was right now. He was picking up his e-mail at a remote location and answering Olivia from that location.

If he brought her here, it would be obvious he'd lied about the dog. Which meant he didn't intend to bring her here. Why would he lie about something like that?

It was just a game. People played these games all the time. Like Olivia said, she would never come to the States.

Ryan might hate Boss, but the feeling was more than mutual.

So what? This was fiction—mostly fiction.

"Okay, I'm just going to tell you the truth. I'm frightened, Sam, and you're the only one likely to give me sensible advice. While I was out today, someone must have got into the house. I know what you'll be thinking— why am I just writing about it now? They searched my darkroom—nowhere else—and I only just went down there. It's in the basement. I probably wouldn't have known they'd been here at all if I wasn't so compulsive about keeping my work organized.

"This is weird, but I think I know what they may have been searching for: the photos for Penny Biggles's London Style *layout. I don't know what made me take all the prints and negs with me when I went out, I just did. Maybe it was what you told me that made me more cautious. I rang up* London Style *a little while ago. They don't know anything about the kill fee that man called to offer me. I should try to explain myself better. As you know, I photographed a London house for Penny. It's a fabulous place in Notting Hill—and some of the shots will be used to illustrate an article being written about her work. At least, I still hope they will. Penny was the designer. Whoever was in here didn't actually take anything in my workroom as far as I can tell, or move a thing in any other part of the house. They must have wanted these.*

*"*London Style *told me they still expect to use the piece. So the call about someone coming here to see me and bringing money, the kill fee, but wanting to have the pictures in case they could place them was a hoax, right? Which means my photographs are valuable to someone. The authorities are the best ones to deal with this now—or they might be if I had something more definite to tell them. My friend, Mark Donnely, is an investigator for an insurance company. He'd probably have a good idea."*

Aiden let the screen go black and stood up. He'd taken the prying too far.

The door opened and he jumped before he heard Vanni say, "Thought I'd find you up here. Jealousy is bad news, buddy. You covet the guy's orchids. I hope he counted 'em before he left."

"Petty theft isn't my thing."

Vanni came all the way into the apartment. Even by the subdued light, his solid bulk and the vitality that hovered around him were big, powerful. He said, "What is your thing?"

"Reading Ryan's e-mail," Aiden said, for the shock value. "Actually, Sam's e-mail. That's who our slimy colleague is when he's chatting up women online."

Vanni chuckled, then was silent. Rain glittered in his dark, curly hair and on his leather jacket. He approached the computer, his substantial shoulders swinging as he sidestepped the chair to stand over Ryan's screen. Vanni tapped the mouse and jutted his chin when he started scanning the list of mail that appeared.

"What d'you think you're doing?" Aiden asked. "Don't you have a conscience?"

"Yeah. Around here somewhere. Probably hangin' out with yours."

Aiden took a seat in the gray-leather chair again and watched while Vanni read Olivia's first epistle, and the second. "Shee-it," he muttered. "What's he up to?"

"If we read on, we may find out. But we aren't going to read on, are we?"

Vanni turned his head to look at Aiden. "Aren't we?"

"Let's say someone's sneaking into Ryan's setup . . ." Aiden swung the chair gently to and fro. "No, let's say someone's hit Ryan, buried him up in those hills, and now the killer's infiltrating Ryan's persona. A crazy, naturally."

"Naturally," Vanni said, grinning. "Poor old Ryan. And we never had a chance to finish figuring out if he's really a cop gone bad."

This was one of Vanni's favorite theories. He was convinced Ryan Hill—and maybe his sinuous little partner, Fats Lemon—were on the take.

Aiden shook his head and took the mouse away. He opened the next piece of mail from Olivia. When had he started calling this stranger Olivia?

You really think I should keep quiet about all this and bring the photos and negatives to America for safekeeping? This seems extreme, but I want to agree. I wonder why you're so against my idea of approaching Mark. You must be reacting as an FBI agent. And you're nervous, too, aren't you? You think whoever's doing this could be anyone—including Mark. That wouldn't make any sense, but you aren't to know that.

Vanni snorted. He gestured as only he could. "Will you look at that? He thinks he's more irresistible as a fed than NYPD. Schmuck. Maybe my ambition's changed. Why help him retire altogether? Why not get him busted down to the beat?"

"Mama," Aiden said, "wouldn't approve of plotting, in particular plotting for no more honorable reason than you don't like a guy."

"Schmuck," Vanni muttered.

"Read on," Aiden told him.

"Sam, maybe I'm overreacting and letting my imagination run away with me, but what if I did come to you and someone frightful followed me on the plane? Wouldn't that be terribly dangerous? They could hold up the plane, hijack it or something."

"The lady's a dramatist," Vanni said.

Aiden said, "The lady's scared. She ought to be. Whatever game friend Ryan's playing—if he really means he wants her and her photos here—there's something very wrong with the way it smells."

"Read the next one," Vanni said, bracing himself on the desk.

"Yeah. Only twenty minutes between the two."

"All right, I'll come if you think it's best to put distance between me and London. Oh, dear, I really am quite frightened now, I must say. We've never met, yet I feel I know you better than I've ever known any man. I don't know what I should do without you. I'm alone here. Mummy and Daddy wouldn't understand, and Daddy would blunder about making such an embarrassing fuss.

"I suppose I could book up and let you know when I'll be arriving. Thank goodness for credit cards. I never thought I'd say that. I hope we'll know each other when we meet—if we meet. We should have found a way to exchange photographs. I have a scanner, of course. I know you don't, but you could have used someone else's."

Aiden looked not only at Ryan's scanner, but at the digital camera on the desk beside the keyboard. Explanation needed—soon.

"I'm very ordinary looking," Olivia continued. *"Brown hair and eyes, sturdy, average height and, according to Penny, a sartorial disaster. Sorry about that. I'll be wearing a hat. I almost always wear a hat. And I know it's corny, but I'll put a flower on my lapel. You could do that, too. We may as well try to lighten things up a bit."*

That was the last post.

"Batty," Vanni said.

Aiden agreed. "Deranged."

"They could be perfect for each other."

"He could be planning to rip her off."

"What's she got to rip off?" Vanni asked. "She doesn't even have the price of an airline ticket."

"It's an expensive ticket."

"Not that expensive."

The bell announcing incoming mail rang on Ryan's computer. OliviaFitz's name showed up together with, *"That man just rang up again. He asked if I'd thought about the kill fee and said he was on his way to talk to me in person. They obviously don't think I suspect anything. I tried to get Penny, but she's not at home and I can't find her. I'm getting out of here. I'll call the airport, then I'll give you the flight number. See you in New York."*

Two

Stress made Olivia hungry. In moments of boredom, anxiety, or when the weather got really gray—which was often in fair London Town—she found herself in the kitchen, in front of the open fridge door with no memory of how she got there. But middle-of-the-night raids on Hampstead's fragrant twenty-four-hour bakery on Heath Street spelled out-of-control emotional upheaval.

She was having one of those out-of-control upheavals tonight, or this morning. It was very early on a clear morning and Olivia FitzDurham, she who was considered slightly wacky but generally cautious, was standing before the display cases in GIVE IN AND DIE HAPPY, prepared to do just that.

The aromas were incredible. Fresh bread, Banbury cakes, Chelsea buns, custard-filled donuts that still sizzled, macaroons and Madeira cake. And those trays of marzipan fancies, the heaps of tender Battenberg slices. She wanted one of each, but most of all she wanted fresh, dissolve-in-the-mouth raspberry jelly rolls coated with coconut shavings and powdered sugar. A fresh batch would soon slide onto a wire rack and cloud the glass case with titillating steam through which she would play peekaboo with the objects of her desire.

With a sigh, she closed her eyes. Then she drew in a deep breath and heard the only other customer in the shop, a man who had just entered, echo that sigh. From the corner of her eye she saw him pick up a French loaf. Light and flaky on the outside, it would be so soft and warm on the inside.

With his teeth, he tore off one end. Olivia watched his reflection in the mirror at the back of a wall case, watched him chew rhythmically—and look at her. Even behind his dark glasses, in profile, she saw how he eyed her slowly from head to foot while steadily turning a mouthful of light bread back into dough.

She averted her face, only to be confronted by herself, and a not very appealing picture she made. Her red woolen boater sat foolishly on the back of her head and did nothing to tame the ringlet-like curls her hair sprang into when there was even a hint of moisture in the air. For the rest, her old tan raincoat belted haphazardly around her middle was a disgrace.

This was all nutty. The truth was that she knew any thought of hopping on a plane to New York to meet a man who had accidentally fallen over her on the Internet—only two weeks earlier—was out of the question. But her rapidly withering hopes for adventure made her want to do it anyway. One of her occasional silly tendencies to be superstitious caused her to fear this could be her last chance at something even remotely daring, and she didn't want to miss it.

She had to miss it.

The man chewed with his mouth open. Olivia couldn't stop herself from glancing at him once more—and finding him staring at her yet again. He made no attempt to smile. His black trilby was pulled well down over his eyes, throwing the top half of his thin face into shadow except for the glint of shoplights on his opaque lenses. A wobbly bag of empty skin stretched from beneath his chin to be gathered in by a starched white shirt collar. His precisely knotted tie was green with some sort of subdued, repeated pattern, and he wore the type of suit favored by most men who worked in the City: black with vertical white stripes. Streaky-bacon suits, some called them.

He kept on staring, and she wasn't about to be the first to drop her gaze. Ridiculous fellow. Old enough to be her father but staring at her in the most inappropriate manner. Threatening in a way.

A squeak distracted her, but she couldn't tell where it came from.

Embarrassment had made her put off letting Sam know she'd come to her senses. She should already have posted to say she wouldn't be going to New York, but he'd think her such an appalling ninny. Thus the jelly rolls. A couple of plump Chelsea buns filled with succulent raisins, currants and sultanas, wound together with cinnamon sauce and topped with sweet white frosting that dripped down the sides would be good with her morning tea, and they'd keep her mind off what she really wanted to do—but really mustn't.

Another squeak.

An assistant returned to the shop with cream-filled meringue pillows. "Won't be long with the jelly rollies, luv," he said to Olivia. Of the other customer, he asked, "Ready, are you, guv?"

The man shook his head but didn't answer. The boy behind the counter shrugged and returned to the kitchens.

Olivia grew increasingly uncomfortable. Her stomach ached vaguely and jumped unpleasantly. Several more squeaks raised her suspicion that she was hearing some sort of rodent, or rodents. The sight of the man dropping crumbs into his coat pockets, then patting them as something moved inside, convinced and sickened her.

When she tore her attention from the squirming pockets she was confronted with the chilling vision of the stranger smiling at her, showing crowded, yellowing teeth while he chewed on. What was left of the loaf he held in both hands and squeezed as if he were strangling a very tiny neck.

"Jelly rollies," the returning assistant sang out. " 'Arf a dozen luverly hot, sticky raspberry rollies with extra coconut and sugar just for you, luv." He put the cakes into a crackly white bag, handed it to Olivia, took her money and made change.

She thanked him and went toward the door.

"And you, guv? Ready now, are you?"

That earned him another silent shake of the head before the man waited for Olivia to pass and turned to observe her when she stepped outside. She went to the curb and waited for a milk dray to pass before crossing the street. In a window ahead she soon saw the rodent fancier take up position on the curb she'd just left.

He was going to follow her.

Fighting against a painful pulsing in her throat, Olivia looked around. No police were in sight, not that she could rush up to an officer and accuse someone of . . . of what? He'd have to do something—like attack her—before she could ask for help.

It was early enough for the night chill to linger. The skin on her face felt tight and icy. The sweat on her back felt icy, too, and she breathed with only the tops of her lungs.

Oh, she was overreacting because of the break-in. She started walking toward home.

He followed. Others passed, but she could isolate the sound of his small, polished shoes clapping on the pavement.

If she went straight home, he'd find out where she lived. It was dark along tiny Back Lane. The street lights would come on again for a while, but not for an hour or so.

Ahead, a steady stream of early workers converged on the tube station. These were the ones who went into downtown London before most people awoke.

Olivia arrived at the station, turned right abruptly, and made for the platforms deep in the bowels of the black earth.

Crammed into a grinding, rattling lift, she held her breath while they groaned downward to one of London's deepest stations. Men in bowler hats silently clutched copies of the *London Times,* and suited women joined in the game of "if I don't meet anyone's eyes, I must be alone." Teenaged girls chattered, displaying pierced tongues to match their pierced eyebrows and noses.

A bumpy stop and the doors opened to disgorge the latest stream of travelers. The thunderously echoing run broke out. On the underground everyone who could, ran. Olivia walked past garish ads pasted to the walls. The London theater scene hawked its rich offerings on tattered posters.

Olivia decided she'd take a Jubilee line train, go one stop to Finchley Road, and double back, making sure she wasn't still being followed.

Commuters swarmed along the platform to find spaces to wait. Across the pit, where electrified rails spat and popped, they stared at more billboards, these huge against grimy cream tiles that covered the walls.

An announcer's voice wa-wa'd, harmonica-like, over the speaker system and not a word was intelligible. Olivia dived behind a pair of passengers and peered between them at those who approached. So far there was no sign of the man with the bread. She glanced repeatedly at the hanging electric signboard where upcoming trains were posted. The next one was no good. It arrived, sucked fresh victims into its too bright compartments, and shot away again.

Olivia backed farther along the platform, catching up a discarded copy of *The Mirror* from a bench as she went. She opened the paper, surreptitiously poked a hole through it and held it before her face. The platform was filling up again, this time with a bigger crowd, but the man wasn't to be seen.

This wasn't the type of excitement she craved. She wanted to go to the States because she wanted to meet Sam. The thought made her ears burn. That wasn't the only reason. There was the *London Style* mixup, but the authorities here could have taken care of it. Possibly.

Olivia FitzDurham's behavior was totally out of character. The thought made her smile. Who would ever have thought it, Olivia doing something wildly unlike her usual ordinary self—make that her ordinary, boring and *prissy* self.

Well, others might think her prissy, but they weren't inside her head where the wild dreams lived, were they?

Even though she'd never seen Sam, she had a mental picture of him and she liked what she saw there. She'd actually had erotic thoughts about a man who was only words on a computer screen.

Thoughts and feelings, and she'd enjoyed them.

There, that was total honesty, and it would be very difficult to go to the local police now. Mark would be disappointed she hadn't gone directly to him, too, which she also couldn't bring herself to do. If she'd intended to report the incident, it should have been done at once. Not long after the fact.

She craved just one outlandish adventure. There had been too few of them in her life, none that she particularly recalled, in fact.

Was it so much to ask? That she go to meet a man who aroused her without a look or touch?

She turned a page and shuffled the paper to clear her peephole. That aberration hadn't followed her after all. Muscles in her shoulders relaxed and she breathed more evenly.

The loudspeaker blared again. More babble. Movement drew her attention to the tracks. Several feet below the level of the platform, they shone dully in their soot-caked trough. Olivia could smell the soot, and she could see rats scurrying back and forth. They must survive down there because they were too light to electrocute themselves on the rails.

Olivia averted her eyes to the tattered hole in her paper and gritted her teeth. There he was, that horrible man, and he was stuffing crisps into his mouth from one of several bags he held in the crook of an arm.

He finished a bag and let it fall to the platform, then tore open a new supply. With the precision of a machine, his hand rose and fell from his lips. He stood perilously close to the edge and divided his attention between the darting rodents and studying the people who came through the entrance to the platform and marched toward him. Repeatedly, he stood on tiptoe to get a better view. Looking for her, she was sure.

Olivia fidgeted. One hand went to her throat, but the newspaper folded away from her face and she grabbed it again. Her train was posted now. Another empty crisp bag, the last one, fluttered to the ground. The man made a motion with one hand. He only watched the passengers now, but he dropped crumbs from his clenched right fist onto the tracks.

He was feeding the rats.

Sickened, Olivia made herself look again. His back shook while he continued to toss crumbs. Laughter. He was deeply entertained by the rats' antics. A small, thin person in a black trilby with the brim turned down. His head and body, in a streaky-bacon suit, seemed all one.

The tracks vibrated, heralding the approach of the next train. Olivia pressed to the wall, gauging her next move. If he got on, she wouldn't. And she'd hope he didn't see her before the train left.

One glance toward the exit. Another glance back. He'd gone. She couldn't see him. Where was he? Olivia looked behind her, cringing, expecting to see him there.

The sound of the train grew louder, but it wasn't loud enough to drown out a great gust of noise, a swelling gasp with a chorus of spine-tingling screams and hysterical yells.

Alarms sounded, then the wail of a warning siren. The train's brakes howled on the tracks and the thing grated and sparked to a stop halfway along the platform. The doors remained closed, and faces pressed against the insides of the windows.

One man's voice roared above the rest, "Is she dead?"

Olivia's legs wobbled. Her insides jumped and she became aware of tears streaming down her face. With her back still against the wall, she slid along behind the straining mass of onlookers. Looking at what?

Faces turned this way and that. Mouths opened and closed, but Olivia couldn't seem to hear what they said. Someone nearby said, "They think she was pushed." "Nah," another said, sneering in an attempt to sound tough, "she'll 'ave tripped. I don't understand why some of 'em gets so close to the edge."

"Excuse me," Olivia whispered, "please excuse me."

No one heard.

She made her shaky way toward the exit. Some poor woman had been in a terrible accident. Just standing there, waiting for a train to take her to work, she'd been hurled . . . Olivia dropped the paper and put her hands over her ears. She couldn't do anything to help.

Stumbling, she carried on until a new spectacle tossed another wave of disturbance into the crowd. Medics, firemen and policemen dashed into view, ordering people aside as they came.

Olivia reached the clearing made by the arriving professionals. She tried not to look at the object of their burst of activity, but failed.

Close to the edge of the platform lay a woman. Her ashen face was turned toward Olivia and blood ran in garish streamers over her skin, but her eyes were slightly open and her lips moved.

A great leap of hope and gratitude all but sent Olivia to her knees.

She stood still, drove her hands repeatedly into her pockets and smiled through tears.

"If he hadn't been so quick, she'd have been down there." A kneeling woman pointed to the tracks, then indicated a man in jeans and a sweatshirt who looked as white as the patient. "She was already going over the edge when he grabbed her. He could have been pulled in with her, but he didn't think about himself."

Olivia made another search for the man from the bakery, but he'd obviously slipped away. Probably because the possibility of meeting the law scared him off. Coward.

The medics had opened a gurney and were immobilizing the woman preparatory to moving her.

Olivia stepped closer. She had to. Someone picked up a woolen hat that rested half on and half off the edge of the platform. He said, "This is a bit tatty but it could have been worse. Her brains could have been in it." His nervous laugh brought a weak, answering titter from a few shocked observers.

The hat was red, bright red.

Reddish-brown curls fanned out from the prostrate woman's head.

The belt on her old tan raincoat had snapped and trailed at her sides.

Olivia tore off her own hat and spun away. She crept into the tunnel leading to the lifts, searching around her with each step. When a lift arrived and opened, she looked inside before entering with a crowd, and facing the direction she'd come from. Sounds bombarded her, and the frenetic beat of her heart joined in the fearsome racket.

The lift doors slowly closed, and once more she gave thanks for her good luck, but an instant before heavy rubber moldings thumped together, the man from the bakery came into view. He ran, held onto the crown of his hat with one hand and waved the other while he yelled, "Wait." He wore dark glasses that should have made it all but impossible to see down here. "Hold the lift!"

"Like 'ell we will," a girl with turquoise dreadlocks said. She knocked away the fingers of someone coming to the runner's aid and the door slid closed. "Some of us has got work t'do. 'Angin' about for one of them streaky-suited City gents? Not likely, mate."

That poor woman down there had almost died, almost been killed. Olivia was convinced there had been an attempted murder, and that she had been the intended victim. The woman had been unlucky enough to bear a marked resemblance to her and to be wearing clothes too similar to be discernible from Olivia's in a madly heated moment.

Now, the would-be murderer—and she knew without a doubt it was the man at the bakery—would make his getaway, but that didn't mean that if he was crazy enough, he wouldn't be back once he discovered he'd not only failed to kill, but had attacked the wrong victim.

From her right pocket Olivia drew out the bakery bag. It was a squelching mass, the inside coated with thick red jelly.

Three

The phone rang.

Olivia didn't know how long she'd been sitting at her desk, staring straight ahead at her computer screen and trying to decide what to do next.

She pushed her chair back.

It could be that nasty person calling about the photographs again. He spoke as if he had cotton wool in his mouth, or as if he was talking through a flannel still wet from washing his face with it. An amateurish attempt at disguising his voice. And if she of all people knew it was a trick, well then, it was silly. But it was very nasty indeed, too. Not that anything would ever be as frightening again after what had happened at the tube station.

If she answered and it was him, she could try to put him off from coming here, say she'd meet him somewhere instead. She picked up the phone and said, "Hello, Olivia FitzDurham here."

"Olivia. It's Penny. Thank God you're back. I've been trying to reach you for hours."

"I haven't been gone hours. Where are you? I tried to call you until late last night."

"There's no time for talk," Penny said. "I'm in France. I haven't got time to tell you what's happened, not right now. I had to run. Now you have to run."

Olivia massaged her eyes. "We'd better contact the police."

"No! Oh, no, Olivia. If you call the police, we're finished. I've been threatened. If there's any police interest, they've said they'll . . . Olivia, they'll kill me."

"You've got to talk to me," Olivia said, falling over her words, driving a fist into her stomach. "Please. I've got to know what's going on. Someone already tried to kill me, tried to push me under a train." She wouldn't take time to explain how she'd pieced the evidence together.

"Oh, my God," Penny whispered. "And they're trying to blackmail me. It's mad. Pack up and leave. Do it. Don't wait, Olivia. For my sake, don't wait."

Olivia bowed her head until her forehead rested on the desk and whispered, "Okay, I'll do it."

Instantly the line was dead. She'd have to go ahead and take Sam up on his offer of a safe haven.

She'd barely hung up when the phone blared again. This time she snatched it up. She wouldn't gain a thing by sounding terrified. "Hello. Who do you want to speak to?"

"Hello, darling. Daddy and I were just talking, and we've decided this would be a good weekend for you to come. We—"

"Mummy." Of all the rotten luck. Mummy calling from Eton now, of all times. "Mummy, why do you and Daddy insist on getting up with the worms. Could I please—"

"Olivia! What can you be thinking of, interrupting me like that? Why, I'm quite bemused by you. That's another thing Daddy and I were talking about. You've changed. And it's up with the birds, not the worms. How unpleasant that sounds. *Worms.*"

A muted chime on Olivia's computer announced an incoming message from Sam, and her already thumping heart positively pounded. She opened the post.

"Olivia: Use this new address from now on. Hackers have gotten to the old one and it's not secure. Get a cash advance so you don't have to use your card to buy the ticket. Just let me know when you'll be getting in to JFK Airport and I'll meet you. Sam."

The address was, <u>MustangMan@Dakota.org</u>. How odd.

"Olivia, darling, what's the matter? Is something wrong? Talk to me at once."

"I'm fine, Mummy. A bit tired. It's already been a long day." And this new day had scarcely begun.

Another e-mail arrived.

"Olivia: Don't open anything else from this address. Contact me at MustangMan with your flight information. I'll be waiting to hear from you."

Dakota was a state, wasn't it?

She heard her mother talking, but to Olivia's father and with a hand partially over the mouthpiece. "She's behaving very strangely, I tell you, Conrad."

"Give it to me, Millicent," Daddy roared. Then he roared at Olivia, "What the dickens is going on? The P.M.'s on the telly, so hurry up, young lady."

"Nothing's wrong, Daddy." Except that a criminal might arrive at her front door shortly, and to escape another man, a would-be murderer, she was about to book a flight to New York, where she would be met by a man she had never so much as spoken to, but in whose hands she intended to place her life. Well, her safety, anyway.

Her mother's voice quavered down the line again. "Daddy says you're all right, Olivia. He says I'm making something out of nothing. I'll be the judge of that this weekend."

There was another message from Sam.

Olivia moved her mouse and highlighted the line. The subject was: "You're too quiet."

"Catch the train up, darling," Mummy said. "I worry so when you drive that terrible old Mini. It ought to be condemned."

"Yes, Mummy. I'll call you later." She slammed the receiver into its base and prayed the thing wouldn't ring again.

Now what would Sam have to say?

She turned cold and pulled her hand back. He'd told her not to answer any more posts from the old address, which meant this one wasn't from him.

It could be. No, he wouldn't be so careless.

The highlighted line gleamed, and Olivia felt sick looking at it.

It was the middle of the night—no, the early hours of the morning in New York. In Hampstead, the clock on the mantel—a little painted, porcelain affair flanked on each of its fussy sides by a shepherd and shepherdess—struck its tinkling chimes eight times. Beyond white-lace curtains at the rounded bay window over Back Lane, pale morning sunlight shone on hanging baskets of leggy fuschias suspended from the crossbar on a black lamppost, but inside the little house Olivia still needed the lamp that stood atop the creaky rolltop desk. Voices reached the second-floor sitting room at Number 2A—voices, and the occasional sound of a car's tires squidging down the steep and winding cobbled road toward Heath Street.

That photograph man could arrive at any time, but she didn't intend to be there.

She must phone an airline, and pack, and drive to Heathrow. Her camera bag was always packed and ready. Where was a decent suitcase? The green tartan grip her brother, Theo, had given her when she'd graduated from art school was the newest.

The grip was in the attic.

But the phone books were on the hall stand downstairs.

Perhaps she ought to find the suitcase, then—No, first the flight, then the case.

Theo was such a dear to let her use Number 2A while he was out of the country. He was always out of the country, and he could sell the house for a lot, she supposed. She suspected he only kept the place because he worried about his "nutter" sister and wanted to help her. Theo was a bit of a snob. Oh, not really, not more than the merest bit, but he did have strong opinions about some things and expected his sister to "marry well," even though he saw no reason to hurry into that state himself. For Olivia to "marry well," he baldly stated that a good address was important. 2A Back Lane, Hampstead, was quite a good address.

The narrow staircase was gloomy, a function of the only windows in the hall below being the stained-glass fanlight over the front door and a matching panel in the center of the door itself. Olivia had taught herself to avoid turning on the vestibule light whenever possible. As generous as Theo might be, he'd had the switches converted to the type of punch-and-run efforts Olivia had detested in France. One punched the button at the top or bottom of the stairs, depending on where one started, and ran as fast as one dared. One was inevitably left in darkness before reaching one's goal. But all this did save electricity.

Theo was in international banking.

Brollies stood, higgledy-piggledy, beneath coats hanging from brass hooks on the mahogany hall stand. A heap of tatty phone books kept company with the pointed ends of the umbrellas where they rested on a green-tinged brass tray at the base of the stand.

Oh, really, everything was taking twice as long as it should. She was tired, that was the reason. After all, a night without sleep was a bit much.

She carried the appropriate book to the bottom of the stairs and sat down to open it in her lap.

Someone used the knocker on the front door. The noise vibrated in the silent little house.

Olivia held her breath. Through the blue-and-yellow stained-glass panel she saw a shadow—a fairly clear outline, actually. Cautiously, she stood up and tiptoed closer.

The head outside might not be as far from the ground as hers.

A woman?

Still clutching the open telephone book, she slunk along the nearest wall and lowered herself to one knee. Sliding the nail on her right forefinger under one corner, Olivia eased the flap to the letterbox inward. No more than half an inch. With her cheek resting against the door, she closed her left eye, and squinted with her right. Pinstripes traveled down a double-breasted black suit jacket.

She clutched the region of her heart and leaned carefully away.

A grunt accompanied the gradual sinking of the jacket, of the person inside the jacket. A tie—green with gold ducks in flight—came into view, then a white shirt collar over which thin flesh waggled like the pouch beneath a pelican's bill.

Olivia extracted her fingernail without disaster and clamped her hand over her mouth. Scooting, she shrank into a dark corner. One of the long macs on the hallstand hung near enough for her to crouch behind it.

A familiar sharp clatter meant Olivia's visitor had opened the letterbox from his side.

Olivia's eyes felt dry, and her throat hurt. *Please let him give up and go away.* The lining in the old mackintosh was torn behind one sagging pocket. She shifted and discovered her second serviceable peephole of the day.

The man rattled the door knocker again. Rude fellow. And he did so while he pressed his face to the open letterbox and peered in. He wore his dark glasses with the small, round lenses. When he moved, evidently to get a different view into the hall, his nose came into view, a bumpy, faintly purple nose like that of the vicar of St. Paul's, where Mummy went to church.

This wasn't the vicar of St. Paul's. Unfortunately.

"Miss FitzDurham? Come on, love. Don't keep me hangin' about."

Well, that definitely wasn't the same voice as the one on the phone. Olivia breathed deeply but felt no relief.

"Let me in where we can talk quiet-like."

She might be a bit dotty on occasion, but she wasn't a fool, and she wasn't letting him in.

"If you had my boss, you'd help me out here, Miss FitzDurham. You have no idea what I go through."

The creature disgusted Olivia. Did he honestly think she wouldn't recognize him?

"Well, I can see I'm going to have to impress you. Here, take a gander at this. Go on, it'll show you I keep my word—and that I'm on the up-and-up." He pushed something through the slot, something that fell to the shining wooden floor with a solid *thunk*. Olivia was almost certain she heard the man mutter, "Blimey," but couldn't be completely sure.

Olivia positioned herself to look downward. The sun sent a shaft past fingers that still intruded into Number 2A. An envelope with banknotes spilling out basked in the spotlight. Well, this was definitely the same person as the one who rang her, but he'd forgotten his flannel this time. She wondered if his pockets still housed rats or whatever.

All was silent for too long. Olivia heard her own pulse against her eardrums. She ached from holding still.

At last he said, "Look, unless you can go invisible, you're in there. I know you are, see. Come on, let me get on with my business, there's a good girl."

His fingernails were well manicured, and he wore a diamond ring on the small finger.

"You wouldn't keep the money and not give me the photos, now, would you?"

She jolly well would not.

"The negatives are all I need if you don't want to open the door. Put them out the letterbox and I'm gone. *London Style* is always reasonable, and we're very sorry for the inconvenience."

Was that a twenty-pound note Olivia could see? The envelope was thick, so there might be quite a few of them. Sam wanted her to use cash to buy her plane ticket; probably so she wouldn't leave a definite trail for someone else to follow. She'd read about that sort of thing.

"Miss FitzDurham?"

Call the airline. Book the flight and arrange to pick up the ticket at the airport. Pack a few things and go.

Olivia cleared her throat. "Who's there?" The man had to be got rid of. She hadn't asked him to push money through the door, but he had, and he was asking for the negatives. Good enough.

"It's the man from *London Style*. If I could come in—"

"No." She pushed the mackintosh aside and stood up. "I see you've brought the money to pay me. I'll just get what you want. Thank you." Perhaps there was enough money on the hall floor to pay for her ticket; then she wouldn't have to worry about getting a cash advance.

She dashed down the uncarpeted stairs to the basement, snatched the envelope containing the Abbey House, St. John's Wood, negatives, and returned to the hall. "I'd like you to sign a receipt," she said, marveling at her resourcefulness under stress.

The man cleared his throat. "You sure you want the neighbors staring at me talking to you like this, miss?"

"Just give me a receipt and our business is done, Mr.—"

"Don't have any receipts. They told me you already had an agreement. I'm handing over the money. You don't need anything else, miss."

Olivia considered his logic. "All right." She picked up the money to make sure it wasn't a bank note on either side of pieces of newspaper. That was something she'd seen at the pictures. She riffled the contents of the envelope. No newspaper.

"Very wise," the man said.

Olivia jumped, horrified that he might be watching her. He couldn't really see her from where he was, but he would have heard her check the money. "Here," she said, pushing the negatives at him.

The letterbox closed. Olivia hurried into the dining room that fronted on the steep street and tried to get a good look at the man. He had paused briefly to check the contents of the envelope she'd given him. A moment later, he was on his way with one hand held behind his stiff back in a studied pose. Small and thin, his black shoes still shone—very small black shoes. The brim of his dark trilby was turned down and from the back his head appeared to rest directly on his shoulders. And she had seen his face again—the purple nose, the lax skin of his neck.

It was definitely him, the man who had fed the rats in his pockets at the bakery, the man who had attempted to push her under a tube train, or who had stood on the platform ready to ambush her but managed to attack the wrong woman.

There wasn't any time, not for worrying—or even being afraid.

She ran up the stairs and back into the sitting room. There wasn't any time for thinking.

TWA had a flight into Kennedy Airport leaving in a few hours. She booked a seat, scrambled up the pull-down stairs to the attic, and located the scuffed green tartan grip Theo had bought her. The neon-pink luggage tag was in a side pocket, and she strapped it to a handle.

The call to her parents was brief because she summoned a rare flash of authority when Mummy started to complain. "I'm going to France on business, and that's that," she'd said, and hung up. Really, they meant well but they did stifle one so.

Despite her brother's conviction that his sister was a "nutter," this absolutely wasn't like her, not dashing off without a good deal of consideration about the steps she intended to take.

Should she go to the police here in London?

And run the risk of getting Penny killed? What would she say anyway? That she'd got carried away by the attention of an American federal agent . . . on the Internet? That she'd discussed some odd circumstances in her life and decided, partially at his suggestion, partially because he'd written what she wanted to read, not to talk to the police here? And would she talk about Penny? And then would she go on to say that she'd just given a man a set of negatives— through her letterbox—and accepted money for them?

Do. Not. Think.

A call to the nearby mini-cab office brought a handsome man wearing a purple-and-gold turban to her door. He said nothing, only jerked his head while looking at Olivia, signifying for her to come with him. While she locked her front door and glanced around before stuffing the key under a flower pot, he flung open a back door on his burgundy-colored vehicle, leaving it open while he slung Olivia's belongings into a boot, where what looked like scrap metal lay in a rusted jumble. He got into the car and started the engine with Olivia still on the pavement. She had to leap inside and drag the door shut or he would have left her behind.

She clung to her seat while the driver—who apparently spoke no English—careened his dented sedan to Heath Street and into the congested morning traffic. Surrounded by lorries and buses, Olivia repeatedly closed her eyes when her driver battled with any vehicle obviously more powerful and well maintained than his taxi. He battled with every vehicle.

If she was slated to die today, she'd die today. But she'd already avoided death once, and now she'd started her daring journey, she felt almost invincible.

She uncurled her sweaty fingers from torn cloth seats and eased against the back.

The airline ticket cost so much she still couldn't bear to think of the figure. The woman booking agent she'd spoken to on the phone had turned all nasal and superior when Olivia mentioned that the fare seemed a bit steep. "When you book at the last minute and you don't know if you're staying over a weekend, what do you expect?"

This wasn't like her. She might prefer to think of herself as spontaneous and, well, artsy, but she was really rather timid when it came to taking risks.

This was not a risk. She was going to meet a perfectly honorable, concerned friend. And there was no longer any doubt that she'd stumbled into some sort of unsavory nonsense.

That was all the thinking she'd do for now.

Making sure the driver couldn't see her in his mirror, she opened her purse. That disgusting, despicable man back there couldn't possibly have given her enough money to pay for the ticket, but perhaps with some extra from a cash point, she still wouldn't have to actually use her card to pay for the flight.

For the first time she realized there were two envelopes rather than one. A second was adhered to the first by leftover glue where a label had been removed. Obviously she hadn't been intended to get both.

Olivia dealt with the first. On either side of the bundle inside the envelope was a twenty-pound note, with a ten-pound note next to them. Not much of a start. After checking the driver once more, she began to count. But not for long. Her fingers grew clammy, then numb and didn't seem to want to move. A fifty-pound note showed its face, and another, and another, and another. She paused when she'd counted five hundred pounds. "Good gracious," she murmured. "However much is there?" The magazine had been going to pay her two hundred and fifty if they printed her photographs. A kill fee because they'd changed their minds should be less. Both she and Sam had certainly been right in not believing the story about a kill fee, even before *London Style* denied all knowledge of offering her one. No magazine would voluntarily overpay.

Olivia uncurled her fingers and looked at the thickness of what she'd counted so far. She tried to estimate how much more money there might be.

"Oh." Surely there was a mistake? Surely there couldn't be that much—a thousand pounds perhaps?

"Oh, crikey!" Either she needed glasses, or she was even more rattled than she'd thought. She continued to count, amazed at how quickly the sum added up in increments of fifty. "Yes, a thousand. Unbelievable." There was still more, so she counted on under her breath. "Fifteen hundred. Sixteen. Seventeen—two thousand. *Fishhooks*, I'd faint if I dared." What she'd soon added up was over four thousand pounds. With trepidation she lifted the opened flap on the other envelope and discovered a used ticket to a film called *Nasty Girls Need Punishment*, a dry-cleaning receipt, and two uncashed checks, apparently drawn on the same account. And she still didn't have a final figure on the cash. The biggest risk in her life—as far as she could see—would be to remain in London while people either attempted to take her life or tossed thousands of pounds at her for something that should have no value other than as part of Penny Biggles's layout for *London Style*. She, Olivia, was an unknown for whom any publisher would offer peanuts, for which she'd be grateful.

Making this trip was absolutely the right thing to do. It was the only thing to do. And she was going to do it.

Four

"No," Vanni said. "Not just no, but hell, no."

Aiden checked over his shoulder. They were in a small office off the squad room, but someone might come in at any moment. "Come on, buddy. What's the big deal? A friend—me—needs a favor, so you'll do it." The open office door and a wall of windows were visible to the swarm in the squad room.

"No." Aiden's partner kept his eyes trained on a computer screen where he was selecting mug shots for a lineup. "Don't ask again. Gimme a hand here. Does that look like him?" He pointed at the blank face of a white male, bald, with the kind of innocent baby eyes guaranteed to raise the hairs at the back of any cop's neck. The guy was a big, strong sunovabitch, and no one you wanted to know was at home behind those eyes.

"Does it?" Vanni pressed him.

"Sure. Put him in." The pictures they chose, a visual lineup, included the real suspect and would be used to try for a positive identification by a victim.

"That's good enough," Aiden said.

"Says who?" Vanni swept a hand in all directions, indicating the scene in the squad room where detectives came and went—at the moment mostly came—and yelled good-naturedly to each other. Suit jackets had been discarded and the sleeves of white shirts rolled up. Mini-consultations were conducted in corners. Vanni waggled his head and said, "See anything out there, partner? We're havin' a busy mornin' in case you didn't notice. Our one hundred percent effort is needed around here. The chief's on his way up; word has it he's stewin' about somethin'. Someone probably closed a loophole in one of his schemes. Probably a crackdown on his free Yankee tickets."

Aiden was an even enough tempered guy and he didn't shake easily, but the last thing he wanted was for the chief to hear Vanni talking wildly about kickbacks. And kickbacks, by any other name, were still kickbacks. "Can it, Vanni. I know you're fooling around, but this place is a zoo. Anyone could hear you and *not* understand. And I'd likely be guilty by association. The chief's just looking for an excuse to get my ass in a sling. What gives with the SWAT guys, by the way?"

"You think someone's going to tell us?" Fats Lemon said, having sidled into Vanni and Aiden's space. He was a skinny guy with a gray crewcut and tight, bronze-colored skin that crumpled into a wrinkled mask when he smiled. Fats smiled a lot, was smiling now, his wide, thin-lipped mouth stretched, and all but closing his eyes.

"Hey, Fats," Vanni said. "How's it goin'? Let us know if we can do anything to help. It's a bummer for Ryan to be gone so long." Vanni was better at making polite small talk than Aiden.

"I'll let you know," Fats said, preening nicely. "Maybe I'll be that hard up some day."

Aiden would have taken him by the neck, but Vanni shot up from his chair and stepped between. "Didn't I hear you're expected at the morgue?" When Fats nodded, Vanni went on to say, "You'd better get on it then. Make sure you don't fall down the steps on the way out of here. I'd hate you to bruise that skinny ass of yours. Give old Carver my regards. Tell him I hope to have something different for him one of these days, something he's never seen before."

It was Aiden's turn to intervene. "I've got to leave," he murmured to Vanni. "Come outside. I want to talk some more before I go."

"Push me some more to get your own way, you mean."

"Whatever."

Fats Lemon still hovered, for all the world as if he was passing time with two good friends and colleagues.

Vanni succumbed to temptation and said, "Carver's been known to get real angry with people who keep him waiting—unless they're dead. Once heard a story—not confirmed, of course—about him asking a tardy rookie to crawl inside a drawer to check something for him. He said the stiff on the table had just been taken out of that drawer and that it wasn't as cold as it ought to be. The cretin rookie did as he was told, and Carver slid the drawer back in, locked it, and went away for an hour."

"Sure," Fats said to Vanni. "I'm no rookie and I can handle Carver."

Chief Friedlander arrived and the noise level dropped a bunch of decibels. A small man, he made up for lack of height with what Aiden liked to call "presence." Muscular and fit, his walk forceful enough to create its own energy, he entered any room chin first and with the type of assurance that told everyone around they'd better listen up— just in case he barked a question in their direction.

He strode into his office with its wall that was half glass and made no attempt to shut the door. Another good sign. If he closed the door and lowered the blinds over the windows, someone was for the high jump. Aiden watched him, noted his fancy, custom-made shirt once the suit jacket came off. Then there was the expensive silk tie and the Gucci loafers that rested on the desk. The chief wore no socks. He was one trendy guy.

He looked up and met Aiden's eyes. Before the moment could turn into a staring match, Aiden turned away. He had an edgy relationship with Friedlander, who had voiced concern about Aiden's reserve and raised doubts about his being a good team player.

Not long enough ago for the incident to have become a memory, Aiden had made the decision to go into a building where a domestic dispute was in progress without waiting for a backup. Things had been getting ugly in there and he feared someone would be dead before the next car arrived.

Turned out he'd probably been right about that, but he'd put himself and Vanni at risk. And if Vanni hadn't been right behind him, Aiden might be singing heavenly music by now. The chief had put him on suspension for a week and hadn't stopped making sure Aiden knew how badly he'd goofed up.

But Aiden hadn't stopped condemning the chief for failing to help Chris Talon, Aiden's ex-partner, to overcome the unnecessary guilt that caused him to quit NYPD and end up with the Seattle Police Department. Chris had blamed himself for the death of a woman charged, erroneously, with the murder of her child. She'd killed herself, but that had been no fault of Chris's.

Aiden and the chief existed in the same work space, but he doubted the other man had the slightest respect for him.

Aiden hadn't needed to hear the chief say what the force thought about maverick cops—they were considered potential liabilities. Before Chris had quit NYPD around four years earlier, Chris had been the kind of tough cop who didn't chatter, but did know how to cut to the core in a few words. The two of them had been a perfect team, a complimentary team. Aiden rarely went through a day without missing his old buddy, but you moved on, you had to. Vanni was younger than either Chris or Aiden, brasher, louder, and he was enough of a contrast to Aiden to make his more senior partner's quiet watchfulness real obvious.

Vanni had tired of the game with Lemon. He motioned for Aiden to follow, ran downstairs, passed two officers at reception and a gaggle of potential plaintives in chairs along one wall, and slammed his way through the doors and onto 51st Street. There were more cops around than civilians, and a casual observer might think the cops were too engrossed in eating bagels and yakking to have noticed even if someone got knocked off on the steps to the precinct house. Any cop knew better.

Vanni pulled Aiden across the street, dodging vehicles whose screaming drivers leaned out the windows to holler insults. Vanni's target was the pretzel stand on the corner of 51st and Third. Vanni liked some predictability in life.

"From here we can see if Fats tries to horn in again. That guy's a friggin' nightmare. I'd like to know who he sleeps with to keep his job."

"He's not such a bad cop," Aiden said. "He got lumbered with a lousy partner—you can't blame him for that."

"He coulda cited incompatibility and requested a different partner."

Aiden managed a one-sided grin. "You make it sound like a marriage gone wrong. You know it looks bad when a cop complains about his partner. Lemon's probably got ambitions, just like you and me."

"Ambitions?" Vanni's voice rose several octaves. "He's already realizing his ambitions. He *likes* working with Ryan. It's got to be Ryan who fixed him up with the fancy duds. Their clothes are almost identical. They're in on it together, I tell you. And Fats is ecstatic about it. For all we know, he's got enough on Ryan to make him pay for silence and support."

"You ever thought of writing a book? I heard imagination's a must in that line of work and you can clean up millions for just a couple of weeks' work."

"I've thought of it," Vanni said. "I'm waiting for my muse is all."

Vanni was a master at sliding away from the problem in hand.

"Would it be okay if I picked up Boss this afternoon and took him to Mama's for a visit?" Vanni continued. "She just loves that nasty-tempered dog of yours, and she says it's been too long since you brought him over."

"Sure you can take him. Now quit avoiding the reason for this conversation. Vanni, you've got to help me. I can't take her back to my place in case Ryan shows up. It would turn too nasty and I don't want to upset her. She'll already be upset—and Ryan could take it into his head to do anything, including accuse me of being a pervert with plans for Olivia's body."

"Not my problem."

"You've got an extra—"

"No, dammit. You've got cold feet. First smart thing you've felt since you got yourself into this. But they're your cold feet, not mine, and I'm not taking some whacko Brit female to my place."

Aiden wouldn't give up until he'd talked Vanni into helping him. There was no one else to ask. "She's not whacko, just a bit naive."

"Like hell," Vanni shouted. Immediately he hunched his shoulders and lowered his voice. "She's making a big trip to a country she doesn't know, to meet a man she doesn't know, spending money she obviously doesn't have, and she could be walking into that airport to be taken away by someone with murder in mind. She's not whacko?"

Aiden thought about all that. "She's all on her own with what could be big trouble. She's coming to me because I'm the only one she knows here."

Vanni snatched two steaming pretzels from the guy with the cart and thrust one into Aiden's hands. "She ... Dammit, but you're a couple of tacos short of a full meal deal. Give me your ear, friend."

Obediently, Aiden bent close to Vanni, who whispered, "She doesn't know you, asshole." He cleared his throat and this time he shouted, "She knows Sam and there isn't any Sam. Got that? She shouldn't be coming. There's a disaster on its way and your name is on it. And hers. What if Ryan's planning to blow her away because she's got something he wants, but he doesn't want her around to talk about it?"

"I'm weighing those odds, partner," Aiden said. "I acted without thinking. I've never done that before, not on a personal level. Now it's my job to help Olivia gain some courage, and to make sure Ryan Hill isn't a danger in the future. I think I can do that."

Vanni narrowed his dark eyes and chewed away at the pretzel.

Aiden looked at his watch.

"Impetuous," Vanni said, swallowing visibly. "That's what it was, impetuous. And you know what? You're right, you've never done a spontaneous thing for yourself since I've known you. You collect scrap heaps you call vintage cars—and they've gotta keep you poor. Who ever heard of renting a warehouse for an indoor junk yard? You raise orchids that drive you nuts because they don't bloom like you want them to. The Wally Loder undercover thing is something else. You're fantastic at it, but when you turn into Wally, it's strictly for business, never to have any fun. You've never even deliberately gone out and gotten tanked enough to fall down."

"I've been drunk," Aiden said.

"Sure, but not paralytic. I never knew another cop who didn't do that at least a few times. Shows a man's got heart."

There was no answer to that.

"Well, hell," Vanni said, waving the remnants of his pretzel in the air. "I guess I've been wrong about all this. I need to encourage you, congratulate you. You're goin' out to the airport to pick up a woman you've never met. You're going to make sure Ryan Hill doesn't get his clammy paws on her. And you're gonna figure out what's goin' on with these photographs. Great. At least it's a start. If she shows up at all, the two of you can chat about what's best for her, then she'll go home again. You will have tasted adventure, boyo, adventure of the real personal variety."

Aiden laughed. Suddenly the whole scenario was ridiculous, and every word that came from Vanni's mouth made it even more ridiculous.

"This isn't funny," Vanni said, but he smiled. "I'll go call Mama now and tell her you'll be bringing someone to dinner."

"I don't think—"

"Shut your face, Flynn. Unless you just want to say thanks and good-bye. My mother will give your new girlfriend the spare bedroom until she can get a flight home. Mama loves it when the house fills up—makes her remember when we were all kids and at home. She'll have a good cry."

"I don't want to make your mother cry," Aiden said, but quickly added, "She's got a heart of gold and you're lucky to have her. I'll take you up on the offer."

"I didn't offer. You asked. And I'm agreeing to Mama's place, not mine."

"Thanks anyway. You think I ought to dress differently to go to the airport—more like Ryan, maybe."

Vanni choked on his current mouthful of pretzel.

"Hey," Aiden said, and thumped Vanni on the back. "Are you laughing at something?"

"Yeah." Vanni controlled his coughing and pulled Aiden against the windows of Azure, the corner delicatessen. The stream of humanity on Third Avenue threatened to bear them both off the sidewalk and into the flow of honking traffic. "Now listen up, Aiden. When you do your Wally bit, you put on a new skin with the weird duds. You hide behind an identity you can convince yourself belongs to someone else, and you're real comfortable because you're a genuine actor—you assume the part. That gives you permission to do and be what you never are when you're yourself. Is that clear?"

"What you mean is clear, Doctor Zanetto, but you've got it wrong. I'm not going to waste time with an amateur shrink today, but I am going to tell you to quit analyzing me. And I'm a happy man, remember that. Happy, contented, doing everything I want to do. Got that?"

"Sure." But Vanni shook his head. "What's that thing they say about doing a lot of protesting? Do you even see the looks you get from every woman at the precinct? No, of course you don't. Damned thing about that is I think the strong silent act *really* turns 'em on. If we held a contest for most wanted male around there—and I don't mean perps—you'd win hands down. You got a string of women ready to stand in line just to eat you up, buddy. I hear they've all got lick-off underwear in their drawers—just in case."

Aiden laughed and it felt great. "Sure they do. But I only have eyes for Margy and I think my love goes unrequited there, so drop it." Margy was the chief's secretary and an unflappable superwoman.

"Margy has children your age," Vanni pointed out. "Not that she isn't too good to you. They're all too good to you."

"Margy is my hero. End of topic," Aiden said.

The shriek of several police sirens, accompanied by pulsing dome lights, gave Aiden the pause he needed. Rain began to fall again.

"Okay," Vanni said when the sirens faded. "You've got what you wanted. You can bring the woman to Mama's. I'll talk to her before she gets there. I gotta get back, and so do you."

Aiden finished his pretzel and tossed the paper in a trash can. "Cover for me, okay? Say I'm following a lead. Whatever. I want to get to the airport early. She's going to need some reassurance when she gets off that plane."

Vanni managed a look of deep sadness. "You are one thoughtful guy. Some woman's gonna be lucky to get you. Would you mind trying not to get involved with this particular woman? Her behavior spells buggso. Got it?"

"You don't know her so you can't make judgments like that."

"You don't know her either." Vanni draped an arm around Aiden's shoulders. "And you're never gonna know her. You can forgive yourself for stepping in as professional greeter because Ryan Hill would have gotten her here if you didn't. You probably did the right thing. But I don't envy you trying to explain how her virtual boyfriend is a real pain in the ass and maybe a kook to boot—a twisted, possibly criminal, kook."

"I'm not laying that on her. I'll be a good listener and see what I can do to help. I could make contact with her insurance investigator friend and ask him to help her out. Then she'll go home and avoid getting cozy with Internet pals in the future."

"And you'll start by tellin' her you're not who she thinks you are."

"I don't want to talk about that anymore."

"You mean you don't want to face it, Aiden. You'd rather go in disguise as someone else and let him do the talking. Listen, you need a place to take her other than some fleabag hotel where she'll be all on her own. I'm arranging that, but not if you show up pretending you're Ryan D. Hill. Got it? Mama wouldn't understand that, and neither do I."

Aiden considered before saying, "You want me to meet OliviaFitz and say, "Hi, you think I'm Sam, but I'm really Aiden?"

"Yeah. Don't let emotion cloud judgment. If you don't want to risk a kidnapping charge, you'd better make sure she knows who you are. It's simple. I'm not Sam, I'm Aiden, and Sam isn't Sam, he's Ryan. Ryan's a crook and I'm here to save you from him.' You can put it in your own words if you like."

Five

Olivia wheeled her bags from the U.S. customs area at Kennedy Airport through double doors to a cordoned-off walkway. Just once, she scanned the crowd of waiting faces on the other side of a black plastic rope. So many excited smiles, so many bunches of flowers and balloons—and signs. *Welcome Home Chad. We love you.*

She saw no sign with her name on it, but she wouldn't expect one.

From the moment the aircraft doors had closed at Heathrow, she'd been overwhelmed by a desperate craving to turn back. At least in London she'd only feel afraid. Here she felt afraid and foolish—really foolish.

She kept her eyes downcast and walked through the phalanx of waiting people. They strained forward, looking for their particular passengers. Languages blended together, and Olivia wasn't sure she heard any English at all. Everything was strange, colorful, yet overlaid with scents of grime. Even the Avis and Hertz car rental desks looked foreign. This was America, New York, and—and she was the only one who knew she was here, except for Sam.

She needed to calm her mind.

Shrinking down as small as she could would be an easy instinct to follow. Perhaps she could book a seat on a plane home—the next possible plane back home.

But she'd always wonder what Sam was like in person. He'd promised to be here to meet her.

She felt light-headed. In fact she might even faint. Clinging to the handle of her luggage cart, she made it to a row of chairs and sat down—and studied her sensible flat brown shoes. Her tan linen jacket had wrinkled badly. She ought to have remembered Penny warning her to avoid linen unless she was certain she wouldn't have to sit down—or go to the loo. The straight, russet-colored skirt was of different material from the jacket and probably wasn't quite the thing, but at least it didn't clash with the jacket.

If Sam wanted to, he'd find her. If he didn't come at all, she'd have no choice but to return home.

He wasn't the type not to show up.

A girl's squeal pierced Olivia's ears and she shuddered. Toddlers charged around, some pausing to cry for no evident reason. But what did she know about children, other than that they were generally inappropriate but often sweet? There were even some little ones who gave her an urge to pick them up.

Where was he?

She made herself look up again.

She didn't have to study faces, only buttonholes. The crowd had thinned out, but she couldn't see a single man with a flower in his buttonhole.

There didn't seem to be many people who had come on their own to greet the plane. Some lone women and men stood by. Most of the women pressed to the rope. Most of the men hung back.

She hadn't told him they should meet in baggage claim, had she? Oh, no, she couldn't have made that mistake when she knew she'd be bringing her luggage through customs. She could go to check the baggage area, but he might come here while she was away.

Now the people waiting had dwindled to a number that allowed a study of each one. Sam wasn't a woman, so that eliminated more than half of the candidates.

A handsome, dark-haired man let out a whoop and swept a little boy into one arm while he wrapped his other arm around a pretty woman who was clearly his wife.

No one who looked like that would be Sam, anyway. Sam was a nice man, an intelligent man, but he'd be ordinary to look at. Guilt attacked. She'd never been into stereotyping people, and this wasn't the time to start. Just because a person was smart, he or she didn't have to be plain. It was just that she didn't care much about how people looked, although—and this was a form of bigotry—she supposed she didn't generally trust handsome men.

Four more excited groups came together and moved away. Three of the lone men remained.

Olivia tried to be discreet while she considered and dismissed a man who couldn't be more than twenty-two. His hair was bright red, that carrot color. White skin and big freckles. A cheerful-looking person, but his T-shirt announced, "Tonight's The Night." Not Sam.

Of the remaining two candidates, one was tall, with dark blond hair, wavy, well-cut, and streaked by the sun. His charcoal-gray suit was a perfect fit, his shirt collar and cuffs very white. His tie suggested he needed ways to express his individuality. Even at a distance Olivia could identify a rather wild, geometric design done in shades of mauve through purple and red. He had the build of a well-toned athlete—lithe and long-muscled—and the loose stance of a runner. No, not a runner, they were too thin. A hurdler, perhaps—or one of those people she'd seen on the telly once in that violent American game where they wore helmets and a lot of grotesque padding inside their clothes. There was one really attractive person on each team, the one who got to decide everything and throw the ball or run, whatever he wanted. All the other players waited for him to decide, then shout about it. He was muscular but slim—and fast on his feet. You'd think whoever was in charge of getting players would twig to it that those other men they chose, the huge ones who could only run a few feet before they fell in a heap with all the other big ones—well, they ought to figure out that what they needed was a whole lot more like the slim, brainy one.

Wild Tie held a bunch of flowers, but one side of his jacket was pushed back and his other hand sunk into his front pocket. Olivia had always been a leg woman, and this man's legs certainly made memorable lines in his trousers. Penny would call him "brilliant, a complete knockout." What a face. And he was tanned.

She flushed and looked at her hands in her lap. *That* wasn't Sam, although there had been a strong resemblance to this man in those fabulous dreams she'd had.

Not Sam.

That left a bespectacled man with a pleasant face, straight brown hair, and a really nice smile. She could say, "Sam?" in a loud voice and see what happened.

Olivia hadn't come.

Aiden identified what he felt as mostly disappointment. Oh, there was a little relief in there, but mostly he was sorry she wasn't on the plane. Evidently she'd come to her senses and bagged it. Vanni was going to laugh himself sick, not that Aiden cared. He hoped Olivia would be okay, that's all.

The guy in front of him made a sudden move, hauled up the cordon, and went beneath to throw his arms around a tired-looking woman with three children. They stayed there, hugging and chattering in Spanish before moving slowly off. Aiden watched them go. They made him feel good.

Maybe there were one or two passengers to come yet.

The woman who had struggled through and sat down on a chair opposite was still there. She looked completely lost, but he'd learned not to gather up anyone he saw who appeared needy.

Another passenger, a man, straggled through.

The seated woman wasn't very old, late twenties maybe. She had a lot of soft brown curls that made her eyes look huge from a distance. If Olivia really didn't show, he could offer to help this woman. If she turned him off, at least his conscience would be happy.

She had lovely legs. A faintly baggy brown skirt didn't reach her knees and even a pair of sensible flat shoes didn't detract from legs that deserved to be noticed.

Maybe he should go to the TWA desk, use his badge, and try to get his hands on the flight manifest. He could even have missed Olivia altogether.

Damn. This was the kind of thing that reinforced a man's conviction that women were unpredictable.

He caught the woman's eye and smiled. She smiled back, and he liked it. She had a sweet face, not flashy, but easy on the eye. When she tossed her hair back, he got a sensation that would only hit a man who didn't have a life.

Hey, a man ought to be able to laugh at himself. He didn't have a life in the accepted sense—accepted by other guys. Not anymore. Only it was okay for him to comment on his isolated private life, but it wasn't okay for Vanni Zanetto and members of his family to have opinions. What they didn't get, partly because he'd never tried to explain, was that he wanted a woman in his life, wanted her very badly, but he was some kind of throwback who believed there was only one right woman and he'd better be careful not to miss her because he was distracted by anything that looked promising in a skirt. He'd been that route, and it was past time to move on.

The worried-looking lady probably wasn't tall—just about average. He'd say her looks were better than average. Someone nice lived behind those gentle, sparkling eyes. She was obviously waiting to be met, but each time she looked in his direction she gave a small, vaguely embarrassed smile. Too bad she didn't have any idea how to put her clothes together, but her figure was good—he could tell that. Nice breasts inside a white blouse buttoned to the throat and secured with some sort of pin. Her jacket looked as if she'd washed it all wrong, then forgotten to iron it.

Average. Brown hair and eyes. Sturdy. A sartorial disaster.

No hat, no flower in the buttonhole, and not what he'd call sturdy exactly. But . . . holy hell!

He held the bunch of flowers as if he'd forgotten they were there. Olivia thought he might be trying to make up his mind what to do. He should stay where he was. Whoever he'd arranged to meet might be held up somewhere, but she'd get there somehow. No woman would stand this man up.

He was smiling again.

Olivia smiled back. The first time, she'd been afraid he wasn't smiling at her at all; then she'd have felt a fool. But he was smiling at her—a conspiratorial smile because they were both waiting and both feeling undecided about their next moves.

Whew, he had the kind of smile a woman might see in her dreams. She looked away and checked that her passport and tickets were safe. There hadn't been time to change any pounds into dollars, but that couldn't be difficult to do.

Why did this country feel more foreign than, say, France, or Italy? It did, very foreign.

If she stayed where she was, how long would it be before someone noticed?

Oh, no, she'd forgotten her own flower. Now look at it. She had taken a daisy from a vase at home and when it had started to droop on the plane, she'd wrapped it in a damp tissue and put it in her bag. Now, since she'd forgotten it was there, it was mangled, rusty-looking, and missing most of its petals.

She managed to pull the stem through the buttonhole on her lapel. Not that it mattered anymore.

The thing to do was find a hotel that wasn't too dear and spend the night there. For a fee she'd be able to change the date on her return ticket. She hadn't known how long to plan on staying, so she'd finally chosen two weeks.

There would be an information desk somewhere.

He was still there, she could feel him, and see his shoes and the bottoms of his trousers when she glanced in that direction. Poor man.

Once on her feet and as organized as she was ever going to be, she caught his eye again and smiled—and stood still. He had a rose in his buttonhole.

If he was Sam, he'd have said something by now.

"Olivia?"

Six

The shop bell chimed, and Rupert Fish gripped the handle tightly. He eased the door open slowly and entered on tiptoe, hoping Winston might be too engrossed in whatever to notice that his partner had finally returned to Bloomsbury.

Winston Moody had noticed. Over the tops of rimless half-lenses, his watery blue eyes sought out Rupert. Reproach. Yes, Winston invariably attacked passively—silently—at first, and with baleful, "how could you do this to me?" stares.

Rupert salivated. He could taste the satisfaction of squeezing Winston's fat neck until those rheumy eyes popped out. But Rupert must continue to wait.

In the fifteen years they had been in business together running Moody and Fish, Antiques, first in less salubrious quarters in Shepherd's Bush, and for the past ten years, in London's exclusive Bloomsbury, Museum Street to be exact, Rupert had learned to dislike Winston more with each day. But Winston had the upper hand and he knew it. He owned the controlling share of the business and had uncomfortable knowledge about Rupert's humble beginnings—and about a lucrative endeavor that went wrong. By handing over certain papers to the authorities, Winston could send Rupert to jail for a long, long time. Rupert knew a thing or two about Winston, too—Winston had unusual sexual preferences—but Rupert didn't have the kind of solid evidence he needed to turn the tables.

Fortunately a tiny, blue-haired woman stood before Winston and gestured extravagantly while she discussed a Michel-Robert Hallet snuff box in a heavy French accent. The box was a valuable gold and enamelled piece and nothing, not even the opportunity to torment Rupert, would divert Winston if he got the whiff of a pending sale.

"Preposterous," Winston told the woman. "A third? You insult me, madam."

"I offer you 'alf then," she said. "We both know this is not one of 'is best pieces. I only consider it at all because I 'ave so many better examples and this is a curiosity."

Rupert smiled. This could continue for some time, and afterward Winston would need to vent his opinions of "bargain-hunting charlatans." He might even forget to interrogate Rupert at all. "Not bloody likely," Rupert muttered. Not given the importance of what he'd been supposed to accomplish in Hampstead.

He flexed his hands. The fine tremor that shook him would be obvious to some. Rupert didn't care. He wanted the FitzDurham woman dead. Dead she wouldn't be a threat anymore; there wouldn't be a reason to wonder just what she knew and what she might do with the knowledge.

It wasn't his fault that another female in an ugly red hat and raincoat had tricked him into thinking she was the one he wanted. Too bad that bleeding heart meddler stopped her from dying. And then he'd had to bide a little time and pay, actually *pay* for the negatives he had in his pocket.

Peace. No Winston. No FitzDurham. Was that so much to ask?

He couldn't bear to remain where he could see Winston.

Soames would have been ignored all day. Winston hated the ferret, more because he belonged to Rupert than because of a supposed allergy to the animal. Rupert made to pass Winston, who was sweating and red-faced, and the prospective client, who was not.

"There you are," Winston said. "Stay put, there's a good chap. I'm almost finished here."

The woman's face was powdered white. Her very dark eyes darted rapidly between Winston and Rupert. " 'Alf," she said as if she spied some advantage in Winston's divided attention. "I will take it with me."

"Not possible. Forgive me, madam, but we're closing now." Winston moved toward the door, bowing his bald head as he went. "Do come back if you decide the piece is worth full price."

Rather than argue, the Frenchwoman gave a delighted grin and waved as she departed, saying, "You will think about my very good offer, and I will give you another chance. Per'aps."

This was their late-opening night, and darkness had begun to seep into the street. Lights in the shop windows cast a yellow wash over items displayed there and onto the pavement outside. A strolling couple stopped to look at a Chippendale commode which they evidently found amusing.

Winston finished shooting home bolts and came toward Rupert in menacing, head-first mode. "Damn you," he said succinctly, stretching his receding chin as far forward as that feature allowed. "Explain yourself, man. At once. Where have you been? It's nine, for God's sake, and not a word from you since last night."

"You could always have done the dirty work yourself. The choice was yours." The choice was always Winston's, but if Rupert had his way, that was going to change before too long.

"You know, Rupert," Winston said in the pseudo-pleasant tone that always boded ill, "no matter how long, or how hard I try to help you overcome your lower middle-class background, you defeat me. Breeding will out, isn't that what they say? I'm not even sure a good school would have made a difference. You are a common man, progeny of a loathsome thief of very little brain."

This was not the time to get shirty. "Whatever you say, Winston." The toad really got his jollies from seeing he'd offended Rupert.

"I say that you have no sense of honor, and a sense of honor is the mark of a gentleman. You are not a gentleman. If you were, you would consider the man who helped you out of the gutter. Where have you been all day?"

"Making sure we're safe." Let the bastard toy with that.

Winston ran a finger under his starched white collar. He favored tweed lounge suits and suede shoes, and smelled strongly of the cigars he smoked. Never a slim man, with age he had broadened and softened and taken on an ever more doughy appearance. How much pleasure Rupert would have on the day he told the chinless pervert exactly what he thought of him.

"I'm waiting," Winston said.

"Did you feed Soames?"

A withering stare met Rupert's question.

"No, I don't suppose you have. I went to Hampstead. Just like you wanted. Found the house. Spoke with the girl."

"And?" Winston produced a rumpled handkerchief and passed it over his moist brow.

"And we did business."

"You got the photographs?"

"Er—yes, that's right." He'd done bleeding brilliantly considering the circumstances.

"Where are they?"

Rupert patted his jacket.

"Have you looked at them?" Winston sweated more freely. "Can you see anything?"

"I've been a bit busy. The girl wasn't easy to deal with."

Winston's eyes rested on Rupert's jacket. "You couldn't have been dealing with her from last night until nine this evening." He'd grown redder and he breathed hard. "Everything depends on this. What's the matter with you? Something's gone wrong, hasn't it? You've dashed well balled it up, you monumental ass. I warned you that—"

"Better calm down, Winnie, or you'll pop a vein." He should be so lucky, Rupert thought. "She did a bunk afterwards, and I had my hands full making sure I knew where she'd gone. Just in case." And that hadn't been easy. Rupert had snoozed in his waiting taxi. If the taxi driver hadn't been alert, he'd have missed seeing FitzDurham take off in her mangy mini-cab.

"Just in case what?" Winnie asked slowly.

That tore it. He couldn't say he'd decided he ought to know where Miss FitzDurham was just in case she tried to use the actual prints, or make a second set of negatives. And he wasn't ready to reveal his sickening mistake with the money. He shrugged. "You never know what might come up. We could want to talk to her again."

"No, we *couldn't*. The last thing we want is to have any further contact with the woman at all. Where have you really been? Not with Kitty. Please say you haven't been with Kitty."

"I haven't seen my dear wife for days." He had seen Nonie at her flat in Shepherd's Bush—warm, welcoming Nonie, who was always ready to help him feel like a man again—had been since Rupert's own days of living and working in the same area. "I don't even know where Kitty is." Nonie knew Rupert was unappreciated by some people and spent every minute of their time together appreciating him enough to make up for the rest.

"Kitty can't know anything. Understand? If that woman finds out we're valuable, she'll find a way to take advantage."

"She won't find out we're vulnerable, Winston."

"Give me the photographs."

Shit. He slid the envelope of negatives from his inside breast pocket and handed it over.

Winston's hand, the hand that held the envelope, trembled. He backed up to an eighteenth-century chair upholstered in a fine example of Genoa velvet, and sat down with a thump that raised dust. What height Winston had was in his torso. His feet swung clear of the ground. He opened the envelope and stared inside.

Rupert sniffed, and laughed, and made for the back room.

"Come here." Winston sounded querulous and unlike himself.

"Just need to see to Soames."

"Back—here—*now.*"

Rupert broke into a trot and scooted into the cluttered sanctuary he and Winston shared. Here they were out of sight of customers, while any customers could be viewed through one-way glass. Winston was very fond of one-way glass—he used it elsewhere, too.

"Rupert?" Through the glass, Winston's frightened expression seemed magnified. "Come here at once or I shall get very angry with you."

In the end, Winston always became muddled and foolish. Good. The time had come to cause a diversion.

Rupert took Soames from his cage and held the creature's face close to his own. "Good boy, beautiful boy. You go and say hello to dear Winston." With that he kissed the ferret's nose, put him on the floor, and hurriedly returned to the showroom.

"What are these?" Winston held the negatives in one hand.

"The negatives. I offered her money, and she finally agreed." He smiled as if proud of the proceedings. "It wasn't easy, but I pulled it off."

"And the photographs? She had to have photographs."

"They wouldn't have fitted through the letterbox."

Winston's eyes grew larger. Light glittered on his little lenses. "What letterbox?"

"The one in her front door. The one she put the negatives through."

"But—"

"She wouldn't open the door, Winston, for God's sake. You can't blame her. She was on her own and didn't know me from Adam. So she passed those out to me through the letterbox."

"And she's still got photographs?" Winston's chin made another valiant attempt to jut. "*Photographs,* Rupert. The photographs that could land us in jail."

"She doesn't know what she's got."

"That's not the sodding point, you moron. What is the point is that she's *got* them. What's to stop her from using them for that magazine?"

"She took the money for them, that's what. And I told her it was a kill fee."

"Oh, yes, oh, of course. In that case she wouldn't think of using them elsewhere. I feel better now, Rupert."

As usual, Winston was blaming him for everything. "Even if she'd given me photographs, how could we know they were the only set?"

"You were supposed to get in there and search."

"I did."

"Another balls-up. You didn't get a thing."

"I couldn't find them. Everything looked the same to me. What did you want me to do, take the lot? Take everything?"

"Yes, Rupert, that would have been a good idea. Then we could have been sure." Winston squirmed and his eyes grew more moist. "Phone's ringing. Don't answer."

Rupert went to the white phone on a tulipwood writing table where sales were conducted and picked up the receiver. "Hello, Rup—"

"Stuff it, Fish."

Kitty. Of all the lousy luck. "Can't talk now." Oh, no, he certainly couldn't talk to his nemesis now.

" 'Course you can. You're avoiding me."

"I'm not avoiding you, Kitty. You're avoiding me. You know where we live, but you don't choose to go there."

"I go there."

Winston had set the envelope aside and was waving his arms and gesturing for Rupert to hang up on Kitty.

"You don't go there when I'm there." He loved Kitty in his own way. She was the sexiest woman he'd ever met, and he still didn't quite believe that she'd ever agreed to become his wife. "I miss you."

"No!" Winston said, then covered his mouth when he realized he'd spoken aloud. He passed a forefinger across his throat and bounced.

"I need money," Kitty said.

Rupert pursed his lips.

"I've been watching you, Rupert." Kitty's full voice took on a singsong note. "Who is she, lovie?"

Now his skin cooled and he avoided even glancing at Winston. Kitty knew about Nonie. "You've got it wrong," he said.

"I followed you to Hampstead."

"Hampstead?" Sweat coated his body instantly. His eyes stung. "What do you mean?" Once the woman began to fall, the platform had become a blur. Kitty could have been there.

"Come on now, lovie. You watched her go into that house and

you waited forever. But then you were pleading with her through the letterbox." She laughed her snorting laugh.

He breathed again. "Yes, well, you've got it wrong. She had something I wanted to buy."

Winston moaned and covered his eyes.

"Oh, reeeelly? You poor boy, you are in a bad way."

"I didn't mean it that way," Rupert said hurriedly. "You know I never look at anyone but you. It was strictly business."

"*Hang up*," Winston howled, then said more quietly, "and don't you dare slip and mention ... *He who is never mentioned* is not to be mentioned."

"Put that little twerp on the phone," Kitty said. "And get me money. A lot of it. Leave it with Vince at The Fiddle."

"Winston doesn't want to talk to you, and—"

"Yes, I do want to talk to her," Winston interrupted. "Bring me the phone."

"Are you diddling that mousy little woman?" Kitty asked.

"For God's sake, Kitty. Miss FitzDurham? *No.* You've got nothing to worry about."

"Bring me the phone, Rupert," Winnie ordered.

Kitty laughed and snorted, "I'm not worried. I'm never worried. Whoever is Winnie talking about?"

Rupert couldn't think what she meant. "What?"

"Oh, you can tell me. Ever so quietly. Whisper. Who's *he who is never mentioned*? Surely not—well, you know who?"

"Your ears are too good for your health," Rupert told her. "You've got the right man. And he's dead now—which means he absolutely never gets mentioned again."

Winston slipped low enough in his chair for his heels to touch the carpet. "Fool," he mouthed. "Bloody fool."

"Dead?" Kitty said, but not as if she expected an answer. "Oh, Rupert, don't tell me what happened. It's better if I don't know. I don't care anyway. Give Winnie the phone, there's a good little lapdog. I'll expect Vince to have something for me."

There came a time to give it up where Kitty was concerned. He hauled on the long telephone cord and thrust the receiver at Winston who put it to his ear as if he expected worms to crawl inside his head. "Yes?" he said, sweating profusely now.

He listened without speaking for a minute or more, apparently unaware that his specs were sliding down his nose. Silently he held the receiver out to Rupert, who heard the line buzz and hung up.

"Bitch," Winston said. "Might as well give her some money to shut her up. She'll only keep pestering you if you don't."

Darn it. Rupert didn't have to ask what Kitty had told his partner. In the throes of—well, in the throes of being quite grateful to her, he'd told Kitty some of the personal bits, including Winston's personal bits. She'd probably just informed him of what she knew. This was going to make it tougher to get some proof of Winston's escapades.

A long, thin, supple body covered with gray fur slipped across the floor behind Winston's chair. Rupert was almost moved by pity to make a dash and head off Soames. Almost.

The gray fur turned silver in the light. Soames's tiny, needle-sharp claws sunk into costly Genoa velvet and he rippled up the side of the chair. While Winston gazed morosely at his flaccid hands where they rested in his lap, Soames flowed behind his head and delved his darling, wet little nose into the ear Kitty had so recently assaulted.

Winston jumped. He jumped, and stiffened. His eyes stretched wide open. "Rupert?" he whispered. "*Rupert?*"

The torturer was tortured and very nicely, too. "Isn't that sweet," Rupert said. "I've always told you Soames likes you."

It was bloody amazing the way lugubrious—a good word, that— the way lumbering, lugubrious old Winnie whipped his sueded twinkle toes onto the chair and stood on the seat. Soames slithered around Winnie's neck like a snug fur collar.

Winston turned deep puce. He squealed, and danced, and flapped his arms—and his jowls.

Another sound reached Rupert. Choking. Flaming hell, if he didn't watch out, Winston would drop dead, which might be brilliant if Rupert didn't still need him. "It's okay. Hold on. Oh, dear me. Come to Daddy, Soames, you're frightening Winston." He grabbed the ferret and stuffed him into an ivory birdcage. "It's all right now. He's gone, old friend. I've taken him away."

With his arms still outstretched, and his legs pressed together, Winston held his pose, but the color gradually faded from his face. His eyes regained focus and he seemed, slowly, to become aware of where he was. Without a word, he lowered his arms and climbed down. He removed his glasses and rubbed the lenses on his damp handkerchief, flipped his head as if tossing back luxuriant hair, and reseated himself.

Rupert waited.

"You can take some of the money and leave it for Kitty, if you like," Winston said while he gathered up the envelope Rupert had given him. "Not that you can make a habit of using business funds."

"Thank you," Rupert said.

Winston took out two individual negatives, held them up to the light, and squinted. Rupert crossed his arms. The storm had passed. Once Winnie saw he had what they really needed, he'd back off.

Another two negatives, and another two were held up to scrutiny. Taking less time with each pair, by the time Winston looked at the last ones he barely raised them before his eyes before dropping his hands again. He gripped the arms of the chair and allowed everything to slide from his lap to the Savonnerie carpet beneath his hanging feet.

"Winston?" Rupert frowned. "Are you ill?"

"You paid her?"

"We agreed I should."

"How much?"

Rupert grew warm. That had been a mistake he'd hoped to rectify at the airport, but there had been no way and now she was gone. And he was bloody well going to have to follow her. "I'm not really sure."

"Give me what's left." Winston held out a hand.

"Can't." He always ended up feeling like a stupid kid.

"What did you pay for those?" Winston pointed to the negatives on the floor.

Rupert puffed up his cheeks and longed for a bag of crisps. "I gave her the envelope, like you told me to."

"I never bloody well told you to give her the envelope, you fool. I told you to see how little she'd settle for. You were supposed to offer her fifty, then up it to a hundred or so if you had to. What the hell are we going to do?" He rocked his head from side to side. "Give me the deposit slip for the checks. Or did you mess that up, too, and forget to go to the bank?"

Rupert glanced at a Japanese ceremonial sword on a credenza behind Winston. Supposedly it could decapitate a man with a single swipe.

Too messy. And too public.

"Rupert?"

"The checks aren't in the bank."

"I should have known better than to allow you to take the bank deposit at the same time. *Where* is the bank deposit?"

"We'll get it back," Rupert said. "I had the two envelopes in the same pocket. They must have got stuck together."

"Oh, my God." Winston flopped back in the chair. "You put everything through her letterbox. No. Say you didn't. There was thousands in cash. And those two checks—three quarters of a fucking *million* in checks."

"She got the lot," Rupert said. "I didn't expect her to hold out the way she did, and I made a mistake. I was rattled. There, that's the way it was." She should have been dead but wasn't. That was also the way it was, but Winnie would never find out that Rupert had botched a murder attempt.

Winston moaned repeatedly and wiped at his mouth. He said, "Tell me you're joking. If you're not, she knows exactly who we are and how to find us." He paused with his mouth open. "And we're going into overdraft. Expenses have been over the top. We had to speculate to accumulate, you know that. The money will start rolling in again soon. I had a plan. We'd tell our latest customer—he who wrote those two checks, in case you've forgotten—we'd tell him his transaction's on hold. That the merchandise is coming. Keep him quiet for a bit and use his money. Then we'd bring our old friends in New York to heel. And they would come. We know what they've all got hidden away. There are private collectors all over the world who would pay to see our list of those paintings. They're all stolen. Those crooks would come when we called, and they'd pay for our continued silence about what they've got."

"And they will still come, and we'll be in clover," Rupert said, rubbing his hands together. "Nothing's changed there. And we'll get to the FitzDurham woman and make sure she's no bother. It'll all be fine."

Winston said, "Not if someone blows the whistle on that other matter. The matter you felt you had to discuss with dear Kitty, who won't let it drop."

"You're wrong." Rupert wished he absolutely believed what he said. "Kitty's not stupid. I've told her he's dead. She'll have figured out it's safer to keep quiet because she doesn't want to get involved. That goes without saying."

"It had better go without saying." Winnie jabbed a toe toward the negatives on the floor. "The FitzDurham woman's got prints, and now she knows who we are. And she's got names and numbers for people who expect us to be absolutely discreet."

Rupert chewed his lip. "You don't know if she saw anything in the photos. You don't even know if there's anything to see in the photos. Anything we need to worry about, that is. We're only guessing and taking precautions." He leaned toward Winnie. "You don't know, do you?"

"What if she's a planter?" Winston said.

"I think you mean a plant, Winston."

"She could be. It could all have been a setup to draw us out. What if they had those photographs and knew there was voluble evidence in them, but they didn't really have any idea who the evidence was voluble to—or who the photographs belonged to? For all you know, she's out there now." He gestured toward the street and sank lower in the chair. "She could be out there watching us and reporting back to the mastermind. Telling him they've cornered us and it's time to close in."

Rupert peered through the windows, then pulled himself together. "That's *valuable*, Winnie. But she's not. They're not. She left for the States. Should be there by now. Just about. You wouldn't believe what I went through to find out where she'd gone."

"That's it then." Winston leaped up and cuffed Rupert one across the ear. "We're off."

The ear stung. Winston inflicted his petty pain and kept Rupert's hate alive and growing. "It's not that bad. We're not done for yet."

"Off to the States, you fool," Winston said. "To track her down and finish her off. And whoever she works for. She can identify us. Besides, she's a swindler. She got our money for the wrong negatives."

Seven

He walked, or sauntered, to stand in front of her. Olivia pressed hot, damp palms against her skirt and did her best not to pass out from lack of air.

"Olivia Fitz?"

Disaster. There was no way she could feel relaxed with him, not when he must see her as a dowdy, dun bird to his brilliantly blue-eyed golden eagle. This was the most embarrassing moment of her entire life.

Sam was waiting.

"I'm Olivia FitzDurham," she said, looking up at him and making sure her gaze was steady. If her eyes appeared shifty, it would be truly horrifying. "Thank you very much for coming to meet me. I'm really sorry to be such a nuisance. I'm sure you're very busy investigating important cases and this is bad timing for you to break away. I've been thinking. I'm sure everything's just fine. I've overreacted. I'm going to see about getting a flight back to London. In fact, you don't need even to wait with me. There's bound to be a plane leaving soon." She stood up and offered him her hand. "It's very nice to meet you. I wish you every success in any endeavor you undertake."

Aiden waited until she finally closed her mouth. He glanced at her extended right hand and placed the bunch of roses in it. She automatically closed her fingers around the paper and stems.

He hadn't expected to be a smash hit with her, but from her reaction, he was one helluva turnoff. "Welcome to New York," he said, and risked another grin.

A smile arched his upper lip away from his teeth, crinkled the corners of his eyes, and made little brackets on each side of his mouth.

"Yes," she said. "You must be an awfully kind man." Otherwise, why would he waste his time with her? Not that she wasn't passable to look at, just not—well, not, that's all. Why was she even thinking about his physical reaction to her when the poor man was only doing what came naturally to him—protecting a potential victim?

"Er, thanks," Aiden said when he couldn't think of another response. *He must be an awfully kind man?*

Olivia couldn't do a thing to stop herself feeling flustered. "I'm not a victim type, you know. I've never been that sort of person. Really, I'm very capable." She longed to be back in London, in Hampstead. What a monumental idiot she was making of herself. And to as much as contemplate his thinking of her as a victim sickened her.

Now he got it; she was embarrassed because she thought she was inconveniencing him. "I'm glad you got here safely. Don't give the victim stuff another thought. You acted, and that's positive"—*Thank you, Vanni*—"because too many people are indecisive under pressure and they freeze. That's when they become victims." There was something to all that stuff about Englishwomen's skin. Although she must be exhausted, Olivia's skin glowed.

"What a nice thing to say, Sam. You're right, of course, but I admit one can feel a bit of a pest—a lot of a pest, actually, for intruding in someone else's life."

This was where he should take her aside and explain about Sam, or Ryan. He should explain everything, right now, before things got any stickier.

"It would be nice to at least spend the night here," she said, and made a motion to stop him from taking her luggage cart. "Oh, no, you don't have to do that. It's on wheels and ever so easy to pull."

Gently, he patted her hand and removed it from the cart handle. "Exactly. So it'll be easy for me to pull, and then I won't feel like a jerk. Or will that offend your feminism?"

"I'm *not* a feminist. Well, of course I'm a feminist, just not that kind of feminist." She chuckled. "Now that's as clear as mud, isn't it? I mean I'm *really* a feminist, but there are obvious reasons for the differences between men and women."

"Uh-huh." If he laughed, she wouldn't think he was kind.

"The strength thing, I mean." Olivia Fitz was getting pinker. "You know, bigger in some places, or ways, differently shaped because we were intended to perform differently. Oh, good grief." And she really did laugh. "Contrary to my brother's opinion, I'm really quite sensible and clear-headed most of the time. I'm not known for saying inappropriate things. Thank you for dealing with my luggage."

Aiden decided he might be able to like the lady. "You're tired," he said, taking a bulging black bag from her shoulder. "I'll handle that, too. Cameras, I bet." He must tell her who he was—or wasn't.

"I don't go anywhere without a camera. Without one I feel there's something missing. Probably like you and your gun. I need to find a phone and call some hotels."

Her brother could be the one with the real inside track to how clear Olivia's head was.

She walked along beside him, and he liked her walk. She didn't mince or trot, but neither did she stride in her sensible flat shoes. "It's amazing here," she told him. "You can feel the energy."

"Wait till you get to Manhattan. Hold on to your hat then. What happened to your hat anyway?"

She slapped a hand to her head and stood still. "I don't remember when . . . Isn't that ridiculous? I'm not sure. I'm not even sure if I put one on. Possibly I didn't. How strange." She started walking again.

"Why would you wear one at all? You've got pretty hair. I'm glad it's not covered up."

That caused her to bow her head so he couldn't see her face. She didn't answer him.

"You do know I can't allow you to stay in a hotel, don't you?"

"I'll be fine there."

He'd managed to make her feel unwelcome. "People are already expecting you."

Olivia knew Sam was trying to be nice, but she wouldn't let him go to any more lengths to help her. "You're awfully kind, but I can't allow you to put yourself out anymore. I don't know what I was thinking of before. Of course I can't stay at your place. What would your family and friends think?"

His sudden sharp laugh and the way he shook his head unnerved her. She had no idea what he found so funny.

Aiden couldn't say what he thought, which was that his family wasn't going to know, but that his friends would be eaten up with curiosity about the woman Aiden-the-loner chose to shack up with. And shacking-up would be what they assumed he was doing. "Y'know, Olivia," he said, and placed a hand on the back of her neck without thinking. Too late to snatch it away. "Y'know, I think it's you who are kind. You've got to be anxious and adrift, but you're worrying about my reputation. In fact, that's downright sweet." They finally reached the doors to the drive-through in front of the terminal and went outside. "Why don't you wait here while I get my car?"

A chill and gritty wind stirred around Olivia's legs. "No, no, it'll save time if I come with you, and it feels good to be moving."

He'd kept his hand on her neck and noted that his touch seemed to reassure her. He shifted to grip her shoulder. "I want to feed you. Then, when you've had some rest, we'll go over everything that's happened to date."

"Thank you," Olivia said. Was she going to talk about believing she'd been a murder target? "I don't want you to feel responsible for me. You aren't. My goodness, is that some sort of game?"

What game? he wondered. "I don't follow you."

"Pedestrians racing with cars and things. It's a sort of chase to see who gets there first, and still alive."

"Oh, that." He kept a firm hold on her and wove a path across the street. "Everyone knows what they're doing." No point in telling the truth—that this was the biggest game of "chicken" on earth and scaring her even more.

"Heathrow's wild," Olivia said, and he realized what she evidently hadn't. She had grabbed a handful of his jacket. "This is wilder."

"Yeah." The crowds and jostle of vehicles looked average to him. "We're going to Brooklyn."

He felt her prepare to ask questions, but they'd reached the elevators in the garage, and negotiating a spot inside the first arriving car made conversation impossible.

Olivia's anxiety only built. He didn't live in Brooklyn. Why would he take her there? "Is Hell's Kitchen in Brooklyn?" The doors were closing and a lot of people were crammed inside, but she couldn't wait to get a clearer picture of what was happening.

"Nope. I'll explain where we are as we go."

Once more he held her shoulder. She wasn't sure if the familiarity felt good, the action of a friend, or if it made her feel threatened.

An elegant woman wearing a butter-colored silk suit, cream hose, and high-heeled, bone-colored pumps stood a few inches from them and very deliberately studied Sam. She was gorgeous, and from the way she looked at him, she thought Sam was gorgeous, too. She started at his feet and moved very slowly up his body until she reached his face. Olivia saw him glance briefly back at the woman, but look away at once. He squeezed Olivia's upper arm and smiled down on her.

Hmm. Yes, the familiarity felt good.

The woman's tightened mouth registered annoyance—probably

because Sam wasn't drooling over her. She switched her attention to Olivia and repeated the foot-to-face sweep. Olivia smiled. The woman didn't smile back. The elevator doors opened again, and Sam propelled Olivia out.

"You hungry?" he asked. "You'd better be. Where we're going, they don't understand if you don't eat three helpings of everything."

"Rather hungry," Olivia said. "I don't want to put anyone out, though. I mean, I've already been enough of a nuisance and—"

"Do me a favor, ma'am. Don't say that again. You're here because you were encouraged to come. End of story. Okay?"

He'd drawn to a halt near an antique car that reminded Olivia of something from a gangster picture—except for the color. She stared at the vast fins and tried hard not to crumple under the weight of her shaky reaction to the irritation she heard in Sam's voice.

"Sorry," she said. "I'll be more careful what I say." She started walking again.

"This is it," Sam said. He opened a back door of the finned monster—the chartreuse, finned-monster—and put her luggage on the seat. "Come on, let's get you settled."

"This is your car?"

"Restoring cars is my hobby. I usually drive a Mustang, but I thought you might enjoy something more sedate."

"It's a Cadillac?"

"Yep. A fifty-nine Cadillac Sixty Special four-door hardtop. Isn't she a dream?"

A Cadillac the length of a frigate and sporting an immaculate chartreuse paint job. "A dream," Olivia said. And, oh, so sedate. She wondered what the Mustang looked like. She pointed at him. "MustangMan. I get it now."

"That's me." Sam ushered her into the passenger seat where shiny black leather felt slippery. "One-hundred-thirty-inch wheelbase," he said. "Overall length, two-hundred-twenty-five inches. Did you notice the dummy air swoops—torpedo-shaped?"

A man and his toys. "I certainly did. They're—memorable."

Aiden slammed the door and ran around to the driver's side. He ought to drive the Caddy more often, but he didn't like to risk having some bored bubble-gummer keying the sides—or worse. Kids with nothing to do could make life nasty.

He slid behind the wheel and sighed at the way the engine hummed the instant he turned the key. "Listen to that," he said. "You had it right. It's a dream."

Olivia supposed the car was interesting. The view down the bonnet went on forever. Once Sam was on the ramps leading down from the garage, she asked, "You were going to tell me about going to Brooklyn."

Now. Now he would tell her about Ryan. "We'll take the Belt Parkway. Brooklyn gets a bum rap from people who don't know it. Some of the views of Manhattan—wait till you see it at night—they're something." She might totally panic when he started talking about not being who she thought he was.

"But Hell's Kitchen isn't in Brooklyn."

"No, Manhattan. Midtown."

"I need a map."

"Sure, to orient yourself." Time enough to explain everything when they got closer to the Zanettos. "You'll soon feel you've lived here all your life."

Olivia doubted that. "I ought to tell you more about what happened this morning—or whenever it was. I'm getting confused on times. There wasn't time to put all this in the last e-mail, but that man—the one who came for the photographs—he was so creepy. He looked through the letterbox in my front door and asked me to push the negatives out to him." The next bit mortified her. "He put an envelope of money inside. Mmm . . . there was enough so I didn't have to use a credit card to buy my ticket. That was good, wasn't it? They can't trace me that way now, through my credit card."

Olivia was aware that her surroundings were more green than she'd expected, but she was too perturbed to take close note of anything they passed.

"Let me get this straight," Aiden said. *He'd better remember it wasn't his job to interrogate her.* "A man came to your home—"

"It was the man who rang up earlier. At first I thought it wasn't, but then I realized he just didn't have cotton wool in his mouth."

Aiden took a sidelong look. She was looking right back. So earnest and anxious. So pretty. And maybe more than a few tacos short of a full-meal deal? Hadn't that been Vanni's line? "Cotton wool in his mouth?"

"Sorry. You say cotton. Inside his cheeks. I've read how people put cotton wool in their mouths to change their voices. Or a flannel— washcloth to you—over their mouths. Or perhaps that was a flannel over the telephone receiver. I knew it was him, though, because he mentioned ringing me earlier about the kill fee."

"Ah, I see."

Olivia heard other words in her head: *He intended to kill me but attacked someone else by mistake.* She said, "When I didn't agree to give him the photographs, he said he only needed the negatives. Then he pushed an envelope full of money and things through the door."

Rather than gaining any reassurance from this revelation, Aiden got a too-familiar feeling of foreboding. "Olivia, did you give him the negatives?"

"He gave me the money."

"So you've said." He could see her hands trembling in her lap. "Just take a deep breath and stay with me on this. Because he gave you the money, you gave him the negatives?"

"I feel *so* awful."

"Save it. We don't have time for you to crack up on me."

His voice had turned hard, and his profile was sharp, the corner of his mouth turned down, and that muscle she'd often noticed in men's cheeks worked back and forth. Oh, dear, he was grinding his teeth. She'd made him really angry.

"I don't mean to snap at you," he said. "It goes with the territory, I'm afraid. I get intense about business and I forget to make nice."

Make nice? "You don't have to pretend to be what you're not for me. I'm a stranger to you anyway. Well, I am really. Oh!" She jerked around to sit facing him. "I didn't give him the ones he wanted. Oh, dear, I see what you thought. He asked for negatives, so I gave him some. But they weren't the ones from the shoot for Penny Biggles."

Aiden shook his head and gave the steering wheel a punch. "Atta girl." He looked at her again. Her head was bowed, and she was engrossed in pulling at her skirt. "But the money—"

"I know, I know." She frowned. "I shouldn't have taken the money, but I decided I hadn't asked for it and I'd find a way to repay it later. I needed a way to buy that ticket without anyone being able—oh, drat—being able to make an excuse to go to the credit card company and find out about my transactions. You didn't want them to, either. *Blast* it."

The side seam of her skirt had apparently been closed into the seatbelt. She'd managed to pull it free, but at the expense of tearing the seam. While he stole repeated glances, she assessed the damage, then took hold of a trailing thread and wound it around a finger to break it off.

"What were the other things in the envelope?" he asked, as much to distract her from obvious distress over her clothes as to find out the answer.

"Not in the same envelope. There was a second one stuck to the one with the money. Two checks, an old ticket to the pictures, and a dry-cleaning receipt. Oh, *no.*"

Olivia was definitely not the kind of girl who wore her skirts slit from hem to hip, but she didn't have a choice—at least not at the moment.

Of all the dreadful things to happen, Olivia thought. She tried to cover her exposed upper thigh, where pale peach-colored garters held up lace-topped stockings.

Aiden kept his attention firmly on the road ahead. "This is the Belt Parkway," he said. "A lot of the areas you see in Brooklyn used to be considered undesirable. Rough. Dangerous, even. Mostly it's all been cleaned up. There are some great real estate buys here now. The Zanettos—that's where we're going—they live in Clinton Hill. They've got this wonderful old house. Mama Zanetto and her husband brought up seven children there. Mr. Zanetto passed away some years ago. I never met him. But Pops Zanetto, the grandfather, is still there. Wild old guy." He was running out of prattle, but she seemed to have grown still now. "Tell me about the checks."

She didn't answer, and he risked another look. Olivia held both of her hands clamped over her left thigh, but she wasn't doing an efficient job of keeping peach-satin garters and the lacy tops of her stockings covered. So the big question was, did that sexy underwear tell the real story about the lady's personality? Aiden hoped so.

He faced resolutely ahead once more. Why did he hope so? What did it matter one way or the other? She wasn't likely to be planning to seduce him.

Shucks.

"I feel ridiculous," she said in a very small voice. "It's nice of you to pretend I haven't ripped my skirt, but we both know I have."

"Yeah. Well, maybe you could turn it around so the seam's at the back."

Olivia stared at Sam. "At the back?"

A faint color rose along his cheekbones. "I guess not. The front, then?"

She sputtered, and started to laugh; she couldn't help it.

Sam grimaced. He shook his head. "Stupid suggestion. When we get where we're going, stand close to me until I can maneuver you somewhere to change, okay?"

"I hope so." The many hours since she'd slept, and the tension packed into those hours, were beginning to blunt her ability to think at all.

"The checks, Olivia."

She opened her purse and pulled out a crumpled envelope. "I couldn't take them out on the plane. It probably wouldn't be a good idea for someone to see me doing that. There's more money in here, too." A lot of money. This all got more weird, and being here felt the weirdest part of it all.

"Who are the checks made out to?" Sam asked.

Olivia slid them out, and the rest of the money. "This one's to Moody and Fish Antiques." She riffled through several more. "They both are, and they're written on the same account. It doesn't have a name, just a number, but there's a New York contact listed underneath, an Alberto Fanelli. Two checks written by one person within a couple of days. Both to Moody and Fish Antiques. Why wouldn't you write just one check?"

"You've got me. They're not endorsed, though?"

She turned them over. "Yes, they are. There's a stamp. Moody and Fish Antiques, Museum Street, WC1. I think that's Bloomsbury."

"Is that in London?"

"Yes. A very good area of London."

"How much are they for?"

Olivia looked at the sum on the first check. Chilly prickles shot out on her scalp. The second one didn't make her feel any better. She found a pad and pen and wrote the two sums down. Several times she added the figures.

"How much?" Sam prompted her.

Her gaze drifted to the window and ugly highrises standing shoulder to shoulder, beside the big road and stretching away into the distance. Theo would croak if he had any idea what was happening to her. She wouldn't allow herself to think about her parents. When she looked ahead again, Sam was steering to the right on a long curve, and she jumped at the sight of a car coming straight toward them.

An illusion. She'd forgotten they were on the opposite side of the road from England. Tiredness had really got the better of her. "I need to count again. I'm having difficulty concentrating."

Once more she added the figures. How hard could it be to add two sums together? Surely she had the decimal point in the wrong place.

"Got it now?" Sam said.

Should she involve him in this any further? He braked for a huge lorry with red, white, and yellow plastic strapped over the loads on two beds. The plastic flapped. Too many images to assimilate.

"Olivia?"

"Yes." His legs fascinated her. Long, very long, and when he gave the car more petrol or pressed the brake, muscles in his thigh hardened and stood out beneath his gray suit trousers. When he took his other foot from the clutch, the fabric caught around his calf.

Yes, Theo, I'm a nutter.

Aiden turned his head and caught her apparently watching his driving technique. He saw the instant she realized he was looking at her. She went back to the checks she apparently didn't want to tell him about.

She'd forgotten the gaping skirt. He narrowed his eyes. The outside of her left leg showed from high-cut peach-satin panties at her bared hip, all the way past matching garters and sleek thighs to her pale, very sheer stockings, to a shapely calf and slim ankle. Too bad about the flat brown shoe, not that there was anything wrong with his imagination. Disposing with the skirt altogether, and getting rid of both shoes, painted the kind of picture in his mind, and resulted in the kind of reaction elsewhere, that made him hope she wasn't studying him too closely.

"I must have this wrong," she told him at last. "If I've got eight hundred and ten, then one, two, three zeros, how much does that say?"

"Where's the decimal point?"

"It comes after all that. Then the final two zeros."

"Shit," Aiden said, applying the brake before he realized what he was doing. Rapidly, he accelerated again. "Match your figures to the checks again. Add them. Then give me your total one more time. Slowly."

He heard her muttering as she did as she was told. Then she announced exactly the same figure as before. "It can't be, can it?"

"Eight hundred and ten thousand? If you haven't transposed numbers, or added wrong, then that little duo represents over three quarters of a million dollars."

"Pounds."

"*Shit.* I forgot. That's got to be more than a million dollars." Something big was going down here. No way was there a chance Mr. Moody and Mr. Fish wouldn't be searching for their million. "I don't want you carrying that. It's not safe."

Olivia felt even more sick. "He wanted to push me under a tube train," she said softly. "It was really early in the morning. This morning. Before I left England. He came into a bakery where I was shopping. I'd never seen him before, so I had no idea he was the man who called about the kill fee earlier, but he scared me. Then he followed me, and I went into the station because I didn't want him to follow me home. He pushed someone who looked like me instead."

The Cadillac slowed dramatically. Sam leaned forward over the wheel, frowning fiercely as if trying to be sure he'd heard what he thought he'd heard.

"The other woman had on almost identical clothes and the platform was really crowded. One minute he was feeding rats on the rails with crisps, the next I heard the screams. He was gone, and that poor woman was on the ground. Someone had saved her, thank goodness."

"Why didn't you tell me this the minute you got off the plane?" Sam's voice sounded different.

"You didn't give me a chance—no, that's not true. I wasn't sure how to say it, or even if I should." She was perilously close to tears. "It was in Hampstead. He sickened me. There are rats on the tracks, and he was feeding them crisps. He—"

"Yeah, so you already said. Sicko." She wasn't to know how much it took to impress him. "Then what happened?"

She told him and added, "So I did all right, didn't I? I mean, I didn't completely panic when I realized he was the man at the door later. And I managed to get away without him knowing where I'd gone."

Her innocent ability to believe in this scenario was disconcerting. "Possibly," he said. Treating her like a child wouldn't help.

The skin on her thigh was smooth and very white. Her head was bowed, and her dark hair separated to show equally vulnerable-looking skin at the back of her neck. He'd like to kiss her neck first, then make his way to her thigh, the inside of her thigh where his tongue and lips and warm breath would tickle and make her squirm.

Holy hell, Flynn. Get a life.

"You did well," he muttered. And what, he wondered, had the man who fed rats done when he discovered what he'd put through Olivia's front door? "You think he just went away after leaving your house? Simple as that?"

Sam sounded so impersonal and tough. But he was an FBI agent, and he had to be tough. "I didn't see him again."

Aiden decided not to push her further on the point. It was perfectly possible this guy had seen her being driven away and followed.

"I know what to do," Olivia said, feeling inspired and relieved at the same time. "I'll mail the checks back to Mr. Moody and Mr. Fish with what money is left. I can put in an IOU for the rest. No, I've got it. I'll write a personal check for the balance and ask him to hold it till I let him know I can cover it."

Oh, my, God. "We'll work it out together, Olivia. I bet beaches and water weren't what came into your mind when you thought of Brooklyn."

"I suppose not. More like gangs and graffiti—only I don't think I've ever thought about it much." The beach looked more like scrubby marshlands to Olivia. "Why are we going to the—the people you talked about?"

"The Zanettos." Who would never let him forget it if he arrived pretending to be Ryan Hill. "They've got a big dry-cleaning business. My friend Vanni's oldest brother runs it for their mother. Several members of the family are involved. We're getting close. I've been told there are similarities to London here. The little shops, the people who've known each other all their lives exchanging the news of their days. It's all neighborhoods and families. I don't think foreigners think about it that way at all. We're just about there. Don't worry with the skirt. Hold my arm when we get out of the car. You don't have a coat? It's cold, kid. Winter's coming on. You need more than that jacket."

This was appalling. "You're going to wonder about me, but I didn't even remember to bring a mac or a brolly."

"Yep, well, hold my arm and stand close to my side. I'll tell 'em you need to freshen up."

"What a bother. I'm so—"

"You said you weren't going to talk like that again."

"No. I mean, yes, I did."

"Good. This is it."

Sam pulled his boat on wheels into a space undoubtedly intended for at least two cars. The shallow roots of beech trees with big, gnarled old trunks popped up cement along the edge of the wide pavement that separated the road from narrow, steep gardens fronting a long row of terraced brick houses. Each house was three stories high, with basement windows visible beneath black iron steps to the front door.

"Sit tight," Sam told Olivia. "I'll get your luggage out, and we'll pretend we're running a three-legged race."

She felt hot, then cold. Lace curtains moved in one of the front windows of a house that was bigger than the rest. No face was actually evident. A boy on a skateboard cut off her view. His stiff jeans were wide, as wide at the waist as they were at the hems. She thought it possible that the jeans were actually attached to the board and the boy would have to climb out of them to get off. Several other boys zipped along on roller blades, leaping over the exposed tree roots and dodging baby strollers. Pushed by mums and dads dressed in chic casual and with "established professional" all but embellished on their brows, these strollers might cost as much as some automobiles.

Sam already had her luggage out of the car, and he opened her door. At the same moment, the front door of the big house opened and a man stood on the top step. Olivia was too preoccupied with her predicament to do more than register his presence.

Sam planted the wheeled cart in front of them and said, "Okay, Olivia FitzDurham, relax and let me manage this, okay?"

She nodded and didn't care that he took her hand to pull her to her feet, then tucked the hand and her forearm under his own arm, tightly against his side. With his left hand, he reached back and slammed the car door.

"Hey there—"

"Hey, Vanni!" Sam roared, so loud he startled Olivia. "Traffic was traffic. Same old, same old. What's for dinner?"

"I'm not allowed in the kitchen," Vanni said. "You know that."

"I sure do." Sam shouted each word. He pushed the cart ahead, then lifted it up a step at a time. "Olivia FitzDurham and I are starving. Vanni, meet Olivia, Olivia, meet Vanni Zanetto."

Olivia exchanged greetings with Vanni, whom she now saw was another star-quality male, only with very black hair and hazel eyes that were startling against olive skin. He stared down on them, his frown magnificent—and foreboding. Actually he frowned only at Sam.

"Poor Olivia's exhausted, Vanni. D'you suppose she could freshen up before she meets the family?" He smiled at her, then at his friend. "I doubt if she's experienced anything quite like the Zanettos."

"No problem," Vanni said, not taking his attention from Sam. Finally he looked at Olivia. "I'm sorry for your trouble, but my partner here is one of the best. He'll work something out."

She hesitated. "You never mentioned being in another business, Sam." Not that he owed her his entire life story.

"Sam?" Vanni said. "That's what I thought." He should have known Aiden would make a mess of it with her. The guy was so awkward around women. For someone who was physically coordinated and really strong, the way he was manhandling a little suitcase up the steps like it had rocks in it showed just how uptight he was.

"Save it, okay, Vanni?" Aiden said.

Oh, no, this was one time when Aiden Flynn's partner had to act fast if he was going to avert disaster. Vanni reached down to sweep the cart carrying a green tartan bag that sported a pink neon luggage tag from Aiden and deposited it inside the front door in a single move.

"We're glad you can be with us, Olivia," he said. "My mother loves company. So does my grandfather. He likes to be called Pops. My mother will tell you she's Mama to everyone. Comes of having seven kids—she's always been Mama."

Both Olivia and Aiden had stopped climbing the steps. Vanni narrowed his eyes at Aiden and said, "You knew what you needed to do."

"Yeah. And I'll do this my way, okay?"

"Not okay. You dragged me into this, buddy." Olivia's skirt was torn. Aiden had her plastered on his side like a coat of paint, but something was peeling. She was no fashion plate to begin with, but flashes of pale orange underwear made an interesting statement against Aiden's dark-gray-clad thigh.

"Just point us in the direction of Olivia's room, Vanni."

Olivia looked up at Sam, then at Vanni. They were furious with each other, and she couldn't think of any way to extricate herself from a very uncomfortable situation.

"I'm going to take a step up with my right leg," Sam murmured. "On the count of three, use your left leg. One, two, three." He stepped up slowly, and so did Olivia, but her leg was much shorter than his and she had to roll slightly toward him to avoid Vanni getting a view she couldn't bear thinking of him getting.

Sam shrugged her camera bag higher on his left shoulder and put his right arm around her, holding her waist. She clung to him.

"Once more and we've made it."

"You haven't made anything," Vanni said. "I don't believe this. How did that happen, miss? Did he—hell, no, he wouldn't touch you. He doesn't have it in him."

Aiden made a note to knock the crap out of Vanni the instant he could get him alone.

"I caught it in the seatbelt," Olivia told Vanni.

"If Mr. True Blue had settled for not having seatbelts—which he doesn't have to have in *that*—it wouldn't have happened. Mama'll mend it for you. I'll get one of my sisters down here with something for you to change into. June! Get out here and help."

She decided she didn't like him much. Too full of himself, and as mean as they came. "Sam's trying to help me. He's an awfully kind man."

"Oh, yeah," Vanni said. "Awfully kind is what I'd call him. And dumb as a post if he thinks it was a good idea to . . . For cryin' out loud, partner, I told you not to come here before you told her the truth. Tell her now."

"Your timing stinks," Sam said. "Let me do this my way."

He spread his fingers over her ribs and rhythmically rubbed her there. Evidently he was too preoccupied to realize he was smoothing the side of her breast with his thumb. She grew so hot all over, she trembled.

Vanni Zanetto studied them with those piercing eyes of his, and Olivia saw that he hadn't missed where Sam's hand was, but she didn't know how to move away without causing even more trouble.

"And I never used to believe in love at first sight," Vanni said. "You make such a nice couple. Such a cozy couple."

"That's it," Sam said. "Get out of my way, but I want to see you as soon as Olivia's somewhere comfortable."

"And I suppose I explain to my family that you're in disguise mode?"

"Not now, Vanni."

"When, then?"

"Soon."

Vanni nodded slowly. "You're vulnerable, Olivia. Aiden here's a nice guy, but he's not exactly Mr. Smooth around the ladies. I'm sorry, old friend, but I'm gonna have to help you out here. Take Olivia up to June's old room—two floors up and on the right. Sit her down and tell her you aren't and never have been Sam."

Eight

Kitty Fish stood in the shadows across the street from Miss FitzDurham's house. A man had paced slowly past, glancing toward 2A as he went; then, after a while, he paced back in the opposite direction. Kitty was waiting to see if Rupert would show up. Rupert and Winston were up to something big and, if her instincts were right, something dangerous. This meant there could be a lot of money in it for her. She could always get Rupert to talk; then they'd have to pay for her silence.

This time the man had stopped, and he certainly wasn't Rupert. The outline suggested someone athletic and young. He looked in all directions before crouching in front of the door.

Kitty's heart took an extra, excited beat. The street wasn't wide. He was close enough that when the light had caught his face, she knew who he was. She didn't know whether to scream, to laugh, or to faint.

Beneath a clay pot of waning geraniums, potato bugs, silverfish, and mud kept company with a key to Olivia's front door. Thanks to the frosty moon and some convenient light from ye olde cutesy streetlight, he hadn't even needed to fumble to find what he wanted.

Women. They were boring opponents—most of the time.

Time was running out. If it hadn't already run out. He let himself into the house and smelled lavender. Figured.

Upstairs or downstairs? He took an instant to think about it. She used the basement, but he didn't think she spent much time on the ground floor.

First upstairs; then, when he'd tried to knock potential disaster off his back, down to the basement—not that he expected to find anything worth having there.

He pushed a button to turn on the light and climbed the stairs.

When he was partway up, the light went out.

Don't let it be a fuse. He put a hand on the wall and climbed as rapidly as he dared while his eyes adjusted to the darkness. His fingers stubbed into another button for the lights and he punched it. The fuses were fine.

In the first room at the top of the stairs he hit pay dirt. A computer sat on an open rolltop desk. Olivia was tidy. Her papers were neatly stacked. Magazines had been carefully fanned on a brass coffee table.

He turned on the computer and got into her mail server in seconds. What he found gave him the creeps. She never deleted e-mail.

Minutes later he was giving thanks for Olivia's old-message fetish. She'd left him all the information he needed, all the explanation.

He wrote a brief note himself and sent it on its way to New York.

There were scores to settle, overdue scores, but first he'd do the Goldilocks bit and hang out in the bed Olivia wasn't using right now. Early in the morning he'd make a visit that wouldn't be expected. Involuntarily, his hand rested on the piece in the waist of his jeans.

Another kind of visit would be good before he went to bed. He smiled and tapped the keyboard rapidly, entered his password to a favorite late-night meeting place, and settled in to see what the ladies were up to tonight. The ladies, and the men who knew how to use them. Sonja was his ideal. She was evil, you could see that, and you could also see how well she bled when she was punished. Bled and screamed. The sound was irresistible. The woman loved every second, even when she was pretending to be dead.

He switched off. Now, bed. He was ready.

The faintest sound reached him from downstairs. He didn't form a conscious thought before extinguishing the light and flattening himself to the wall inside the open door. His Sauer was in his hand and poised beside his head where he could feel the cold metal. That was a sensation that calmed his mind.

The hall light came on. He heard footsteps, very slow, unsteady footsteps, on the stairs. Through the space between the door hinges and the jamb he had a direct view of the top of the staircase.

The big question was whether the newcomer was aware that there was someone else in the house. That and one even bigger question— who was arriving here when the place was supposed to be empty for at least a couple of days?

Slow, slow footsteps.

The light went out, and he held his breath. Now his blood was really pumping, and it felt so good.

Whoever was out there continued to make crawling progress upward. He could hear breathing now. The footsteps stopped.

If it was Olivia, he'd have reason to celebrate. No reason she shouldn't get to join in.

The next sound didn't immediately compute. Soft, slithering.

Light flooded the space outside the room.

In that light he saw a woman, her head bent forward, concentrating on unzipping her short, brown-silk skirt. Long blond hair fell over her shoulders in tangled curls. He could smell her perfume, a rich, musky scent.

The skirt slid down over slim hips, revealing a silver garter belt and sheer gray stockings. No panties. The lady wasn't a natural blonde.

Darkness blotted everything out once more. He held back a curse, but he knew how to be patient, especially when he was given an unexpected gift.

The woman's humming made him smile grimly. She was enjoying her "private" show, enjoying herself, the ritual of taking off her clothes. He'd put quite a wad on his loving whatever fantasy was playing inside that bleached head.

She turned the light on. She felt like seeing what she was doing again.

Good thing, because he felt like seeing what she was doing again, too.

The skirt was on the floor and she wobbled atop high-heeled, transparent plastic mules. His gut told him she was fried, which meant she'd be coming down soon unless she had more of whatever she was on.

He couldn't take his eyes off the dark, lush bush. She repeatedly pressed her thighs tightly together, at the same time fumbling to undo buttons on a silk blouse that matched the skirt. She jerked and grabbed for the railing that ran along the short landing. Her shudder brought parts to his south springing to attention. She cradled her breasts and moaned. Selfish, selfish girl.

Another second and he listened to her sighing in the blackness. Fucking light could drive a guy mad.

This was one show that was worth the irritation.

She hummed some more, and he visualized her swinging those naked hips in time to the beat. More light donated a whole new view. She hadn't quite managed the buttons at her cuffs, but the rest of the shirt trailed from her elbows. Her headlights didn't need any help, but she was into coordination. A silver bra, strapless and boned to her minuscule waist, offered up a pair of the biggest brown eyes on milk-white tits. Few men would call those handfuls, unless a man were a freak, or a basketball player.

He was going to have to find out the extent of his ball-handling skills.

Finally she managed the cuffs, and the shirt joined the skirt.

With both hands she massaged her softly rounded belly, naked between the boned piece at her waist and the low-slung garterbelt.

Maybe he'd waited long enough. He was tired, but not too tired to have some fun. Yeah, fun. A girl shouldn't waste so much, so selfishly.

Another plunge into the night left him with her sounds and a picture that glowed in his brain. Sleep was good. Several hours of entertainment was better. It would be a humanitarian act. She'd either be careful where she performed solo in future, or she'd make sure she was never alone, maybe never, ever alone.

He smiled and squeezed his crotch.

And there she was again. Oh, God. One by one she undid the row of tiny hooks down the front of the bra. They'd been hidden by rosettes of silver ribbon. As each one popped open, his judgment was proved as perfect as ever. The satin window dressing was just that. Those brown eyes stayed right where they were. When she wriggled a little and dropped the stays—he guessed that's what they called them—he couldn't look away. Disposing of the belt scarcely broke his concentration for an instant, although he decided he ought to remember how much he liked a woman in nothing but sheer stockings and transparent mules.

Now she deserved a partner, if only because this partner could teach her some lessons she'd never forget.

He wanted her away from the top of the stairs. It would be a waste if she fell and broke her neck before he'd finished with her.

"Come closer, bitch," he mouthed silently. "Come to your very own nighthawk and see what he's got for you."

Hot damn, she must have heard his brain. She swaggered closer until she stood with her back to the facing doorjamb. He couldn't see more of her face than pouty red lips and the tip of a pointy tongue gripped between real white teeth.

He didn't care if she *had* a face. He also didn't care that her boobs didn't jiggle the tiniest bit and had probably cost plenty. They'd do what he needed them to do just fine. "Come to daddy, mama." He salivated. Every muscle in his body tensed hard.

The light did its disappearing act again, but this time it was back on without a pause. Gradually the woman sank down the doorjamb, spreading her legs as she went. He could see sweat on her skin, and how moist and slack her mouth was.

She started pulling on the lips of her vagina before her ass met the carpet. With the soles of her feet together, she gave the task her all, pausing at intervals to play with her nipples and pant even louder.

Mission accomplished.

Two for you, zero for me—so far.

She got up and strutted into the room, switching on lamps as she went. Her butt was reddened from action on the carpet, but it was nice, very, very nice. Standing in front of the window, she languorously closed pink velvet curtains. A writing table stood at an angle near a white-marble fireplace, and she went to search the surface. A cigarette and lighter materialized from a wooden box. She lit the cigarette, sat on the desk, and inhaled deeply. When she tipped her head back, smoke rings issued from her pursed lips.

In that movie-star move copied by thousands, she ran her fingers through her hair, shook it out, and tossed it back. Without looking at him, she said, "Welcome to London Town, Ryan. You have no idea how surprised I am you're here. And very glad, too." She laughed— propped her hands on the edge of the table and laughed from the gut. "I was following a hunch. Staking this place out to see if a certain little dickhead was jerking me around. And along came Ryan the stud. You can't blame me for thinking of old times, and how much fun it would be to see if you've still got what it takes to do your thing. You used to be so good, Ryan. I've missed you."

Being a master of quick recovery was a priceless asset. "I didn't realize I was watching the best alley cat in the business," he said. "The bleach job threw me. And you're older, of course. But I was too busy enjoying the show to care who you were and how many more wrinkles you've got. You and I have things to do, Kitty. We've got bargains to strike."

Nine

"Vanni, you big lump, out of the way and let the girl in. She's got to be exhausted. You come right on in here at once—Olivia, is it?—yes, Olivia, Vanni told me." This small lady with gray-flecked black hair wound on top of her head had to be Mama Zanetto.

Still reeling from the angry exchange between Sam and his partner, Olivia felt disoriented by the appearance of the ebullient Mrs. Zanetto. The woman couldn't be more than four-foot-ten, and a plump figure inside her belted black dress suggested that she ate a good deal of the excellent cooking Sam and Vanni had alluded to.

"Where you from, Olivia?" Mrs. Zanetto asked.

"England."

"England where?"

"In and around London most of the time. My folks live in Eton."

"You know any of the Bocellis? They live in London, too. Fine family. Eight sons. Two daughters. And they're all in the family business." She aimed a disapproving glare at Vanni. "Unlike some people, they know they owe it to their parents to look after things. They're in buttons. Biggest button-making business in London. You know them?"

"I can't say I do," Olivia said, but didn't add that London was a big place.

"Next time you go there, I give you a letter to take. They'll make you very welcome. Good people. And *mio figlio biondo.*" She crooned this last, took hold of Sam's hands, and smiled at Olivia. "I call him my blond son. That's what he is to me, a son I wish I had given birth to. You being a good boy?" She patted his cheek. "You stay away too long and that makes Pops angry with you. He is my father-in-law," Mama told Olivia.

Sam smiled down on Mrs. Zanetto. "He's angry because he misses trying to rile me."

She shook a finger at him. "You should humor a sick old man. He has few pleasures. Watch this one, Olivia—he is a heartbreaker who doesn't even know when he hurts you."

"Mama," Sam said, "you embarrass me."

Olivia smiled, but she filed away the comment. What had Vanni meant about Sam telling Olivia the truth about himself and not being who he said he was? And what was their business? She felt sick—and very hungry, and tired.

And she felt angry, really angry, and so scared. And if what Vanni had said was supposed to be some sort of joke, he was way off base. It wasn't funny. She stared hard at Vanni, who avoided her eyes.

"What happen to you?" Mama Zanetto asked. She inclined her head to see the side of Olivia's skirt. The single brow she raised at Sam almost made Olivia laugh. "Hmm. Well, I get June to lend you something of hers."

Another woman appeared, this one perhaps in her twenties, and spoke in Italian to Mama Zanetto, who said a good deal and gestured eloquently. The woman ran up the stairs.

Only moments passed before the striking, dark-haired girl trotted back down to the hall. She put one end of a blanket in Vanni's hands and muttered in Italian, the other corner of the blanket in Sam's hands and said, "Hold it up. Look straight ahead." Over the top of the blanket, she passed a full black skirt to Olivia. "This will be nice for now. Give me your own skirt."

Olivia did as she was told and felt immensely grateful to be properly covered again.

"This is my younger sister, June," Vanni said. "June, meet Olivia from England."

June greeted Olivia briefly and slipped instantly away—after snatching the blanket from Vanni and Sam, to whom she offered angry glances.

"I guess we've offended June," Sam said. His smile at Olivia was uncertain.

"That's easy to do," Vanni said, then suddenly added, "Prepare yourself. Canine attack on the way."

Startled, Olivia saw the surge of heavy muscle beneath shiny black-and-brown fur. She stepped backward. The biggest, ugliest German

Shepherd she'd ever seen surged from gloomy regions at the far end of the hall.

"Hiya, Boss," Sam said, dropping to his haunches and holding out his arms. "Come here. Maybe I've got something for you."

The dog stopped in flight, used his heavy legs and feet as brakes on the shiny floor. Intelligent dark eyes went from face to face and lingered on Olivia, who now felt completely unnerved. "Oh, my," she said. "Boswell, of course. He really is quite large, isn't he?"

"He was bred in Germany, where they concentrate on strength and performance, not how pretty they can make them," Sam said. "Come on, old guy. Be nice. He doesn't accept strangers very easily."

"Thanks for the reassurance," Olivia said. "I think I'll go outside."

Sam shook his head. "No need."

Boss spared his owner the briefest of glances before he went back to staring Olivia down. He lowered his belly and took several steps closer.

Wasn't Sam going to do something? The dog was getting ready to attack her.

Boss's upper lip lifted. It actually curled and turned up at the corners. The animal had vast teeth, and the fang-like eye teeth were capped with glittering metal.

Olivia stood her ground, but she longed to flee. "He's quite a dog." Throwing up in Mama Zanetto's hall would be mortifying.

"One of the best the canine corps ever had. If he didn't have a bit of arthritis, he'd still be on active duty."

"And if they'd provide him with beds to climb on," Vanni said. "And I don't mean the kind they make for dogs."

"Unfortunately, he does have a couple of idiosyncracies. Quit drooling over the lady, Boss."

"He looks as if he'd like to have me for dinner," Olivia said.

Aiden glanced at her, then studied Boss, and he couldn't stop a too-wide grin. "That's not what this is about. He likes you, the traitor. He doesn't like many people."

As if to prove that Aiden knew what he was talking about, Boss loped to Olivia, turned his head sideways, and rested a cheek on her legs. He sighed.

"No loyalty," Mama Zanetto said. "I gotta get back to my gravy. You call me Mama, understand, Olivia? All my friends call me Mama. Ten minutes we eat. Maybe five. Set the table, Giovanni."

She marched away in black shoes with crepe soles that squeaked on linoleum tiles.

Aiden punched Vanni's arm lightly. "Better do what your mama wants, Giovanni."

"You'd better do what I've told *you* to do," Vanni said.

Boss growled, deep and low, and only the glittering eye teeth showed. He took a menacing step toward Vanni.

"I guess man's best friend is telling you to back off," Aiden told Vanni. "He doesn't like the way you talk to me."

"You're cruisin' for trouble, buddy," Vanni said. He left, and an atmosphere of anger hung where he'd been.

Surely Olivia was going to ask about Vanni's comments. She'd make it easier if she did because he'd just have to tell her the truth.

"Boswell, you're very handsome," she said softly, holding out a hand to the dog. Aiden heard her swallow and saw the trouble—no, the frightened expression in her eyes, dammit—

Aiden would have liked to take hold of that hand and pull her away somewhere completely private. If he could be completely alone with her, he'd find a way to explain what had happened without making himself sound like a snoop. But this might be his best chance at trying to put her mind at rest. He spoke very quietly, "Please trust me, Olivia. This must all seem scary and too much for you, but I promise I'll take care of you. And you're safe with me. Okay?"

"I don't really know you, do I?"

She'd be a fool if she didn't doubt every word he said. "No, you don't. Bear with me. Once we get through dinner, I'll make sure I explain the mixup. There isn't time now."

Boss had eyed Olivia's hand for a long time; now he approached and put his wet nose in her palm. There was no missing the slight trembling in Olivia's hand and arm. But the old canine womanizer rested his big, ugly head on the woman's palm, showed his fearsome teeth in his version of a besotted smile, and studied her with liquid eyes.

"Oh," Olivia said. "He's smiling at me, Sam. No wonder he's so special to you. He's an absolute love."

Boss inclined his head and proceeded to lick her forearm with a tongue large enough to make the journey from wrist to elbow in less than a second. A paw rose and hung in midair until Olivia held and shook it.

Aiden made a mental note to let Boss sleep wherever he wanted to sleep tonight. The dog deserved a medal for excellence in diversionary tactics.

"Dinner," a voice shouted from somewhere.

"That means what it says," Aiden told Olivia. "You don't keep Mama and Pops waiting. By the way, don't let Pops get to you. He's got an evil sense of humor and a mean mouth—but he's one of the best. Give him a chance. And give me a chance, okay?"

"We'd better go to the table," Olivia said. She couldn't promise him anything.

Sam nodded and ushered her ahead of him into the Zanettos' dining room. Despite the generous size of the area, a huge table filled the space. Spread with a green-and-white cloth, every inch was all but covered with oversized dishes. The smells attacked Olivia's taste buds and they watered. Bowls of pasta, bowls of red sauce, bowls of salad, baskets of bread, platters of meat and cheese, a block of Parmesan on a tray with a grater—she had never seen quite such a feast. In the center of the table stood an old and elaborate piece of brass with a naked boy holding up a large bowl overflowing with fresh fruit. Candle holders encircled the bowl and unlikely prisms of crystal dripped from the oddest spots. Red candles flickered in the holders. Sam put Olivia in a chair between himself and an ancient, bent, and grizzled man at the head of the table.

June, wearing an apron, waved her hands at Mama and talked volubly in Italian. A man who resembled Vanni but who was a slightly older and more heavyset version, nodded to Olivia and took a seat opposite. To his left sat a thin woman with black hair pulled severely back from a beautiful, sad-eyed face.

"Sit," the old man said in a husky voice. He coughed and his whole, thin body shook. He waved an elegant, if gnarled hand. Nicotine stained the fingers, and the grooved nails curled like a parrot's claws. "Show some respect for the food that is prepared."

Sam joined Olivia at once, and Vanni sat to Sam's right. June threw up her arms, but sat down. The stocky man took a seat between her and the lovely, quiet woman. Mama, grinning as if no gathering had ever been more perfect, took a chair facing her white-haired father-in-law.

Shouting across and around the table made conversation, or even understanding, impossible. Sam leaned toward Olivia and said, "That's Basilio and his wife, Pia. Basilio runs the business."

"What are you whispering about, Biondo?" Mama asked. "Speak up."

"Perhaps he is making love to his new lady," Pops Zanetto said. "Is that what you're doing, boy?"

"I was explaining who's who to Olivia," Sam said. "She's tired, so I thought I'd make it easy on her."

"June," June said, shooting a hand across the table for Olivia to shake. "We're glad Biondo has finally found a woman to bring here. We offer him good Italian girls, don't we, Mama? He turns them all down."

Mama nodded, her expression one of deep despondency.

"We bring wonderful Italian women," June continued. "And we leave them alone to get to know each other. But always it is, 'She talks too much,' or, 'She eats too much,' or 'She is too forward.' Have you ever met a man who thought a woman was too forward? And when we tried to get him to explain what he meant, he couldn't. So we asked the girl and she said she got a little close to him on the couch, then she put a hand on his chest, then she looked up at him, and moved her hand to his leg. Then she undid her blouse—"

"June," Mama snapped.

"Let the girl finish her story," the old man said, pointing a shaky finger. "At my age, stories about other men's good fortune are all you have. Go on, June."

Olivia sucked in her mouth to control an urge to grin.

Sam leaned forward and rested his chin on a braced hand. His expression revealed nothing of what he was thinking.

"*Mange, mange,*" Mama ordered. "The food is getting cold."

"You *mange,*" Pops said. "Tell the story, June."

Bowls and platters began to make their way around the table, and heaping forkfuls of rich food were piled on plates.

"As I was saying," June said, a righteous annoyance turning her lips down. "This beautiful Italian girl with big young breasts any man would be grateful to see, opens her blouse for him. She isn't wearing anything underneath, and she moistens her lips and closes her eyes. And she waits. And nothing happens."

Olivia put her hands in her lap and bowed her head. She had an irresistible vision of her mother witnessing this scene.

"Get on with it," Pops ordered. "Then what?"

"When he didn't kiss her, or touch her, she moved her hand the smallest distance, just enough to touch the big salami and—" Roars around the table drowned June out.

Very discreetly, Olivia put her hand on top of Sam's on his thigh. He turned his hand up, laced their fingers together and squeezed. Already amazed at her own forwardness, Olivia was too surprised by his immediate response to know how to react. Poor Sam was probably so mortified, he didn't know what he'd done. Right now he would cling to any kind person.

As the laughter subsided, Basilio said to his sister, "How do you know how big Biondo's salami is?" And his sister tapped his face a little harder than might be considered friendly.

Pops chuckled. "*She* doesn't, although she might like to. But Olivia could tell you right now. Pass the gravy."

With all eyes on her, and on the forearm and wrist that disappeared beneath the table, Olivia grew hot and knew her face would be the most unbecoming shade of tomato red. Sam took her hand and held it on top of the table.

There was a small silence before, undaunted, June said, "That poor girl was all but naked and holding his burrito and what does she get for her trouble? Nothing. He tells her she's a nice girl—"

"Which she isn't," Pops said.

"Then he gets up and turns his back so she can button her blouse. And he never asks to see her again."

"The babaloos couldn't have been so good," Pops said. "Maybe you've done better this time, huh, Biondo?"

Olivia felt all eyes go to her chest but managed not to cross her arms over the region.

"Enough," Mama said. "You are a bad influence, Pops. Eat, eat, all of you. There's plenty more and we got one or two present who need more meat on their bones."

Olivia didn't doubt she was among the one or two.

Pia said, her voice surprisingly full and low, "Basilio's working too hard. How we going to have time to make babies when he works all his life away for his family?"

Sam cast Olivia an apologetic look.

"Later," Mama said. "Our Basilio is a tower of strength to this family. We're in dry cleaning, Olivia. The best dry cleaning in New York, maybe in the world. June works with him, and his brothers Adamo and Emilio. Then there is Sophia who is—well, you will hear anyway. Sophia considers herself an *actress*. But she is a good girl. Every mother should have such good children."

"You forget Lucan." Pops' face became expressionless.

"Him, we don't talk about." Mama crossed herself and turned to Sam. "How come you bring your girl here instead of Hell's Kitchen?"

"Lucan is living in sin with a *Protestant*," June said. "Pass the Parmesan."

Aiden knew he was supposed to be Mama's diversion from the

subject of Lucan and scrambled for something, anything, to say. "A leak," he said. "Yes, there's a leak in my place."

"Where?" Vanni asked.

Later, Aiden thought, he would have to tell Vanni that a man's friends should try to make his life easier. "In the bathroom. Makes the whole place cold."

"It's always cold. You like it cold," Vanni said.

"He's old-fashioned," Mama said, smiling. "He doesn't want temptation right under his nose, so he wants his girl to sleep here. Eat, Olivia, eat. It's not you don't look good, but you could be better covered in places. And you are welcome in our home for as long as you want to stay. Just watch that Biondo, where he puts his hands. I see now that he's no different than the rest."

"What places?" Pops asked. "What places she needs better covered?" He pushed a small serving of spaghetti and sauce around his plate. Olivia hadn't seen him take a mouthful yet.

"Pops," Mama said. "You got to give an example to these young people. Don't teach them they got to be personal all the time."

"Like you are, you mean?" Pops said. "So where does Olivia need fattening up? Not the babaloos. This I can see." He kissed his fingers while eyeing Olivia's chest. "But Biondo maybe likes a little more here or there."

"*Don't* feed that dog," Pia said, bringing a skinny fist down on the table. "It's not healthy, him slobbering in here."

"Where?" Pops persisted. "Where she needs the fattening up, boy?"

"Nowhere," Sam told him. "She's just right as she is—in my opinion."

Olivia's eyes filled with tears. She had to be beyond exhausted or she'd control her emotions better.

"Now if you said things like that to me when you got home, it wouldn't matter how late it was," Pia said to Basilio.

"You're beautiful," her husband told her, and from the look in his eyes, Olivia knew he meant it. "I am a lucky man."

"Get her to bed," Pops said. "Never mind dinner, go do the thing before she forgets what you said."

June slipped Boss a chunk of pepperoni and followed it with a saucer of meatballs.

"She's feeding the dog at the table again," Pia said. "It's disgusting."

"Welcome to our home," Vanni said to Olivia.

"It's lovely," she said. "Thank you for letting me be here. I've never experienced anything like it."

Evidently Pops found that funnier than anything he'd ever heard. He laughed and coughed and wiped at streaming eyes with the backs of his hands. When he gasped for breath, he used two hands to take a goblet of red wine to his lips and suck it down in gulps.

"Stop it," Vanni said, abruptly and loudly. "Pops, you stop that now."

"Leave him," Mama said quietly.

"I'm not leaving him," Vanni said. "He shouldn't get excited because of his heart, you know that."

Pops produced a handkerchief and blew his nose. "What does it matter?" he mumbled. "I lived long enough already."

"Don't," Mama said. "Think of Vanni."

"Think of Vanni, think of Vanni," Pops said. "What's the matter, you're afraid I'll die laughing? Seems like a good way to go to me."

"Our grandfather needs a heart transplant," Basilio said, and the big man's open devastation made him seem smaller. "According to the medical profession, he's too old."

Pops said, "They're right. When it's time to go, it's time to go."

"What they mean," Basilio continued, "is that he's not rich enough. At least, he refuses to tell them he is and won't let us spend the money on him."

"I worked for that money for my children and my children's children," Pops said. "You think I like the idea of being chopped up like a pig carcass, then, if I should be so *fortunate* as to live, watching all of you try to pull things together without having enough money left to do it with. No, thank you. Kindly drop the subject."

Olivia watched this family interact and felt strangely bereft. She loved her parents and Theo, but she'd never known displays of emotion, other than tightly contained anger, and there had rarely been a sense of really close ties. The FitzDurhams loved each other, but didn't know how to let each other know.

"I need all of you to help me." Vanni's announcement silenced everyone. "We all love Aiden, but he's making a big mistake that could ruin his life. We don't want him to do that. By the way, Olivia thinks Aiden's name is Sam because he hasn't managed to explain that it's not. It's not Sam, and it's not Ryan. Ryan Hill—some of you may have heard that name mentioned—he lives upstairs from Aiden. Ryan's been corresponding with Olivia by e-mail and calling himself Sam."

Very carefully, Olivia shifted backward in her chair.

"Vanni," Sam—or Aiden—said. "I have a problem to work through here. But it's my problem, not yours."

"This is a close family and you're a member," Vanni said, his handsome face so hard he didn't look like himself. "I gave you your chance to clear things up, and you failed. Now we gotta help you."

Olivia couldn't quite swallow. She frowned around the table. When she tried to remove her hand from . . . whoever he was, he tightened his grip on her.

"Do you think you're being fair?" he said to Vanni. "Do you think this is the place to drop all this on Olivia?"

"We both know there isn't anything you can say here without knowing it's absolutely safe. We joke around, but nothing goes out of the room unless one of us tells the others it should." Vanni looked at each Zanetto. "We got big trouble. Not one word gets repeated outside the family—okay?"

Mama wrung her small, plump hands and said, "You don't have to say it even. Let us help you, Aiden."

Aiden. So that much was obviously true.

"Okay with you, Aiden?" Vanni asked.

Aiden looked at Olivia. "I'm sorry," he said. "It all happened so fast that I didn't get a chance to break it to you before you left England. I thought you were in danger. Now you and I both *know* you are. I did what I did because I wanted to help you. I don't know if you can believe that. You don't know me, so why should you, but I'm still asking you to give it a whirl. There's something rotten going down with Ryan Hill—he's the guy you know as Sam. I happened to be looking after his orchids—he lives in the apartment above mine—and I saw your messages on his computer. My machine was on the fritz so I was going to do my own e-mail from his. And I admit it—I read his mail, your mail. I should say I'm sorry, but it would be a lie because I think you need my help."

His long speech left Olivia silent and unsure what to say. She looked into his clear blue eyes and thought she saw an honest man. She also noticed the small gold hoop he wore in one ear—and liked it.

He cleared his throat. "You may not want my help, but you must find someone you can trust."

"You're in danger," Vanni said, and his mother hugged herself and rocked. "Somehow Ryan Hill found you, and you were a threat to him. There's no other explanation. He's safely tucked away upstate, or he has been. I'm betting he's on the move now and it'll only be a matter of time before he tracks you down. The thought of him finding you alone isn't something I want to think about."

Olivia couldn't feel her hands. She was terrified, and when she looked from face to face she realized she was also among total strangers.

"Cut it out, Vanni," Aiden said.

"Because it's true? What good will that do? We gotta have a plan."

"First Olivia has to be convinced she hasn't been grabbed by a maniac—me—who can't be trusted."

"I do trust you." She hadn't had any intention of saying that, but she did. And her instincts about people had always been good. "What would you have to gain from me? Certainly not my fortune, or my ravishing person. Right?"

Pops chortled again, and again tears squeezed from the corners of his eyes. He pointed at Olivia. "You got to like the girl. But you got to wake up, Olivia. You dress yourself like an old lady, but you're a woman a man likes to think about putting his hands on—and other things on. Am I right, Biondo?"

Basilio said, "You are right, Pops. Now remember you're the head of the household and supposed to be an example."

"I thought I was," Pops said, shrugging, a devilish glint in his eye. "I was telling the truth, just as my father taught me, and your father taught you—and you, Basilio, will teach your children when you and Pia learn that it can take passion to put those little meatballs in the pan."

Olivia found her voice. "Sam—Aiden, you and Vanni are also in the FBI?" she said.

"*No.*" Vanni could be a little overzealous with his annoyance. "And neither is friend Ryan. He's NYPD. We all are. He must have decided you'd think FBI sounded more romantic."

"Mama," Aiden said, with absolute conviction that he had to take back control of the situation. "Could I get Olivia settled? Vanni said she's to be in June's old room."

"Now that June thinks Sophia's room is more elegant," Pia said, examining her fingernails. "I think Sophia's room is a nightmare. All that red and black."

"Of course," Mama said. "If you've had enough to eat, both of you, go on up. Everything you need is there, Olivia. Our home is your home, for as long as you like. Vanni, how can we make Olivia at ease about us? This must be so difficult for her."

"I'm easy," Olivia said.

Pops coughed. "Wouldn't advertise that, if I was you. Boss, you gotta job. You go look after our new friend, hear me?"

"That's a great idea," Aiden said, and he felt relieved. He'd have to return to Hell's Kitchen, which for some reason bothered him. He wanted to be close to Olivia.

"Thank you," Olivia said. She got up. "I'm really very tired. Don't make Boswell stand guard over me. I'll be fine." She stepped back from the table and Aiden rose at once. So did Boss. The dog fell in behind Olivia with a look of delighted anticipation on his long-snooted face.

"I need to tell you one or two things, partner," Vanni said, also getting up. "One or two developments at the precinct."

"Oh." Olivia paused and looked at the two men. "You're *police* partners."

"Yeah," they both said.

The Zanettos chorused good nights and Olivia felt their warmth.

"I think the girl needs a human guard," Pops said. "Get Aiden the cot, Vanni. He can sleep in the corner of Olivia's room."

When Olivia looked back at the old man, he'd developed a sudden appetite for his pasta.

Aiden picked up Olivia's bags in the hall and led the way upstairs. Vanni was behind her, Boss beside her. Aiden had the briefest thought that he'd got himself into something deeper than even he had imagined. The biggest potential complication was that he found the woman interesting, a development he didn't remember happening since his old partner, Chris Talon, met Sonnie Giacano, the woman who subsequently became Chris's wife. He'd envied Chris then. Now he was really glad for both of them.

June's old room was childlike, with a patchwork quilt on a single bed, looped lace curtains at the windows beneath chintz drapes pulled all the way back. Pictures of pop stars covered the walls, and gathered pink fabric ran around the kidney-shaped dressing table and a small stool. Teddy bears were heaped on the bed.

Olivia and Boss followed Aiden in, then Vanni, who closed the door and listened as if he expected someone to follow and stand outside the door.

"Now," Vanni said, "listen up. We've got really big problems."

Aiden took in Olivia's strained face. "We know," he said. "First thing in the morning, we'll have a powwow and decide on the next step."

"Too late," Vanni said. "By tomorrow we've got to figure out how to get Olivia out of here and you with her."

Aiden took an instant to hold up a hand. "She's got to rest, Vanni. And you've got to be a whole lot clearer."

"Sorry," Vanni said. "Sit down, Olivia. Or stretch out on the bed. You can sleep if you like. Aiden and I will take care of everything."

There were times when Vanni showed no sign of understanding the comfort zones of other human beings. Olivia dutifully sat on a chair, but her back was straight, her slim ankles crossed, and every line in her body screamed that she was on alert.

Boss sat beside her and rested his head on her lap. Lamplight glinted on his titanium grin.

There would be no stopping Vanni. "Okay," Aiden said. "Spit it out but keep it simple."

"The chief got a message from Ryan."

Aiden frowned and waited for more.

"He blew the whistle on you. Bad cop in cahoots with a British thief—female."

"That's goddamn ridiculous." He paused. "But let me guess. The old man bought it. He's been waiting for me to take another wrong step so he can get rid of me."

Vanni didn't answer Aiden. Instead he glanced at Olivia, whose brown eyes were huge. "Art theft. Seems Olivia's job lets her be in the right places at the right times. She has the opportunities. And according to Ryan, you're the one with contacts in the States, Aiden. Collectors who don't care how you get what they want. You've been *helping* these people find their hearts' desire. Ryan, so he says, has been quietly investigating you, but now he knows you're on to him and he's afraid for his life. So he's asking the department to apprehend you."

"But"—Aiden turned the puzzle pieces over in his mind—"but there's absolutely no evidence against me except for what Ryan says."

"No, and that's why all this is being dealt with unofficially at first. But Fats is backing Ryan up. He says he's scared of you, too, but he hopes if you know your cover is blown, he'll be safe."

"What a crock. What an absolute, friggin'—sorry, Olivia. What a pile of—garbage. Not a word of it holds water."

Vanni leaned on the wall and propped an elbow. He wiped at his face.

"What?" Aiden said. "C'mon, Vanni. We can shoot this apart in minutes."

"How? Do we hand over Olivia? They're looking for her in London now."

The whitening of Olivia's already pale face distressed Aiden. "I'm going in to talk to the chief," he said.

"Whatever you think," Vanni said. "I'll do my best to take care of Olivia. Maybe I can find a place to hide her until everything blows over. If it blows over."

"Aiden," Olivia said, so softly he could hardly hear her. "Vanni wouldn't say all this if it wasn't true, right?"

He wanted to say it was a joke. "No. No, he wouldn't. Something has gotten really screwed up."

"You stepped right in the middle of a plan Ryan must have been working on a long time," Vanni said. "All he's doing is fighting back."

"What's my alternative to going to the chief?"

"Get out of sight until I can work things through," Vanni said. He took a deep breath. "And pray I can do it."

"Why can't Olivia stay here?"

"She can't, and you can't. They know Olivia's in the country now. They're already looking for her. They'll come here."

"And Ryan? Has he said he's returning to duty?"

"Yeah. In a few days, he says. He's coming back to help find you."

"I'm not running from that little creep, Ryan D. Hill."

Vanni nodded slowly. "Your call, partner. Whichever way you go, I'll be right there on your side doing what I can."

"This is my fault," Olivia said. "Don't worry. I'm going to the police at once. I'll explain that I don't know what they're talking about and that'll be that."

She found herself under scrutiny from two pairs of eyes, and they didn't look as if they thought she'd just had the winning idea.

"Ryan's made a good job of this, hasn't he?" Aiden said.

"The best," Vanni said. "And you shoulda heard that creep, Fats. He just about had the chief offering him a safe house. By the time Lemon finished, you sounded like a psycho who's probably got half-a-dozen should-be floaters doing the Hudson polka in concrete shoes. The cars came up. Your cars. What the collection is worth and so on. How does a guy do that on a cop's salary?"

"He doesn't," Aiden said, mentally cursing the unfairness of having to address this. "I inherited from my mom. My dad died years back. I don't have any siblings, so it all came to me. End of story."

"I'd suggest you just go out and get lost in a cabin somewhere,"

Vanni said, "but if they put a manhunt together, I'd rather they didn't find you alone out there."

"I'm not running," Aiden said. "I'm clean, so I'm not running."

"You're with Olivia," Vanni pointed out. "And even if you can get the chief to buy your own story—" He stopped and pressed his lips together. "Olivia, you already heard me say they think you're a big time art thief. I don't know all the details, but there's evidence. If you did turn yourself in, they wouldn't just apologize and say they must be mistaken."

She stood up. Aiden watched her and experienced the strongest emotional reaction to a woman he ever remembered having. Olivia raised her chin, and he saw her throat move. Tears filmed her eyes and her mouth quivered, but only until she tightened it and pulled the corners down.

Vanni waited for her to answer.

Aiden wanted only to keep on looking at her.

"I've already said I'm ready to go to the police station. Now I insist. You can't know whether or not I'm this thief some people think I may be. I'm as badly off here as I would be with the police, right?"

"You are with the police," Vanni said. "Some of us are open enough to know we ought to wait for more proof before we jump in. But in the ways that matter, what I believe—or Aiden believes—doesn't count. If friend Ryan has gathered enough phony evidence, they're going to follow everything up and if you're really unlucky, innocent or guilty, you'll be thrown in the slammer."

"But you think if I take her and run, you can find a way to string Ryan up?" He'd never been good at relying on someone else.

Vanni hunched his big shoulders and said, "I hope I can."

Olivia knew what Alice in Wonderland must have felt. In this cozy little girl's room, the two men were oversized and out of place, and they were both angry and worried.

"The chief came at me like I was on trial," Vanni said. "You'd have thought you were in the running to become the next Unibomber."

Aiden made up his mind. "This is going to put you on the line," he told Vanni. "You ready for that?"

His partner averted his face and nodded.

"The force means everything to you," Aiden reminded him. "Still sure?"

"It means everything to you, too. That makes us even. I'm ready."

"So you think I should take Olivia somewhere we're not likely to be found?"

Vanni nodded again.

Aiden said, "Olivia, you're confused. You've got to be."

"I'm in a country I've never visited before, thousands of miles from home, with people I hadn't met before today. And I'm accused of being a thief. But I'm not as confused as you think I am. I've been going through one shock after another for days."

"So you'd consider going into hiding with me?"

She looked at the floor. "Yes." And she was frightened but also excited. So much for all those people who told her she needed to get out more.

"Okay. Tomorrow we get a plane out of here."

"They'll be watching the airports," Vanni said. "Still unofficially, of course."

"Not unless they think you've been singing to me."

Vanni ran the fingers of both hands through his thick hair. "I didn't think of that. I'm getting ahead of myself. There's a briefing at 0600. They were talking about how you and Olivia must have known each other—probably been lovers—and you'd be hanging out in New York at least until you got wind that you were under suspicion. Maybe you're right. Both of you get some sleep, then leave early in the morning. Where, though?" He frowned. "Where will you go? Key West?"

"Too obvious," Aiden said. "I've got a reputation for liking it down there. I'm going to Chris. Most people here don't know he's on the force in Seattle now. In fact, I don't know who does other than you and me."

Vanni nodded. "I should have thought of that."

"He's perfect for a lot of reasons. He'll find a place to put us, and if someone does track him, he'll be so convincing no one will ever believe we've been near him. And he's the best man we could invite into our corner."

"Okay. Sounds good. You should get out on the first available flight, though."

"I think Ryan D's going to show up the minute I'm out of the way," Aiden said.

"Absolutely," Olivia said. "He'll feel really safe then. And when you run away, you look guilty. That won't hurt his story, right?"

Aiden smiled at her. "We could use you on the force. But you are right. If I go, I look guilty. But if I stay, they're going to come after you anyway, and once they've got you, Ryan will return with all his carefully constructed accusations. Apart from those two scenarios, both of which can be overcome, there's the matter of the guys in London. We can assume Mr. Moody and Mr. Fish wouldn't be anxious for you to talk to someone like me, but I've got to find out where they fit in here. And I want to know which one came after you with murder on his mind. The best way to buy the time to do that is to let everyone think I'm otherwise occupied—as in saving my own skin."

"Where did you say your friend lives?" Olivia asked quietly.

"Seattle," Aiden told her. "He retired from the force here, then ended up there and joined up again. They're damned lucky to have him."

She didn't look convinced.

"It'll be okay," he told her, and wished he could be completely sure it would. "Wait'll you see the guy. He'll make you feel safe."

"You make me feel safe," she said, and turned her back. "I should go to sleep and so should you. Thanks, Vanni. I'm awfully sorry to be such a pest."

Vanni took a step toward her, but Aiden shook his head and Vanni retreated again. "Nothing to feel bad about," he told her. "You aren't responsible for the lousy people in the world."

"The room next door's empty, isn't it?" Aiden asked.

"Yeah. But I'm not going to my place tonight so I thought I'd use it. You can share, though." Vanni took a piece of paper from his pocket and handed it silently to Aiden who recognized a short computer printout. "What I don't know for sure is where this originated."

"I'll get ready for bed," Olivia said, still facing the wall. "Then, if it wouldn't be too much trouble, and if he wouldn't mind, I'd be grateful to have Boswell in here after all. Stupid, I know, but it's all been too much."

Vanni wiggled his brows, then mouthed, *"Lucky Boswell."*

"No problem," Aiden said. He took Boss by the collar and led him to a rug at the bottom of the bed. "Guard, Boss." He clicked his fingers and the dog dropped, rested his head on his paws, and darted his eyes from side to side.

Aiden read the paper Vanni had given him: *"Olivia here. Hope you get this in time to stop you from leaving for the airport to meet me. Sorry for all the trouble. I've changed my mind. I won't be coming to New York, at least not at the moment. Thank you for all your kindness, Sam."* The e-mail had supposedly been sent from Olivia's address some hours earlier, while Olivia was already on her way to New York. This was a last desperate effort to stop Olivia from meeting up with Aiden.

Too late, but evidently whoever wrote it—and Aiden would bet it was Ryan—hadn't been sure when she left England. But he must have figured out he'd not only posted after the fact, but that by doing so, he'd made sure Aiden knew someone was following Olivia. Now Ryan was moving in to cover for himself. Aiden met Vanni's eyes, and they exchanged a bleak glance. Vanni hadn't been wrong about the presence of danger.

Olivia opened her bulging tartan grip and started pulling things out, and Vanni left the room.

She stood up and dropped her hands to her sides, toiletries in one, underwear in the other.

Without warning, she walked into Aiden's arms. She rested her face on his chest, and he couldn't tell if she was crying.

"Sorry," she said, very muffled. "Look what I've done to you. I don't know what to do, but I've got to save you from all this."

For a moment or two he stood there, his hands raised. Then he wrapped an arm tightly around her, and stroked her hair with the other. "I told you to quit apologizing. And I'm the pro at this sort of thing, so I'll work our way out. We'll end up heroes." Mostly, he didn't want either of them to end up dead or in jail. "Meanwhile you'll get to see some of the most beautiful country in the world. And I'll get a vacation I never expected." *Some vacation.* "Stick with me, kid. I'll make sure you have a time to remember."

Olivia looked up at him, at his lean and smiling face. Now she knew he was lying, or at least embellishing. He'd look after her, but he wasn't—couldn't be—looking forward to it. "You're an awfully nice man," she told him.

Aiden smiled through gritted teeth. Tonight he'd learned something; "nice" wasn't a word that made him feel—*nice.*

Ten

"Toast?" Ryan asked. "No, toast isn't what you want, is it?"

"Damn you, Ryan," Kitty said. He was used to people being afraid of him. Ryan Hill didn't frighten her—she knew how to manage him. She still shivered with excitement at the memory of seeing him outside the front door of Olivia FitzDurham's house.

Ryan clasped his hands behind his neck and stretched. The man had great muscles.

"I want some sleep, and you know what I want before that," Kitty said. For hours he'd taunted her, played games with her all over the Hampstead house. He really got off on having her do weird things nude, like slide down the banisters. At least he was naked, too, and that was worth the admission price.

Ryan was hungry, and a lot more tired than he intended Kitty to find out. He stuck his head into the all-but-empty refrigerator in the FitzDurham woman's Delft-tiled kitchen and groaned. "Butter. No margarine. And only whole milk. Bacon. Eggs. Sausages. That's it. Not a piece of fruit or a vegetable in sight. You could hold an orgy in here, it's so empty. And one look at the food she does have, and my arteries sound *Taps*." The bread he'd dropped in the toaster was butter-top-egg.

"For God's sake, Ryan, shut the refrigerator door before you freeze off something you don't want to lose. Forget your bleedin' arteries and *fuck* me again. And *finish* it this time."

Kitty wasn't too swift. "You don't learn fast, do you?" he said, turning from the refrigerator with a bottle of milk in hand. "Push me and I get real unhappy. What I decide to do, I do in my own time." His white-blond hair fascinated her, and the sweeping Slavic bones in his face. But his eyes were pure ice and the less she looked at them, the better she felt.

She let her head hang back. "How much more time do you need? You're not human. What kind of man keeps a hard-on for hours?" *A sick man with a problem.* He definitely wasn't normal. "I've forgotten how many times you've pulled out and left me like this."

"Shut up." He controlled an urge to slap her mouth. "My women don't complain. They line up for their turn. Men like me don't come along very often. I've got special talent. Enjoy it."

Deliberately strolling, he got close and rolled the cold milk bottle back and forth over her breasts while she squirmed and her nipples puckered up hard. If she cried out, he'd decide he'd found a new form of torture to use again.

Kitty pursed her lips.

He'd handcuffed her wrists behind her and to the back of the tall bar stool where she sat. One ankle was tied to each of the front legs. Two of the stools, each with blue poppies on their upholstered seats, stood at a counter that divided the kitchen from a minute and very dark room where several tweed chairs crowded, arm-to-arm, around a TV in an ugly cabinet.

The toast popped. He'd eat it dry. "Sure you aren't hungry? Maybe there's some cereal," he said.

"The only thing I'm hungry for doesn't come in a bowl."

He didn't comment.

Kitty knew she must have marks on her wrists and ankles. It didn't make sense that Ryan would risk doing something she could show Rupert. Whatever Ryan was really up to, he couldn't want his old partners in crime, Rupert and Winston, to get any hint of it.

She shook back her hair and pouted at Ryan. Whatever game he was playing, she'd play with him, at least until she could duck out and still be safe. "My wrists hurt," she said, wriggling.

"And you love it. You're insatiable."

"It's a good job I am," she said, blowing at strands of hair that stuck to her mouth. "What you've done to me would kill some women."

He grinned at her. "But not you, horny babe. Only woman I know with calluses in her nookie. Let me get my toast." He'd already poured a mug of coffee. "Then I want to watch you do the squeeze number again. Never saw a woman get off that way before."

"Sick bastard," she muttered, but remembered to smile.

Ryan put his plate of toast on the counter and pulled his stool close to Kitty's. Time to get real serious. He sat on the stool, took a swig of milk from the bottle, then drank some coffee and followed it up with a mouthful of toast. "Why did you come here tonight?" he asked, deliberately offhand. "It wasn't because you knew I'd be here." He'd been timing this question since he'd realized it could be the most important he ever asked.

He didn't fool her. He tried to sound nonchalant, but the way he kept his eyes downcast warned Kitty that he was fishing for something he really needed to find out. "I thought Rupert might be here."

Ryan's eyes rose to hers instantly. "Why would he be?"

"I followed him here yesterday and I thought he might come back again." She could keep it vague, at least for now, and until she found out what the exact information might be worth—or how dangerous it could be to reveal. "I needed a way to get some money out of him, so I hung around tonight."

Ryan breathed a little faster. "He came to this house? He came into this house?"

He was getting angry. Kitty couldn't guess why, but it scared her. "He didn't come into the house," she said, praying it was what he wanted to hear. "He looked so stupid—not that that's hard for him to do. Talking through the letterbox in broad daylight."

"About what?"

"Couldn't hear." Might as well take a risk now. "He left and waited in a taxi around the corner till the woman who lives here came out with a couple of suitcases and took a cab. Then he followed her."

Shit, Ryan thought, Fish probably found out Olivia was on her way to New York. "Then what happened?" he asked.

"Don't know. Later on I called him up at the shop and accused him of having an affair with her, but he denied it. Said she had something he wanted and he was trying to get it back. That's all. Mind my own business. Same stuff he always says if I ask him about anything."

Ryan relaxed. Fish had come here trying to get the photos. Moody would have sent him. "Did he say whether she gave him what he wanted?"

"No." She'd hold off on the envelope she'd seen passed through. "But he wouldn't, anyway."

"When did you say this was? Yesterday?"

She looked at the yellowing ceiling and frowned. "I suppose it was only yesterday. It feels like years ago—so much has happened since then."

Ryan did believe Kitty was being straight with him. What she said fitted in with Olivia's movements, as best he knew them. Unfortunately, since Rupert hadn't got what he wanted, and those photos must be so important to him, it made sense he'd try to catch up with her. Rupert was Winston Moody's follower and wouldn't leave the country without talking to him. The way Ryan saw it, Rupert would have returned from Heathrow to the antique shop, and he and Winston could have left for New York by now. Ryan decided that if they had, he'd have to make sure they didn't get in his way.

"You're something special, babe." He held the bread to Kitty's mouth, but she turned her head away. "You need to keep your strength up." He laughed.

"You're a piece of Yankee shit," she told him. "Damn you, you're getting crumbs all over me."

Every word from her mouth made him feel better. She didn't know a thing that mattered. If she did, she'd be more careful, much more careful, around him. Most likely she wouldn't be here at all, unless she was so twisted that fear turned her on.

Kitty was that twisted, she had to be. She'd followed him in here, hadn't she?

"Get the crumbs off me. They itch."

He glanced at her naked white body. "Can't allow that," he said.

Kitty liked the way he looked at her. He leaned forward and blew on her breasts. She squealed. He stood up and bent over her, getting into the blowing thing. His warm breath started her writhing. Ryan blew and followed up with brushing hands, and the brushing hands dealt practiced tweaks and slaps. And her skin flushed with intense arousal.

Ryan saw when her eyes lost focus. She was starting to come again.

He sat back on his stool and tasted the coffee again. "Not bad, but then, I made it."

"You *bastard*. Finish it. *Finish* it."

"Did you see me tonight, Kitty, or this morning?"

She tried to squeeze her thighs together but couldn't, the way her ankles were tied to the chair made sure of that.

The heat faded. Ryan looked into her eyes intently and said, "Did you? Have you seen me in the last twenty-four hours?"

"I'm seeing you now, aren't I? Creep."

"Wrong answer." He tapped her leg. "You haven't seen me at all. The question isn't likely to come up, but just in case it ever does, you haven't seen me since you nagged Rupert into taking you to New

York last year. Remember how much fun we had when Rupert wasn't around?"

"Why do you need me to be quiet about you?" The instant she asked the question, she wished she hadn't.

Ryan turned his next tap into a slap that left the red impression of fingers on her thigh. Grimly he observed the tears she couldn't hold back. "I've got plans for you, Kitty, plans for you and me. You're going to like them, but not unless I'm convinced you deserve what I'm going to offer you. I'm going to tell you what I'm offering, and what I'll expect from you." The idea had come to him shortly after she'd showed up last night.

"I'm all ears," she told him, blinking the tears away. Her leg still stung, but she was even a little excited, not that she intended to let him know. After the last few hours, he'd have difficulty believing it, but she was known for playing hard to get.

"A swank apartment in New York and an allowance you won't be able to spend fast enough to make a dent in. How am I doing so far?"

"Go on." Her heart had speeded up.

"Your mouth shut unless I tell you to open it."

Orders again. "You'll have to spell that out, especially the reasons and what I'm going to get out of it."

"Not a big enough carrot yet, huh? You don't change, Kitty. I'm going to make more money than your little brain can visualize. I'm going to make so much money, I'll be running with people you've only read about. A woman I could train to fit in as *Mrs. Hill* could be a real asset to me."

He couldn't be suggesting he wanted to marry her. Kitty managed to sit up straighter. "Aren't you forgetting something? Like Rupert?"

This was where he trod carefully, but said what she wanted to hear. "You were always too good for him. We might have to be patient, but not too patient. A trip to Reno or Vegas will deal with the small stuff. In the meantime, Rupert's a nobody among the people who matter. They don't know he exists. This is for you and me, baby."

Kitty swallowed. No matter what else she did, she had to remain cool. Seeming too eager could make her a whole lot less appealing to Ryan and she wanted him, at least until she got her share of all that money he was talking about.

"What do you say, sweets?" Ryan did what he didn't much like to do—he kissed Kitty, a deep, tonsil-touching kiss that brought her breast on a search-and-titillate mission. She brushed her nipples across his chest and panted. He pushed his hands into her hair and made the kind of meal of her mouth that was guaranteed to start her begging for him to come inside her. Well, he knew how to do that. A little slight of hand, so to speak, and he could do it just fine, but not before he had her so starry-eyed at her prospects with him that he'd be able to believe her when she agreed to everything he wanted from her.

When Ryan pulled his lips from hers, Kitty knew what it would feel like to have a plunger used on her mouth. He prolonged the sucking contact and she heard a faint "pop," when skin parted from skin. She kept her eyes closed and sighed. "Lay it on me, Ryan," she said

"Anything you say, baby." And he moved between her legs to rest his rock-hard dick on her belly. "Okay?"

"Almost."

"What do Rupert and Winston say about me?" He kept a smile on his face, but he watched her minutely, searching for even a flicker of some reaction that would mean he had to rethink the next move.

There was no flicker in Kitty's eyes. "They don't talk about you at all. The last time I mentioned you, Winston said you were none of my business."

Good. Not that he'd expected anything different. Winston and Rupert had every reason to want to keep their association with him real private. "Let's play it their way, then," he told Kitty. "In fact, we've got to. You're going to witness a miracle, baby. By the time we've finished with Moody and Fish, everything they've got will be ours. And all their connections, too—you do know about the connections?"

She frowned, as if thinking was unfamiliar. "You mean those people they deal with in other countries? The ones who pay them so much money?"

"Those are the ones," he said, making sure he sounded a whole lot more patient than he felt.

Something tapped the kitchen windows.

Ryan stared into the darkness outside but didn't see a thing.

"What is it?" Kitty craned around to look and her eyes grew huge. "Ryan, someone's out there watching us."

"That's the problem with forgetting to cover the windows."

Men were so unobservant. "There's nothing to cover them with. See who it is. Don't let them get away."

He executed a sloppy salute and strode to the door.

"You're *naked*," Kitty said in a harsh whisper.

"Lucky world," Ryan told her and threw open the door. He'd picked up his Beretta on the way and stood back from the thick gloom in the tiny garden behind the house. A stiff breeze raised gooseflesh all over him. It didn't do what it might be expected to do to a man.

"Close the door," Kitty moaned. Nude and shackled, she was in a direct line with the door. Vulnerable didn't come close to describing how she felt. "I'm cold."

A black cat shot into the kitchen. Sinewy and tall, he jumped onto the chair Ryan had vacated and from there fell upon the barely touched toast.

Kitty screamed. "Get him out of here. I hate cats. I'm allergic to them."

The diversion came at a good time. Moody and Fish wanted to forget he'd ever existed. When he'd first suspected they intended to cut him out of the action he'd been right. Turning the tables, cutting them out instead, would be a delicate operation, but screeching on a stool behind him was the answer to his prayers, an answer he hadn't even thought of until she'd followed him in here and put on her show.

"Ryan!"

"It's okay. Just be quiet and let me think." Trees rustled. There was no moon, and he couldn't see anything but shadows. Those flowers the English went bugs over, the ones that smelled at night, layered their heavy scent into the wind. He could barely make out a path of broken slabs of stone with moss in the cracks. Everything in this country was on a miniature scale. Made him want to throw out his arms and push for more space.

"It's climbing on me!"

He closed the door and went to Kitty. The cat had discovered the residue of crumbs that still clung to her skin.

"Please, Ryan. I'm going to be sick. His tongue hurts."

The critter was no dummy. With a long, sandpaper tongue, he lavished a bath on Kitty, and he wasn't missing many places. Ryan wasn't keen on cats either, but he stroked the animal and hid a grin when it arched its back and drove sharp claws into Kitty's legs and stomach.

Her slitted eyes and the way they glittered at him suggested he'd had enough fun with this if he hoped to gain her trust. "Off you go." He tossed the cat down and it immediately disappeared into other regions of the house. "This is the plan. First you tell me how hard it would be for you to go on vacation—alone, or so-called alone."

"I do what I like. Sometimes Rupert doesn't see me for days or weeks." She didn't add that she frequently stayed away until she needed money and she might sometimes let her husband look at her in exchange for what she wanted, but they hadn't made love for months.

This was perfect, Ryan decided. "He never appreciated you. But I do. Do you love him?"

Kitty laughed. "Love him? No. He had money and I didn't—end of story."

Better and better. "So there aren't any loyalties hidden away?"

She shook her head. "No, Ryan. You shouldn't have to ask. Come here. I want you back where you were before that sodding cat arrived."

Obediently he rested himself on her stomach again. Kitty contrived to move beneath his erection. The tightness inside him intensified. This time he couldn't make an excuse to go to the bathroom and ease himself.

His face, the sincerity in his eyes, wasn't what she expected of him. "I want to hold you," she said softly, looking down at dimensions any man would love to show off in the showers. "I want you to believe that you are the answer to my prayer. I need you. I can't believe I was lucky enough to find you tonight. It was fate, Ryan. I'm going to be whatever you want me to be." And he would pay for the honor.

The faithful Doberman stare worked every time, Ryan decided. "Will you marry me, Kitty?"

Her heart pounded and her skin fired up from underneath. She couldn't quite get a breath.

"Kitty, honey? Will you come to the States with me and be my wife, partner?"

"Yes," she finally managed to say. "But—"

"No buts, baby. I'll take care of everything, but you've got to promise me something."

"Undo the cuffs."

He chucked her under the chin and rubbed their noses together. "Soon. I've got a present for you first. But you've got to promise you won't say a word to Winston or Rupert."

"I wouldn't!"

"I know, I know, you don't think you would, but you could be tempted if one of them gets smart with you. And I wouldn't blame you." With a knuckle, he circled first one big, brown nipple, then the other—and he pinched the bud between finger and thumb and pulled, more gently than he'd have liked to.

Another explosion was building for Kitty. When she had time to think, she'd try to remember how many times she'd climaxed since they'd been together. "Oh, God," she moaned. "You're killing me."

Not yet, babe. "Kitty, if you did say something to Rupert or Winston, you'd ruin everything."

"I won't."

"Not a single word? As far as they're concerned, this night never happened, and if anything ever comes up about me, you're going to be puzzled because you'd forgotten all about me. Okay?"

"Oh, yes, oh, *yes*, Ryan. I love you."

Sure she did. "You're sure they've never said anything about me recently?"

"Not a thing. In fact I asked when we'd see you again." She lowered her lashes. "I've kept hoping, you see. Winston called me a meddling bitch. He told me if I said your name again, he'd shut me in his storage room. I know all about that room. It's got one-way glass and things happen in there. Rupert told me. But saying that to me has cost that little pervert plenty, and—"

"I believe you, honey. How soon can you be ready to leave— maybe leave for several weeks if things don't go as smoothly as I hope?"

"Really quickly."

"Good. I'll book the plane tickets. We won't travel together, or be together in the States—"

"Oh, Ryan, you said—"

"Hush." He pressed his fingers over her mouth. "Let me finish. We won't be together until it's safe and all the details are fixed. But we'll talk a lot. And you'll talk to Winston and Rupert."

She frowned and shook her head. "I don't want to. Why would I waste money calling them?"

"You won't be paying, remember. And you'll call them because I have to know every move they make. I've got to get back to New York. I'd ask you to stay here, but I can't bear the thought of you being so far away."

"Oh, Ryan."

"Oh, Kitty, I know, babe." Real soon he'd know this had been worth every gut-twisting second he'd suffered through. "I don't know why I didn't do something about us a long time ago. Of course, I don't want you to tell them you're in the States." And she'd only be there because he, Ryan, had to be one hundred percent sure he could get to her fast—and control her. "I won't be able to stay away, you know that. I ought to, but how can I? You'll have to help me be strong."

"What kind of car do you drive?"

Poor Rupert Fish. "A BMW. Just got it. Gold with an ivory interior."

Kitty mmm'd. "You never told me where you live."

"I've got a place upstate. In the hills. Fabulous view of a million miles of forest. Windows everywhere. Indoor pool. Sauna. Hot tub just begging for you and me, the night, the stars—or maybe some snow falling."

"Oh, Ryan."

Shee-it. "We've got to quit talking, babe. I'll arrange a ticket and you'll pick it up at Heathrow. You'll go where I tell you to go in New York and wait to hear from me. I'll make sure you've got money, plenty of money. Just stay put, okay?"

"Anything you say, darling."

"Okay. Let's move it."

"Ry-an. You promised." She wanted to part knowing she had something of him with her. Wow, she never remembered feeling this sentimental over a man. And he was the biggest, handsomest son of a bitch she'd ever had—almost had since they'd been together in New York before. Every inch of him was muscle. He had the kind of definition men dreamed of while they sweated in their gyms.

Ryan had almost convinced himself he could get away without this. "Don't worry, Kitty, I'm going to give you something to remember me by." He left her long enough to switch off the overhead lights. Dawn tickled the sky but not enough to find its way into the house.

His glutes hardly shifted when he walked, Kitty noted. When the lights went out, they showed pale in the gloom, and she shuddered afresh.

"Ready?" he said. He gave a short laugh. "Ready or not, here I come."

"Lovely cliché," she told him. Sweat broke out, and she was instantly drenched.

Sometimes a man had to make huge sacrifices to get what he really wanted. He'd known he needed a go-between to keep tabs on Moody and Fish, but he hadn't expected that to become so complicated. How could he have guessed they might follow Olivia to the States. Ryan had intended to take his time dealing with Fish and Moody, but it didn't look as if that was an option anymore.

Thank God for Kitty. She was an answer to a prayer. With her in place, he'd finish what had to be done in a fraction of the time—unless his fucking nemesis, Aiden Flynn, proved harder to get rid of than Ryan anticipated. At least he could be fairly certain good old *MustangMan* (real inventive screen name for a man who collected old Mustangs), that as long as Flynn was keeping up with his e-mails, Ryan could hope the man hadn't gone to the airport to meet Olivia FitzDurham. She would be wandering around New York with no-where to go. She'd have to be dealt with, and the damn photos she was probably carrying, too, but she was no major intellect. She'd come back here and wait for him to get in touch—and he wouldn't disappoint her. What she wouldn't be expecting, was her "Sam" in person.

"Ry-an."

The palms of his hands itched. He had very strong hands. "Coming. Just wanted to give you plenty of time to be the best you can be."

"You don't even know what best is, big man. Come on."

Blessing the darkness, he returned to his place between her thighs. For the required length of time—not long—he played with her, kissed her, delved into the place Kitty lived for. He took a deep, calming breath and wrapped his left elbow around her neck until her face rested against his. He could still reach forward over her shoulder and fill his hand with a breast. With his other hand he alternated between stimulating her and stroking his shaft with the practiced, featherlight strokes he'd learned to use to gain release.

Kitty sobbed into his shoulder and poured forth words of endless devotion.

Why didn't she shut up?

He felt it start. Gradually the sensation gathered power, the power that promised ecstasy, then peace. But then just as it always happened, what he thought of as a metal cinch circled the inside of his penis, with a flood of semen dammed behind it, swelling, burning, but finding no way to escape. The cinch was slowly relaxing.

Kitty didn't care that her wrists were probably bleeding. She struggled against the cuffs, strained to reach out to Ryan. She had never felt what she felt now.

The ejaculation started, and Ryan thrust up and into Kitty, the force of his locking thighs picked her up from the seat of the stool. He flooded her.

"Don't stop," she shrieked. "No, don't stop. Oh, Ryan. Oh, baby. Yes, yes, yes, yes."

Yes, yes, yes. The cinch clamped down again, and this time he was grateful because it let him pull off the illusion she had to have.

"Oh, Ryan." Her head fell on his shoulder. "I really love you."

He pulled out as slowly as he could endure. "I love you, too."

Eleven

Chris Talon had never been a man to tread lightly on someone else's feelings. Not unless the feelings happened to belong to his wife, Sonnie.

With a battered, sweat-stained fedora settled low on his brow, Aiden stood outside a women's room at JFK waiting for Olivia and replaying what he ought to have told his ex-partner on the phone. Terminal 9, or 8 and 9, or whatever American Airlines called the ongoing construction site where it serviced both its international and domestic flights, teemed with so much humanity that it ought to be easy to blend in. If Aiden weren't a cop, he might be able to convince himself of that and dispense with one of what the department called his "Wally" disguises. When he needed to get lost, or to blend in somewhere, he always relied on one of his many "Wally Loder-looks," a legacy from his narcotics days.

Chris thought Aiden was an ass for putting his career on the line over a woman he didn't know and who shouldn't mean a thing to him.

That announcement should have made it easy for Aiden to squelch the sanctimonious bastard. He could have reminded Chris that he'd already walked away from his career when he met Sonnie, but then he'd gone ahead and put his *life* on the line for a woman he didn't know and—hell, who decided if a woman should or shouldn't mean something to a man?

He felt Olivia's presence at his elbow. She looked in every direction and didn't have the training to do so without being obvious.

"Vanni decided to use the men's room," Aiden said.

Olivia already stood very close. She dropped her bulging carryall and edged in even closer until he felt her pressing against his arm. He carried the camera bag over his shoulder.

"You're afraid you're going to be arrested," she said.

Now she put it like that, he supposed he was. "No way, lady. Don't let your imagination run away with you."

"This is perfectly terrible. Those men over there? They're police, aren't they?"

"You mean the Sky Caps? No, Olivia, they aren't cops—they work for the airports here. They handle baggage."

"You're awfully kind, but I know exactly what's going on."

"There's nothing going on. Well, yeah, there is, but not what you think." *Come on, Vanni.* "I just want us on our way before this town wakes up, okay? There's not a thing to worry about."

Olivia looked up at him. Really, it could be so annoying to have a man treat one like an idiot. "I suppose that's why you're wearing that grotty hat, and the—what do you call coats like that?" It wasn't like her to be snippy. After all, he would look scrumptious in anything he wore—or nothing at all.

Her mind must be tottering.

"Don't like this antique, huh?" he said. "It's an old letterman jacket."

"Thank you, Aiden. That explains a great deal. Blue, with white leather sleeves, and striped cuffs and hcm, or whatever? And a rocket in the pocket?"

He bent forward from the waist and laughed.

"What's so funny?"

"Oh, you'll never know. You do have a way with words. Rocket *on* the pocket. For the New London Rockets. Look around you. Versions of this all over the place. This one happens to be very precious to me. It's a souvenir of my soccer-playing days, but you don't like it."

"No, no." She could be so careless with her words sometimes. "Forgive me, please. I'm so sorry. It's really very—well, very interesting now you've told me all about it."

"You are wonderful," he said, straightening and scanning the area. *Bingo.* He dropped his voice. "Now don't scream or faint, just go along with me, okay?"

To Olivia's amazement, Aiden slid his arms around her and held her close. And he pressed his face into her neck and rocked her gently— as if he—*liked* it. "Make sure you don't look shocked," he said. "There's a lot of heat out here. Much more than there should be. The last thing I want is to be recognized by some over-zealous suit. Put your hands on my shoulders, or neck, or anywhere else you're comfortable putting them. Smile, or hide your face. Or kiss me, dammit."

Kiss him. "I can't kiss you—oh, of course I can." He wanted her help, so she lifted his face from her neck, closed her eyes, and pressed her mouth to his.

Hot damn, Aiden thought, this hadn't been what he expected. The instant before his vision blurred, he noticed that Olivia's dark lashes had bronzed tips. She held his face so tightly, she was going to leave nail marks on his temples. The effort was costing her a lot. A woman who did a lot of kissing didn't clamp her mouth shut and slam so hard against a guy she almost broke teeth—for both of them.

A white cotton sweater had replaced the blouse and pin of yesterday. Her own skirt had been mended, and the rest of her baggy outfit was the same, but she proved that the clothes didn't make the woman. Inside her duds she was one holdable female. He breathed in deeply and experimented with mapping the interesting places on her back and waist—and below.

She withdrew her mouth a fraction and muttered, "Is it all right yet?" without opening her eyes.

"No." This time he did the kissing. He might need to get a life, but he hadn't spent all his nights tending orchids in Hell's Kitchen.

Step one was to soften up those kissable lips of hers. He barely touched his mouth to hers, almost bounced there softly, skimmed lightly back and forth, keeping his eyes slitted to judge her reaction. Her features smoothed, even the line between her brows. She'd been frowning since early in the morning when he'd found her sitting on the edge of her bed, dressed, packed, and with Boss's head in her lap.

"Everything's going to be okay," he murmured, and parted her lips a little, splayed his hands over her back, and eased her in tighter. "Mmm. Yeah, just fine. Friend Ryan took advantage of a chink he saw to try to dig himself out of trouble. I'm the diversion."

She had a mouth made to be kissed. So soft and giving. He felt himself sinking into her. He couldn't get close enough.

"Ryan Hill's picking on you because of me," she said unevenly. "If you hadn't been too much of a gentleman to ignore my e-mails, you wouldn't be in this position."

Being a gentleman had nothing to do with snooping in someone else's mail, and he liked it just fine in this position. "Hush a minute. Pretend you're enjoying yourself."

Olivia barely stopped herself from moaning. How disgusting of her. She was enjoying herself more than she ever remembered, and that couldn't be nice when she and Aiden were strangers. He was making a very good job of pretending to be in a state of passion, though. Aiden parted her lips more. He had such a wonderful mouth, firm and mobile, and talented. He turned his head a little, one way and then the other, stroking his lips over hers, opening them more and more. She moved her hands to his shoulders and could feel how solid they were, even through the horrid coat. Under the coat he wore a gray polo-necked jumper. When she ran her fingers over his chest, there was nothing but hard muscle and bone there. How very nice. Oh, it was extremely difficult being British and passionate at the same time. A man she would never have expected to give her a second look was kissing her as if she were his last meal, but she couldn't stop analyzing things that should just be accepted.

She wasn't, Aiden decided, touching him like a stranger going through the motions, not anymore. The tips of her surprisingly long fingers made patterns on his chest, and down his sides, and around to his back, then returned to his chest. Like little homing pigeons, those fingers found Aiden's nipples through the thin knit sweater and he went weak at the knees. She opened her mouth and her breath came hard. His came harder, and sweat broke out on his brow. Their tongues were fully involved, and so were other parts of Aiden. Her breasts made their presence wonderfully evident, and the only thing that would have improved the way they felt would be the removal of their sweaters—and her bra.

Aiden held himself rigid. It might not do to let her feel that this was no longer a purely strategic maneuver.

She loved kissing him, loved his big hands straying over her back and bottom. She knew from the heat that flashed over her skin that she'd turned red. Aiden splayed the fingers of one hand wide on her bottom and pressed her into his hips. Oh, dear, he did feel so good. Penny Biggles often announced that she was "horny" but that "a hard man was harder to find." Not from where Olivia was standing at this moment. This type of thing—a wildly enthusiastic response to an inappropriate occurrence—happened when a woman was edging up on becoming an old maid. She was too vulnerable. Oh, yes, she was vulnerable.

This was playacting. The simple but clever disguise he'd put on—down to corduroy trousers and sandals on bare feet—changed everything about him, even the way he walked. "You're so good at this," she whispered.

"Why, thank you, ma'am. You're excellent at it yourself."

She could hardly say she'd been referring to his mastery of disguise, not his prowess as a lover.

He kissed her again, shutting off anything else she might have said. And he resumed the slow, circling dance with her pelvis. The loose corduroys he wore were amazing. They left absolutely nothing to the imagination, and Detective Flynn was extraordinarily well—what would be the way to describe that?—not hung, that was frightful. Well loaded? Just as frightful, but quite descriptive, really. He kissed her chin and followed with more kisses, short and firm, down the length of her neck.

Her breasts stung, and she ached between her legs. All purely sexual, and wonderful, but inappropriate. But the ache intensified, and she wished she could feel his skin on hers. He'd have a fit if he knew what she was thinking. But she'd like his skin on hers, his thighs between hers, and him inside her.

She'd lost it.

"I like the way you smell," he said, and she thought his voice sounded funny, not that she wanted to try speaking at all herself. "What is that? Cloves?"

She giggled. "Eucalyptus. Thanks. I rather like it. And you? Rosemary?"

"Huh?"

"Rosemary. The herb. Such a pungent aroma."

"Margy gave the stuff to me. Waves On The Wind, or something dumb. I think it's supposed to be sexy—er, forget I said that. Everything's supposed to be sexy."

She would not feel disappointed. "Margy?" Oh, that was really nonchalant.

"Great gal. She's the chief's secretary and thinks she's my mother."

Relief wasn't appropriate, but she was relieved.

Aiden realized he was rocking with Olivia, that he'd been rocking with her for some time, and holding her in ways that weren't necessary to making sure no passing cop would recognize his face.

They were kissing again. Gradually, keeping his mouth on Olivia's, he angled his head until he could look past her.

Vanni stood close by with his arms crossed. He raised one hand and waggled the fingers, and Aiden almost heard his partner's sigh. Vanni shook his head and looked heavenward. He made a signal for Aiden to stay put, and walked swiftly away.

Shucks, he'd have to keep on kissing Olivia.

He smiled against her mouth.

"What is it, Aiden?"

"Under the circumstances, this is not a good thing to admit, but I sure hope I get another chance to hide out by kissing you."

"Oh."

Vanni returned at a barely restrained run. "Follow me," he said as he passed them. "Watch for my signal and *go* there."

Aiden spun Olivia around. "Relax," he told her. "This is a good reason not to have anything to do with cops. Too much hype that turns out to be nothing worth worrying about. Here we go."

She hung her bag over an elbow and said, "We've got to get to the plane." They walked rapidly in Vanni's wake, dodging wheeled transports loaded with baggage and those who couldn't or wouldn't walk.

"We've got time. Stay cool."

It was all very well for him to tell her to stay cool, Olivia thought. Passionate kisses must be commonplace for him. She had just experienced the best kiss she'd ever had and was shaken because she couldn't feel guilty. Not only that, but he had other clothes he could get his hands on. Everything she had with her in the States, apart from her camera case, carry-on bag and papers, was in her suitcase and probably already in the belly of the aircraft.

Airport employees sweeping debris into dustpans moved with excruciating slowness and were always in the wrong place when Aiden and Olivia drew level. Vanni's thick, black curls were impossible to miss when he stood a head taller than most people. He wore a black leather jacket and swung his shoulders in a manner Olivia might find arrogant if she didn't know he was another nice man.

With the concourse behind them, Aiden cursed silently at the thought of having to go back through security. They'd be damned lucky to make the flight at all, and taking a later one would only increase the danger of his being stopped. After the chief had his meeting—for which Aiden would not show—it was very likely that even if the current crop of suits weren't hanging around here for him, there would be a fresh batch who *would* have Aiden Flynn on their minds.

"I know you don't want me to mention this," Olivia said, and he didn't miss her longing glance at a Starbucks coffee stand, or the way her eyes lingered on scones, and Danish, and muffins. "I've done this to you and I can't forgive myself. If I'd remained in Hampstead I could have gone to Mark and he'd have helped me."

She surely could, and later he'd find out why she hadn't. "You're hungry. Hang in there and I'll feed you."

"You don't have to worry about me at all. Vanni just took a right turn. There—" She pointed, and he slapped her arm down. "Sorry, didn't think. He pointed and turned right."

He wouldn't burst her bubble by saying he already knew. "Lead the way."

She took his hand as naturally as if they'd been friends since childhood and led him into a corridor that opened to the right. She could really move. "There he is. Now where's he going? Oh, Aiden, we're definitely going to miss that plane."

Aiden thought so, too, but said nothing. Vanni had scooted out of sight into what looked, from a distance, to be an airline club room entrance. When Olivia pulled Aiden to a stop outside the door, it said, "Maintenance."

"Stand still," Aiden told her. "I want to make sure no one's interested in what we're doing." He pushed back the old letterman jacket to give him easy access to his gun and braced a hand on the wall. He played with Olivia's hair for several seconds before looking over his shoulder. People surged by the end of the corridor in an endless, yammering tide. No one seemed to as much as look his way, and the corridor itself was empty.

Aiden pushed Olivia behind him. He took the gun from his waistband, held it in his right hand, turned the doorhandle, and shoved the door inward with his left.

Vanni stood amid buckets and mops and shelves piled with plastic trash bags and cleaning supplies. "Get in here and shut the door," he said. "Lock it."

Last in, Olivia followed Vanni's instructions and locked the door.

"I almost blew it," Vanni said. His complexion seemed white under his olive skin. "Honestly, I opened my big, stupid mouth to one of the suits back there and just about ruined this for all of us. I asked who they were looking for. Can you believe that? I might as well have said he was obviously a badge and admitted I had a reason to be nervous about his business out here. Lucky for me, the dumb shit blew another gum bubble and told me to move along. I was so darn lucky, Aiden. He wasn't smart enough to smell something rotten."

"Cool it," Aiden said. "The last thing we can afford is panic." He didn't add that he'd never seen Vanni panic before and he couldn't imagine why he'd start now.

"This has got me rattled," Vanni said, as if he heard what Aiden thought. "I keep thinking I ought to be able to go to the chief and tell him the truth. But you're right. He wants to take you down. I called in really early and told Margy I was tied up but I'd be there. The chief was already in. You know he doesn't do early mornings. He came on the phone, and the first words out of his mouth were about you. He wanted to know where you were and if I could get you to the meeting without letting on you were in trouble."

"What d'you say?" This was how it had to feel to face an electric chair when you knew you were innocent. Close, anyway.

"I said you were following up leads on the Carreras case. That's the one where the strawberry's giving blow jobs while her partner rips off the dealer."

Aiden hardly dared look at Olivia. She said, "What's a strawberry?" but showed curiosity, not shock.

"A female who does sex acts for cocaine. Gang types usually."

"Thank you, Vanni," Aiden said. "Sometimes I wonder about you."

"I wonder about you *all* the time," Vanni said with a grin.

Olivia said, "Poor thing."

Aiden gave up. "I know the case. What am I supposed to be following up? Just in case I need to know."

"I dunno. Make it up as you go along. Aiden, old buddy, you can't fly out of this airport now. You may not even be able to get out of this airport, period, but we're going to try."

"You want to make that clearer?"

Vanni leaned against some shelves, and all three of them were promptly showered with hundreds of plastic bags. They swatted them away from their heads until the avalanche stopped and they stood knee-deep in garbage sacks.

"Clearer, please," Aiden repeated, kicking at the bags that only settled around his legs again.

"Did you see how much heat there was out there?"

"Sure I saw. They wouldn't send that much artillery after me."

Vanni looked miserable. "Look, I don't want to say this, but I've got to. I had a few words with Fats Lemon this morning, too. Ryan's doing a real number on you. Now we've got narcotics possession added to art theft. Apparently you've been transporting fortunes in balloons. Heroin. The balloons get rolled inside canvases. Look, this is crazy and crazy-making, but I won't let it happen to you. They aren't going to pin it on you. I've got to get you out, both of you."

"She shouldn't be here," Aiden said. "She'd be safer in England.

You need to do what you've suggested, Olivia, and go to your insurance investigator friend. Mark, is it? And to the police."

"Why?" She braced her feet in the slithering plastic sacks and said, "You're afraid I'll slow you down, or get in the way. Well, I won't. And I think I'd be in greater danger back in England. Those men know where I live. I've got some things that belong to them, too. And I already know they don't care what they do to make sure I'm not a threat to them anymore."

"Why would you think you'll be safer here?" Aiden asked. He needed to move fast, and she was already slowing him down.

"Because you're here, and I trust you just as you said I should." She raised her chin. "I'd rather die with someone who had at least given me a chance than all on my own waiting to see if someone in England will help me. Also"—and she'd regret saying this—"you'll think this is silly, but you may need me and I want to be here for you." She didn't look at either man's face.

"She's here," Vanni said after too long a pause. "And I doubt we could get her out without her being stopped anyway. So this is the way it's going to be." Vanni shook his head vehemently. "Don't you start arguing with me, Flynn, because I'm putting everything that matters to me on the line for you."

"Don't do that—"

"Shut your goddamn ungrateful mouth. You, I care about." He looked at Olivia. "And now I care about her, God help me. And Pops and Mama would never forgive if I let something happen to the two of you. They're already hearing wedding bells and thinking about how they'll pull the wedding off in the Church."

Aiden and Olivia groaned in unison.

"Yeah, well, you can't blame 'em after all the years they've known you, Aiden, and you've never brought a woman home before," Vanni said. "Enough of that. You'll be driving across the country. I can get the route mapped on the computer in minutes. I'll pick out places where you peel away from the beaten track and get some sleep when you absolutely have to. Even with you taking it in turns to drive, you're going to get exhausted out of your minds."

"Hold it." Aiden put his face close to Vanni's. "All I have to do is get Olivia and me on a plane. If we go to the gate now, we can dash aboard the instant before the doors shut and hope to be safe."

"What if someone who's looking for us is already on the plane?" Olivia asked in a small voice.

"I'm willing to take the risk that they wouldn't board if we hadn't showed up."

"But they may have," she persisted. "People do the oddest things for money."

Her way of stating things tended to have a cooling effect. And he already knew his idea wasn't a great one. "Okay, so we give up on flying, damn it. It'll take us about three days to get to Seattle from New York, and that'll be with very little sleep." He narrowed his eyes at Vanni. "No stopping at all, except for the obvious reasons."

"I like driving," Olivia said. "It'll work. Oh, dear, I wish I had my suitcase."

"June'll be happy to donate some stuff," Vanni said. "And there's stacks of Sophia's stuff in her room. I'll see to that. Aiden, we've got to go now."

Vanni opened the door and stuck his head out. He didn't seem to notice that a river of slippery bags seeped out into the corridor. Carrying Olivia's cameras while she continued to clutch the vast bag she referred to as her grip, Aiden held the door open for her and she shuffled out. He followed and barely stopped himself from falling.

Olivia took a step, slipped, and dropped her bag.

Vanni grabbed for her, but she slithered out of his reach, wildly fighting to regain her balance. The plastic bags behaved like ice skates on the sloping stone floors and she spread her arms, wobbling dangerously and zipping forward.

"Stop," Aiden yelled, and narrowed his eyes at the sound of his voice. He started to run and instantly knew his mistake.

"Oh, *shit*," Vanni hissed, inclining his head. "Will you look what heard you?"

Aiden looked. Coming toward them was a large, muscular, plain-clothesman. His attention was all on Olivia. He kept his feet clear of danger and snatched her out of harm's way.

"Shit, shit, shit," Vanni muttered. "That's it. We're done for."

Aiden executed a snazzy sideways hop and landed on firm ground. He had nothing to lose now. "Thank you, sir," he called out. "You okay, honey?"

The cop seemed disinclined to release her arm.

"Topping, thank you, darling," Olivia said, or almost sang. "This lovely man saved me."

The *lovely* man exuded too much interest in his "topping" armful. Aiden waited for the guy to take a good look at "Topping's" companion. When he did, Aiden said, "Thanks. I'm going to report this mess. It's dangerous."

"It certainly is, sir," the cop said, returning his attention to Olivia, who appeared charmingly mussed and soft—just out of bed, in fact. Very sexy. This flight of fancy was costing Aiden his predictable life and the career he cared about.

"All right, then," the cop said, with the briefest glance at Aiden and Vanni. "Don't worry about the report. I'll make it. Look after the lady."

Gaping, Aiden watched him till he was out of sight.

Vanni's soft chuckle did nothing for the mood. "What are you laughing about?" Aiden said.

"You," Vanni told him very quietly. "You *do* have a case on the woman. If you got out more, you wouldn't get carried away by the first skirt who—"

Aiden gripped Vanni by the neck. "I've had it with that. Got it? The next comment like that, and you're going to be looking for a really good dentist."

"Oh, don't," Olivia cried. "What's the matter? Did I do something wrong?"

"She needs some therapy," Vanni said, holding Aiden's wrists. "It's not normal to take the blame for anything and everything that goes wrong. Want to get your hands off me?"

"I meant what I just said," Aiden told him.

Vanni bowed his head and said, "Yeah. Okay. I'll try not to make that mistake again."

Aiden let him go. When he saw Olivia's face, he felt ashamed. "Just kidding around," he said. "That's how we keep from getting too serious."

She didn't say anything.

"Follow me," Vanni said. A service elevator tucked into an alcove was his objective. They soon traveled rapidly downward to the basement of the terminal, where orange-suited employees tossed baggage onto moving belts and there was too much activity for three interlopers to be noticed.

"You know your way around here," Aiden observed to his partner.

"Not really. Let's hope I can find us a way out."

He did, and within another fifteen minutes they were in his unmarked police car—a green Pontiac in need of soap and wax—and heading for the Brooklyn Bridge and Manhattan.

Olivia slumped low in the back seat. She didn't respond to any of Vanni's or Aiden's attempts to make her talk.

"Let me go in to your place first, okay?" Vanni said. "Just in case someone gets sent over there after the chief's meeting. If it's all clear, you can grab whatever you need. Then we'll go back to Mama's to get some stuff together for Olivia."

Aiden waited, but she didn't acknowledge that she'd heard Vanni's comment. Great, now he had a sulking female on his hands.

"Your pink panther is in good shape, isn't it?" Vanni said.

"Pink pony. It's in great shape. So's the Caddy. But I won't be taking either of them on this jaunt."

Olivia glanced at the backs of the two men's heads. One so dark-haired that a weak winter sun shone blue there, the other light with traces of the sun's bleach job glinting. They were all business. Surely if she put her foot down and said she wanted to go it alone—in this country (she certainly wasn't going back to England at this point)—they'd have to bow to her wishes.

"You want my car?" Vanni said.

"No, thanks." Aiden cleared his throat. "Nice otter, buddy, but you need that Four Runner. Nice vehicle for hauling things."

"In other words, you don't think much of my wheels."

"They're great. I need one. But I've got something else in mind. You'll approve."

Of course they wouldn't bow to her wishes. Men were never more than boys grown larger. They smelled a challenge, a game to be won, and they wouldn't be diverted.

The scenery was all industrial and alarmingly large. They'd driven on a road called the Van Wyck Expressway. Like the motorways at home but blown to enormous scale and with vehicles also on a large scale. Then the Belt Parkway which she remembered from yesterday and this morning. Kennedy Airport sat on the edge of a marshy, sandy, bog-like area. At least there was some blue water dotted with green islands to be seen today.

Unfortunately, the air wasn't at all fresh. It smelled of low tide, even though it wasn't, and her nostrils tickled at the scents of oily sludge and exhaust fumes.

"You're very quiet, Olivia," Aiden said, turning to look at her over his shoulder. "It's a pretty day, huh?"

She supposed all things were relative when you lived in a huge city. "In a way. Yes, it is pretty. Like an industrial miracle."

He beamed and his upper lip arched away from strong white teeth.

"Exactly. Not very many newcomers view the area as clearly as you do. It's fabulous. You'll be surprised how quickly it gets into your blood."

The way he smiled mesmerized Olivia. "Yes, you're probably right." People talked about blue eyes, but they were usually more gray-blue nondescript than blue. Aiden's were blue, neon blue.

Her life was in danger. Aiden's life was probably also in danger—because of her. And for all she knew, Vanni's life was threatened for the same reason. And she was obsessing on Aiden Flynn's physical charms.

He continued to smile at her. There was question in his eyes, as if he couldn't decide if he should say anything else.

"Don't worry about me," she said. "I've never had an adventure, and I've always moaned about it. So now I'm having one, and I intend to enjoy it."

"She's bugs," Vanni said.

Aiden inclined his head and said, "I don't think you should talk about my friend like that."

Olivia shrugged and said, "It doesn't matter," although she had no idea what Vanni meant.

They took the Midtown Tunnel and entered the city. Olivia gripped the edge of her seat while Vanni seemed to drive much too fast for the dense traffic and the waves of pedestrians that surged into the street at every intersection.

"I live off 49th," Aiden said. "Not far. People don't realize it, but nothing's too far in Manhattan. Take a look at the stores. Everyone says they're something. I've never had time to notice."

Olivia tried to notice. A shop with a huge bear outside revealed floor upon floor of toys visible through its windows, but Vanni passed too quickly for her to make memorable impressions. He made a turn onto another street, and another until Olivia no longer knew in which direction they were heading. "I'm going to park at the end of the block," Vanni said at last. "Okay?"

"Yeah," Aiden said, "Okay. But I don't have to like it one damn bit."

When Vanni finally pulled alongside a curb and stopped, Olivia looked out to see shopfronts, many of them still barred shut from the previous night, and what appeared to be flats above. Groups of men clustered around doorways smoking and laughing. Some sat on upturned crates and waved their hands to emphasize what they were saying.

"This used to be a rough area," Vanni said, "like the Bronx. But it's a happenin' place now. Gettin' to be one of *the* places to live, right, Aiden?"

"Right. Some great apartments here. Get going, Vanni."

"Yes, master."

Vanni got out of the vehicle, tossing the keys to Aiden as he went, and sauntered up the block. He stopped in front of a barred window and looked in as if he was deeply interested in whatever he saw.

"Jewelry store," Aiden said. "Russian family. Good people. The grandfather owns the building and the ones on either side."

"I see." Olivia would like to see much better. She'd like to get out a camera and start shooting. Everywhere she looked she saw something that coalesced into a natural composition. "What's the shop on the corner, the open one?"

"Deli."

She assumed that was supposed to be so self-explanatory that further questions wouldn't be necessary. People, mostly men, came and went from the deli.

"Why does Vanni keep on standing there?" she asked. "Isn't he going to go inside your place?"

Aiden was wondering the same thing, but he couldn't make a move until Vanni gave him the nod. "He's looking around. That's all."

"He's not looking at anything but the shop window."

She was right, but he didn't want to discuss the point. "Be patient. He'll signal when he's ready."

Not a dozen feet from Vanni, eating voraciously from deli sacks, two men faced each other. They managed to talk and gesture without pausing between the food they stuffed into their mouths.

A yellow cab stood at the curb, and the driver had swung the passenger door open. His light was off, and Aiden decided the two guys were his fares.

So what? Couple of saps just off an all-nighter and in the hungry phase.

Vanni still wasn't moving.

"So you live in that building?" Olivia asked. The waiting frightened her. "Above the jewelers?"

"Yes. Ryan Hill's place is on the top floor, but I already told you that."

"I like it here," Olivia said, not entirely truthfully, but it was only nice to compliment someone on the place where they lived.

"So do I." Aiden liked it a lot. Here he'd finally found a place where peace was his for the taking—and all the shadows could be shut outside his door. "I hope I get to spend some time here again before too long."

"Yes." Before she had time to heap on more guilt, Olivia studied two men, men with nasty tempers, who were eating and shouting at each other on the pavement. "I say," she said softly. "Oh, I say. Oh, Aiden. I think I know one of those people."

"What people?" He jerked around in his seat. Her face registered shock, and he didn't like it one bit. "Quickly. What people?"

"I must be wrong. It's because I'm tired. I don't see too well at a distance."

Aiden undid his seatbelt, searching in all directions as he did so. "You ought to wear glasses if you can't see."

"I do." She delved into her huge bag, pulling out small pouches, a change purse, envelopes of documents.

"Forget it," Aiden told her when he couldn't bear the wait any longer. "Tell me what you think you see."

"Here they are." Triumphantly she held a case aloft. She removed dark-framed glasses and put them on. Her eyes were vastly magnified. "Oh, dear, he mustn't see me."

Olivia slipped from the back seat of the car to the floor and crouched there, twisting her head sideways toward Aiden.

"*What* is it?" he said.

She took off the glasses. "They only work for distance," she explained. "Do you see a taxi at the curb with its door open?"

"Yes."

"And two men arguing and eating?"

"Yes." He must find the patience not to hurry her.

"The shorter one. Not the plump person in tweeds and suede shoes. The little, thin one. Very straight back. Sandy-colored person. If you saw him really close, he's got one of those bumpy, purple noses. Probably from some sort of excess." She didn't like to give real labels to people, like drunkard. Mummy and Daddy did that. "He's the one in the streaky-bacon suit—that means the type that has the thin white stripes in the dark fabric. See him?"

"I certainly do." He'd have to be blind not to after that description. "You know him?"

"He's the one, the one who fed the rats."

Rats? Aiden took a second to make any connection at all. When he did, he turned all the way around toward Olivia. "You mean the man you believe intended to push you under a train? The one you gave the wrong negatives to? The one you thought you'd successfully lost in London? Either Fish or Moody of the fat checks you've got in your possession?"

"That's him."

"You're sure?"

"I know it seems fantastic, but I am absolutely certain."

"Okay." One choice he didn't have was to arrest the guy. At this point he had nothing on him but Olivia's accusations. "That's the man who probably tried to kill you. Shi—shoot. Vanni's listening to 'em. The fact they're here, outside Ryan's place—and mine, of course, but it would be Ryan they're trying to reach—well, that proves there's a connection between them and my upstairs neighbor."

Olivia's rat-lover fed the residue of his meal to a rangy mutt prowling the spilled contents of garbage cans at the curb and got back into the cab. His fatter friend followed, after throwing his paper sack on the sidewalk.

"Isn't that the way it always goes?" Olivia said. "You decide someone is absolutely awful—not a single redeeming quality—but that nasty little man likes animals. He's always feeding them."

Aiden grunted. The cab didn't move. Vanni waited a respectable time longer and walked slowly back in the direction of the Pontiac. He got in, took the keys from Aiden, and drove off.

Once he'd put several blocks between Aiden's home and the car, he said, "Did you see those two guys eating and—"

"I saw them," Aiden interrupted. "Olivia knows them."

"I don't know them," she protested. "The thin one wanted to kill me, and he came to Hampstead to try to get the photos from me. I've already explained all that."

"Oh, yeah?" Vanni said, sounding disappointed that he'd been scooped. "So you're the woman they were talking about. They think you're here in New York looking for Ryan. They know where he lives."

"Slow down," Olivia yelled, and both men lurched around in their seats. "Look back there." She'd been keeping watch over her shoulder.

Vanni slowed down. "Geez, don't do that to me. I'm not doing more than thirty. You just took ten years off my life."

"No," she said, pointing through the back window. "I don't care how fast you go. It's Boswell. See him?"

Vanni speeded up again. "Boss is at Mama's. You're seeing things."

"No!"

"No," Aiden echoed. "Pull over. He's done it before, remember, gone home looking for me."

The car stopped, and Aiden jumped out. Olivia couldn't take her eyes off the way he walked, then broke into a run. The man and the dog ran toward each other.

"That's all we need," Vanni said. "Now we got to worry about the canine."

Olivia wasn't interested in anything but Aiden.

Boswell, drawing the eye of every passerby, loped with the kind of long, powerful strides that belied even a twinge of arthritis. He reached Aiden, but instead of leaping at him as Olivia expected, the dog instantly dropped and waited. Aiden stood over him, and Olivia had no doubt he was talking. Even at a distance, Boswell's ears could be seen perking up and flattening.

Aiden bent to rub the dog's head and press their faces together, then set off back toward the car. When they arrived, Aiden opened the door beside Olivia and said, "You might want to ride up front with Vanni."

"May I ride with Boswell, instead?" she asked.

Aiden didn't answer her, but he let the dog climb in and returned to the front seat himself.

With a huge sigh, Boswell flopped down and looked puzzled by Olivia's position on the floor.

"He's too old to be running for miles like that," Aiden said. "All the way from Brooklyn. Crazy old devil."

"Loving old devil," she said. "I interrupted you, Vanni. Those men. What are they doing?"

"Yeah," Vanni said. "Okay. Their plan is to hang around Aiden's building until they see you show up trying to find Ryan, or come out from his building. They seem sure you must already be in New York, but they think you're lost. Evidently they've got some way of knowing Ryan wouldn't be able to meet you."

"How would they know that?" Olivia said.

Aiden said, "Only one way. They're in touch with him. But why wouldn't they think you came looking for him at his place yesterday and gave up when you didn't find him?"

Surreptitiously, Vanni pressed a silencing finger into Aiden's thigh.

"That's right," Olivia said, and she felt better. "They don't have any idea where I am. They're just guessing. So I'm all right. Actually I never did have Sam's—Ryan's—address. All I knew was that he lived in Hell's Kitchen."

Vanni gave Aiden a pained look.

Olivia saw that look. "What is it?" She got up from the floor and resumed her seat. "I saw the way you looked at Aiden." Boswell settled his head on her knee.

"It's nothing," Vanni said. "Where to first, partner? Do we pick up whatever car you're going to drive, or go to Mama's for some things for Olivia?"

"Car. Then Mama's." Aiden knew Vanni would soon find a way to tell him something he wasn't going to like.

"Stop trying to keep things from me," Olivia said, her voice rising. "I'm a very calm, sensible person. Ask anyone who knows me. I won't panic, no matter what you say."

"It's nothing, really—"

"Yes it is! Now tell me."

Aiden looked straight ahead. Vanni was heading for the warehouse Aiden rented for restoring and storing cars.

"Okay, but don't flip out on me. They said they're sure you must be with Aiden by now. You just didn't get back to his place yet. They've had it staked out all night."

"Great," Aiden said. "Just frigging great."

Olivia said, "Oh, dear." She found some comfort in Boswell's heavy presence.

"Anyway, Laurel and Hardy think they've got everything worked out."

"Why didn't I think of that?" Olivia said. "They remind me of Laurel and Hardy, too."

"Yeah," Aiden said. "The most obvious thing here is that friend Ryan's got something going on the side with those two goons. Fats— Fats Lemon is Ryan Hill's partner—he's in on it. Has to be. So why can't I get to the chief and make him see what a fool he's going to look when all of this goes down?"

"Exactly," Olivia said.

"I don't know what to say anymore." Vanni kept on driving, but much more slowly. "We could try getting someone to listen, but what if the groundwork is as good as it looks to me?" He brought a fist down on the steering wheel. "I'll go in and talk to the chief again, I guess."

"No," Olivia said. She wasn't given to premonitions, but one had just smacked her so hard that she felt disoriented. "There's something else, isn't there? Something you're not saying, Vanni."

"I'm going to do whatever you tell me to do," Vanni said to Aiden. "You know how much you mean to me, man, and to my family. Those guys back there intend to track you two down. They were talking in what they think is some sort of code, but I didn't need any road map. There's a whole, goddamn network involved in this. The money has to be huge. And some of the players are definitely way out of any league we've ever played in.

"Aiden, I don't think Laurel and Hardy have anything to lose. Or Ryan and Fats. They've got to stop you or they're finished. The one thing they probably haven't anticipated is that you'll try to flee across the country. They expect you to go by air—and they sure don't sound worried about Kennedy or LaGuardia or Newark."

"Because they're all staked out," Aiden said quietly. "We're being looked for at every airport for miles around. Every airport with flights to South America or other parts where they probably couldn't get at us."

"Yeah." Vanni had reached an area of narrow gray streets with windowless buildings lining the pavements. Children tore down the middle of the street, yelling and shoving at each other. "Makes you envy schoolteachers, huh? Hey, good thing nobody knows about your change of plan. Why don't you wait at the warehouse while I go pick up what you need?"

Aiden didn't like the way the future was shaping up. He was still alone at thirty-six because that way he knew exactly who he was responsible for and, at the end of the day, who would have to share his bad times; no one. "I'm thinking we should just leave and pick up anything we need along the way." It was the "we" that ruffled him.

"Good call," Vanni said lightly. "How much cash do you have on you?"

"Enough to get by for a while."

Vanni nodded. "I'll give you what I've got, too. Then I'll wire more if necessary."

"Because we shouldn't use credit cards, right?" Olivia said in a small, tight voice. "But we could change some of my pounds."

Vanni glanced at her in the mirror. "Better not in case someone tries to check you out. We'll keep in touch. We'll have to be careful, but it can be done. You'll have your cell phone, Aiden. Leave it on.

I'll do all the calling. That way we don't risk tipping our hand if you call at the wrong time."

"Would you just be honest with me, please?" Olivia said. "What else is there? What is it you're not saying because of me?"

Aiden caught Vanni's eye and nodded.

"Okay," Vanni said, "I could be wrong. But back there it sounded as if there's been a decision. They want you dead—and Aiden."

$Twelve$

One of a pair of large, metal double doors swung inward without a sound. Daylight swept over the inside of the warehouse and its contents. From where Olivia viewed the scene, an indoor scrap yard was a perfect description. Cars shrouded by tarpaulins, cars in various stages of repair, pieces of cars, benches loaded with tools, hoists, piles of tires, piles of hubcaps, bins of hardware, swags of unidentifiable objects contained in mesh and festooned from grated catwalks on all sides of the cavernous space.

Aiden threw a bank of switches, and yards of neon bulbs shot startling white light over the scene. Olivia looked upward, past the catwalks she'd already seen, to the grime-caked windows of cubicles lining an even higher balcony. Heavy ropes and rusted pulleys decorated every overhead space and swags of cobwebs made unlikely garlands.

"Welcome," Aiden said. He moved between the clutter like a man who knew every piece of what he surveyed.

Olivia searched around her before she knew what she was looking for. "Where do you keep your Cadillac?"

"In a garage near the apartment. My Mustang's there, too. Will you excuse me while I make a phone call?"

He was all business. Olivia nodded and said, "Of course."

"Close the door."

"Certainly." She wouldn't have thought rudeness was his style, but perhaps he was preoccupied. Just outside the door, for all the world as if he was trying to make himself invisible, sat Boswell. "You are going to be in trouble," Olivia whispered. "You were supposed to go with Vanni. How did you get out of the car?"

Solving that mystery didn't take a brilliant mind. He'd got out of the car because Vanni had let him out—no doubt because Vanni thought the dog might offer extra protection—but Aiden had said there wouldn't be room to take him.

"The door," Aiden said, louder than Olivia considered necessary.

"You heard," she told Boswell. The dog put his long snoot inside, then slithered in and disappeared behind a heap of scrap. Olivia closed the door. Boswell would make her feel better, and he was a lot more even-tempered than his master right now.

"Bo?" she heard Aiden say. "Aiden. No. I'm in New York. I need a favor."

Olivia sat on a car seat artfully placed at an angle with a rusty engine block in front. Pop cans littered the top of the engine. She didn't have to go anywhere. With Aiden, or alone. She could hide right here in New York and try waiting out all the fuss. As soon as he got off the phone, she'd tell Aiden that was exactly what she intended to do. There had been too much of doing what someone else wanted her to do in her life.

"I know, I know," Aiden said, his voice rising. "Are you on a cordless? Yeah, well, I can't hear over the racket in that seedy bar of yours. Walk out back. I don't have time to hang around asking you to repeat yourself."

He had the nerve to call someone up asking for a favor, then be nasty and actually tell them he was in a hurry. Boswell slunk from his hiding place and climbed onto the seat with Olivia. He sat upright beside her, gazing into her face.

"No, it's not completely finished," Aiden said into the phone. "Sure it's taking longer than you expected. You think I don't know that? I had a little setback with the paint job. Look I could just have taken off in it, and you wouldn't have been any the wiser, but I'm an honest guy so I'm calling to ask ... okay, okay, I'm calling to tell you I'm taking your car across the country because I've never been seen in it, or with it. Not a soul is likely to know it's here. I haven't had any reason to talk about it. I need anonymous wheels. I'm ... Let me finish. I'm going to Chris. If someone does find out I'm in your car and they contact you, you don't know what they're talking about. They'll probably expect me to be on my way to Key West. If they suggest that, you still don't know what they're talking about. Got that? They'll get in touch with Chris for sure, but he'll back me up. He'll say he never heard from me. Doesn't expect to see me. And as far as you're concerned, the Rover isn't in the main warehouse, and you don't know where the other warehouse is."

Amazed, Olivia watched Aiden gesture, and pace, and spin absolute fibs, one after another.

"There isn't a second warehouse, Bo. That's just so they stop looking for the car here in New York. I don't want those jackhammer brains poking around my stuff. They could break something."

Olivia eyed the debris surrounding her and wondered how he'd know what was or wasn't broken.

"I don't have time to explain it all now. You and Roy doing okay? Good. I'll get down there to see you again soon. In the Rover! But I'll call and tell you more about what's going on. Huh?" Aiden stopped pacing and grew quite still. "Who made you an authority on covert maneuvers? No it wouldn't work just as well for me to stay here and hide out. Out of the goodness of my heart, I set myself up. I'm making it easy for a bum cop to cover his tracks. My own people are looking for me. If they keep looking, they'll find me in this city no matter where I hide. It's tougher for a cop to hide than a criminal. I've got to buy time to figure things out, and that means I need distance from here, Bo. Yeah, thanks, I'm glad to have your approval."

Well, Olivia still thought staying here was a good idea.

"Aren't I always on my own—when I'm not with Vanni these days? Sure I miss Chris, I'll always miss Chris, but he didn't want to be a cop in this city anymore."

Was he saying he was going on this trip alone? Olivia stung at the thought that he'd dismissed her like that. Let him dismiss her. If he was so intent on going, he'd be better off alone. And it would make it easier for her not to have to tell him she'd changed her mind and intended to go her own way.

"Actually, I'm taking a friend with me. She's in the same trouble I am. We were going to fly, but we weren't quick enough to beat the stakeout. I'm going now, Bo. Hi, Roy. Good to hear you. No, I'm not hiding a mad, passionate affair from you guys. Get back to serving beer and oysters. And give my love to Key West. I miss it."

He hung up and didn't look in Olivia's direction. Instead he darted around a trestle table piled high with more black and oily paraphernalia, and with the air of a conjurer revealing the lady he just sawed in two, whipped a filthy tarpaulin off a vehicle.

Olivia knew a beautiful old Rover when she saw one. This looked as if it might be about a 1970. Perhaps '68. The bonnet was long, and turn lights sat immediately above each front wheel. All the lines were elegantly curved. The silver-gray body gleamed, and she caught the flash of a red-leather interior.

She got up and went closer, and winced. The paint, so perfect at a distance, showed numerous cracks, and in some places tiny chips had fallen off to reveal metallic bronze paint beneath. This must be what Aiden had been telling his friend about.

Aiden hadn't wanted to look at the Rover 100 for a week or two, until he'd recovered from the disappointment of having the paint blister and then crack for no reason he was aware of. The choice had been taken away. At least he knew the 1960 sedan was in perfect mechanical order and capable of getting him out of a tight spot if the need arose.

"Who are Bo and Roy?"

He hadn't forgotten Olivia was there, just wished she weren't. "Friends. Very good friends. Roy is Chris Talon's brother. Bo's Roy's partner. This is Bo's car. I'm renovating it for him. We're going to use it to get to Seattle. No one's going to think to look for me in this."

"So why did you ask Bo to tell all those lies?"

"I didn't." He looked at her. "I made suggestions just in case someone gets smarter than I think they will. I don't think I've ever mentioned this one, but who knows?"

"Bo's right. It's pointless to race off across America, supposedly to hide from bad people, when we can hide from them right here in New York."

Aiden bundled up the tarp and set it aside. "When did you get to be the expert in logic?"

Words couldn't be taken back, and he wished he hadn't spoken them, but she was the woman who had probably become infatuated with a man she'd never met. And she had traveled halfway across the world to meet him. He stuffed his hands in his pockets. Olivia looked away. She held her mouth firmly shut, but it still trembled. Her hands hung at her sides.

His mother's hands used to hang just like that when she felt completely helpless—usually when Aiden's father had disappointed his small family yet again.

"Don't blame Flynn," his mother would say. "He should never have married. He doesn't set out to hurt me, he just isn't interested in the way I feel. He's only good at taking care of what matters most to him—Flynn."

How long had it been since he recalled his mother talking about his father? She'd invariably gone on to tell Aiden that having him had been her idea, not his father's, and that it was ironic that the child she'd borne to become the companion she'd never found in her husband had inherited so much more from that husband than from her.

"I'm not logical at all," Olivia said, her voice sounding unused. "I've known that most of my life. I'm sorry if I sounded presumptuous, but I think I'm a little angry. I'm not very often. Angry, that is. But I've been drawn into something really horrible for no better reason than my having taken some photographs. Honestly, I can't imagine why anyone would get upset about them. They're nice, or I presume to think they are. Of course, that's purely subjective and many, possibly *most*, people wouldn't think they were—"

"Olivia. For God's sake, stop putting yourself down every other word. If you've got something to say, spit it out." Oh, great, she'd gone into her "I'm useless" mode because he'd scared her into it, and now she had the same just-kicked look all over her. "What I meant—"

"You meant, get to the point. I will. I took shots over two days. For Penny Biggles. They're of the interior of a beautiful old Notting Hill terrace house. Two terrace houses made into one, actually. Penny was the interior designer for the renovation."

Aiden slapped the heel of a hand to his brow, and Olivia jumped. He was being perfectly awful, or perhaps he was being himself after putting on a show of good behavior. "What is it?" she asked. "What have I done now?"

"You haven't *done* anything," he told her. "I have. Where are the frigging pictures? I can't believe I've been dragging you around since yesterday and I haven't asked about the *pictures*."

Dragging her around. "I should have remembered to show them to you," she said coolly. "I'd prefer not to take them out here."

"Why?"

"Well—" She searched for a clean and clear place to spread them out. "There isn't a good spot to set them. I don't want to get anything on them. Sorry."

For a moment he just stared at her. Then he said, "Why? No, don't answer that. Fine. You're sorry. We'll get on the road as fast as we can. Tell me more about the photos while we finish up here. See that refrigerator over there? There's soda and some beer. Apples. Clear everything out into a cardboard box."

The refrigerator wasn't like any she'd ever seen. It reminded her of a pink sarcophagus standing upright. It sounded like a cement mixer filled with gravel. "Penny did a fabulous job." She emptied plastic cases of new drill bits from a box and began filling it with cans and food—mostly cans. "If you like really contemporary interiors. I don't, but I appreciate when they're well done."

"Hurry up."

Olivia paused. Had she actually said she was going with him? "The shots for *London Style* are of the most important rooms. The conservatory at the back is fabulous. The whole top floor—third floor—of the two houses is an art gallery. That's quite a lot of space. The people who own the place collect post-World War II paintings."

"Paintings?" Aiden shouted from beneath the raised hood of the Rover. "The paintings you stole?"

Olivia slammed the refrigerator door. "I've never stolen a thing in my life. Well, there was a pencil once in infant school, but—"

"I was thinking aloud." *Fuck, fuck, fuck, everything that came out of his mouth made the situation worse.* "I mean I was remembering what Vanni said about you supposedly being an art thief—which I know you aren't. Maybe the stolen paintings are the ones in your photographs."

Unable to lift the box, she dragged it toward the car. "If I were going to steal art, it wouldn't be Abstract Expressionism."

"Really?" He was one of those people reduced to saying, *"I don't know much about art, but I know what I like,"* when asked.

"Really," Olivia said, dusting off her hands. "Do you like Gorky and Jackson Pollack and that group?"

He shrugged.

She said, "Well I might if I understood them. I don't, any more than I do non-objective stuff. I guess my intuitive responses are missing. Abstracts in general are hard for me."

He could, Aiden thought, learn from Olivia FitzDurham. She wasn't afraid to be wrong, or to admit ignorance. "Whatever. Those photos are key, I know that. This is ready to go. Boy, is she ready. What a beaut. Okay, the box goes in the trunk. Put your bag in the back seat. The more room up front, the better. What the—" Boss was doing his roadkill impersonation on the company couch. "Where did you come from, you big dope? Boss, you're gonna be the death of me. Damn Vanni. Did you see Boss come in here, Olivia?"

"Yes."

"For—" *Shut it. Just control it.* "O-kay. We have a problem, a big problem. This is a sedan, but I just don't see it as a family car."

"Do you have a family?"

He worked his lower jaw. So the lady with the innocent brown eyes thought she could be funny. "This is wasting valuable time. I'm going to have to contact Vanni and tell him to come get Boss when he can. I don't want anything extra to think about."

"I'm not leaving Boswell here."

"He likes it here."

"How do you know? He'd pretend anything to keep you happy."

"This is wild. That's my dog. He can't come with us because it isn't convenient. He'll be fine here until Vanni can pick him up."

"No," Olivia said. "You won't stay here because you're afraid bad people would find you here, but you're prepared to leave a helpless animal. What does that say about you?"

"That is the least helpless dog you're ever going to meet." He slung the box in the trunk, marched to pick up Olivia's bulging bag and cameras, and put them in the back. "Those teeth are steel and titanium. He could bite through bricks with the things."

"You exaggerate. He absolutely could not. And he certainly couldn't catch a bullet with them, unless it was on the way to his brain. There's plenty of room for him in the car."

"Omigod. I'd have thought photographers needed good special skills. Get in. We'll take him to Brooklyn, dammit."

He issued commands for Boss to go to the car while he opened the doors to the street.

By the time he got back to the Rover, Olivia was in the passenger seat, crammed against the door, with Boss wedged between her hip and the gears.

Both stared straight ahead.

He approached, picking up his fedora and the jacket Olivia loved so much on the way. He opened the driver's door. Ducking down, he peered inside before tossing his jacket behind the seats. The hat he slapped on his head.

They still stared straight ahead.

Aiden got in and started the engine. "Listen to that," he said.

No response.

"Traitor," he said into Boss's ear, and drove into the street. Leaving the engine running, he hopped out, closed and locked the warehouse, and got back in.

"There's plenty of room," Olivia said, aware that she wasn't being entirely truthful, but they could manage. Men could be so stubborn, so difficult.

"No, there isn't," Aiden said. "In the back, Boss. Back! Now!"

Boswell's eyes and jowls drooped, but he crawled slowly between Aiden and Olivia, sat behind Aiden, and stared out the window.

"In case you're interested, we're now about to head in the opposite direction from Interstate 80, which is the route we're taking on our way to Seattle."

That was another thing about men, Olivia decided, they fixated on unimportant details so they could avoid what really mattered. Once again she was going to ask a question she thought mattered. "Are you absolutely sure we should run rather than stay and hide here?" No guts, no glory. That's what Daddy always said.

"Yes. I'm still convinced we need to put distance between us and Manhattan." A Pontiac, gray rather than green like the one Vanni had been driving, turned off 11th Avenue and crawled toward them. "I don't believe this," he muttered.

Olivia looked at him, but Boswell pushed his head between them and watched the Pontiac.

He said, "Back and get *down*," to Boss and shoved the dog to the floor behind Olivia. To Olivia he said, "Kiss me, dammit," through his teeth and pulled her face beneath the brim of his fedora.

There wasn't even time for Olivia to take a breath before Aiden was kissing her. At first there was just the pressure of his mouth on hers, and the discomfort of being hauled across the shift and the hand brake. Within seconds he was doing it again, sucking her bottom lip between his teeth, repeating the process with her upper lip, licking all sorts of sensitive places and making sounds that suggested he really liked what he was doing.

She really liked it.

Aiden took his mouth slowly from hers. Touching her was incredible. She was nothing like any woman he'd ever dated or wanted to date, or even imagined existed, and he couldn't get enough of her. He kissed her brow lightly and rested his cheek there.

"Don't look over your shoulder," he told her, watching the Pontiac through the clouded-up back window. "We won't be going to Brooklyn."

Olivia opened her eyes slowly, more slowly than goose bumps sprang out all over her body. "What's happening?"

"You're getting a lesson in knowing when to take directions from a professional. An ambitious cop just passed us and parked. Name of Fats Lemon. You've already heard the name. Good old Ryan Hill's partner—probably in crime as well as on the force. I think he was too busy checking the numbers along here against what he's got written down to notice there's anyone in this car."

She wondered if he always resorted to, *kiss me, dammit,* as a diversionary tactic.

"Fats is no big brain, but he's found out about my warehouse, gotten the address, and he's about to force his way inside. Does that give you a hint of how good an idea it would be to hide in New York?"

This was one time when he would not get the last word. "It gives me a hint of how long Boswell would have had before he was catching bullets with his teeth."

Thirteen

"You should never have got us involved with a New York policeman, Rupert."

"I didn't. You did. And this car's a bleedin' boat." Still in a stall at the Budget rental agency, they sat in a rather splendid black Cadillac with dark-tinted windows. "Let's exchange it for one of those nice little things over there."

"You don't even know what those *nice little things* are. But they look cheap." Winston intended to make absolutely certain there was no question about the chain of command here. "And none of this was my fault from the beginning. From the day you lost your nerve— right here in this city, at The Dakota. If you'd been more careful, we'd never have been seen going into the apartment there."

"You panicked. Ryan Hill was a dolt, anyone could have seen that. A so-called detective doing *security* work at a New York apartment building. Anyone knows a good American detective should be able to find a less arduous way to augment his income."

"You are not to mention that man's name again," Winston roared. "I thought you understood that. And what the devil are you talking about? An *apartment building?* It's *The Dakota*, Rupert. Central Park West. Doing security work at one of the most salubrious addresses in New York could hardly be called anything but a highly intelligent manner of putting oneself in the way of good opportunities. In case you've forgotten, some very rich people live at The Dakota—including our very good customer, the one who wrote the checks you chose to give to the FitzDurham woman."

"What does that have to do with anything, Winston? That a lot of rich people live there, I mean?"

"You know very well. There's so much money in that building, it's a wonder it doesn't sink. That's why *we* have done a good deal of business there. Those people have so much, they simply can't keep track of it all. So, if one borrows a painting here and there from them, why should they complain—particularly if we only choose paintings that were previously stolen? Those greedy, underhanded people know they have no right to them anyway, so they can hardly report theft, can they?"

"You said it," Rupert agreed. "We like the pieces they keep hidden away the best, don't we? The really valuable stuff. Greedy farts. Owning for owning's sake and getting their jollies from private viewings of what doesn't belong to them anyway. Crooks."

"Yes," Winston said. "I didn't panic, you know."

"You did. Ryan—sorry—the detective said he'd seen everything, and he'd turn us in if we didn't give him a share, and you agreed to whatever he asked for. The crook."

"They're everywhere," Winston said. "One begins to wonder how many honest people are left in the world. But you were the one who asked him not to report seeing you go into that apartment—even if it *wasn't* your apartment. Those were your words. You as good as told the man you were planning to—well, *borrow* something."

"You didn't have to dissolve into a blubbering heap and promise him everything but our souls. Look what you accomplished with that." Rupert indicated the Cadillac and pointed toward the exit where vehicles on East 43rd were so tightly crammed, they could have been welded together. "Nothing but trouble ever since."

"We weren't to know he couldn't be trusted, or that he wasn't working alone and intended to turn on us." Very soon, Winston knew, he would become miffed enough with Rupert to resort to less gentlemanly behavior. But then, Rupert was no gentleman. "Hurry up and drive. If we can believe the latest report, your Miss FitzDurham and friend have a good start on us by now." Winston landed a smart cuff on Rupert's ear. It made him feel better to see the lout cringe.

Rupert clutched his reddening ear and said, "You'll regret that."

"I doubt it," Winston said. "Ought to give you comfy, familiar feelings. After all, when your mummy and daddy did that, you thought they were showing how much they loved you. Get on with it. This car is costing hundreds a day."

"I know." Rupert edged the Cadillac gingerly forward, repeatedly reaching for gears that weren't there and feeling for the clutch, which also wasn't there. "We could have saved a bit if you hadn't insisted on an automatic transmission. Bloody awful nuisance, if you ask me."

"I didn't," Winston said. "You heard what the man said. You're going to need whatever help you can get just to deal with the traffic and stay on the right side of the road. You'd never manage the shift as well. You're a dreadful driver."

Amid blaring horns, a blur of shaking fists protruding from car windows, and yelled epithets, Rupert entered the traffic on East 43rd at a crawl. He hunched forward against the wheel, over which he could just see, and peered through the windshield. "Damn these tinted windows. Feels like being on the tube when the lights fail," he told Winston.

"Stay on this street until I tell you to turn. Can't you go faster, Rupert? You seem to be making other drivers rather upset."

"No, I can't go faster. Do we go past the Empire State Building? Now that's a building, that is, and I've never had time to take a good look at it. All we've ever done here is hang out in antique shops and apartments that don't belong to us."

"For crying out loud, Rupert," Winston shouted. "You've got no sense of direction, you *git*. Empire State's nowhere near where we're going. Turn! Right on Lexington Avenue. No! Not Lexington, one more block, *then* right. Omigod, you nearly hit that bus. Wiggle your way around and keep Grand Central Station on your left. See it?"

Rupert looked out of his window. "Got it. More like a Roman bath than a station."

"We're on track," Winston said.

Nervy little poofter, Rupert thought. Winston ought to drive while he, Rupert, snapped orders so quickly they ran together.

"Left! Two blocks, then right on Madison."

Winston would have to go. The opportunity would arise, and Rupert would take it. Winston would be no more.

"Ree-ight. Right, right, right, moron."

"Right you are, Winston," Rupert said, feeling a calm spread inside his mind. He missed dear Soames. There was something so comforting about the spineless little body that it relaxed one. Just thinking about his ferret gave Rupert solace. If he saw a pet store, there were bound to be some nice rats to watch. He liked the white ones best.

"Tricky bit coming up," Winston announced. "Left on 51st and past St. Patrick's. Too bad there isn't time to pop in and light a candle."

"What for?" Rupert decided Winston was going a bit soft up top.

"I believe in hedging my bets," Winston said.

Rupert ignored the comment.

"Turn right!" Winston pounded a pudgy fist on the dashboard and yelled, "Ouch. I can't relax for a moment. *Right.*"

Rupert squeaked around as the lights turned red. "You've got to give me more notice. Can you turn right on red here?"

"How should I know? Shut up and do as you're told. You're the driver. I'm the navigator." He rustled the maps spread over his lap. "According to that man, Fats Lemon, we may have to cross the entire country."

"I remember now," Rupert said. "You can't turn right on red."

"Shut up. I'm concentrating."

Rupert groaned, then yelped. An ambulance, lights flashing, headed directly toward them.

"On the right," Winston screamed. "Get on the *right!*"

"It's a one-way street," Rupert wailed. "And we're going the wrong way, you blithering idiot." He veered to the curb, narrowly missing first the ambulance, then several yellow cabs swerving in to pick up passengers, and slammed on the brakes. Sweat ran into his eyes and burned. Beneath his suit jacket, his shirt adhered to his back and the collar, already sopping, began to turn cold.

"What are you stopping here for?" Winston looked over his shoulder, his half-glasses steaming up. "Can't you read the bloody sign?"

Rupert looked, too. "Which one? There are at least eight signs on that lamppost. No Parking Alternate Tuesdays? Is it Tuesday? Is it an *alternate* Tuesday? Or do you mean, No Parking During Loading Hours. How should I know when loading hours are?"

"I mean," Winston said through gritted teeth, "the sign that says, DON'T EVEN THINK OF PARKING HERE! It's the one at the top."

"That's mad," Rupert said.

Winston made to hit him again, but Rupert covered his head and ducked. "Hit me one more time and you'll drive."

"Haven't got a license with me."

"We'll get you one."

"No time. Back up. Now."

Rupert formulated an argument, but there was nothing for it but to get himself facing the right way as quickly as possible. Reversing slowly, following the endless stream of taxis swerving in and out to the curb, he finally reached the corner and managed, by some miracle, to back around it.

"There," Winston said, studying a map through a magnifying glass. "That wasn't so hard, was it? Now, keep your wits about you. Get out the toll money for the George Washington Bridge. We get to Interstate 80 and away we go."

Very deliberately, Rupert turned off the engine and set the emergency brake. "This is a legal parking spot."

"Congratulations."

"You are at my mercy."

"I can ruin you," Winston told him hoarsely, taking hold of his sleeve. "Don't you forget it. I can leave you with nothing. So don't cross me."

A wise man knew when to back off and save the heavy artillery. Rupert disengaged Winston's hand, set it on top of the maps, and patted it. "We're overworked. It's getting to us. Let's decide what we're going to do. Specifics, Winston."

"You push me," Winston said, all petulance.

"We don't know what kind of car the FitzDurham woman and her boyfriend are driving. Or where we're supposed to intercept them."

"Lemon said he'd be finding out soon. We've just got to get some miles behind us or we'll never catch them, regardless of whether we find out about the car."

"You're right. And we'll get going as soon as we know what we're doing. Exactly."

"I've decided that once we're past Chicago, we take Interstate 90 all the way."

"I thought staying on 80 would be a better choice."

"Why, dammit?" Winston said.

Rupert hadn't given the route any thought at all, but he was always proud of his ability to think quickly. "Well, since we aren't sure exactly where they're going, other than somewhere on the West Coast, if we haven't already been told which road to take, we'll be in a better position on 80, if they're heading for California, which is very likely."

"Why?"

"The weather, of course. Why would anyone go to the West Coast when winter's starting, and *not* go to California?"

"Logical," Winston said, gratifying Rupert. "Now can we go?"

"Not until we decide."

"We've decided, Rupert, old sport."

"We haven't decided how we're going to do it when we catch them."

"*Do it?* You have such a crude turn of phrase."

"We get what we want," Rupert said. "The photographs, the

checks, and what money she still has. Then we kill them both. I thought that was already decided."

He could have predicted the shudder that jiggled through Winston.

"The question is, how?" Rupert continued. "When we go in after them, we've got to be armed and ready."

"*Armed?* No guns, Rupert. You know how I feel about guns, and with good reason. We don't have one, anyway."

"This isn't the time to be squeamish. We'll get a gun because that's the most likely way for us to kill them."

"No, no, no." Winston shook his head, setting his jowls wobbling. "Absolutely not. They've changed things here. You have to wait before they'll let you have a weapon. And they ask questions."

Rupert restrained his temper. "Everyone who wants a gun, gets a gun. Still. This is a big, violent country. You still watch those John Wayne flicks. Nothing's changed. We'll kill them, and no one will even know. We'll be out of the country again before some bumbling sheriff with a plate-sized star on his chest starts trying to solve the case."

Winston said, "I think we should hire a hit man."

A policeman walked toward them with measured steps. Rupert sat, absolutely unmoving, and said, "Winston. That policeman's coming to us. Smile. No, don't smile. They suspect you if you're obsequious. Gimme that." He pulled a map between them. "We'll tell him we're lost and ask him for directions."

Winston plopped a stubby finger on the map and traced random lines there, leaving a damp trail as he went.

Rupert's heart pounded sickeningly.

"Where is he now?" Winston whispered.

With studied nonchalance, Rupert glanced up. The policeman was having a discussion with a barefoot gentleman about the finer points of the law relating to urinating in public.

"All clear," Rupert said. "He's got more important matters to deal with than us now. We haven't done anything, anyway."

"A hit man's the thing," Winston said, his eyes unusually sharp over his lenses. "Tonight if we can arrange it. But no guns. Let's have them forced off the road and into the water somewhere. They'll drown, and no one will know the reason. We'll be in the all-clear."

"Clear," Rupert said. "We're not talking about a blitz. That's amazing, Winston."

Winston smiled and said, "Thank you. I think it's rather good."

"But we'll still have to get our hands on the photos and checks, won't we?"

"The water will probably ruin them."

"Mmm," Rupert said. "Can't have that, can we? I think we're back to a gun."

"Strangling's what I really have in mind," Winston said. Really, he wasn't accustomed to figuring out how to kill people. These things invariably got out of hand, and he liked predictability. "I was only testing you to see if you were concentrating. You weren't."

Once more Rupert opted for moderate restraint. "The boyfriend is a strapping young detective. That much we do know. But we're going to be able to strangle him?"

"No. We'll get a really strong hit man."

"Hit man equals bullets, equals guns."

"Sex!" Winston laughed and clapped his hands together. "Of course, sex. It's always involved, and men will be men."

"Meaning?" Rupert asked.

Winston sighed loudly. "Why do I have to spell out every tiny point for you? We'll save the money for the hit man. *You* can get them while they're, you know, *doing* it."

Rupert sniggered. "Moving targets might not be that easy."

"You're disgusting," Winston said. "You wait for the moment. *The moment.* Make it look like a murder-suicide."

"When?"

Little wonder Rupert was so fond of rat-like creatures, Winston thought, they shared similar IQs. "They'll get tired," he said, trying for patience because Rupert showed signs of having one of his rare attacks of stubborn resistance. "Tired and horny and they'll go to a motel. It'll probably happen tonight, even if it's late."

"Where will it happen?"

"When they're in bed!"

Rupert turned his mottled purple nose in Winston's direction, assumed his best attempt at a superior sneer, and said, "I meant *where* will this motel be? Which state? On which road? Where, dammit? We can't just drive around the countryside looking for them, not in America."

"Hardly." Winston ran a finger beneath his collar and stretched his neck. "What do you think I am? A fool? We'd better call that number Lemon gave us."

Rupert crossed his arms.

"We don't have a choice," Winston pointed out. "He said he'll be waiting to hear from us."

"I know we don't have any choice, but he's up to no good. I know you never liked Hill, but I'd rather deal with him than Lemon."

Winston raised his hand to land another slap on Rupert's head, but thought better of it. "I'm going to pretend you didn't say that, Rupert. Call the number."

With a very bad feeling, Rupert located the cell phone they'd acquired at Fats Lemon's insistence and slowly punched in the number the detective had told them to call.

"Yeah," Lemon said as if from an outer space location.

"Hello, this is Rupert Fish. You told me to ring this number and get directions."

There was the slightest pause before another voice said, "Yes, love. I can't tell you how pleased I am to hear your voice. You're finally going to understand what I've been through and how much you mean to me. Where are you?"

Rupert's left hand had turned numb on the wheel. He pressed the mouthpiece against his jacket and said, "It's Kitty."

Fourteen

"Making conversation with strangers isn't easy," Olivia said, breaking a silence that had lasted a long, long time.

Aiden's posture at the wheel was mostly relaxed, but by the pale dashboard light, she could see signs of fatigue in his frown. Occasionally he shifted position and rolled his head from side to side.

Evidently he didn't have any opinion on the ease of conversation with someone you didn't know.

"This is Indiana, right?" she said. It was, but the total quiet was making her desperate for a topic.

"Has been for some time," Aiden said, checking his rearview mirror.

"We've been on the road around fourteen hours? You've been driving that long?"

"I like driving."

"So do I. Please let me take a turn and you can rest."

Aiden laughed, and she didn't think it was meant to be a grateful laugh. Since they'd left New York, the only stops they'd made had been at what he called "rest stops," where travelers didn't rest. They used the bathroom and got "free" coffee from a stall where Aiden said you always paid more than you would anywhere else because it was a donation. Olivia hadn't worked out what the donations were for, but she'd appreciated even the worst coffee and shop-bought biscuits.

"I really am a good driver, Aiden. I got my license when I was seventeen—on my first try—which isn't what usually happens in England. And I've been driving ever since. Even Mummy says I'm what she calls *passable*. Mummy isn't big on praise."

Aiden was coming to like the sound of Olivia's voice. Soft and a little husky, she spoke clearly and the accent pleased him. She didn't chatter, or hadn't for some time until now, and she was polite—even when he wasn't. Also, given their extraordinary situation, she was calmer than should be expected of her.

"I'm sure you drive well. The truth is, I'm a lousy passenger."

"That's an excuse," Olivia said. "You need a break."

"I wouldn't get it with you driving on the side of the road you're not used to."

"We're on motorways. What difference does it make?"

"It makes a difference."

Boswell stood on the back seat and rested his head on her shoulder. She hugged his massive neck. "There's hardly anything on the road, Aiden. Please change places and get some sleep."

"No, you're not driving."

She watched stars in a black sky, and the dim shapes of sparse trees, the occasional glint of water in some small lake. "There's no way you can just keep driving like this. You'll fall asleep at the wheel, or starve, whichever comes first."

"I'll take another apple."

"They're all gone. So is the cheese. There's no food left, except for a jar of something called pimento spread."

"That can be tossed at the next opportunity." He glanced at her, but didn't smile.

Olivia's stomach did a little flip. It flipped every time he looked at her, or she looked at him, or thought about him—which was all the time. All of which didn't mean anything. Not really. She was justifiably aware of him because regardless of everything that pointed to him being trustworthy, she had no proof that he wasn't part of some terrible plot, perhaps the same plot that had brought her here in the first place.

If Mummy and Daddy ever found out what she was doing, they would never again allow her to as much as protest when they questioned her common sense. They would feel fully justified in adding to their ode to Theo's brilliance and bemoaning the mystery of producing so accomplished a son while their daughter was an incompetent nincompoop.

"Are you sleeping?" Aiden whispered.

"No," she said sharply. "Just thinking."

"I was afraid of that. I think it's dangerous for you to do too much thinking. Keep your eyes peeled for an eats sign."

"A neat sign?"

"*Eats*. An *eats* sign—for a place where you can eat. Diner, or something. You gotta be starving. You've given just about everything we had to me. We'll stop and get some hot coffee and some food."

She didn't fool herself into thinking the only reason he would stop was to feed her, but she'd enjoy thinking it was part of his motive. And she salivated at the prospect of food.

Ahead a signboard gleamed and Olivia leaned forward, pulling out her glasses and cramming them on just in time. "The next exit," she said, not caring that she sounded ridiculously excited. "What luck. Can you believe it? You asked, and here we are. Food and lodgings and services, it says. *Usterbee*. That's the town. Population . . . That can't be right. Population, eighty-seven?"

"Real metropolis," Aiden said. He still got a kick out of the little, almost-forgotten towns across the country, although tonight, or this morning as it was now, he wasn't getting pleasure out of too much. "Let's do it. We're both hungry and you have to be so tired, you're punchy. You haven't had much sleep in several days. You'll feel better once I feed you. Pray the local eatery isn't closed."

The lights were on at *Dierdre's Want To?*, set all alone in the middle of a large, lonely parking lot. Shutters covered the bottom halves of the windows, but there was movement inside. A swaying neon sign over the door advertised, "Cozy Cabins For Rent." Ranged around the edges of the area were the dim forms of clapboard huts with steeply sloped roofs. The advertised lodgings, probably. The absence of any cars outside these suggested zero occupancy.

Aiden parked, got out, and stretched. The air delivered a cold blow, reminding him that his feet were bare inside his sandals and the jacket was too threadbare to be much protection against the weather.

Olivia wore the cotton sweater and linen jacket. Unwilling as he was to accept complete responsibility for this all-but-helpless foreign woman, he did feel that responsibility. The heater in the Rover was one of the things that hadn't been brought up to full function. Geez, a little more planning and there could have been blankets and a pillow in there for her. She had to have more clothes—and so did he. Nothing could be done about that till morning, when he'd make sure they found a small town with some sort of store.

"Come on, Boswell," he heard Olivia say. "Let's go over here and attend to things. Good boy. Such a good boy."

He turned and saw her trotting, albeit stiffly and with Boss at her side, toward a dark area. He didn't want her off anywhere on her own, not even with the dog, and he followed at a distance, flexing his shoulders as he went.

More compliments were showered on his no-good canine before Olivia headed back toward Aiden.

Olivia saw something move. She stood still and reached for Boswell's collar. "It's all right, boy," she told him. "I'll take care of you." A big shadow blocked out the light from the café. The shadow moved toward her.

Aiden's shout of laughter brought enough relief to turn her knees rubbery. "Just me," he said. "You're going to take care of Boss? That's cute. You're cute. Come on, let's eat. And don't wander off without me again—not even a short distance."

She didn't argue with him or try to explain that she was only reacting out of shock, and he shouldn't shock her in future because she'd been known to become unpredictable under such circumstances.

"Aiden," she said, catching up. "We're in a real fix, aren't we?"

Unless he was overreacting, which he didn't tend to do, they were in something more than a "real fix." "We're going to be careful," he told her. "If you can put some faith in my experience, I'll try not to let you down. And we're going to get help from a guy who is the best, absolutely the best."

"Chris Talon?"

"Yep." Although he'd watched the road behind them all day and into the night, he'd seen no sign of anyone who might be following, and they hadn't been buzzed by any aircraft. But he'd never had a stronger sensation of being followed. "It was a good idea to stop. We both need to stretch our legs. Bring your bag. If it seems okay, I'll take a look at those shots of yours."

With Boss stationed outside the door of Want To?, Aiden automatically rested a hand at Olivia's waist when they entered the diner.

She shouldn't like the warmth of his hand so much. She absolutely should not have unbalanced thoughts about preferring this, being with him even under dangerous circumstances, to the quiet existence she'd always lived.

"Whoa!" The shout came from a tall, extremely thin man in a white shirt and trousers, white apron, with a round white-paper hat on the back of a head of thick black hair. His face was deeply lined, and his brows overhung dark eyes. "You two just took ten years off a fella's life. What the Sam Hill you doin' in the middle of nowhere at this time of night?"

"Sign on the highway says you're expecting us." Aiden pulled

Olivia to his side. "We're just passing through. Been driving a long time. Any chance of some hot coffee and whatever you've got to fill two empty stomachs?"

"Wait till Dierdre hears about this," the man said. He laced his hands around the handle of the broom he'd been using. "She's goin' to be so bummed out she missed ya. Don't get no one out here at night. Almost never. Except for when people wants a cabin. Daytime is different. But those folks don't want to come back here this time of night. Too lonely. Come on over and take a booth. Make yourselves comfortable. I'm Cal, Dierdre's boyfriend."

By Olivia's calculations, despite a pretty good dye job on his hair and eyebrows, Cal must be pushing seventy. She'd really like to see Dierdre. Aiden led her to the booth Cal indicated and waited until she was seated before slipping in opposite.

Cal went to the counter, returned, and plopped down two glasses of water, two mugs, and a palmful of small cream containers. He filled the mugs with coffee. He'd carried everything in his two large hands and finished by pulling several packets of crackers from a pocket in his apron and tossing them on the table. "You're probably peckish," he said. "Nibble on those to get you going."

The menus were under his arms. These he spread, one before each of them, with some ceremony. "How long you been driving?"

"Fourteen, almost fifteen hours," Olivia told him.

"Yeah." He closed the menus again and removed them. "You look it. Both of you. Got some of the best black bean chili you ever had the honor to get a whiff of. I'll start you off with that. Stick it to your insides. Then we'll talk about givin' you some choices. Mebbe."

He left them, and Aiden rubbed the heels of his hands into his eyes. "You meet the craziest good people out in the sticks."

Olivia said, "Yes, and the nicest," and felt them run out of things to say.

She had that slightly tousled thing about her again. Soft and sleepy. Aiden hadn't seen darker eyes that he remembered, or eyes that had the same mix of brilliance and innocence. Not that she was dumb. No, sir, not this woman. Just out of her depth and walking on quicksand, foreign quicksand.

Irritation had swept at him in eddies ever since he'd met her at JFK, but they'd gotten farther apart. The initial instinct to encourage her to make the trip, and to want to meet her, still bemused him. For a man who avoided personal attachments, his behavior had been over the top. Still was.

He liked being with her.

Kissing her hadn't been a chore. The thought was dangerous. It brought him close to laughing and awakened the sexy reaction he already knew she could arouse in him.

Olivia opened a packet of crackers and ate one. His five o'clock shadow was darker than she'd have expected given his light hair. His eyes were on her. She checked her mouth for crumbs.

Ice clinked and she glanced up. He drank water, looking down at her over the glass.

She really liked the single gold earring he wore in his left ear. Strange, since she usually disapproved of such things.

They made jokes about Americans having perfect teeth. She didn't find anything funny about Aiden's teeth, or his mouth. She had the sensation that she felt his lips on hers again, and rolled her own together, capturing that touch.

He put down the glass and ran a forefinger around the rim. He turned his face aside and bowed his head. Then he looked sideways at her through his spiky lashes.

Olivia drew short breaths. Lean and long, tough-cut but sensitive, his features weren't classic but they went together in a way that scrambled every sensible thought she might have had.

Again he looked away, and again his brilliant blue gaze returned like some sort of seek-and-destroy weapon.

She couldn't keep on looking at his face.

Without the jacket, his shoulders bulged beneath his soft denim shirt. There was a suggestion of hair at the open neck. He'd rolled back his cuffs over forearms she'd like to touch. His hands were all male, broad across the prominent knuckles, the backs covered with a tracing of bronzed hair—and scars that had to have a story. They were expressive hands, as well as capable.

Olivia loved men's hands if they were nice. Aiden's were more than nice. She thought about how they might feel on her skin if he really wanted them there.

He'd felt sexual tension enough times, but this was different, this was electric, and he had become more engaged than the usual. Great. Perfect timing. He stirred and made to get up. "Boss needs water."

Stinging all over, wobbly in her tummy, Olivia rose promptly, her glass in hand, and headed for the door.

"I got it," Cal shouted. "He's got a bowl and a blanket. He's havin' a good ol' time."

Olivia returned to the booth, aware of Aiden watching every move she made.

She had a walk, what a walk. Maybe it was because she was walking slowly, looking at him, almost telegraphing that she felt the same physical connection he felt. "Cream in your coffee?" he said, and poured in the contents of two containers anyway. "You had cream at Mama's. Juice might be good. Give us some quick energy." He felt more edgy than tired, and as aroused as hell, but despite all the right signals in her eyes, Olivia's wan features worried him. All he needed was a sick woman on his hands, a sick woman he wanted to sleep with.

She put her elbows on the table and propped her fists under her chin. "Now," she said. "I know you've told me. I think you have, anyway. But would you spell out for me exactly why we're doing what we're doing?"

"I have told you." He saw the door open an inch and carefully slid his hand to the butt of his gun. "But I'll tell you again, because I like you." He forced a smile. Keeping her from overreacting was essential.

She smiled back at him. Damn, but she had the best smile. How many women had he met with the kind of open, grateful smile that made him feel they didn't have any hidden agenda? None, except maybe Vanni's sisters, who thought of themselves as Aiden's sisters, too.

The door eased open a little more.

"You're such a nice man, Aiden. I do know I've pulled you into all this, you know. You didn't have to try to help me. I've really made life hard for you."

"Try not to call me *nice* again, Olivia. Salads are nice sometimes. Soups can be nice. An ice cream is a nice way to finish a meal, especially on a hot day. An inoffensive but ordinary pair of shoes is nice enough. I'm not nice, ma'am. I can find people who will tell you just how nice I'm not."

Still she smiled; in fact, her eyes sparkled with the intensity of that smile. "You were going to tell me something."

Yeah, he thought, and someone's trying to come in here without giving advance notice. He leaned forward, allowing himself a good hold on the gun, and easing it from his waist. "We're getting away from New York because Ryan Hill has pulled off the feat of turning the entire NYPD against me. He has them thinking I'm a criminal, and that you're a criminal, too. With Vanni's help in New York, and

Chris's help in Seattle, I think I can get the evidence I need to bring us out winners, wrap this case up, and leave Ryan Hill in jail afterwards. With Fats Lemon, if he's an accomplice, and I think he is. Traveling, staying on the move, is the only solution I can come up with that'll give me a chance to do my job and not be stopped. If I'm locked up, I'm stopped, Olivia, with a capital S."

Aiden was on his feet and braced when the door opened all the way.

Olivia kept her mouth shut, but swung around in her seat.

No one came in.

He edged sideways from the booth. "Put your head down," he ordered Olivia. "Keep it down."

A glance showed Cal with his back to them and working over a steaming pot.

Without incident, Aiden made it all the way to the booth nearest the door. "Shit," he said, and slammed the hand that held the gun over his heart. Boss lay on the floor, his head on his paws, with a look in his eyes that swore he needed anti-depressants. "Darn you, buddy," Aiden said and sank to his knees. "How come you've turned into something like a lap dog? What happened to all that training?"

"Guess he got old like the rest of us around here."

Aiden shot to his feet, gun at the ready again, and confronted a woman who didn't reach his shoulders. Her breadth pretty much matched her height, and the gravelly voice he'd heard went well with a flat, masculine face onto which the lady had applied liberal paint. Her tight platinum curls were held in place by a black net decorated with tiny colored beads.

"You gonna shoot me, cutie?" she said, grinning as if the idea appealed. "That'd liven things up a bit around here. Probably be good for business. What do you say, Cal?"

Cal had approached, bearing a steaming bowl in each hand. "Don't you hurt my Dierdre," he said, and his voice shook. "You need someone for target practice, use me. Just don't hurt Dierdre."

Embarrassed, Aiden put the weapon away. "Sorry," he said. "Habit. Blame him." He pointed at Boss, who was attempting to make his way toward Olivia.

"You're a cop, ain't ya?" Cal said. "I thought you was when you come in. Then there was the dog."

"No," Aiden said. "Just a man who carries a gun for protection."

"If you say so," Cal said, but didn't sound convinced.

"He does say so," Dierdre announced. "Came back to check up on you, Cal. I was going to suggest you close up early."

Aiden wondered what these people considered late.

"What's he feeding you?" she asked Aiden, and sniffed. "Black-bean chili. Good start. You been traveling awhile, I see. Eat. Then we'll see to fixing you up with a place to stay. Get something aired out."

"Um, well, we weren't actually thinking—"

"Eat," Dierdre interrupted. "Don't give 'em any booze, Cal. Not till they've eaten. Don't want 'em falling asleep in their plates."

At last Aiden returned to the booth and sat down in front of his bowl. Olivia, an annoyingly amused grin on her face, had dispensed with manners and eaten almost half of her own chili. Boss sat sideways beside her. He wouldn't have fit any other way.

"What the hell's gotten into you, Boss?" Aiden said. *"Down."*

"Please leave him," Olivia said. "Stop trying to control the world and eat. Please, Aiden."

"The dog's fine," Cal yelled.

"I know when I'm beaten," Aiden said and found that the chili tasted better than any he'd had. A large platter of bread coated with melted cheese appeared in Dierdre's hands, and she placed it between them without a word.

Cal came to refill coffee and drop another heap of cream containers.

"Don't you get travelers at night all the time?" Aiden asked. "You can't treat them all like returning prodigals."

"We've been here thirty-five years," Cal said. "Reckon both of us are pretty good judges of character. I can tell two things about you. You're in trouble. And you're good people. And a third thing is you left wherever you came from in too much of a hurry to bring what you need." He inclined his head to look significantly at Aiden. "And four, you may not have known each other a real long time, but if you don't already have something going, you will."

He walked away.

Olivia turned hot—not an unwelcome development—and couldn't look at Aiden.

"He's right about most things," he said.

She stirred what remained of her chili. "All but one," she told him.

"Yeah. You're a good person. My character's questionable."

The breath she took caused her to choke, and she gulped water.

Dierdre left the diner, but Cal continued to push food on them. Olivia began to worry about the bill but didn't know how to bring this up to Aiden without sounding rude.

"You full?" he asked her quietly. "I am. I was some time ago."

"Really full," she said. "I don't suppose they'd be able to change some pounds for me?"

"Uh-uh. I've got us covered."

"I pay my way. But thank you." She peered into her bag, but one of Aiden's long, tough hands descended and stopped her.

"Not this time," he said.

Cal brought yet another plate, but put it in front of Boss. "Steak pie. I'd only have to throw it out, anyway."

Boss put a paw on the edge of the plate to anchor it and loudly sucked up the pie.

"Don't you have a health department around here?" Aiden said.

"Not in the middle of the night," Cal told him. "You gonna turn me in?"

"You're a very kind man," Olivia said. "This is only my second day in the—"

"Olivia hasn't done a lot of traveling by car, so this is a new experience." He frowned at her.

So now she was supposed to be suspicious of everyone, *everyone*, and make sure she didn't give out the most unimportant information about herself.

Dierdre reappeared. She came directly to the booth and slapped down a key. "Number seven. It's not fancy, but it's got the newest bed and the heater works. And the shower gets hot. Just don't run it too long without giving it a chance to recover."

Olivia pulled a shutter aside and looked outside.

"It's three in the morning," Dierdre went on. "Where you're coming from and where you're going is no business of ours. But we know good people in trouble when we see 'em. Get four hours of sleep, or just three, then get going again. You'll do a whole lot better than if you keep going now."

He ought to refuse, Aiden thought, but another look at Olivia made him change his mind. "We'll need two cabins," he said. She wasn't a woman who'd get cozy with a man she hardly knew.

"Oh," Dierdre said. "I—well, I'll see what I can do with Number two. That's not so bad. Maybe you should park around back? Back of the cabins? Just an idea."

This woman had a nose for trouble all right. "I think I will," Aiden told her.

"Would it be a good idea—tell me to mind my own business if

you want to—but would it be a good idea if I hadn't seen anyone like you two passing through tonight? Just in case I'm asked?"

Aiden figured that if he agreed, he was taking a chance on these two not turning him in to the nearest law. But the only way this whole caper was likely to favor the good guys was if they took some chances.

He'd take this chance. "It would be a good idea. Thanks."

"We'll manage with just Number seven," Olivia said, putting her nose on the window. "And we're grateful to you for being so kind."

Aiden caught Cal's grin and shook his head slightly.

"Fair enough, then," Dierdre said. "You got bags? Clothes?"

"Well—"

"Didn't think so. Something about you. I put a couple of emergency kits in the cabin. We carry 'em in case—you know, in case of one of those disasters we've been going to have since World War II. There's basic stuff in there and I've kept 'em updated. Here." She darted back behind the counter and produced a bottle. "In case you're too tired to sleep. A nip of brandy always helps. Now, off you go if you've had enough eats."

Olivia automatically took the brandy Dierdre thrust at her. Cal gave Aiden a battery-operated lantern, and the two waved them out as if they were children who had to get to school in the morning.

Boswell loped along beside Olivia, showing his own signs of tiredness.

"You don't want to stop," Olivia said. "They're just being kind, I'm sure of it, but that doesn't mean we have to do what they suggest."

"No." And just in case Cal and Dierdre were contacting the authorities, he wanted a chance to check. "I'd like you to sleep for a couple of hours if possible. I'd also like to see if I can buy a blanket for the car from them. I'm going to get you inside, move the car, and make my way back to the diner."

She'd have liked to ask him not to leave her alone, but thought better of it.

Aiden unlocked the cabin door and reached inside to switch on the light. "Home, sweet home," he said automatically. Rustic could be pretty rustic once you left the beaten track in these forgotten places, but the place seemed cheerful enough. "Lock yourself in."

She did as she was told and went immediately to peer through faded chintz curtains at the single small window. Aiden's tall, broad-shouldered shape was impossible to miss. He walked directly to the Rover and got in.

What would she do if he decided to leave her here?

He wouldn't. She didn't know what made her so sure, but she was sure. The Rover's engine came to life and she heard it pass around to the back of the cabin. A door slammed and footsteps crunched on gravel, passing the cabin in the opposite direction. When she peered through the curtains again, she saw Aiden's unmistakable silhouette heading for the diner.

She shouldn't feel so happy at the sight of him.

At a doggy grunt, she looked over her shoulder. Boswell had leaped onto the cabin's one bed. Only a double, it was piled high with a down comforter covered in red, white, and blue striped flannel. A heap of pillows, no two with matching cases, rested on top. Two businesslike heavy plastic boxes, white with blue hinged tops, also rested on the comforter. In blue marker to match the lids, someone had written "His" on one white box and "Hers" on the other. Olivia had to smile. She dragged "Hers" to the cabin's one chair, an over-stuffed, cracked vinyl recliner in a shade of faded purple.

She had to look out the window again. This time she could see Cal and Dierdre standing near a booth, talking, but not the person to whom they talked. Olivia didn't have to see. It would be Aiden. She didn't like being parted from him, and that was absolutely ridiculous.

Except that given her situation, she might be forgiven for not enjoying her own company too much.

He was being a gentleman, of course, staying out of the way to give her privacy.

An examination of Dierdre's emergency box produced items of clothing, a toiletry kit, sealed packages of rations, a first-aid kit, sewing kit, flares, bottled water, a radio and batteries, an axe, a multi-purpose knife, flashlight, and silver thermal blanket.

The clothing and toiletries were all that interested Olivia, and she carried several items to the bathroom, together with the nightgown and clean underwear she kept at the bottom of her bag for moments just like this.

The bathroom was a cubicle behind louvered doors where it was necessary to walk all the way inside before the doors could be closed again. Towels were heaped on a shelf over the toilet. Everything was clean and warm.

Feeling horribly vulnerable, she undressed and showered as quickly as possible. Her skin wasn't completely dry when she pulled on the panties and nightie. They stuck to her, but she didn't care.

Over the nightie she pulled on a huge green sweatshirt emblazoned with "Purdue University Wrestling," and a pair of thick white socks that reached her knees.

She rinsed out the delicate, rose-colored underwear and pale stockings she'd worn that day and hung them over the shower enclosure. This wasn't any time to be coy about such things. Her horribly creased jacket, rumpled sweater, and the skirt Mama Zanetto had mended, Olivia hung on a hanger. She hoped they'd improve before she had to put them on again.

A tap at the outer door caught her combing her wet hair. She finished the job quickly and went to let Aiden in.

"You didn't look through the window," he said, bringing a burst of cold air into the cabin with him. "You just opened the door. I could have been anyone. Never, *never* do that again. Ask for a name first."

"Sorry. I will." He was right, of course.

Geez, he thought, she couldn't be expected to get all of this in one gulp. "It's okay, you weren't to know. You're not used to this type of thing."

"You were gone a long time." Did that sound like something a possessive wife would say?

If it did, Aiden didn't react that way. "Those two are something. They've been here forever. They just want to talk, and I didn't want to shut them up in case they said something interesting. They're okay, by the way. Let me look at the photographs."

In her too-large socks, Olivia scuffed across pink-and-blue carpet tiles and rummaged in her bag.

"Did you hear the other car arrive?" Aiden said.

"No," she told him. "I was probably in the shower."

Aiden glanced at her. "I've got to do that. A car pulled up to the diner when I was walking back. I hope it's someone else who wants a cabin. I don't think there's a lot of money made around here."

Looking directly at him disturbed her. She shifted her attention back to her bag and located photos and negatives. She left the negatives where they were and took the pictures to a table with a laminated top over which a naked bulb hung. "I wish I had some idea what we're looking for," she said, and spread out the photos.

"You smell nice," he said.

Olivia said, "Thanks," but he was already absorbed in her shots from the Notting Hill project.

"Wow," he said. "Could they use many more colors and patterns in one space?"

"Dierdre could give it a try," Olivia said, and giggled when Aiden ran his gaze over the cabin and grinned.

"Is this kind of thing expensive?" He tapped one picture.

"Really, really expensive," Olivia told him.

Aiden pored over the shot. "Some library. I like it."

"That's my favorite room," she said.

Their eyes met briefly.

"This must be the art gallery." A series of photos confronted Aiden, some showing a single painting or sculpture, some taking in an entire wall of pieces and displaying them to smaller, less detailed advantage. "Why would one couple need this much stuff?"

"Some people never have enough."

"I see what you mean about what they like. I guess I don't know cubism from futurism. Every painting here looks abstract to me." He turned photographs this way and that. "So does the sculpture. Wisest plan is to get somewhere safe and spend a lot of time with these."

"Absolutely. I need time to study each frame. Although there may be nothing to find in them. I've always thought that."

He agreed. "Still, there are other people who don't think so, and they're willing to do just about anything to get their hands on them."

"I'd have said *anything*," Olivia commented.

"And I guess you'd be accurate," he told her. What he'd like most of all would be to gather her up and dive under the covers with her. They'd probably fall instantly asleep, but at least he'd get to hold her.

"I'm grateful to Cal and Dierdre," Olivia said. "I don't think I've met people like them before. There are toiletries and some clean things in the boxes. You'll probably want the one labeled, 'His.' "

"I guess I will." He opened the top and started pulling out contents. "Cal and Dierdre are hanging around over there. I figure they always do when they've got guests. Is that the other car now?"

Olivia returned to the window, made a peephole between the two curtains, and surveyed the grounds. "Yes, it's parking down at the other end. Good. I don't want to be near anyone else."

Aiden considered all the possible meanings of that comment, but didn't say anything.

"It's a big car," Olivia noted.

"Uh-huh," he said, finding toothpaste, then a brush and comb. "Big black Caddy. Looks like a pimpmobile, or a mafia job."

"What do you mean?"

He ought to feel guilty at the sight of her startled expression. He took his armload to the bathroom and inclined his head to study her. "Mmm. Nice outfit. Especially the sweatshirt and socks. You might not want to stand with the light behind you. Get some sleep."

The doors shut behind him, and Olivia looked down to see her legs clearly outlined through her thin silk nightie.

Fifteen

Olivia listened to the shower—and to the surprising sound of Aiden Flynn humming the tenor part of the "Hallelujah" chorus. Really, people never failed to surprise one.

The sound of a phone ringing shocked her more. There wasn't one in the room, but she knew Aiden had a cell phone with him. This could be very important, was bound to be important for someone to call here.

The sound came from the dreadful jacket, from an inside pocket. Gingerly, Olivia took out the instrument and turned it on. "Yes?" she said softly.

"Olivia?"

How many more periods of horrible tension could she tolerate? "Hello, Vanni. Aiden's in the shower."

"Oh, is he?"

The very familiar heated sensation flash-fired her body. "Yes. We've stopped for a couple of hours, then we'll be off again. Shall I get him?"

"No, just give him a message and tell him I'll be in touch again soon. I've got to pick my times. Calls from his end aren't an option. But you know that. Ryan Hill—in the flesh—showed up at the precinct late this afternoon—yesterday afternoon now. Evidently the guy's got quite the stash of evidence against Aiden and you. If the chief had his way, there'd be an APB out for the pair of you now. Ryan talked him out of it. Said he wanted to avoid getting you killed by some hick with zero experience and itchy fingers. Wants to make sure you're brought in alive and with whatever evidence you've got with you intact.

"That's his story, you understand. What he really wants is to get to you himself and make sure anything you've got on him *never* makes it into official hands. He's been given the all-clear to pursue you himself. In the absence of material evidence, it's still unofficial. Says he'll ask for all the backup he needs, when he needs it."

Olivia paced and worried. "I wish we knew what he thinks I've got. Evidence against him, I mean. We looked briefly at the photographs and couldn't see anything. There hasn't been a chance to really study them."

"Just don't flash 'em around," Vanni said. "Keep 'em safe." He was quiet for a few moments. "Look, Aiden will try to say he doesn't need me, but if things get too rough, I'll find a way to be with you. And I'm ready to wire money. Tell him that, will you? And remind him I'll be calling back when I can. He's gotta make sure he doesn't risk an incoming call reaching me at a bad time. I'm trying to figure out how Ryan knows for sure that you met up with Aiden. He could have found out what plane you took from London and decided that since Aiden's gone and there's no sign of you—well, I guess that's what happened."

"Yes."

"Is the car running okay?"

"Beautifully. Aiden was ticked off when he realized Boswell was in the warehouse."

"Mad, huh?" Vanni said. "He would be, but Boss can be useful. Where are you now?"

"Ohio. Look, Vanni, I want to be off the phone when Aiden comes back. I'll give him all this gently if I can—the stuff about Ryan. When you talk to him tomorrow, he'll have had time to think it through." She swallowed before saying, "Do you think Ryan intends to—well, kill us?"

"Yeah."

"That's what I thought. Thank you for your honesty. Please give my regards to your family. Good-bye, Vanni."

"Er, yeah, so long."

She turned off the phone and stuffed it back in Aiden's coat. He continued to hum over the sound of the water. Any moment now it would turn cold and he'd get out.

There were some things a decent person didn't do, and one of them was drag someone else into their trouble.

"Okay, okay," she said aloud because the sound of her voice seemed a normal thing in the middle of a great deal that was bizarre.

"You are not a brave woman. You're not a coward, but you aren't about to join any bomb squads, either. But you have to release this man from your problems. Otherwise he may lose his career, and even his life."

But how could she do that? She sought about in her mind, desperately chasing avenues that led nowhere. There was only one way. Leave him, get away before he could know she'd gone. Heaven knew what she'd do once she walked out that door, but there was no alternative she could live with.

He'd think her such an idiot.

She could handle that, but not the prospect of causing the destruction of another human being.

Scrambling, she dragged a pair of green sweatpants from "Hers" and pulled them on over the socks. She stuffed her nightie down inside and grabbed for a hooded, zip-fronted sweatshirt to wear on top of everything. Her shoes didn't want to fit over the socks, but she forced them on and slung her bag over her shoulder. Taking the entire camera case would be too much, but she managed to stuff her Nikon into a space in the bag.

The shower continued. Aiden had moved on to "Rocky Mountain High" and kept muddling the words.

Olivia planted a kiss on Boswell's long nose and whispered, "Be quiet and good," in his ear. Several pillows shoved under the comforter made her feel juvenile, but when she looked at the effect, she decided that if she was lucky, Aiden would think she was sleeping and it would hold up for long enough.

She slipped outside to a full-throated rendition of "The Irish Blessing." By now the water must be icy, but evidently the man was made of sturdier stuff than she was. Very gently, she closed the door. There were probably about five miles between her and the motorway, but walking had never intimidated her. Avoiding the open spaces in the parking lot, she sped toward the wide driveway, passing the large black car on her way. A light shone at the window of a cabin, and she could hear people arguing inside.

What a shame to quarrel when they must need rest.

Hitchhiking was so dangerous. Women got carted away and raped all the time, and murdered, or left to die in deserted places, like the bottom of the Thames.

Perhaps a police car would come along, and . . .

She was mentally challenged, that was the problem. The last thing she dared risk was attracting the attention of the police.

Olivia began to sweat. Bushes beside the road were losing their leaves and becoming scrubby, but in the gloom they seemed thick and gnarled, their branches like reaching, beckoning fingers. The wind had picked up, and it whined in the rustling limbs of taller trees.

In the not-too-far distance, she heard the drone of passing vehicles. The motorway wasn't far at all. If someone stopped, she'd take a good look at them before getting in and ask them a few pleasant but sensible questions. She was a good judge of character, and she'd trust in that.

Soon the sky would begin to lighten, but for now it remained pressed down and ominous upon the land.

If—no, when—Aiden figured out what she'd done, he'd come after her.

She shouldn't have done this. Talking things through and making him understand she must find her own way would have been the thing.

She broke into a run, stumbling over rocks at almost every step.

Insects set up a clickety-clack and hiss in the grass on either side of her. *Please don't let a snake come near me.*

A sensation that the air had been ripped apart stopped her. A swishing noise started, like a large bird flying low. Olivia threw her hands over her head.

Instantly, her sleeve was grabbed and her arm jerked to her side. When she dared to look, she saw the glint of silvery fangs and the glitter of eyes before she was knocked to the ground. She tripped and hit, knees first, knocking the wind from her lungs. Her head landed on her outstretched arm and her bag made a whumping sound.

A voice whispered harshly, but with the buzzing in her head, she couldn't make out a word. Everything shook.

Standing over her, his lips wrinkled back from metal teeth that looked terrifying in the darkness, was Boswell. All sign of soft, doggy friendship had vanished. He growled insistently, and she knew better than to move, or even say a word.

"Okay, Boss." This time there was no mistaking Aiden's voice. "Good boy. Release."

Boswell stood aside at once, only to be replaced by his boss. Olivia wasn't sure which of them was the more frightening. Aiden settled a toe on her upper arm. She couldn't have moved if she'd wanted to. She didn't want to. Olivia wanted to disappear. The next best thing was to close her eyes.

"Don't you pass out on me now, you little fool. What in God's name got into you? Where did you think you were going?"

She squeezed her eyes more tightly shut and didn't answer him. She'd play too shocked to react.

"Okay." He caught hold of her beneath the arms, hauled her up like so much rubbish, and tossed her over his shoulder. "You badly hurt anywhere?"

She gave a short shake of her head.

"Good. I'm going to be moving fast because I don't want anyone to see this. Open your mouth, and I'll shut it so you won't make the same mistake again."

He ran and she jounced, pounding her stomach each time she met his hard shoulder. Approaching the cabin from the back, he kept close to the side and got them inside so smoothly, she doubted anyone would have noticed even if they'd been looking. Boswell had the gall to resume his comfortable spot on the bed.

"Down," Aiden ordered, and the dog obeyed at once. The reason for removing the dog was quickly obvious when Olivia landed on the mattress hard enough to bounce.

Aiden locked the door and slid on the chain. He turned the lantern down very low. The only light in the cabin, it didn't allow her to see his face clearly.

Damn him, she thought, she'd been trying to do him a favor. She rolled onto her side, facing away from him.

With a rough jerk, he lifted her by an arm and a leg and dropped her on her back again. He said, "I want you looking at me."

"That hurts," she said. "My knees really hurt. I wasn't trying to do you any harm."

"What *were* you trying to do? I've lost count of how many times you've told me I'm a nice man who doesn't deserve to be pulled into your problems. But you've never been stupid enough to suggest there's any alternative but for me to work a way through this now—for both of us. How did you think it would help if you ran and ended up either dead or taken into custody by the local boys?"

"I did think of that, but I'd already committed. Sometimes it's hard to turn back when you're committed, right?"

He glared down at Olivia. Dressed in his soft denim shirt, unbuttoned, and the corduroy pants that rested on his hips because he hadn't taken time to put a belt on, his chest rose and fell with exertion.

"Isn't that right, Aiden?"

"I ought to go away," he said through his teeth. "I shouldn't stay here now."

She didn't know how to respond, but unzipped the hooded sweatshirt and raised her shoulders to wriggle out of it. "Too hot," she said apologetically, knowing he must be cold.

The woman didn't have a notion what was going on inside him. And the feelings he had were so alien to Aiden, he didn't know if they'd fade, or if he really ought to put distance between himself and Olivia.

"I've made you so angry. Please forgive me."

The explosive sensation in his head only swelled. "If someone had picked you up on that highway ... Don't you have any sense at all? You dropped everything to come halfway around the world without knowing what you were really doing, except running away. I thought by now you'd be getting it that being impetuous can be a killer, and you have a big problem, *and* that I've put everything I am on the line to help you. Was I wrong?"

Inside, Olivia pulsed. Part fear, part excitement, the pulsing grew in parts of her that made her question if she was as civilized as she thought she was. "Why should you care if someone weird picked me up?"

"I don't," he shouted, and ripped off the shirt, casting around as if looking for something else to put on. "There are little things in life, little unexpected facts, know that? Like, we *aren't* strangers. Maybe we never were."

The shoes really hurt, too. She used her heels to kick off first one, then the other, and reached down to tug off the thick socks. "Where did that come from, Aiden? Who said we were strangers?"

"You did. You said it's hard to make conversations with strangers. But it's the quality of time two people spend together rather than the length. And it's the way a person makes you feel. For some inconvenient reason, I'm getting the feeling you and I have been on a collision course. Maybe it was inevitable that we stumbled on each other, then met." He was going to hate himself for pouring out this drivel. "Those kisses we had weren't the stranger kind." He was doing the thing he'd avoided all his life, saying too much about Aiden the man.

Before she considered what she was doing, her hand was on her mouth. "No," she said. "No, they weren't."

"Do you kiss a lot of men, Olivia?"

"No."

He didn't want to retreat now. "When you do kiss them, does it feel the way those felt?"

"Never." She pushed her hair back. "No one ever kissed me like that."

"You kissed me back."

"You made it easy." The pulsing became almost unbearable. "I'm sorry I've upset you."

"Do I frighten you?"

"No," she lied.

"Then your instincts aren't real good." He turned aside and threw everything on the recliner to the floor. "Don't say another word. Don't make another sound."

He extinguished the lantern.

Olivia listened to him settling into the chair. Her heart beat painfully, and every breath caught in her throat.

The comforter ruckled beneath her and there was no pillow under her head. The sweat pants, several sizes too large, twisted around and made her too hot.

Very cautiously, she pushed the pants down until they were around her ankles.

"Don't move," Aiden snapped. "Try anything again, and I might not be able to stop myself."

"Stop yourself from what?" she murmured.

The sound he made was terrifying. An animal noise in his throat.

"I'm sorry," she said. "The sweats are hot in here."

She heard him rise from the chair. Then he was over her again, tearing off the sweatpants, then pulling her up and dragging the sweatshirt over her head. Olivia's hands flew out and met his naked chest.

He fell on top of her, his face beside her head, his mouth against her ear. "You should have done as I told you. I warned you not to make any noise. You don't seem to sense trouble when it's coming your way."

"I don't understand you."

"Don't you?" He took one of her hands and pressed it between his legs. "Does that mean anything to you? Do you know about men and danger, and the effect it can have on them? I want you, Olivia. I've wanted you since I first saw you."

"We only met a couple of days ago." He was on top of her, and she gripped his shoulders. "You mean you want to have sex with me to punish me for disobeying you, or for doing what you didn't expect me to do?"

"You don't know when to stop analyzing, do you?"

His skin smelled clean, and when he pressed his cheek to her mouth the taste was faintly salty. "I'm trying to understand," she whispered.

Her breasts strained against him. She felt him all over her, even in places he wasn't touching.

"Tell me to stop. Slap me." He raised his head, held her arms down, and looked into her face. All she saw was the glint of his narrowed eyes. "Hit me. Go on, hit me."

Even if she wanted to, he was restraining her.

But he released his hold on her right arm, and at the same time fastened his mouth on one of her nipples through the thin silk nightie.

Olivia let out a small cry and raised her hips from the bed.

He pulled harder on her flesh, then opened his mouth wide and sucked as much of her as he could pull inside.

Olivia writhed.

"Hit me," he said, pulling the gown off her shoulder and baring her breast. He gathered the flesh into his hand and pushed it against his face, all the time groaning. Her legs were locked between his.

She should stop this. This was a carnal reaction and nothing to do with Olivia FitzDurham, a quiet woman for whom passion was a mystery.

Her hand connected with his face. She drew back, and hit him again. The fingers felt burned. She didn't know she cried until she tasted her tears and heard sobbing that could only come from her. "I'm sorry, Aiden. I'm sorry. No, I didn't want to do that, you made me."

"Oh, no, sweetheart, you don't blame me for what you want. Why are you sorry?"

"I've never struck anyone. The last person I should hurt is you. You're the best man I've ever met."

"Even if I am taking you apart?"

"Don't talk," she said. "Please."

If he knew her for a lifetime, he'd never understand this part of her. Sex drove her now, sexual need, repression freed and demanding. "Don't talk?" he whispered. "I think I'm going to have to. For God's sake, don't cry. I can't stand to hear you cry." He couldn't hold back much longer, not unless he walked out into the cold early morning and found a lake to jump in.

"Okay," she choked out. "I won't cry." But he kissed her, kissed her while their bodies strained together.

He undid his pants and rolled away enough to get rid of them. Her nightgown was easy to skim over her head and toss aside. She had the kind of body wet dreams were made of, only he was going to have his wet dream between those lovely legs. She hid herself under those dumpy clothes. Someone ought to figure that one out. The underwear was easier. In the bathroom he'd carefully set the expensive, flimsy, rose-colored bra, panties and garter belt, and pale stockings with lace tops aside. He'd put them where he could see them through the clear glass of the shower. Thinking of her in them had almost made him come right there, only he'd known, even then, that he wasn't having moments like that all on his own. He believed the real Olivia was the woman in the rosy silk, not the one in shapeless linen.

Soft, yes, she was soft, but she was also supple in just the way Aiden liked—or did now he'd given the matter some thought.

She wound her body around him. Their sweat mingled. He reached to knead and kiss every part of her until she fell back, still sobbing quietly but only with the desperation of what she felt.

Aiden left her, and the lantern light came on again, just the tiniest bit, enough for her to see him, and for him to see her.

He didn't smile. His face was set in rigid lines and his eyes swept her body again and again, just as hers swept his.

"This is too much," she told him.

He lifted her hips, draped her legs over his shoulders, and said, "Some things only get better," before he buried his face in the hair that covered the entrance to her vagina, and used his tongue and teeth until her arms fell from him, helpless. He reached to cover and play with her breasts, and she rose on the searing tide of the climax she both wanted and resented. He could do whatever he wanted, and she was helpless to resist. She didn't want to resist.

Aiden took her, and Olivia gave herself up to him.

Pushing his head away, she tried to reach his penis, but he was still in control. "Can I come into you?" he said, and she stared up at him. "Olivia?"

"Casual sex," she murmured, alarmed even while she wanted him.

Aiden leaned over her, pushed her hair away from her face. "I can't make you believe it, but this isn't casual for me. Yes or no, Olivia?"

She nodded and he entered, at first with some restraint, but very quickly with enough violence to drive her up the bed. They moved together, but not for long before he burst the dam within her again and joined his shout with hers.

He'd been too far gone to last long enough to give her real pleasure. Next time.

Aiden fell away from her. There had been other times almost like this, but never when he'd been sober and with a woman like Olivia. She didn't move. He raised his head to look at her, but her eyes were closed. Her body showed signs of the roughness of his lovemaking, and he felt shamed by the red beard burns. He also felt triumphant. She couldn't have initiated what had just happened, but she'd become a willing participant.

Or was that his excuse?

They were in a world apart, together, and probably racing for their lives. But they'd just been as alive as a man and a woman could ever be together.

"Olivia?" he whispered. "Are you okay?"

She was asleep. He felt the leaden weight of sexual lethargy overtake him. He pulled her into his arms, managed to pull up the quilt, and allowed his eyes to drift shut. Satisfied, pleasured, he felt the world spin away.

Olivia wasn't asleep.

The sound of water awakened Aiden.

He rolled to his back, slowly recalling the previous hours, so few hours ago. Rubbing his face and pushing his fingers through his hair, he looked toward the louvered bathroom doors. Steam drifted through the slats.

She probably hoped to be dressed before he got up.

A glance at his watch brought him to a sitting position. After eight. They should have been on the road at least an hour ago. He buried his head in his hands. He could smell her fragrance. Something subtle but memorable. What he'd done was to make sure they could never again look at each other without remembering being together, a scene of urgent sex—no, sex was heavy in what they'd done, but he couldn't shut out the conviction that they had made love as well as sex.

Aiden got out of bed, not without noting that Olivia had made certain he was well covered by the quilt when she left him. Boss whined at the door and he let him out. "Be quick," he ordered.

He gathered his shirt and pants and pulled the toiletry kit out of "His" box once more before knocking on the bathroom door and going in. "Okay if I get started?" he asked, not looking into the shower. The water had been turned off.

"Yes."

Naked, he stood before the sink, ran cold water over his head, and washed his face. He considered shaving but thought better of it. As soon as they hit a town large enough, he'd go shopping for a new look. It was time to cultivate a different face. Keeping his eyes down, he brushed his teeth and toweled his face.

The shower door opened. "Are you going in?"

"Yep," he said. "Won't take me a couple of minutes."

Wearing the pink bra and panties, she was standing back to let him pass. Aiden's gut hit his spine. Other parts of him ought to be covered, if not for his dignity, then for her comfort.

Olivia stood her ground. If he thought she would run at the sight of him with no clothes, he was mistaken. She liked looking at him that way, even if he did make her tremble.

"Last night," he said. "I don't know what to say."

"Don't say anything. It happened. It's over. We're not kids."

He pressed a forefinger to her mouth and said, "It's not over, Olivia. You know it and I know it."

"It's over." It had to be, or when this incredible interlude was behind them, she'd be left in little pieces—if she wasn't already in little pieces.

He moved too fast for her. With one hand behind her back and the other cupping her bottom, he pulled her against him. Her toes barely touched the ground. The stark expression she'd seen on his face early that morning returned.

She breathed hard. "Aren't we running late?"

"Yeah. Would you rather we didn't do this?"

He would taunt her into encouraging him, Olivia thought, if that was what it took. She ran her hands over his shoulders and up his neck.

"When I figure out exactly what's going on, and if we get through alive, I'd like to buy underwear for you. Lots of it. Anything you fall in love with. It's a passion with you, isn't it?"

She blushed, but nodded.

"I may also want to keep you in the rest of the stuff you wear."

"You mean my ugly clothes? You don't have to pretend. You think they're awful, right? I don't have much idea about those things—or maybe I don't care."

The expression in his eyes let her know he'd stopped listening. He used her mound to push his penis from side to side and gritted his teeth. He carried her into the shower and turned on the water.

Olivia yelled. "I've got to wear these. They weren't dry, but they were better than nothing."

"Matter of opinion. Live dangerously. Go without. You'll only be with me."

And that was supposed to make her feel better? He placed her directly under the pounding water while he soaped himself all over and scrubbed his hair. Suds streamed down his body. His legs were very well developed. Everything about him was well developed.

She considered trying to slip around him while his eyes were shut, but didn't. Aiden Flynn had opened something up in her this morning, a certainty that she hadn't known an accomplished lover before.

"Now you," he said, swiping at his face.

Despite her efforts to stop him, he soaped her, too—without removing her bra and panties. Olivia grasped his wrists and looked at him askance, at his white grin, and followed his narrowed gaze to soapy, transparent underwear that acted only as a stimulant. From Aiden's face, and his penis, he thought so, too.

He kissed her, held their slippery bodies together, and kissed her until she clung to his neck. Pulling her panties down enough, he pushed himself inside and against her throbbing flesh. He anchored her by spreading his thighs on either side of her hips. The cups of her bra slid beneath her breasts easily enough. His thumbs working back and forth over her nipples drove her wild, and she took him by the waist, used all of her strength to force him to bend his knees, then guided him into her.

"Olivia," he said, and managed to unhook the bra. "That's what I want, to feel you against me."

This time he'd take longer, he'd hold back longer—if he could.

The desperation was the same as the first time, the helpless abandon even more irresistible.

They finished with him holding Olivia high while she locked her ankles behind him.

He felt the water begin to cool but saw no sign that she had noticed. Slowly she relaxed her legs and slid down to stand.

Limp and pliable, she leaned against him, ran her fingers through the hair on his chest and down to his navel, the base of his penis and beneath to cradle him. He put a hand on the wall and locked his elbow. Something was happening again, the supposedly impossible at this point. Olivia hadn't missed the fact. She slipped lower, held his legs and kept right on gliding her breasts downward. Gentle fingers took hold and rubbed him over her nipples.

Blood plummeted from Aiden's head. He used both hands on the wall. Just watching her caused an ironclad erection. But then she took him just a little way inside her lips. The tip of her tongue sought his erogenous places. "Olivia?" What did he want to say?

She raised her flushed face to look at him, and her eyes sparkled. The woman could destroy him, but he'd gladly be destroyed by her.

Strength rushed through him, and he picked her up, turned her around, and bent her forward. "Brace yourself, sweetheart," he told her, guiding her hands to the wall. The water was close to stone-cold now. He'd have to remember that she seemed to like it that way, and the falling temperature wasn't cooling anything for him.

Holding her breasts, he entered her from behind, reveling in the pounding together of their flesh, in her exultant gasps.

At last, and with the water finally turned off, only their rasping breath filled the space.

"This is crazy," Olivia said, and she meant every word. "I have never done anything like it before. Not . . . well, not, that's all."

Aiden retrieved her bra. The panties would never be the same.

Banging on the cabin door stilled them both.

"Who would it be?" Olivia whispered. "What are we going to do?"

"You're going to stay here," he told her.

In a moment, he was wrapped in a towel and closing the bathroom door behind him. He looked through the curtains to see Dierdre standing there with a tray of steaming food in her hands and a world-class frown directed at Boss, who eyed the food and slobbered on her coat. She raised a foot, and he figured out why the pounding had been so loud.

"Hold on," he yelled. "Coming, Dierdre."

He opened the door an inch or so and smiled.

Dierdre smiled too, only she wasn't looking at his face. "Breakfast," she said shortly. "Stand back. I'm coming in. You've got trouble, and you won't be leaving unless we give you the all clear. You own a Morgan?"

Already standing back to let Boss pass, Aiden blinked and took the tray from Dierdre as she entered. "You're breaking the record for changing subjects. Why would you ask a question like that?"

"Cal and I are supposed to be using this cabin, remember," she said, and closed the door. "I asked about the Morgan because I need to know."

He really didn't have much choice but to pile on yet another chance confidence in this woman. "Yeah, I own a Morgan. Why?"

"And you lied when you said you weren't a cop?"

"Maybe."

"Good enough. Eat. Take anything you want from the box with you. It's all cheap and it can all be replaced. Besides, you'll pay us back."

Olivia emerged from the bathroom wearing a towel and a sheepish smile. "Good morning, Dierdre. You're too kind to us."

"Two men came in last night," she said, ignoring Olivia's comment. "Arrived when you were on your way back here," she told Aiden.

"Yes," Aiden said. "In the car that's parked at the other end of the cabins?"

"That's the one. I wanted you to get some sleep or I'd have come earlier. Cal and I have been watching. If you'd showed signs of coming out, we'd have stopped you from being seen. They asked a heap of questions. But we haven't seen a big, blond man with a dark-haired woman. The big man is a cop. The woman is English. She doesn't dress so well."

Aiden and Olivia looked at each other.

"Mad as wet hens, they were. Probably still are. Seems they think they've been led on a wild goose chase by someone called Lemon. How's that for a name? Just wait till they get their hands on Lemon. He's their contact. How are they supposed to get things done when they can't trust their contact."

"Names?" Aiden asked.

Dierdre smiled with one side of her mouth. "Smith and Brown."

"Of course," Aiden said. "I should have known."

"Oh, dear," Olivia said.

Aiden hitched at his towel and said, "Whoever it is isn't here by coincidence, sweetheart. Next thing we do is get away and do some figuring."

"No problem," Dierdre said. A sequinned green beret had replaced the beaded hairnet. "Leave it to me. You'll see a red truck—that's mine—leaving. I'll be guiding a black Caddy to the highway. They'll be in it. Give 'em a head start before you get on your way. Okay?"

"Okay," Aiden and Olivia said in unison.

Dierdre went out and started to close the door, then poked her head back inside and said to Aiden, "If I was thirty years younger, I wouldn't be letting you leave so easy." Her laugh wasn't completely silenced by the shutting door.

"I want to get on the road as fast as I can," Olivia said.

"Because you feel . . ." He stopped himself from saying she was embarrassed to be with him like this after they'd been intimate.

She gave him a shrewd stare. "Because we can't afford to let more time get away from us."

Aiden took up a styrofoam cup of very hot coffee and drank gratefully.

Standing to one side of the window, Olivia pulled the drape out a fraction. She ate toast and watched.

"That's my job," he told her. "Sit down and have your breakfast."

"Try not to be condescending," was his reward for being thoughtful. "There's Dierdre's red pickup. She must keep it parked on the other side of the café."

Short of getting physical and hauling her away, he'd have to let her play sleuth. "And?"

"Nothing else yet. She's out of the pickup and going inside. Not inside, just looking inside. Now she's returning to the pickup and getting in. That big black car is by the café."

Aiden tapped a bare foot.

"Stop that," Olivia said. "Daddy does that. Makes me nervous. Here come two men. One thin, one heavy. The thin one's going to drive. He's—"

"What?" Aiden asked, taking hold of her when she leaped away from the window. He managed to look from the window himself and saw both Dierdre's red pickup, moving now, and the black Cadillac, also moving, or jerking forward in spurts.

"Those were them," Olivia babbled. She tore a Nikon out of her bag and returned to the window to start taking rapid shots. "At least I've got the car and its license plates. All these hours we've been as good as neighbors with Mr. Moody and Mr. Fish."

Aiden watched the smooth way she handled the camera. "Moody and Fish," he said slowly. "That's who I thought it was going to be."

"Right," Olivia said, still clicking. "Of course you did. I haven't been around criminals long enough to think like one."

He let that pass. "Ryan Hill has to have a connection to them—which would explain why he's after the photographs, too. They're all in it together."

Olivia left the window. "Get dressed," she said, and it was an order.

Her businesslike recovery amused and pleased Aiden, but he hadn't forgotten the other issue between them. Olivia had thrown her towel aside and hopped around naked, pulling on the oversized green sweats with only a cotton T-shirt underneath.

"You're going to make a great partner—in more ways than one," Aiden said. He got rid of his own towel and took her by the shoulders. "You've got it right. We've got to move fast now. But repeat after me. It's *not* over."

Sixteen

"Is it a long way from Des Moines to Dubuque?" Olivia asked. Aiden was driving fast toward this Dubuque and chortling about Cal's announcement that Moody and Fish wanted to go to a meeting in Dubuque but Dierdre had sent them in the wrong direction.

Aiden wanted to shout with relief at the sound of Olivia's voice. Since they'd left Usterbee, she had shut him out of whatever she was thinking about. He knew what she was thinking about. "Long enough to take 'em more than three hours to make it back," he told her. "If they get all the way to Des Moines, anyway. And by then they'll already be three hours or so late. For a meeting in Dubuque. It's great. I don't know why Dierdre and Cal decided they liked us, but we're lucky they did."

"And Moody and Fish think you're driving a dark blue Morgan."

They had to have been given that tip by Fats, Aiden decided. Fats knew about the Morgan, but not the Rover. He'd seen the Rover's discarded tarp at the warehouse and hadn't been smart enough to check around thoroughly and make sure what car Aiden was driving. "I think Fats Lemon gave them that brilliant information. He knows I've got one. And I don't know exactly how he knows, but Lemon's telling them where we are."

"If he is," Olivia said, "how would Dierdre be able to get them to go the wrong way?"

Aiden was wondering the same thing. "They could be out of touch with him now. And look on the bright side. His crystal ball could have clouded up so he can't get a make on us anymore."

"I'd drink to that," Olivia said. "Who do you think they're supposed to meet in Dubuque? Fats?"

"Makes sense. Cal heard them mention the name."

"They were shouting when I went by last night—earlier this morning," Olivia said, and regretted the reference when she'd vowed to herself that the events at the cabin would not be repeated or mentioned, or even thought about again. "They must shout at each other so much, they don't notice. Cal couldn't believe the way they talked about looking for an American policeman with a dog and driving a Morgan."

Aiden knew he was taking a risk on her sense of humor, but said, "They probably know Boss's with me, too. That should be enough to scare the pants off 'em."

Olivia was smoothing the place between Boss's eyes. She looked sharply at Aiden and grimaced. "Oh, right, very funny."

He felt his shoulders lower an inch or so at the prospect of resumed talks. But minutes ticked away to fifteen, then thirty that passed without another word from Olivia, and Aiden couldn't think of any way to trick her out of her withdrawal again. His shoulders stiffened once more and he gripped the wheel tightly, concentrating on the road to keep his mind off the woman beside him—and other things. But he had to glance at her occasionally. She'd crossed her arms. The hand he could see was fisted, the knuckles white. Was she regretting what they'd done together? Dumb question. He visualized her in the shower, in the dark pink underwear turned darker by the water, yet at the same time transparent.

He took his right hand from the wheel and made a move to touch her. Instead he rubbed Boss's head where the dog balanced between them.

"Cal and Dierdre didn't have any doubts that Moody and Fish were following us," he said when he couldn't stand holding the peace another second. "When I went into that warehouse, I intended taking the Morgan. Luck was on our side. We're going to have plenty of time to catch up with Fats and hide this car. More than plenty of time. I'm going to pray Laurel and Hardy aren't too tired to keep on yelling when they do turn up."

"You want to hear their plans so you'll understand what they're up to, right?" Olivia said.

"I want to hear what route they plan to take so we can try to make sure our paths never cross again. Now I'm looking for a likely place to get off the interstate and look for some stores."

"Why?"

"Hey, if you've decided you prefer going without panties, we won't bother." And that comment, he thought, was a *big* mistake.

From the angle of Olivia's head, she might be examining the occasional yellow birch between wide shoulders at the edge of the highway, and the fields of golden corn stubble beyond. The fields stretched to the horizon on either side with many miles between farm houses and their scatter of buildings and grain elevators. Blustery wind tossed up fine debris from shorn corn stalks and speckled a gunmetal sky with low clouds. Every mile or so, a billboard flapped like a garish sail on a square-rigged man-o'-war.

Aiden doubted his passenger was actually seeing much of anything out there. "We can keep on going for another hour, if you prefer."

Olivia couldn't bring herself to look at him. "I'd like to stop soon, please."

"No problem. We'd have to sooner or later. We need new mugs."

"Excuse me?"

"New . . . disguises. We need disguises. Doesn't take much. I'll get us fixed up."

"I'm not the type of person who dresses up. I always detested fancy-dress affairs. Wouldn't go if I could help it, and I'm not starting now."

Aiden saw a road sign. "You are starting now." When he was older and had more time, he might be able to humor dense females. Not now. "This isn't a party, ma'am, it's a friggin' war, and we need uniforms the enemy isn't going to pick off at a few hundred yards." He considered mentioning red coats and white tights on English soldiers supposedly blending into forests, but thought better of it. "Just go along with me. I'm the one who really needs a change of face. But I can't risk you looking so out of place with me that you draw attention. Clackitakit Mall next right. That'll do."

If he thought she would follow him like another dog, he was wrong, blast him. "You don't even know what shops they'll have. You don't just go to any town and expect them to have a fancy-dress shop."

Fancy-dress shop. "We call them costumes here, not fancy dress. I'm not looking for that kind of costume. Leather's good. Easy, and we need easy."

Olivia did stare at him now. *"Leather?* What can you mean?"

"You'll see. Hey, we're in luck, Wal-Mart. Who needs a mall? I love Wal-Mart. Whatever you need, they've got. And since money's tight, we need some deals. They've got deals."

"Money," Olivia said quietly, and frowned. "*No,* I don't believe this." Was she petrified or disgusted, or both? Aiden would be so incredibly angry with her. She buried her face in Boswell's neck and closed her eyes tightly. How could she have completely forgotten Vanni's call?

"What did you say?" Aiden pulled off the road and drove a long entry access to the store. With hunched shoulders and rigid posture, Olivia was clinging to Boss. Her face was obscured in the dog's fur. "Olivia?"

When she lifted her head, her white face alarmed him. Her eyes were huge and even darker than usual. "Tell me now. *Now,* Olivia. What the hell's wrong?"

"Ryan Hill's back in New York."

He shot into the first vacant parking place and slammed on the brakes. "What did you say?"

"Oh," she said, her features crumpling. "Have I made a hash of things by forgetting to tell you? Perhaps it doesn't make any difference. Vanni called while you were in the shower and I . . . it just went out of my head."

When he didn't shout at her, she felt even worse. Daddy always shouted when he was really cross and she hated it, but at least one knew where one was. Aiden could look so menacing with absolutely no particular expression at all on his angular face—except for deadly disbelief in his intensely blue eyes.

"Honestly, it didn't as much as enter my head from that moment to this."

Oh, my goodness. The way he switched off the car and turned sideways to face her was devastating. His nostrils flared, and a white line formed around his mouth. He propped his upper arm on the back of his seat and made motions with the key he held between finger and thumb, small but threatening motions. At least, she thought they were threatening.

"Before or after," he said finally.

She didn't understand him.

"Before or after—no, you were in the shower before I got there. And I left the bathroom before you. When Dierdre came."

This was getting worse. "Not this morning," she said, aware of how silly and small her voice sounded. "Last night. When you were in the shower last night. Before I tried to—" She couldn't bring herself to finish.

"Before you tried to run away? Before I took you back and we slept together—until this morning when we showered together? Didn't all those things happen after you took a call from Vanni, I assume on *my* phone? Then we dressed, and packed the car, and went to talk to Cal, and ate breakfast. Are you mad, or did you decide to help the enemy?"

He was going too far, and she wouldn't put up with it. "That's silly."

"Silly? *Silly?* You decide to withhold vital information and I'm silly to be angry?"

"First, I didn't do it on purpose." She felt someone watching them and glanced out of the window at two teenaged girls leaning against a pole. They gestured at Aiden and Olivia and giggled together. "I've told you now. Stop trying to frighten me, and I'll tell you the rest."

This was, Aiden decided, a nightmare. To be trapped in the company of an airhead female who couldn't seem to understand that she was in danger of being very dead, very soon.

"You're so wise to be quiet," she said, raising her chin. "It'll make matters much quicker and more pleasant. Vanni said Ryan Hill's got a lot of evidence against us."

"There isn't any, so he can't—"

"Don't interrupt, please. He *says* he's got evidence. Your person in charge wanted to send out an ABP, but there was some question about the qualifications of certain people. Apparently one of them might not have the right skills and could kill us by mistake. So they aren't doing one of those things. The investigation is still unofficial."

Aiden prayed for patience. "APB, not ABP. All Points Bulletin. Why didn't you get me from the shower?"

Her expression brightened. She gave him a delighted smile and wagged a finger. "Vanni told me not to. He said he didn't have time— or I think he did. He *told* me just to give you a message. You see?"

"I see that you didn't give me the message."

The lovely smile dissolved. "I am now," she murmured. "Vanni said Ryan wants to make sure we're never able to present any evidence we have against him—not that I think we do have any. And—oh, dear. Ryan Hill will be pursuing us himself. That's the way Vanni put it. And he said you've only got to say the word and he'll come to help us. And he'll send money. That's what made me remember. When you mentioned money."

Ryan was tailing them, had been tailing them since when? Probably yesterday. He took her by the shoulders, gently enough, and shook her slowly back and forth. "How could you have done anything else but tell me about Ryan the second Vanni mentioned him?" He shut his eyes. "That gives me one good idea about how we're being traced. If Ryan is all over the precinct, he's perfectly capable of snooping around and getting information Vanni's got on his computer. Damn it. I'll have to warn Vanni."

"Vanni said for me not to get you. And you know he doesn't want you to call him back."

"I know all about that. Vanni has to call the shots on when we talk now."

"Yes, and he'll call again. He said he would."

Aiden rested his brow on Olivia's. It helped to feel how softly feminine she was, because he could switch on his natural protective urges then, rather than follow other instincts and break every one of her tiny bones. "Okay, okay. I don't understand, but I'll have to accept that you don't always fire on all cylinders. Now it's even more important to make sure we aren't recognized. We don't want to be seen at all if we can pull that off. Let's go shopping."

They got out of the car and Aiden said, "Show's over," to the grinning teens. They giggled and sighed, and Olivia didn't have to guess who was turning their oversexed minds to mush.

She had to trot to keep up with Aiden's long, loose-limbed strides. They went into the shop and Aiden took a cart. "What size are you?" he said.

"What size are *you*?" she snapped back, incensed at his audacity.

"Big," he said. "Underwear first."

She ran her eyes over racks of serviceable cotton panties, then some made of nylon. "I prefer silk."

"Those are silk," he said, pointing a long finger. "It says so." And before she could study the selection, he whipped a black, lace-trimmed thong from the bar and held it against her.

"*Aiden*," she said through her teeth. "People are watching us."

"Again? Think of us as public servants. We're providing entertainment. That looks like the right size." The minuscule black panties landed in the bottom of the shopping cart, to be followed by similar garments in an array of colors. "Now, the other. Thirty-eight?"

Olivia sputtered.

"Thirty-six?"

"Thirty-six D," she told him in a croaky whisper. "I can see to it myself, thanks."

He glanced around and, as if he hadn't heard her, located silk bras. From what Olivia observed, he apparently thought it best to add every one he could find in the right size before he swung the cart toward another department. This time his quest was for his own underwear.

"You don't need to try any of these on, do you?" he asked suddenly, picking a red silk bra to waft aloft. "I didn't think of that."

"No, thank you. That won't be necessary."

"Good. There must be some extra toiletries you want. Are you going to need tampons or something?"

"This isn't happening," Olivia said, crossing her arms and staring at the floor. "I'm sure you grew up with sisters, and none of this means a thing, but you're embarrassing me."

"I don't have any sisters. I'm an only child. I'm practical, that's all. Sorry if I'm too brash. Damn. I should have asked you about birth control."

Olivia's eyes filled with tears.

"Oh ... Hey, hey, it's okay." Aiden gathered her into his arms and silently dared anyone to offer help. "We're both under a lot of pressure. I'm sorry. It'll be okay. I used protection this morning, but last night kind of got away from me. But don't worry. If you're pregnant, you and the baby will never want for anything."

Her tears broke loose.

This was, Aiden thought, what came of not spending enough time around females—a guy missed little things like learning how touchy they could be. "You're exhausted, that's what all this is about. Hell, *I'm* probably exhausted. If you want to cry, cry. You've got a right. You've been through too much." He stroked her hair and became even more conscious of the spectacle they made.

"It's not that," she said through sniffles. "I take the pill—not for birth control, for something else."

"Not that?" he said, casting around for what other reason there might be for taking birth control pills. "What then?"

"I forgot the other thing Vanni said. He's absolutely sure Ryan intends to—to kill us."

They were doomed to misunderstand each other. "Why do you think he's following us? Because he misses my company?"

*   *   *

This would, Winston Moody decided, be the last journey he took in the company of Rupert Fish. In a manner of speaking, the forced trip to America was fortuitous. Getting rid of someone was so much simpler in a big country than in a little one. Rupert would simply have to disappear. Perhaps Detective Lemon would help with that— particularly if Winston pointed out that Rupert couldn't be trusted to remain loyal. Of course, Lemon had proved he couldn't be trusted either.

"You should have made sure you didn't give me the checks and the money together, Winston. The envelopes couldn't have stuck together then," Rupert said. "I'm almost relieved not to be in London right now. I just know those people are telephoning to demand their merchandise. They *expect* to get it once they've paid. I don't want to talk to them until we've got answers."

"What repulsive countryside this is," Winston said, giving himself time to prepare the most demoralizing onslaught possible. "Uncivilized. All looks the same."

"I don't give a flying fuck about the scenery." Rupert could manage a nicely clipped accent when he remembered.

"Charming," Winston said. "Your fly's unzipped."

Rupert looked into his lap and Winston promptly clutched a handful of his partner's hair and yanked his head back and forth. He dug his fingernails into Rupert's hairline, deep into his hairline. The car zigzagged back and forth between lanes.

"Pull yourself together," Winston shouted. "You're driving erratically."

"My God," Rupert howled. "You're psychotic. You want to be killed. I can't see, you fool. There's blood running in my eyes."

Winston took him by the ear and peered to see what damage had been done. "Very little blood," he remarked. "The rest is tears and sweat. The people you keep harping on are *criminals*, Rupert. Those checks are payment for stolen property. What are they going to do— have us arrested? They can wait. We've got to get the FitzDurham woman and her bloody photographs. And that cop. *Before* they slip through our fingers and start blackmailing us. Then we have to make them dead. *Then* we'll deal with the greedy ones in New York."

This was it, Rupert thought, absolutely the last straw. He found a handkerchief and wiped his face. "You're right, Winnie old boy. I never did have your clear head." Flattery got the old bastard every time. "D'you think Fats Lemon will decide our idea is clever? If he's there to meet us when he's supposed to be? He should relate very well to our hiring a hit man." And while Flynn and FitzDurham were being executed, an extra bonus to the shooter would take care of Winston, too.

"I think Lemon may approve. After all, he doesn't seem to have an original idea of his own." And once Flynn and FitzDurham were done for, Rupert would be despatched the same way. "I never thought I'd be glad he was in on everything, but I am. Without him we'd be up a gum tree."

"Lemon's useful to us now," Rupert said. "I hope. But we're not going to like any three-way cuts." *And he, Rupert, couldn't even work up enthusiasm for sharing at all.*

"Lemon won't be getting a cut of anything," Winston said. "Although, if you don't object, we might send him on his way with one prize. Kitty, do you think? Since she's apparently so chummy with him. She knew him before. I can't get over that. And they've been planning to get together all along? Mark my words, she's been spying on us. And now she's acting as his go-between with *us*, if you can imagine such a thing."

Rupert knew when to tread carefully. He had other plans for Kitty—after she'd been taught the error of her ways, of course. She had a lot of bravado but no real courage, and she was away from her support system at The Fiddle. Yes, indeed. Give him a few days with Kitty, alone, in a remote place, and she'd sing a different tune about how forceful he was or wasn't.

Winston slapped his ear yet again. "I asked you what you thought about making sure Lemon's forced to get Kitty from wherever she is and take her with him."

"Perfect." Rupert almost grinned. Why waste energy on the old bag of wind? "But concentrate on our two pigeons first, Winnie, there's a good chap."

"You know," Winston said, "when we get back to New York we should celebrate. Why not pay a little visit to The Dakota and look up some old friends?"

Rupert shuddered and raised his shoulders to his ears. "The ones waiting for their . . . well, you know, waiting?"

"Yes, indeed, Rupert. How quick you are. We visit them—or *him* really. The communications always refer to 'we,' but I think it's a one man operation, one very powerful man. I know he'll want to fund this trip we've had to take to protect his interests. I imagine he'll show us a jolly old time."

The cell phone Winston still didn't like rang, and he picked it up cautiously.

"Answer the bloody thing or give it to me," Rupert snapped.

Winston applied the tip of a forefinger to the "on" button and raised the instrument to his ear. "Yes?" he said.

"What the hell happened to you last night? We expected to hear from you."

Kitty. "What the hell happened to *you?* We couldn't reach you, and you gave us the wrong instructions. They weren't at that dump."

She was quiet for a while, and the dead sound suggested she'd covered the mouthpiece.

"We don't want to discuss that," she said when she returned. "I was just told to check in with you."

"How lovely," Winston said. "Consider us checked. Good-bye."

"Hang up and you're dog meat, you old fart."

"So ladylike. I'm curious. When exactly did you and Lemon get so chummy?"

"None of your business."

"Of course it's my business. I thought you had a big thing for Hill. When did Lemon take over as crown prince?"

"I forgot Hill the moment I met Fats. I know a real man when I meet one."

Winston found it difficult to imagine Kitty choosing wizened Lemon over beefcake Hill. Hell, what did it matter anymore. "What do you want?"

"I was asked to find out where you are."

Winston held the phone away and said, "Where are we, Rupert? What did that last sign say?"

"We're on the interstate," Rupert said, glaring. "Is that Kitty? Let me talk to her."

"Which interstate?" Kitty asked. "And tell Rupert I can't talk now."

"Which interstate, she wants to know. She doesn't want to talk to you."

Rupert scratched his itchy scalp and wrinkled his nose at the flakes that peppered his face. Dry skin was a curse. "I don't want to talk to her either."

"Watched any good stuff lately, Winnie?" Kitty asked.

Winston hated it when Kitty reminded him of what she knew

about him. "What bloody road is this?" he asked Rupert. Everything beyond the car windows looked the same to him.

Rupert said, "Interstate 80, of course."

"Eighty," Winston told Kitty.

"That's not . . . I'm checking a map." Winston knew when she put her hand over the phone again. He assumed Lemon was with her. "You mean you're on 39 heading north, don't you? You should really be on Highway 20 by now and going west, but Rupert was always an old lady behind the wheel. How much farther to 20?"

"She says we're not on 80, we're on 39, and how much farther is it to Highway 20?"

Rupert pushed his face forward over the wheel and squinted through the tinted windshield. "It's not 39, it's 80 west. We're already almost in Des Moines; we can't have much longer."

Winston relayed this message and settled more comfortably in his seat. It was heated and he wiggled from time to time to spread the warmth evenly.

Kitty came back on and asked to speak to Rupert. "She wants you," Winston said, giving up the phone.

"Listen, you dumb shit," Kitty told Rupert. "You've messed up everything you've ever touched in your miserable little life, but this time you've gone too far. You're going in the *wrong direction*. Turn around. If you do everything I tell you, you'll only be six hours late to meet Detective Lemon in Dubuque."

Aiden and Olivia hunched low and ran up a rocky track that took them to the top of a shallow knoll. Following Aiden's instruction, Boswell stuck to Olivia's side. He wanted the dog with her when he sent her back to the car alone. Below them stretched a stand of mostly beech trees. The Rover was a mile behind them and hidden behind a barn in a farmer's field of spent corn.

"I want you to go back now," Aiden said, taking her by the arm. "I've got to watch my rear. If you're in the Rover with Boss, I don't have to watch yours, too."

"You're right," Olivia said, with no intention of letting him too far out of her sight. "I'll just come far enough to see where this place is, then I'll go." She had her Nikon stuffed beneath the revolting black leather vest she wore over a skin-tight white nylon shell with long sleeves. As Aiden's request she'd put a peach-colored bra on underneath the shell. He said it was to help the effect. She wondered who he thought was going to be looking at her, apart from him.

Aiden also wore a leather vest, with nothing underneath and the front designed to show off a man's chest. In this case a smashing chest she knew much better than she should. He'd picked up two long, heavy silver chains with oversized crosses dangling from them. He wore the chains around his neck and the crosses nestled in the bronzed hair on his chest. A rolled red bandanna circled his head, allowing the hair in his gray wig to fall over it, sexy tough-guy fashion. Temporary tattoos of snakes circled his upper arms and might as well have been the real thing. Actually, he looked intimidating and not a bit cold, which he should given the weather.

"You ought to wear tight black-leather pants all the time," he said to Olivia, pausing to check her out slowly. "I'm going to have to find me a Harley, baby. We're wasted in that old man's car."

The trousers he spoke of were stiff and creaked when she walked. Her bandanna—also red—was tied, kerchief-style, around her hair. She'd jammed a quite smashing wide-brimmed black felt hat on top and tilted the brim low over her eyes. She wore enough heavy makeup to clog her pores and make her hot. Aiden had applied the makeup, including black lipstick, and green lines around her eyes that gave her a Cleopatra look. Dangling earrings, cheap silver rings on every finger and her thumbs, and boots finished the outfit. Awful, but there was no point in being self-conscious when you weren't yourself. Boswell was holding up well given the embarrassment of wearing yet another red bandanna, this one tied around his neck to make him look like a "good old boy's" dog. Whatever that meant.

"I'm going in now," Aiden said and slipped over the ridge, heading toward the beeches. His manner, the fact that he'd stopped looking back, suggested he'd moved into solo mode and didn't expect her to go any farther.

Olivia ran rapidly along the hillside, traveling to the left and waiting until she was sure Aiden wouldn't see her before going over the top. Her doggy escort never left her side. Quickly, she dropped down and entered the trees herself, working downhill until she could hide behind a large trunk and still have a good view of what was spread before her.

The place was Bobby Mobo's, a motel, steakhouse, tavern and "entertainment establishment." The vertical siding was painted in gold and black stripes, and cattle horns made a garland around the roofline. Trucks were parked everywhere, and the men and women she saw wore either bib overalls and check shirts, or jeans and check shirts, or in a few cases, the kind of leather getup she and Aiden wore. Boots were *de rigueur;* so were push-up bras. This wasn't where mummy and daddy took the kiddies for breakfast after church.

A movement to her right and below had to be him. He might be hidden from her, but she had great visual recall. His trousers didn't creak, and he wasn't awkward in them. For some reason they clung to his very long, very muscular legs as if he'd been born in them. They clung everywhere. He had a ring at the outer tip of his left eyebrow, and several others ranged around one ear. He had amazed her by getting into the car wearing boots with a spur on one heel. A heavy rope of chain, with one end hooked to his belt and the other inside his pocket, clanked with every move he made.

And still he was so appealing, she couldn't concentrate on serious matters the way she should.

This wasn't her, wasn't Olivia FitzDurham of Hampstead, struggling photographer. Yes, yes, of course that's who she was. She eased out the camera and took a couple of shots of the area, making sure she got good angles on Bobby Mobo's.

A vehicle parked away from the rest caught her attention, or rather the man leaving a brown truck did. It was one of those trucks you saw a lot here, the ones with a top on the part that would otherwise be open, a top with windows on the sides and two doors at the back.

She'd only seen the man for an instant before, when he drove past the Rover on his way to Aiden's warehouse, but she remembered his thin features and tanned skin, his gray crewcut. Thank goodness details were her thing.

She was a photographer. That's what she did. And she was going to take photographs of anything that could be useful.

Dropping to her haunches, she picked a course through the trees in the direction of Fats Lemon's truck. He'd gone inside Bobby Mobo's where, with luck, he would get drunk and do whatever else would keep Aiden safe.

That's when she felt Boswell grow more alert, and she saw Aiden. He broke from the trees immediately behind the truck and approached it nonchalantly with his hands in his pockets.

Olivia worked her way closer, taking more pictures as she went.

Aiden looked around, then circled the vehicle, looking sideways into the windows as he went. Standing by the back once more, he scanned the area, then hooked some fingers under a door handle.

Boswell grew restless. He paced away from Olivia and stood still, his nostrils quivering and his attention focused on Aiden.

"Get back here," Olivia whispered.

The dog didn't waste a glance on her before slipping away, homing in on his master but moving along the edge of the trees like a low-lying, black-and-tan shadow.

Amazingly, the back of the truck hadn't been locked. Aiden opened the door a few inches.

Boswell ran now, a big, beautiful animal who could keep his belly down and still cover ground unbelievably fast.

A man, bent double, sped from the trees. Olivia used her telephoto lens to get a closeup and recoiled at the sight of his expression. Handsome in a Teutonic manner, he also had a crewcut, but his hair was white-blond, as were his brows, and his eyes appeared pale blue. He had paused for an instant, and there was no doubt he looked at Aiden with unveiled hate. He knew him—even with Aiden in disguise, he knew him. The man ran on and reached Aiden only moments after he must have heard him and started to turn around.

Olivia clapped her hands on her mouth and held them there tightly. Screaming wouldn't help a thing.

The man, tall but not as tall as Aiden, and more thickset, raised something in his right hand and brought it down so hard that Olivia heard it thump against Aiden's skull.

Terrified, but determined, she kept shooting pictures and inching forward.

What was the man doing?

What he was doing took so little time she couldn't even have screamed in time to attract attention.

Aiden's attacker threw open both doors at the rear of the truck and picked Aiden up around his waist. He hung there in a way that told Olivia he was unconscious. Then the man stuffed Aiden all the way inside.

That was the moment when Boswell left the ground. He threw himself toward the man, sailed past him, and landed with Aiden. That's where they were when the doors were slammed shut. Olivia heard the blond-haired stranger curse, saw him beat on the door with his fist, and kick at a bumper before he ran around to jump in behind the wheel and drive fast toward Mobo's.

Olivia was already scrambling from the trees and running.

She'd made too little progress before the man appeared again with Fats Lemon and a blond woman wearing a checked western shirt that strained over her considerable breasts and jeans tight enough to cut off circulation to her vital and some not-so-vital organs.

Lemon and the hip-swinging woman all but threw themselves into the front seat of the truck and the other man drove away.

Seventeen

For the third time, Chris Talon dialed Aiden's cell number.

Still nothing.

He watched the flight departure screens, following updates on his flight from Chicago to Seattle. A delay had stretched from thirty minutes to "waiting for replacement equipment." Chris had called his wife and been relieved to hear there was no sign of her going into labor. Their second child wasn't due for a month, but their two-year-old daughter had been delivered early, so he was on edge.

Eight years as NYPD partners had forged something deeper than friendship between Chris and Aiden Flynn. They had a connection. When Chris had heard what Aiden had fallen—no, jumped—into with the British woman whom he didn't even know, Chris had come close to telling his buddy he needed therapy, or a wife, or both. Ever since Key West, when Aiden had helped Chris with Sonnie Giacano's—now Sonnie Talon's—case, Aiden's private loneliness had become a regular topic in the Talon household. Sonnie was a very sensitive woman, and she noticed Aiden's wistful glances when she and Chris were together, especially since Anna arrived. Aiden was the best honorary uncle a little girl ever had.

Where was Aiden? He'd promised to call as soon as he and this Olivia were on the road. He hadn't and that wasn't like him.

One more try, then Chris would give up until he got back to Seattle.

"Good news, ladies and gentlemen," the counter clerk announced into his microphone. "The replacement equipment is here, and as soon as we have a crew aboard, we'll start boarding passengers."

Maybe he'd better wait to try that call again.

*   *   *

Spots of blood squeezed from scratches and small punctures on Olivia's palms and fingertips. The wounds stung but she kept running.

The truck with Aiden and Boswell in the back had squealed, spewing a rooster tail of damp grit, from the grounds at Bobby Mobo's, to the rutted access road between Mobo's and the more main road Aiden had taken to get there. Olivia hadn't wanted to be seen, but she ran as if she were a fast jogger while she tried to see which way they would go. The race was hopeless, and she'd turned back filled with dread.

Now she wanted to reach the Rover as fast as possible and try to follow the truck.

Slipping, hands first, into the corn stubble hadn't helped the damage already done by several falls on gravel. The skin needed to be cleaned.

The barn came into sight. At least Boswell was with Aiden. She'd like to see someone try to hit that dog over the head.

Would they shoot him?

The thought didn't improve the painful ache in her throat. Each breath grew louder in her ears and hurt her straining lungs. She could drive the Rover and manage the roads here, of course she could. She could do it for Aiden.

There was no help anywhere.

She reached the car and got in. Aiden had deliberately left the key in the ignition, "just in case," he'd said.

Sweating, but chilled just the same, Olivia pulled on the rocket jacket Aiden had left behind his seat. She held the striped neckband to her face and struggled with a sweet-sad sensation she got from the familiar wood-and-rain scent of him. How could she have thought there was anything of his she didn't like?

The engine turned over easily. Olivia swallowed, unsure if she was glad, but she must try to find him. Next she tried the wipers. They didn't completely clear the windscreen.

A shrill ringing close to her heart shattered her last shreds of control. Olivia turned off the car, shuddered at the next reverberating peal from the phone while she fumbled to get it from Aiden's inside pocket.

She stared at the buttons. Which one, which one? She'd answered it before, but she couldn't seem to decide what to do.

Another ring sounded. Vanni would hang up. Oh, please don't let him hang up. She punched the right button and whispered a shaky, "Yes?"

The babble of many voices reached her, and bells, and laughter, and announcements.

Then it fell quiet. The phone had gone dead. He'd hung up on her.

Regardless of what Vanni had said, if she had his number, she'd call him. She turned on the phone again and tried punching and holding down various numbers, hoping for an automatic dial Aiden might have programmed. If he had, she couldn't find it.

Rain started to fall, the kind that began abruptly, and instantly slashed sideways. Cold and damp from her efforts, Olivia shivered.

Once more she turned on the car. For some time she fiddled with the gears and clutch, making sure she wasn't likely to ruin the gear box, or stall the car at an inconvenient moment.

The phone rang again. Olivia snatched it up, turned it on and whispered, "Yes," terrified it might not be Vanni at all, or that he wouldn't want to talk to anyone but Aiden.

"Speak up." A deeper voice than Vanni's, a different voice with a different accent—Southern. The background noise was the same as on the other call. "Damn, it's good to hear your voice. You do like to scare a guy. Wait a minute, they're making another announcement."

Olivia waited. The car windows steamed up, and her clamminess increased.

"Yep, that's my flight. Look, I've got to board, but I'll call you the minute I get to Seattle. Okay?"

"No."

"This one's already late and they're in a hurry, so I'd better go. It can wait, can't it?"

"No!" she shouted. "No, it can't wait. There's trouble here, a lot of trouble. You're Chris Talon, aren't you?"

For a beat or two, all she got were the background noises. "Yeah, Talon. Is this Olivia FitzDurham?"

"Right. And I need help."

"I'd have thought Aiden was all the help you should need until you get to Seattle. Put him on, please."

He didn't sound friendly.

"Hurry up, please."

"Aiden isn't here. He's unconscious in the back of a truck, and they've taken him away. I'm going to try to follow but I need advice."

"Repeat that," Talon said. "All of it and don't leave anything out. If I'm missing my flight home to my very pregnant wife because of some whim, you'd better not stick around long enough for me to find you."

Olivia sat straighter. Sweat in her eyes felt miserable, but if this man thought an unjust attack would reduce her to blubber, he was mistaken. "I'm sorry to interfere with your plans, and I do wish you and your wife all the best," she said, and went on to explain exactly what had happened since they left New York.

"Did you get a good look at the guy who hit him?" Chris asked.

"White-blond hair, about as tall as Aiden but more stocky. Pale-blue eyes. Cold-looking. And I should have said the other man, the one who got in the truck with the woman, was Fats Lemon—at least I think it was."

Chris didn't immediately answer. When he did, he snapped out his words so fast that Olivia held the phone hard against her ear to make sure she didn't miss anything. "Interesting," he said. "Just goes to prove I can't trust that boy Aiden on his own. Listen to me and don't interrupt. You are not to drive anywhere. Got that?"

"I have to find Aiden."

"Your loyalty is impressive. Given the choice, I'd rather hunt for one victim than two. You said there's a motel at that place?"

"I'm leaving the moment I switch off this phone."

"So am I," he said—through his teeth, she thought. "And I'm coming there. Might as well start from the last place you saw him. I take it there is a motel. Get a room. Lock yourself in and stay there until you hear from me again. Leave the phone on and I'll call when I'm close."

"There isn't time for me to wait. It'll take you far too long to get here."

"Any time is too much time. I'm at O'Hare—Chicago—and I can be there in two hours. I wish it could be now, but this is better than being in Seattle and having to get to the airport and *still* having a flight in front of me. Tell me you'll get that room."

She couldn't bring herself to say something that might not be true.

"Olivia, do you really care what happens to Aiden?"

"I most certainly do," she told him, furious at the question. "He's the best man I've ever met and I'll never forgive myself if he ... I care."

"Sounds as if you do." His tone changed. "That didn't take long to happen, but we won't talk about it now. If you care about Aiden, you won't go after him because you'll only make things worse. You could ruin any chance he may have for freedom, rather than help him escape."

"Every minute I stay here is another minute they could be doing horrible things to him."

"Olivia—" Chris Talon paused. "Are you in love with Aiden?"

Her heart beat very, very fast. "That is absolutely stupid. I hardly know him." Other than as a lover who could take her apart with a look.

"Sometimes people never get over the pain of losing someone they love," Chris said, ignoring her denial. "Particularly if the one left behind has to live with knowing she did something dumb that made sure the one she loved was murdered."

"Well, this is a fucking mess," Fats Lemon said, leaning across Kitty to get closer to Ryan. "Where are we going? It's going to start getting dark soon."

Ryan was already sick of listening to Fats whine. "You afraid of the dark, partner? Maybe you need to spend some time locked away. Immersion, they call it. I could fix it."

Fats sniggered nervously. "Only Kitty's with me, and you aren't messing with our good times."

"Knock it off." It wouldn't do for Fats to figure out Ryan didn't give a flying fuck about Kitty, or that Ryan was a man only into the visual turn-on that left him alone to do his own thing. The days and nights he'd spent with Kitty would make it easy to get rid of her once it was safe. She'd earned some special attention, very special. Ryan had always enjoyed practicing his surgical skills. He had a knife he kept for the job and he didn't believe in anesthetic. Yes, Kitty was due.

Kitty wasn't sure how much she enjoyed sex with Ryan. He was a good-looking devil, and he did things to her that no other man had ever done, things she'd miss later, but there was something creepy about him, something not right.

Fats might be a skinny little man who spent too much time on tanning beds, but she'd often found the least likely ones could be the most satisfying. They always spent a lot of time telling her all the things a girl liked to hear and that made her feel even sexier.

She put a hand on Ryan's thigh and squeezed. "We're all on edge, lover. Let's get along." When she shifted the squeeze to Jolly Boy, he smacked her hand away with a vicious swipe that made her fingers numb. Well, she'd have to do something about that. "Where are we going?"

"Not far," he told her. "First likely motel and we stop. We've gotta decide what to do about them." With his head, he indicated the man and the dog in the back of the truck.

Her stomach turned at the thought of the dog. She'd found the courage to look behind her once and the dog, an ugly great thing with huge, shiny fangs and lips that snarled, stared right back at her. The man on the floor didn't seem to have moved at all.

"You could shoot the dog," she said.

"We have a little problem. That moron back there loves the dog. That means the dog's life could help us get what we need faster. We need that interfering prick back there. He's our link to the woman. That's also the main reason we're not traveling far yet. He'll hold out, but by the time we finish with him, he'll tell us exactly where she is. Now keep your mouth shut. Chatty broads bore me. I don't keep boring things around."

Fats had taken advantage of Ryan's preoccupation to slip a hand, palm up, under Kitty. She wanted to squeal and wriggle, but knew better. Fats had good fingers.

"You're right about everything," he told Ryan, leaning close to Kitty. "We get a room and find a way to get Flynn out without Boss. We can have some fun with Detective Flynn. He was always too big for his boots."

Surreptitiously, Fats put the fingers of his free hand under Kitty's arm and fondled the side of her breast. The view he had down the front of her shirt—wow, casabas like that deserved a lot of attention and he was willing to dedicate himself to them. He could feel her growing hot against his left hand, but apart from pressing down harder on him, she showed nothing of her feelings.

"I'm betting the woman's back there somewhere," Ryan said. "Probably waiting for him in the Morgan. But we couldn't stick around with him in the truck."

"How are you going to get him out and into a motel with the dog there?" Kitty asked.

Ryan looked sideways. Did the slut think he didn't know what she and Fats were doing? "Real carefully," he said. Fats was redesigning her cleavage, not that it needed any help. "I can deal with the dog. I'll hold him through the cab window"—he indicated the window behind his head—"while you get Flynn out. Then I'll drive in circles with Boss for a while. Maybe I'll let him go, maybe I won't. He doesn't know the area—he'd get lost anyway. Whatever I decide, I'll tell Flynn the dog's in the truck. You and Fats can keep Flynn company while I'm gone. Make sure he doesn't have a good time."

Fats controlled an urge to grin. His dick was already looking at the sky and ready to fly a flag. "We'd better hope for a big room," he said nonchalantly. "It's going to get cozy with four of us."

"We'll get two rooms and I'll be next door to you. See to it. Make sure there's a plug for my laptop." He had a disk to play just to get in the mood for anything that came his way. "We don't want to risk me being seen if the two stooges show up, remember? They don't think I'm anywhere near, and I want it that way until I'm ready to surprise them."

"Those fools?" Kitty said. "They'll never find us now."

"I want them to find us. First we make sure Flynn tells us where the woman is, then we wait for the guys from London to arrive. Flynn doesn't necessarily have to be around for that. He thinks he's so tough. I'll enjoy finding out just how tough he is." He took a knife from his pocket, flicked it open, and tested the blade on his thumb.

Fats felt the ripple of Kitty's climax and marveled at her ability to sit still and not make a sound. He said, "I don't think I know what you have in mind for Moody and Fish."

"Of course you know," Ryan said, squinting to see an upcoming signboard. "I don't want to risk a murder rap, but I want Flynn dead. I've got a big enough beef with him to want him real dead. I'm going to have Rupert and Winston do that little job for me—after I get him ready."

Bobby Mobo's wasn't the kind of place where the desk clerk asked if you needed help with your baggage. The man had asked Olivia how long she needed the room for. Flustered, she'd said, "Just one night, please." To which he'd replied, "A long one, huh," and given her a grin that made her itch.

The room smelled strongly of cheap perfume and disinfectant. Olivia stood up as long as she could, but eventually sat on a wooden chair beside a chipped vanity. She held the keys to the Rover and Aiden's phone on her lap. She'd also carried his jacket with her because it brought some comfort. Her bag was on the floor beside her.

Predictably, when the phone rang she jumped hard. But she got it turned on in record time. "Hello?" she said.

"Olivia, this is Vanni. Gimme Aiden."

"He's not—"

"Goddammit! Tell the bastard to keep his mind on the job. I've got trouble here, and I don't need any extra irritation."

Olivia felt as if she, personally, had done something wrong. "I'm sorry, Vanni, but there was nothing I could do to stop him."

"Hold," Vanni said and she heard him talking to someone in the background. When he came back on, he kept his voice lowered. "I'm at the hospital. My grandfather's been admitted."

"Oh, I'm so sorry," Olivia said. "He's a dear man."

"He's an ornery old devil, but he's my grandfather. If he dies because they won't operate, I . . . I don't know what I'll do."

"Perhaps they really can't operate," Olivia said.

"Sure they can, if the price is right. That means these greedy bastards want enough to buy another island somewhere."

The transmission was breaking up. "Vanni, we've got to be quick. Aiden was knocked unconscious and taken away. I'm almost sure Fats was one of the people in the vehicle, but there was another man and a woman I hadn't seen before."

"Oh, my, God," he said. "If he . . ." Vanni's voice was cut off.

"Hello?" she said. "Hello, Vanni?"

"Yeah." He sounded very faint. "Where's Boss? Running loose?"

"No," Olivia told him. "I don't know. He followed Aiden and jumped in the truck with him. I'm afraid those people will shoot him."

"Son of a bitch," Vanni said. "What a mess. Get that phone charged. I'll call back later. I'm going to have to come to—"

"Vanni," she cried, "Chris—"

"Sure," Vanni said. "I know, don't worry, you'll be okay. So will Aiden. Mama said I should tell you—"

That was that, the battery failed, and she didn't have the vaguest notion where the charger was. Probably in the Rover, but she didn't want to leave the room until Chris arrived. And now he wouldn't be able to reach her on the cell phone.

The room was on the second floor. Olivia went to the window and looked down on the parking lot. Cars, trucks, and motorcycles arrived constantly. People ducked and ran through rain to the building. She could feel a base thundering somewhere below her. The Rover was parked closer now, barely on the other side of the ridge, and she'd locked everything in the boot. She wished she and Aiden had bought some food. Chocolate, anything would do. They hadn't thought about it.

She returned to the chair and tried to keep her feet still. They didn't want to remain on the floor. What was happening no longer felt like an imaginary adventure. This was real. She was scared, but she still wasn't sorry she'd come. If she'd remained in London, she would never have met Aiden Flynn and she didn't even want to think about that.

Penny Biggles had a way of analyzing Olivia. According to Penny, her friend was a war victim, a victim of a quietly defiant war between her parents.

Bunk.

It was true that Mummy and Daddy disliked each other. In the years of their marriage, Daddy had only sharpened his gift for the genteel insult, while Mummy's skills as a bombastic whiner were probably the best to be found in any human being. And Olivia's parents had used their children as a buffer between them.

The FitzDurhams liked to tell their daughter she wasn't capable and shouldn't be on her own because she needed to be looked after. Sometimes she wondered if they might be right—like now, when she ought to be able to make decisions without waiting for help. And that's what Daddy would say, that she was proving how right he was to want her at home. Mummy and Daddy didn't approve of the photography either. They had told her how "silly" they thought it was.

But they were wrong. So was Penny. It had been a struggle, but Olivia hadn't let her parents ruin her self-confidence. She'd broken away from them to find her own way, and she had the makings of a good career. And she would never return home to live. The idea appalled her.

She found the bulky envelope of photographs she had with her and spread them on the bed. In addition to putting on her glasses, she located a magnifying glass. The other envelope, the one containing the money and checks, was also in the bag. Olivia pulled it out and glanced at the checks. The sums were as huge as she'd remembered.

Mr. Fish had posted them in her letterbox by mistake.

The dry-cleaning receipt was for a shop in Belgravia. As for the theater ticket, he had been to a cinema that showed pornographic films. Olivia didn't even recognize the address.

Again, there were no clues there.

Kneeling, she pored over the photos. Walls covered with paintings. Art Deco furnishings. Extraordinary rugs. A little whimsy here and there. Sculptures, some of them dreck, some exquisite.

She couldn't ignore the furnishings. Since Fish and Moody were antique dealers, it was to be supposed that they dealt in more furniture than art. Not necessarily, but in the absence of knowing for sure, every possibility must be examined. The Art Deco furnishings weren't reproductions.

Olivia started from the beginning, studying even more slowly. From time to time she got up and went to the window. She had no idea what Chris Talon looked like, but somehow she expected to know him. The rain had turned to sleet that flew directly toward her and made minuscule icy halos against the encroaching darkness.

She put her nose to the window, and a cloud of fog blossomed on the glass. Her glasses fuzzed up everything. Aiden was somewhere out there, and he wasn't with friends. What did she know about him? Almost nothing. He was an only child. His parents were dead. He was shy around women.

Now there was an interesting observation she hadn't even recognized before. How could she think that a man capable of making love the way he did was shy? Because there was a reticence about him, a watchfulness when he looked at her. It fell away when they—had fallen away when they'd been together.

Oh, really, she had been shameless, and enjoyed it.

Olivia returned to the bed. She was ambivalent about most of the paintings she'd photographed in Notting Hill, although a Kandinsky that was a study for another work charmed her. The next shot was of what she supposed would also be called non-objective, a piece heavy with brilliant geometric splashes of color and apparently random lines. She tried for the spiritual meaning, the intuitive response devotées of the form spoke of. Perhaps she was old fashioned but all she saw was red and purple, lavender and pink. But then, a sculpture made of mirrors and granite and with a many-angled surface like framed blocks of rock candy entranced her, and it was certainly very modern. A sorcerer's palace, or perhaps a house of glass for someone with nothing to hide.

There wasn't a single incriminating piece of evidence in any of these. She shuffled them together like cards. When they were buried at the bottom of her bag with the negatives once more, she felt safer.

She used a hand to scoop water from the faucet to her mouth and peered into the mirror over the sink. Nothing would help the way she looked. Olivia grinned. She looked awful.

"Olivia?" A voice whispered very close to the door.

Her bag was hooked over her arm. She let it slip to the threadbare green carpet, kicked it gently under the bed, and took a step backward, away from the door.

A light, steady tapping began.

"Chris," she said, but couldn't even hear her own voice. Very cautiously, she approached, listening. She must learn to be cautious and smart. She didn't know who was out there.

"Olivia?"

"Yes?"

"We don't want to attract attention here."

With her heart punching at her eardrums, Olivia unlocked the door and pulled it open enough to give her a clear view of a good slice of corridor. Empty corridor.

Blood receded from her brain fast enough to make her feel faint. She slammed the door.

Slammed it against a black shoe.

"Go away," she said, as loudly as she could manage. "I'll call the police."

The door opened with enough force to knock Olivia onto her bottom, then smashed against the wall. She opened her mouth to yell, but not a sound came out.

A windswept, dark-haired man holding a gun stepped over her. "Don't move," he said and toured the room and bathroom, where he repeated his shattering entry. A ripping sound jarred her all over again. If the shower curtain hadn't been torn from the rod, she'd be amazed.

Finally this human whirlwind in a dark suit, white shirt with tie dangling, and mud spattering the lower halves of his trouser legs relaxed a little. He didn't put the awful gun away, but he did stop gliding about and making a lot of unpleasant noise.

He closed the room door quite gently and locked it.

Olivia swallowed. He had greenish eyes and black eyebrows that flared. And he was so big. And he stood over her, staring as if she were an enormous puzzle.

"Don't just sit there," he said. "We've got places to go."

She had no choice but to let him pull her to her feet.

"I'm Chris Talon," he said.

"Yes. Thank you for coming."

He looked her over again and shook his head. "I'm gonna have to have Sonnie talk to you. There are some rules about these things, and something tells me you don't know any of them."

"What things?" She didn't like his disapproving expression.

"Man-woman things," he said.

She didn't need a lecture on the birds and the bees from Chris Talon, and keeping her dignity was essential. "Let's decide on the best thing to do. Aiden's cell phone battery's dead, and I don't know where the charger is. Vanni's going to call back, and he won't be able to reach us."

"Leave that to me. You ever ridden a Harley?"

Olivia frowned.

"Motorcycle. Big motorcycle."

She shook her head emphatically. "Never. I absolutely would not want to."

"You're absolutely going to have to. I borrowed one from a friend in Chicago. First things first. I've got to check distances around here, and possible places they might take Aiden. They won't have gone far."

"How do you know that?"

Chris sighed and patted her shoulder. "Because you're here. Unless Aiden's got everything wrong, it's you they're after, you and what you have, or know. They'll hole up and figure out how to use him to get at you. Only we're going to get to them first."

He pulled maps from his inside coat pockets and opened them one on top of another on the bed. She stood close beside him.

Chris turned his head toward Olivia. "I'm gonna give you one piece of advice I know Sonnie would approve of. Don't let Aiden pick out your clothes again."

Eighteen

Improv theater was a great outlet for people who had difficulty communicating on a personal level. They learned to act out a scenario with little or no warning. A person could pretend they were someone else. That made it easier, distanced you. The classes Aiden had taken years ago also came in real handy when he needed an Oscar-winning performance to save his skin.

Tonight, putting on a convincing impersonation of an unconscious man had at least postponed the beating he knew Ryan and Fats would have enjoyed giving him. If things didn't start looking up, there would be another opportunity for the gruesome duo to work him over.

"Watch him," Ryan said. "I still think the cuffs should be behind him."

"Oh, no such thing," the woman said. She was obviously from England. "You've already put those things on his ankles, too. Where's he going to go? Anyway, he's been unconscious so long, it's scary. Maybe he won't ever wake up. He could have a seizure or something after you hitting him on the head like that. With his arms behind him, he'd probably break them. Then where would we be? You've already said you want to keep him in one piece until you don't need him anymore. Look at him lying there, poor man. White as the sheets. Does he look like someone who could do us any harm?"

"Fucking bleeding-hearts society," Ryan muttered. "It's a good thing I recognized him through the Halloween getup. He's never gotten over his stint in narcotics. Thinks he's still undercover as a punk. Okay, leave the cuffs in front. You keep your eyes on him, Fats. Anything happens to him before I'm ready, and you're dead. Understand?"

"I understand," Fats said with his habit of letting his dislike show through a coat of spurious, insincere respect. "You don't need to hang around here. Go lose that canine."

"When I need you to give the orders, I'll let you know." Ryan was at his foul-tempered best. "Damn dog. I got hold of him by the collar while you were dragging Flynn out. Got him from behind. Look at my hands. That dog pulled so hard, his friggin' collar took chunks out of my fingers. And my wrists. This is from the glass when I was reaching through from the front to grab him."

"Sorry, Ryan," Fats said. "We gotta think of a way to get Flynn to lead us to the woman. It's turned out to be a good thing he met her and they took off."

A pause before Ryan replied suggested Fats had hit an unpopular topic. "Olivia hooked up with Flynn. Fucking, bleedin' amazing. How could I know the bastard would snoop around the way he did? As soon as I sensed something wrong, I went after her. I was too late. Again, nothing I could do about it. But everything's gonna be fine. He's gonna die. She's gonna die. I'm gonna get what I want—everything. You want to keep on talking about this?"

Fats swallowed so loudly, it sounded as if he'd cracked something. He said, "Nah."

"Good. You'd better start praying those two clowns we're stuck with remember to turn on the cell phone," Ryan said. "Damn, but I hate dealing with civilian morons. And remember, you do not mention me to them. No reason to let them think I'm close enough for them to use me as leverage to get what they want."

Fats said, "What exactly do they want from you?" so offhandedly that Aiden came close to grinning. He risked slitting his eyes enough to see through his lashes.

"Just do as I tell you," Ryan said. "Mess up, and you'll go where I send the dog. I'd have nothing to lose anymore."

Ryan took the keys to the truck, holstered his gun, and let himself out of the overly warm room. Aiden had seen that the place was called Sleep In Peace, but didn't know where it was. He thought the name of the motel could turn out to be too appropriate.

All he could do for Boss was send good thoughts in his direction. Ryan might try to let the dog go, but if Boss made it too difficult, he'd buy himself a bullet.

Damn, his head ached. How could he have been so careless as to leave his flank vulnerable? He wondered where Olivia was. It would be just like her to try to find him, but she wouldn't go far, particularly since she was likely to get hopelessly lost. He didn't like thinking about her out there like that. She led with her heart—a bad idea in most situations. They'd met at the wrong time, in the wrong circumstances. Somewhere up there someone was laughing and thinking what Aiden already knew: he and Olivia had come together because he'd meddled in somebody else's business, but he wouldn't have met her at all otherwise.

"You think we ought to cuff him to the bed, too?" the woman, Kitty, said. "Ryan would be pleased we cared enough to do it, and we wouldn't have to watch quite so closely. After all, no play makes boys and girls dull, and we're not dull types, are we, Fats?"

Aiden swallowed distaste at Kitty's suggestive tone. He'd assumed she was with Ryan exclusively. Evidently the lady liked to spread herself around.

"Where's he going to go anyway?" Fats said in a voice that sounded thickened. "We cuff him to something and he's more likely to come to while we're doing it and make a nuisance of himself."

"And that would certainly be a shame," she said. Aiden felt her breath on his face. The pressure of her lips on his and the sensation she caused when the tip of her tongue slid into his mouth infuriated him. He'd have liked to bite that tongue and take the consequences. Only the thought of Olivia, alone somewhere out there, stopped him.

"Now this man's got a mouth," Kitty said. "And a body. Whoa, what a body." She demonstrated what she thought of that body by running her hands all over him. Lying still on a bed had never taken such willpower. "Don't you love tattoos on the kind of muscles he's got in his arms?"

Aiden heard a slap, followed by a yelp from Kitty. "What do you think you're doing? Who do you think you're pushing around? I don't let men hit me, Fats. If that husband of mine does show up, he'll tell you it's not a good idea to underestimate me."

"I don't give a shit about Rupert Fish," Fats said. "Ryan says he's a little asshole. How come you married a man like that?"

"I guess it's because I've got a thing for little assholes, Fats."

Aiden wanted to laugh. He was also struggling with the idea that Kitty was Mrs. Rupert Fish.

"You led me on, and I want what you promised," Fats said, and if a pout was something you could hear, Aiden heard this one. "I don't want you threatening me with your husband, and I don't want to listen to you talkin' nice to unconscious jerks."

"You're jealous," she said, all coy. "I think that's really lovely. I'm just one of those artsy types who appreciate beautiful people, and he's beautiful. It's only academic. He's probably no good in bed."

This was no time for Aiden to consider defending his male pride.

"I'm damn good in bed," Fats said. "I know how to give a woman what she wants."

"How long do you think Ryan will be gone?"

"Maybe an hour. We can lock the door and put the chain on." Aiden heard Fats slip on the chain. "There. That way if he does come back at an inconvenient moment, we'll have time to recover."

"Recover from what?" Little Miss Innocence asked.

"Take your clothes off," Fats said. "Not too fast."

"Ooh, I do love masterful men. Why should I undress for you?"

"Because you want to. You got off in that truck with all your clothes on and Ryan sitting on the other side of you. I don't want anything between you and me but skin. And you owe me, so start paying back."

Aiden didn't want to listen to this, but his only hope of escape was tied to the lovebirds getting it on.

"What about him?" Kitty said, and Aiden didn't need a map to figure out she was talking about him. "I don't want him watching."

"He's not watchin' anything," Fats said. "C'mon, Kitty. I want you, baby. Come here. Come on, sweet thing. I'm going to do something really special for you."

Throwing up now might be really inconvenient, Aiden thought.

"Okay," Kitty said. "You wear a girl down."

Aiden heard the sounds of passion-on-demand. Heavy breathing, smacking lips, forced keening from Kitty's throat. Fabric rubbing together. He risked opening his eyes a crack again but immediately shut them. Yep, he still had good ears.

"Oh, baby," Fats groaned. "These are really something. Did they have help, or did you grow them like this all on your lonesome?"

The next hefty slap needed no imagination.

"I don't have to take that from anyone," Kitty squeaked. "The nerve. Take a real good look and tell me if you see anything you don't like."

Fats was sucking air through his teeth. "You don't have to get violent. You know I don't see anything I don't like. Oh, man, no wonder Ryan brought you back to the States with him. He wasn't about to leave these behind."

As a mere mortal, Aiden struggled with an urge to check out these wonders. He'd always been a man of highly developed self-control.

Something came loudly unsnapped and unzipped.

Kitty said, "Oh, that feels so good. Oh, yes, yes."

"Don't hold yourself back," Fats said, "I'm all yours too, sweet thing. Let me make things easier for you."

More unsnapping and unzipping followed.

"Oh, Fats," Kitty moaned. "Oh, *my.*"

Fats laughed, "That's what women always say. Surprised, huh? You didn't expect this, did you?"

"Get back to what you were doing, dammit," Kitty said. "Leaving a woman on the edge doesn't make her give a damn what you've got in your pants."

Aiden longed to put a pillow over his head. That way, if he did make a mistake and laugh out loud, he'd have a chance of not being heard.

"You asked for it," Fats said. "You've got it."

A series of female yelps followed, punctuated by shuddering wails of ecstasy. "Oh." Kitty said in only seconds. "Oh, yes. Oh, yesss. Oh, oh, oh. Don't stop. Faster. Harder. Yes, yes, yes." Her voice rose to a thin shriek before it fell away into sobbing gasps.

"My turn," said Fats, Mr. Smooth, Lemon. "You've got the best tits, Kitty. Sheesh, what muscle tone. They don't even jiggle."

"You made me sore," Kitty said. "You're too rough."

"And you love it." Fats's voice changed and Aiden knew he was hearing a man who would do whatever it took to get what he wanted now. "Kneel down."

"Like hell," Kitty said.

"Do you like it when a man gets really rough?"

"Hit me again, and I'll tell Ryan you tried to rape me."

"Real soon you'll be able to say I did rape you."

Kitty's giggle sickened Aiden. "Not here," she said. "Not with him on the bed. Come on."

Aiden felt them pass him on the way to the bathroom. Their voices became more muted. Apparently modesty had kicked in, and they'd pushed the door all but shut.

This would be the only chance he got, and this one was like a ticking bomb. Aiden watched the bathroom door. The action on the other side slammed the door all the way shut. If he didn't know otherwise, he'd think a platoon of Rangers was practicing maneuvers in there.

He swung his feet from the bed and scooted to sit on the edge. He doubted he could stand up without falling down. A lot of older motels had old-fashioned phones with dials. Aiden thanked his good fortune that the one on the bedside table was Touch-Tone.

His hands were numb. The cuffs had cut his wrists. To get to the phone, he'd have to stand up.

"Fatsy! Fatsy!"

You go to it, Fatsy.

Aiden put weight on his legs and wanted to yell at the pain in his ankles where the second set of cuffs ground into bone.

"We gotta be quick," Fats said loudly. "He'll get back. If he finds us like this, he'll kill us."

Don't hurry. Aiden managed to shuffle a few inches and bring himself near enough to bend forward and rest his forearms on the table. He felt faint.

"Sit on the loo," Kitty said. "Oh, yes, I like playing horsey."

Unbelievable, Aiden decided, but as long as they kept on having fun, regardless of the weird pictures they conjured in his mind, he was still alive and still had hope.

He got the receiver from the cradle and slid it into his left hand. Punching in numbers made sure he bled freely from his wrists.

Kitty screamed. "We've broken it. Fatsy, it's come off!"

Aiden didn't want to consider what they'd broken off. One by one he depressed his own cell-phone numbers. Ringing started, and he dropped his face into his right hand, pressing the receiver to his left ear.

Three rings. *Please answer me, Olivia.* All he wanted to do was give her something she could pass along to Vanni. The name of this place would be better than nothing.

Four rings.

Answer me, Olivia.

"The party you're trying to reach is unavailable. At the tone, please leave a message."

A stab of pain burned through his right wrist. Where was she? On foot? In trouble?

He hit redial.

Four rings, then, "The party you're—" and Aiden depressed the cradle.

"Get it together, baby," Fats said. "No, leave that for last. I gotta make sure I can see 'em in my sleep."

He had to get himself back on the bed.

Using both hands on the receiver again, he rotated it and lined it up with the base before gently setting it down. Gritting his teeth against pain, he resumed his position on the bed and was grateful to be still and close his eyes.

Hopelessness wasn't a luxury a police officer allowed himself, but he sure couldn't see any way out of this now. Not a chance without a miracle.

The handle on the door to the room shook. He hadn't heard the key turn in the lock but it must have because the edge of the door rattled against the chain.

"Shit," Aiden heard Kitty say distinctly. "Hurry up."

"Damn it," Fats sounded ready to cry. "Oh, baby."

"Baby and Fats are going to be dead if we don't move it," Kitty said.

Aiden managed to make himself sink into a more deeply relaxed state.

The chain was in danger of being yanked from the wall. "Open this," Ryan said. "Now. Open the goddamn door."

Kitty and Fats erupted from the bathroom. Aiden could hear their labored breathing. "He won't know, will he?" Kitty whispered.

"You'd better hope not," Fats told her. "Comin', Ryan."

Fats fumbled the chain off, and from the thud that followed and the man's cry, Aiden visualized Ryan smashing the door into his partner and knocking him down.

"What's the chain for, you cretin?" Ryan said. "And don't tell me you're making sure Flynn doesn't go anywhere. He looks like he's dying to me. You two were screwing, weren't you?"

"No, Ryan," Kitty said. "I was frightened someone else might come, so I asked Fats to put on the chain. I don't know what to expect next."

"Really?" Ryan's footsteps were heavy. The sound of fabric tearing followed. "Just helping you out, baby. That shirt was buttoned all wrong. And will you look at that? I must be losing it. Last time I was in there I could have sworn you were wearing a bra. Remember that, babe? When we stopped for Fats to take a leak, and you and I waited in the truck?"

Silence reigned.

Then Kitty gasped.

"You don't like being pinched?" Ryan asked. "I kinda wondered how sensitive plastic ones were."

"Watch your mouth," Kitty said. "They're very sensitive."

"I'll have to run more tests," Ryan said. "Any calls from that husband of yours and his partner?"

"No."

"Time to call them. They're inconveniencing me. People who inconvenience me make me vindictive."

"I don't want to call them," Kitty said.

"I didn't ask what you wanted. Did you hear me ask what Kitty wanted, Fats?"

"I sure didn't, Ryan. She must have imagined it."

"Yeah," Ryan said. "Just like you're imagining I'm blind. Did you enjoy fucking Kitty, Fats?"

"Kitty?" Fats asked, sounding stupid.

"Yeah. Kitty. You feeling good now? Ready for a long, warm sleep? Too bad there won't be time for the sleep, but I'm a reasonable man. I insist you get a good fuck in. Frustration isn't good for a man. I'd never ask that of you. Go on, get it done. Don't mind me."

Aiden had detested Ryan from the day they'd met. He'd thought Ryan crude then, and by now he knew the man had a filthy mouth and a mind to go with it.

"You're all wrong about this," Fats said. "Isn't he, Kitty?"

"All wrong," Kitty said, and laughed. "You wouldn't want to watch us doing it, Ryan. You'd hate that. Anyway, it's sick. We've got plenty of other stuff to think about."

Kitty cried out.

"Don't hit her," Fats said. "She's not worth the effort, Ryan."

"Shut up," Ryan said. "Bitch. Leave the shirt the way it is. You like showing your tits off, and Fats is going to need something to hold on to. Ever seen any good snuff?"

Fats said, "You're making too much out of this."

"Great stuff," Ryan said. "Best sex you'll ever see. I've got a new disk with me. If I watch it later, I may let you see, too. In the meantime, I'll be the director and you two get to be the actors. Sometimes the women don't really die. Sometimes they do."

"How'd it go with the dog?" Fats asked quietly, sounding shaken.

"It went. Took too long, but it's gone."

Aiden made sure his face didn't move but he felt tears in his eyes.

"Unzip it, Fats. A good live show is exactly what I feel like."

"Well, I don't feel like it," Kitty said.

"But you love putting on a show," Ryan told her. "That's what you do best. Have you shown Fats how you can—"

A cell phone rang.

Ryan said, "Shit, that had better be the call we're waiting for. You're on, Kitty."

Kitty said, "Hello," and her voice was shaky. She didn't say anything else for some time.

"Hey," Ryan whispered. "Tell 'em to hold on, and give me a rundown."

"Just a minute, Rupert," she said, then to Ryan, "They're at Bobby Mobo's. They're exhausted, they say. Kept getting lost. They're going to get a room and sleep for a few hours. Then they'll—"

"They're coming here," Ryan said. "Now. I know they said the FitzDurham woman fobbed 'em off with just a few photos and she kept the rest. I want to see what they've got. If Flynn decides to come out of his long winter's nap, he's going to help us get the rest. That woman's got to be wandering around out there not knowing what to do next. She won't go far at night, but come morning she'll try to take off.

"Tell Fish where we are. Very specific instructions. Dangle the promise of a night's sleep—with you. But you want to meet them in the café first. I'll make sure you and Fats know exactly what to say, but I'll be close enough to hear just in case something backfires. Tell them."

"I don't want to meet them."

"And I don't care what you want."

Kitty sighed. "What about him? You can't leave him here alone. I'll stay and watch him."

"As soon as you finish on the phone, I'm putting Flynn back in the truck and making sure he can't move," Ryan said. "Any other questions?"

Kitty said, "No," and gave remarkably good directions to Fish and Moody. Then she brushed off their obvious complaints. "I'm looking forward to seeing you, Rupert," she said at last. "I miss you, and I've been frightened. Well, anyone can get mixed up in something, then be out of their depth. We'll work things out. See you soon. Bye."

"Very good," Ryan said when the call was finished. "Fats, make sure she doesn't open her mouth about me. We'd lose our trump card if she did. Can you stop her?"

"It'll be my pleasure," Fats said.

"Why can't we just kill them when they get here?" Kitty asked.

Devoted little wife, Aiden thought.

"Because they can be useful. We're going to leave them holding the bag. We get their pictures and the ones FitzDurham has. Then we leave Fish and Moody with Flynn and the woman—and Flynn's gun. Nice of him to bring it for us. Fish is the cold one. He'll pull the trigger if he's told to. Probably enjoy it. We'll make sure someone finds out about it—when we're far enough away to enjoy the headlines. Sweet, huh?"

"Yeah, sweet," Fats said.

Nineteen

The battery in the Rover was deader than dead. Chris had worked over it, using the Harley battery, but there had been nothing. They were left with the bike and might as well make the best of it.

Chris did spare a thought for how difficult it would be to return the Harley to the Chicago friend who'd brought it to him at O'Hare. If he and Olivia were lucky enough to find Aiden alive, they'd never get to the airport with the three of them on the bike, not without being stopped by the police. It was a risk he wouldn't take anyway.

He'd face that one later. "You're sure that's the same car?" he asked Olivia. He hadn't moved the bike an inch yet, but she sat stiffly on the pillion seat, clutching her hat in both hands, and each time he looked back at her, there was no change in her petrified expression.

"Same car," she said. "Rupert Fish and Winston Moody. They've been following us in it."

The car, a big black Caddy, was parked at the motel office. One man had gone inside; another stood outside talking on a phone and showing signs of agitation. Finally he opened the passenger door and threw the phone inside. Then he went into the office and returned shortly with his companion.

Their voices carried clearly. "I'm not going anywhere now, Rupert," the second man said. "That's the trouble with you, you're too easily pushed around. And by that dreadful wife of yours, too."

"They always shout," Olivia told him. "Really, they never stop shouting."

"Just as well right now."

"She's with that Fats Lemon," Mr. Fish said. "He's dangerous, I tell you. Kitty sounded frightened. She said we had to come at once. I've got the directions."

"You're telling me we've got to go at once because that round-heeled sex addict is frightened? Don't be absurd, Rupert. She won't have any trouble finding someone to cuddle her."

"*Don't*," Rupert said. "No, Winnie, just don't say anymore. We're leaving now. It's not far. They were waiting for us to make contact."

"How touching. Must be because they miss us. All right. Let's go, but if they kill us, I shall blame you."

Chris held his tongue on the subject of what he thought about idiots with the power to cause trouble. "Give me your hat or you'll lose it," he told Olivia, and stuffed it inside his jacket. "Hang on to me. Lean against my back. You'll probably like the ride. My wife was a real skeptic, but she loves it now."

The Cadillac took off, and Chris didn't give it much time before following. He drove along the access road and eventually turned onto the highway.

Olivia clung. She put her arms around Chris Talon's wide back and clutched his jacket. He had plugged Aiden's phone into a place on the motorcycle that was meant for it.

Her legs felt boneless. Chris drove fast, and the wind and rain tore at them. Several times he patted her hands. Another nice man with a gruff exterior. She liked him, but then, making snap decisions about people was becoming a habit. She'd even managed to make the kind of snap decision that had allowed her to feel wonderful about sleeping with a man she scarcely knew. Naturally, she had moments of awkwardness when she thought about what they had done, but she was a good judge of character.

And she'd fallen in love with Aiden.

The wind blasted inside her too-big helmet, turned her ears icy and made them ache. She almost welcomed the discomfort because it pulled her attention from the outrageousness of what she'd begun to admit to herself. If this could all be cleared up, she'd return to London and resume her life . . . wouldn't she? Trying to forget Aiden would be the hardest thing she'd ever done . . . if she had to do it.

He was a good, decent, absolutely stunning man and he'd taken risks for her. Look where he was now. He could die because of her.

How could there be so much air and wind around when she couldn't seem to catch her breath?

Aiden Flynn would have put himself out there for anyone he thought was in danger and whom he believed he could help. No. Yes, he would do that, but although almost anyone would scoff at the way their intimacy had happened, she believed he felt something more than casual sexual attraction for her. He wasn't that kind of man.

Wouldn't that theory make a lot of people she knew laugh? And she wouldn't be able to blame them.

He might already be dead. The tears in her eyes weren't all the work of the wind.

Olivia wondered how far they'd ridden. She couldn't see the road ahead, or wouldn't. There was absolutely no question of her leaning one way or the other on the nasty bike in order to look.

Chris slowed down, and Olivia prayed that meant he was stopping.

He veered right, tipping at a terrifying angle, and they roared around a circular exit from the motorway. The exit kept turning and turning and Olivia closed her eyes.

The bike straightened.

A lighted green arrow flashed on and off, advertising the Sleep In Peace Motel. Chris passed the entrance, drove the motorcycle onto a verge, and stopped. He got off, kicked down a stand, and helped Olivia remove her helmet.

"What a horrid name," she said. "Sounds like an undertaker's."

Chris smiled. "Off you come," he said.

She tried, but nothing would move.

Chris lifted her from the bike and held on while she waited to feel her legs. "That happens," he said. "Stamp your feet."

Obediently, she did as she was told. "Is this where they went?" She took off the helmet and hooked it on the handlebars.

"This is where they turned in." Chris chuckled. "You're right about the name. I thought the same thing. We're going to find somewhere out of the way and see if we can figure the place out. Can you handle that? Being cold but keeping quiet?"

"Of course I can." He might have asked if she could also keep quiet when she was really, really scared. She could do that, too. "You've got to be cold in your suit. At least I've got this awful leather stuff on."

Chris held her hand and they slipped along close to a hedge that smelled like fir trees. "I don't feel the cold," he said. The darkness was complete now.

Lighted windows showed through an opening in the hedge. Chris stepped to the other side of the gap, pulling Olivia after him. They made a rapid tour around a building with a coffee shop and office at the end nearest the road, and a single story of rooms that formed an L shape.

Chris didn't like anything about this. Too many unknowns. "We stay here," he told Olivia when they'd reached the cover of some prickly bushes near the last unit. No lights showed there, and there wasn't a car parked in front. Occupancy looked to be low tonight.

"That's it," Olivia said, pointing. "The truck Fats and the other man were driving with that woman. With Aiden and Boswell in the back."

Only one vehicle matched the description she'd given. It stood in front of a room where light glowed through an orange print curtain. "Stay put," he told Olivia.

"*No.*" She made a grab for his sleeve and held on.

So much for even one thing being uncomplicated. "Yes," he told her quietly. "I won't be longer than it takes to see if Aiden's in the truck."

She released him immediately. "I'm sorry," was all she said.

Chris took off, blessing the darkness. He kept his lapels folded over his white shirt, but prepared to fall back on being a civilian motel guest on his way to the café if he walked into someone. There was no need. He got a good look into the empty truck and made it back to Olivia without incident.

"He's not there, is he?" Olivia said. "I don't know if I'm relieved."

Neither did Chris. "The Cadillac's still near the office, which means those guys aren't checked in yet."

She went to her knees in the dirt and huddled against the wall. "We don't know if Aiden's here at all," she muttered. "They could already have killed him."

Chris crouched beside her and patted her back. "I think it's far more likely they've got some good reason for wanting him alive." In truth, he shared her fears. "I need to get into that room without shooting the place up—and possibly hitting the wrong people. From the description you gave me, the man who ambushed Aiden had to be Ryan Hill. I didn't know him well, but what I did know, I didn't like. Cold son-of . . . Cold guy."

"I keep forgetting you've got a gun, too," she whispered, not wanting to think about guns or what a cold man Ryan Hill might be.

"Cops carry guns," he said with as little inflection as possible. "That doesn't mean we all love 'em. They're part of the job."

A sense that something was gliding through the darkness nearby instantly became a conviction. "Hold still," he told Olivia. "Do not move a muscle until I tell you it's okay."

She didn't squeal, or even draw in an audible breath. His opinion of her began to climb.

He drew his gun, but before he could even line it up on something, a panting shadow barrelled forward and slunk rapidly toward Olivia.

"Boswell," she said, much too loudly. "Chris, it's Boswell."

"Keep it down. Hey, you old reprobate. Remember me? I met this good guy before I left NYPD. Aiden had a thing for him even then."

"He's so sweet," Olivia crooned, hugging the big, muddy dog.

Chris said, "Sweet? I don't suppose anyone else ever called him that. Let's give him a look-see."

Olivia said, "I'll do it. You are a good, pretty, and very faithful dog. Let me look at you." She ran her hands over him. Boss suffered the indignity until she seemed almost finished. Then he yelped. "Help me see what this is," Olivia said.

Chris hooded his small flashlight with a hand and trained it on the back of the dog's neck.

"He cut himself," Olivia said. "Poor boy. I'm sorry."

Chris looked more closely. "Bullet crease, I think," he said. "Winged the back of his neck, but it's superficial. We'll get him taken care of as soon as we can."

He felt Olivia watching him and met her eyes. Darn, he wished she weren't so pale. "Aiden's not in the truck," she said and swallowed. She passed a hand over her eyes. "He could be anywhere. Boswell was with him, and now the dog's here, alone, and with a—well, a bullet wound. Aiden could have been shot, too."

She was echoing his own conclusions, but he wasn't about to tell her that. "He could also be just fine and in that room over there. I'm going to ask you to stay here again. Boss will follow orders and stay with you. He obviously relates to you. I'll call him if I think he could be useful."

"I don't want to stay," she said, her voice breaking. "Please let me come. I want to find Aiden."

If Aiden was okay, there could be interesting days ahead. This woman had a big-time case on him. If Sonnie liked her, and he thought she would, his wife would be ecstatic. "Listen to me, Olivia. There could very well be shooting, fighting, all you could do is get in the way. You could jeopardize the outcome we want. D'you understand?"

"Of course I do," she snapped. "I'm not an idiot."

"I didn't say—"

"Sorry," she said quickly. "That wasn't called for. Please do whatever you can. And be careful."

Chris didn't waste more time before starting off. He hadn't made more than twenty-five yards when the door next to the orange-curtained window opened. It wasn't difficult to recognize Fats Lemon, even after at least five years. The guy walked as if his feet were on springs, and he had a way of jerking his head sideways as if his neck hurt. With him was a woman whose silhouette suggested she was well built and liked to show it off. She had a lot of blond hair. They trotted toward the opposite end of the building.

Chris slipped away from the building and walked, bent over, next to a hedge. When the couple went into the café, he crossed back and stood close enough to see everything that went on inside. They went to join two men at a window table. Fish and Moody.

Chris knew what he had to do now. Go into that room.

Once more he stayed close to the walls.

There was only one way to play this one. Arriving at the appropriate door, he squared off, used a foot to send it crashing open and followed it inside, gun at the ready.

Aiden lay on the bed. Barefoot, wearing a getup that would make his mother pass him by, he was cuffed wrist and ankle. Chris couldn't believe his luck. The fools had left him alone. "Aiden," he whispered. "Can you hear me? It's Chris."

His old partner's electric-blue eyes opened, met his, and filled with alarm.

"Olivia's with me," Chris said. "She's doing fine."

Aiden jerked his head to the left, toward another door where the bathroom must be. Only then did Chris hear water running in a sink and the toilet flushing. He dropped to the floor, put the bed between him and the bathroom, and waited.

If Lemon returned, he was probably dead meat. He prayed no unsuspecting civilian wandered by and got curious.

Seconds passed.

Water kept splashing in there.

Only inches from the box spring, he edged toward the foot of the bed. What the hell was keeping Hill?

Chris calculated what it would take to close the door behind him but discarded the idea as too dangerous.

"Chris?" Aiden's whisper was hoarse. "He's armed. And for some reason, he doesn't want Fish and Moody to see him."

"He's not going to have the piece in his hand," Chris replied. "I hope." He wanted any small advantage he could get. Hill might be quick, but the moments it took to draw might be all Chris needed.

The water poured on.

Small hairs rose on the back of Chris's neck, then on his spine.

In the distance, he heard a cry. A female cry.

So much for trusting a civilian woman to keep her cool under pressure.

The shout came again and this time, "Chris!" was real clear, dammit.

"Olivia," Aiden whispered.

"Okay, you fuckers, let's keep it down, shall we?" Chris didn't have to look to know he was hearing Detective Ryan Hill behind him. The guy must have left the bathroom by a window and circled back. "I'll shoot if I have to. Put the piece on the floor, Talon—slowly and carefully. Keep your hands where I can see them."

Cursing silently, Chris followed instructions.

"Good," Hill said once Chris withdrew his hands from the vicinity of his gun. "I didn't expect your chicken-shit ex-partner to show up, Flynn, but did you think I wouldn't notice blood on the sheets and the phone? You think I didn't figure out how you used your time while Fats was screwing Kitty?"

Hill had entered the room and taken up a position where he could keep Aiden and Chris in his sights—and the open door.

"Fortunately I don't need your help now, do I? That's her out there, isn't it, Talon? All we have to hope for is that she's dumb and gutsy enough to try to help. *Help.*" He laughed. "Oh, come to me, baby, and help."

"She won't walk in here," Aiden said. "By now she's calling the police."

"Is she? You're fugitives, and I'm bringing you in. If I hear sirens or see a light I don't like, I'm gonna have to kill you for resisting arrest."

As always, Hill was too in love with the sound of his own voice. It had been known to distract him.

"It's great to have you with us again, Ryan," Aiden said, and Chris kept his grin facing the floor. "Since we know we're going to end up dead before this is over. Why not tell us all about it? What the hell have you been up to?"

"Stuff it," Ryan said.

Dread drove Aiden onward. "Whatever it is, it's damn clever.

Geez, you were always slick. Come on, at least give us a chance to enjoy it, too."

Ryan's attention wavered just the smallest bit. His eyes flickered before he concentrated harder on staring Aiden down and keeping a self-satisfied sneer in place.

"C'mon, Ryan," Aiden said. "Share. I didn't think you'd seen the blood."

Ryan sniffed and said, "Get up, Talon. And I want to see each muscle you move."

"This art theft I'm supposed to be involved with," Aiden continued. "You're in on something big there. Am I right? Listen, we could work something out and—"

"Shut it, or I may forget I care about making noise."

"There's going to be noise at any moment," Chris said. "Once Olivia brings the local heat our way."

"She won't," Ryan said, his voice icy. "I corresponded with her for two weeks before you decided to horn in, Flynn. She's no fool. She won't risk jeopardizing the two of you."

Aiden let the comment about meddling go. His greatest fear was that Ryan was at least partly right and that Olivia was hatching some plot that would only kill them all.

Chris figured it was now or never, now while Aiden had Hill all riled up and focused on him.

There couldn't be more than a yard between Hill's feet and where Chris was stretched out on the moldy-smelling carpet.

"How did you get Olivia to trust you so much that she'd get on a plane?" Aiden asked.

"Trust?" Ryan said. "Hell, she was out of choices. Ripe for the picking."

"How did you find her in the first place? Someone must have given you her name and said she'd taken the photos. But I don't get *why* you wanted her here."

"Forget it, asshole," Ryan said. "You read the posts. You don't need a PhD to figure out I didn't want her. I wanted those photos here, and in my loving care."

Aiden sniggered. "You and those two jokers who are supposed to be antique dealers wanted the same thing."

"They're also cracked. You like rats, Flynn? Fish is a rat lover. Likes to keep rats in his pockets. Maybe I can arrange for him to send some along to keep you company."

"How will you do that?" Aiden said. "You don't want him to know you're here."

Hill braced his elbow. His lips parted, and his eyes moved away. Aiden knew he'd gotten too close to something Hill wanted kept very quiet. "I'm losing patience," he said at last. "You've got one chance. I get the photos—all of them—and you can leave."

"I don't have the photos to give you," Aiden said, with the kind of innocence guaranteed to infuriate.

"I don't have time to get mad," Hill said. "Where are they? How's she transporting them? They are with her, aren't they?"

"Hey," Aiden said. "Hey, Ryan, I've got a deal for you. You tell us what's in those shots and we'll consider letting you have them."

Chris figured Aiden was trying to give him time to make a move, but the smallest mistake could cost Detective Flynn his head.

"Tell me what you're driving, Talon. I'll have Fats go get what I need and I'll tell him not to touch the woman. If he lets me know he's got the photos, I'll walk out of here and you'll never see me again."

"Don't believe him, Chris," Aiden said. "The way I figure, he's really running out of time and what he can't afford is to have Fish and Moody find out he's here. Isn't that right, Ryan? They want the photos. You want the photos. Your life depends on getting them and getting away. Isn't that the way it goes?"

"You don't know anything and won't." Hill's voice grated with anger. "You're expendable and your time's about up."

Chris pulled in his elbows and shot himself toward Ryan, rolling rapidly over to collide with the man's ankles. Ryan hollered as his knees buckled and he came down on top of Chris.

"I can't do anything," Aiden yelled. "These damn cuffs."

Chris didn't have time to answer. He lunged upward toward the hand that held the gun, but Ryan raised that hand high and, at the same time, kicked at Chris's head, landing a solid one on the side of his jaw. Chris crawled up him like Jack on his beanstalk. He grappled with the guy's clothes and let loose a flurry of short jabs. A punch to the crotch sent the guy mad. He struck out at Chris, using the hand that held the gun, dragging in sobbing breaths as his arm rose and fell.

Chris needed the keys to Aiden's cuffs. Attacking Ryan again, he landed the two of them across the bed, on top of Aiden.

Ryan rolled away and Chris made to follow.

"Uh-uh," Ryan said, leering. He held the muzzle of his gun to

Aiden's head. "Games are over. I want answers and quickly. Where are the photographs? Exact location? Inside what?"

"Photographs?" Chris said. He stood on the opposite side of the bed from Ryan, the side where his own weapon rested on the floor near the bed. "Aiden was only stringing you along. We don't know anything about any photographs."

"Don't bullshit me," Ryan said. "You know the photographs I'm talking about. Olivia took them at a house in Notting Hill in London. She fobbed some useless stuff off on Fish and Moody, accepted a bunch of money from them, and took off. All I'm trying to do is get their property back."

Chris didn't answer.

"Okay," Ryan said. "Help me get those pictures and I'll take you somewhere and let you go. It'll be a long way from civilization, but you'll make your way back."

Aiden waited for Chris's reaction. When he didn't say anything, Aiden stepped in. "That's an interesting proposition. Of course, it would have to be carefully drawn up."

"I'm not negotiating," Ryan said. "I'm telling you how it's going to be. And the FitzDurham woman is too much of a loose cannon to leave around. Get her to give up the shots, and you won't have to worry about what happens to her. I'll take care of that."

Aiden's gut felt like it was braided. "Sounds like a great idea." He was itching to strangle the bastard.

There was no warning.

Boss came through the door in midair and flattened Ryan Hill. Hill swore and struggled. "He should be dead," he shouted. "Call him off! Fats is coming back. He won't ask questions. He'll kill you two as soon as look at you. He hates you, Flynn."

Aiden didn't care who hated him. He sat on the edge of the bed and tried to figure out how to get the keys to the cuffs.

Through it all, Hill held his piece in a death grip. He was working the muzzle in the direction of the dog who stood over him, snarling, showing his metal fangs and a whole lot of gum. Chris grabbed up his weapon and aimed it at Ryan. "Give it up," he said simply. "You just lost."

"Aiden?" Olivia said in a tiny voice and walked through the door.

Chris groaned. "Step back out, would you please, Olivia?" he said, trying to sound like a Sunday school teacher directing kids into church. "Go wait by the bike."

"We meet at last, Olivia," Ryan said, and Chris didn't like the sound of his voice. "You're not as ugly as I expected. Don't move, okay? Just tell me where the photographs are."

"Um," Olivia said, her eyes wide open. "What—"

"*Don't* jerk me around. You know what photographs."

Olivia's mouth formed an O, then she said, "Oh, I see what you mean. They're probably in Seattle. I put them in my grip and checked it through. Then we couldn't catch the plane from New York, you know. It was awful. Lots of running around, and—"

"My gun is trained on you, Olivia," Ryan interrupted. "Tell your lady friend I don't have a sense of humor, Aiden. Tell her I run down little old ladies who accidentally step off crosswalks."

"I wasn't being funny," she said. "I decided it was safest to pack them. They'll be fine. I'll get them later, I expect."

Aiden said, "Please step outside, sweetheart. Everything's going to be fine."

Chris heard the "sweetheart." So did Ryan, who said, "I guess you two didn't waste your time alone, huh?" he said. "Well, the face is Miss Next Door, but the body's got possibilities. Nice breasts, Olivia. Am I right, Aiden?"

Olivia's face flamed, but her mouth set in a firm line and whatever flashed in her eyes, it wasn't submission.

"Shut it, Ryan," Aiden said when he trusted himself not to goad the bastard into action. "Olivia. Out."

"Right," she said. "Out I go. Come on, Boswell, pet. Come with Olivia."

At first Chris missed her intention, but when Boss tramped across Ryan, he got it.

Aiden beat Chris to it. Cuffs and all, he launched himself like a stunt diver and landed on top of Ryan.

Rather than leave, Olivia shut and locked the door and ran to Ryan. She knelt and grabbed handfuls of his hair. Then she thumped his head on the floor.

"The gun!" Chris yelled. Boss had ruined Ryan's view for some seconds, but the guy could see again now and the instant he managed to remove Aiden's knees from his shoulders, he'd start shooting.

Olivia shuffled to Ryan's right side and grabbed his wrist. This she banged up and down with even more enthusiasm than she'd used on his head.

A roar escaped Ryan. Rage contorted his face and he surged upward. Aiden was thrown aside. Olivia landed against a wall and her skull made a sound like someone punching a melon. She sat where she was. Boss sat near her, his ears cocked and twitching, waiting to be told what to do next.

"Okay," Ryan shouted, on his feet again, his stance wide. "Come and get me, Talon."

The guy was all muscle. His white-blond crewcut and Teutonic features had earned him the nickname of Führer. The weirdest things about him were his eyes, very pale, and a mouth that came together in a tight gash with almost no lips.

"C'mon, c'mon," he taunted, the palm of his free hand turned up, the fingers beckoning. His gun was aimed at Olivia. "Shoot me, Talon. You three will fry for it because you'll never get around my ground-work. It's too good."

Chris couldn't risk holding back. This might be the best, and last, chance. He sprang on Hill and landed a punch guaranteed to wind the guy.

"Fuck you," Hill gasped, but came back fighting. He ducked a shoulder and rammed Chris who, jammed the back of a knee against the bed and fell.

Hill bombed down on Chris, whose gun sailed from his hand and slid against the baseboard near the door.

Chris was all over the guy. Again and again he slammed the wrist that held the gun while Hill sobbed out his wrath and fought back.

Chris saw Olivia go to Aiden, but couldn't risk taking his concentration from Ryan Hill.

When Olivia moved in behind Ryan, Chris almost ordered her away—until he saw what she was doing. She shot a hand into each of Ryan's pants pockets. The man started, and Chris closed his hand over the gun.

"Get off me," Ryan yelled. "Get the bitch off me."

Olivia was into the guy's pockets in earnest, and when her hands came up empty she instantly went for the back pocket.

"Shit." Ryan exploded. "What the fuck are you trying to pull?"

She jumped away from him and went to Aiden.

"Damn you, Hill," Aiden said. He got awkwardly to his feet, threw his arms over Hill's head, and ground his cuffed wrists into the other man's throat. His feet were free and Olivia danced around the edges of the action with the cuffs dangling from her fingers.

Chris collected himself and took the gun from Hill's flailing right hand. The guy gurgled and his face darkened.

"You're a really bad man, Mr. Hill," Olivia said. "I can't think of a single nice thing to say about you."

Aiden grinned.

Chris said, "You're killing him."

"What a pity," Aiden told him.

"That's not a good idea," Olivia said. "Really, it isn't. You know how things can go. My friend Mark, who investigates crimes, talks about how criminals get away with murder but good people don't."

"You're right," he told her. "But I think I'm prepared to take the risk." He jerked the cuffs a little tighter.

"Oh, dear," Olivia said and from the corner of his eye, he saw her bend down beside Ryan.

"Don't touch me," the man managed to sputter. "Stop it! Stop her. I'll kick your teeth in, you bitch." He tried to kick her, then screamed.

"Stand still and let me do this," she said. "I haven't bitten anyone since I was a child. I only have Mummy's word for it that I did then. But I'll bite you again if you keep kicking."

"She's fucking mad," Ryan said, and he was crying. He screamed again and Aiden met Chris's eyes.

"She bit me again," Ryan said.

Chris stood ready to move in, but Olivia was busy snapping the available cuffs on Ryan Hill's ankles. This done, she stood up and crossed her arms. "I think we should get away fast."

"Good idea," Aiden said. "Let's get these cuffs off my wrists."

"Hold Mr. Hill's arms, please, Chris," Olivia said. "Point one of those guns into his ear if necessary."

Aiden shouted with laughter. "You get us organized, honey," he told her.

Olivia was quick to transfer the cuffs from his wrists to Ryan's.

"Wouldn't it be better if he didn't shout?" she said.

Aiden said, "Surely would, ma'am," and threw the still struggling Hill over his shoulder to carry him into the bathroom.

"I'm going to win," he gasped. "I'm not done yet."

"Need my tie?" Chris called.

"No, thanks," Aiden said. "Check outside."

Chris did so. A blast of cold through the door felt great. There wasn't anyone in sight. He closed the door again. "Still clear."

"Great. We're out of here."

A glance into the bathroom showed Ryan Hill with the band of a red bra between his teeth and wrapped around his neck. The hooks and eyes were fastened at the front of his neck. The cups made passable blinkers. Aiden had tied the straps on top of the man's head. "Courtesy of Mrs. Rupert Fish," he said.

Olivia's laughter surprised Chris. He wouldn't expect her to see the humor.

Chris opened the door a crack. "Okay, all, stay close behind me."

"Even if three of us could ride the bike, four of us can't," Olivia said. "And we've got to get away from here with Boswell, haven't we? Probably to that airport?"

"You bet your boots," he said.

"Whoa," Aiden said, sounding suddenly strong. "What about Bo's Rover?"

Chris looked over his shoulder at him. "The dead Rover, you mean? It's in a cornfield where you left it. If we come through this, we'll arrange to get it towed. Now we have to hope I haven't forgotten how to hot wire."

"You haven't," Aiden said, "but you don't need to. Ryan the control freak insisted on being the keeper of the keys." He held up the objects in question and reached under the bed at the same time. "Keys to the castle—truck, that is. And I need my boots." He tore off the spur.

"I'll be right back," Chris said, and made a dash from the room to the Harley. He retrieved Olivia's things from the saddlebags, remembered just in time to take Aiden's phone with him, and ran back the way he'd come.

Aiden, holding Olivia's hand, went silently to get into Fats's truck. Boss was shut into the back but promptly moved forward and shoved his head through the window that opened into the cab.

"You come up with the darndest things, Olivia," Chris said, sliding behind the wheel. Even if he'd wanted to, Aiden's wrists and ankles were in no condition to allow him to drive. "What would make you say those photos were in your luggage and in Seattle?"

Her attention was only for Aiden. Vaguely she said, "I don't like telling lies and I didn't really. Not completely. Actually, I have one set of photos with me. The other set *is* in the bag that went to Seattle."

"Both sets were the same?" Aiden asked.

"More or less. They were taken on consecutive days. Penny wasn't sure I got everything just the way she wanted it the first time."

Chris didn't trust himself to speak. Somewhere, presumably at Sea-Tac airport, stood a piece of luggage containing evidence people were willing to kill for. Now at least one of those people knew about it.

"You should rest, Aiden," Olivia said. "You've had such a hard time. Feel free to put your head on my shoulder."

"Thank you very much, I'll do that," Aiden said, sounding almost British himself. "I'll do that. Some forces are too strong to fight, Chris. Get us to O'Hare."

Twenty

Fats leaned on the trunk of the black Cadillac and took deep breaths. Of all the complete screw-ups. And now he was supposed to keep on mincing around like Ryan's lap dog, doing whatever the master told him to do while the master stayed out of the line of fire. Balls to that. Ryan had shown just how smart he was—and wasn't. Now it was time for someone else to take over, someone whose intelligence could be relied on. Ryan Hill couldn't be cut out of the picture—that would be asking for more trouble—but he'd have to let Fats call the shots from now on.

He opened the driver's door and looked down into Rupert Fish's face. God, he hated the man, and his bulbous purple nose, and his continual bickering with his buddy, Moody, who was as bad if not worse.

"All change," Fats said. "Give me the keys."

"I can't do that," Fish said. "I'm the only driver on the rental agreement. No one else is allowed—"

"Move over," Fats said, "or get out. The choice is yours."

"Do as he says, Rupert, dear," Kitty said from the back seat, her voice dripping sympathy. "Mr. Lemon knows the road so much better."

Huffing, Fish did as he was told, drawing muttered complaints from Moody about being crowded. "Get in the back, then," Fish said.

"With *her*? I think not. You get in the back, Rupert. You're the one who made the mistake of marrying her."

Fish stayed put in the middle and didn't answer his partner.

Fats got in and took the keys from him. "I don't like talking when

I'm driving," he said. Mostly he didn't want to have to answer the questions that were bound to come.

"What was that phone call you got?" Moody asked.

Fats ignored him and concentrated on finding his way back to the interstate.

"I say," Moody said when Fats settled in at a very fast but steady pace. "I say, Lemon, I asked you a question. You got a call in that execrable café and started rushing about. What was that all in aid of?"

"We're on our way to O'Hare. That's the Chicago airport."

"We know that," Moody said.

"You know sweet frigging all," Fats said. He was long overdue to be in charge. "Flynn's going there. I know what his plans are and why."

"You said Flynn was under control. You said the photos would be in our hands before the night was out."

Fats felt Kitty's hand on his shoulder. She smoothed his neck and played with his earlobe. Trying to calm him down, he guessed. Kitty was something. Maybe they could keep on having good times together. He was going to need her help, and he'd have to trust her.

"We will have the photos," Fats said. He twined the fingers of his left hand into Kitty's and squeezed. "I know what has to be done."

When they got to the airport, they'd have to move fast and there couldn't be any mistakes. Ryan had been right about one thing; it would be a disaster for Fish and Moody to arrive in Seattle in time to ruin everything by getting their hands on FitzDurham's bag.

"If you know where they're going, why not say?" Moody asked.

No harm in them knowing now since they'd have to find out soon. "Seattle."

"Where's the FitzDurham woman, then?" Rupert said. "You said you separated that lot. Don't know why when it's dangerous to have her running around flapping her mouth."

"She's *not*, goddammit," Fats said, and instantly knew his mistake.

Moody leaned forward to see past Fish. "Well, now, isn't that interesting news. Where is she?"

Rupert snickered, and wiggled in his seat. "She's with him, isn't she?" He elbowed Fats. "Isn't she? Caught up, didn't she? Rescued him from under your nose. And we're supposed to take instructions from you? That's rich, isn't it, Winnie?"

"Rich," Moody agreed.

This time Rupert burst into snorting laughter. "They took your car," he blurted out, "didn't they? What did you do, leave the keys in the ignition? Oh, rich, very rich."

"Next time you'll know better than to leave a prisoner unattended, I hope," Moody said. "Our photographs are with Olivia FitzDurham, and she's about to slip away with them. We both know what could result from that."

"Only if she really caught what happened on film," Rupert said, petulance personified. "We only heard her take photographs. We didn't see what she was photographing. And if it was *you know what*, we don't know she took a close-up that showed—"

Thwap.

Fats jumped and braked. "What the hell are you doing?" he yelled. "What was that?"

"One more word from you and you won't live to be shot," Moody said.

Fats swerved onto the shoulder. "Want to repeat that?"

Without a word, Fish grabbed Moody.

Fats undid his seatbelt and hauled the guy off. "Are you nuts? We don't have time to throw away. What's this about shooting me, Moody?"

"I was talking to Rupert, not you," Moody said with hauteur. "I only tolerate him out of kindness. He comes from the scum of the earth. I taught him everything he knows, which isn't much. I'm the brain."

"And I suppose he's the brawn," Fats said, feeling weary. He got on the road again.

"If it weren't for me," Moody said, "he'd have spilled the beans about what's in those photos ages ago."

Fats shook his head. Either he was in Never-Never Land or having a nightmare. He thought over the words that might fool Moody into saying more. "Good job he's got you. Photographic evidence can be a killer. That one small thing the crooks never dreamed the cops would see."

"Exactly," Moody said. "You're an understanding man, Lemon."

"We should have been well away from Notting Hill," Fish said. "You're the one who got us late. And that's what put us in the wrong place at the wrong—"

Moody took him by the throat and said, "Shut *up*."

"Ah," Fats said. "Don't you worry about me hearing things, Winnie, I can be trusted." Excitement raised his pulse. "Something was stolen, something worth a lot of money, and the woman caught some evidence on film that can incriminate you. Or she may have. That's it, isn't it? Happens."

There was absolute silence before Moody said, "That is *not* what happened in this case."

"I must say," Fats commented, with feeling. "I must say I'm real hurt you don't feel you can trust me after all the support I've given you."

"Oh, we do trust you," Fish said. "Don't we, Winnie?"

Moody didn't respond, but Fats didn't need more drivel from Fish and Moody. He'd found out what they thought the pictures might show: evidence of a theft in a ritzy London house. And Fish and Moody would be implicated. Ryan had done a lot of talking about how much money they stood to make as long as the law didn't get its hands on those shots, but he'd refused to explain why.

Extortion had a potentially high profit margin.

Now it was Fats's turn to be in charge. Let Ryan stew, at least for as long as it took to get to Olivia FitzDurham's luggage before she did.

Olivia longed to put on some of her own clothes. She'd been into the washroom and done what she could with her appearance. The makeup was gone and she'd combed her hair through. With the new hat she'd bought at Wal-Mart—one of several—she felt more comfortable. But she still wore the frightful leather togs, including boots, and felt watched. The United gate for the Seattle-bound flight was crowded. They'd arrived at O'Hare when the next plane for their destination wasn't due for over an hour.

She sat down beside Aiden, who was slumped, legs outstretched, chin on chest, looking like death. His eyes were closed. He'd taken off the gray wig but made no attempt to remove either the tattoos or the profusion of silver jewelry.

"Let him sleep," Chris Talon said, arriving beside them. He'd been pacing back and forth across the concourse, always staring at the security point not far from the gate. He seemed more cross than tired. He picked up her carry-on bag and camera case. "Come with me."

Olivia got up again and followed him while he threaded a path through streams of passengers. He and Olivia dodged a motorized cart and stood near a row of seats with televisions attached. Every seat was taken by someone engrossed in a screen.

"I just tried to call Sonnie," Chris said. "She's not there, which concerns me. I left a message explaining what I'd like her to do. I've told her to ask one of her friends to go with her to Sea-Tac to get your luggage. Now I want the damned plane to get here."

The anxiety in his eyes worried Olivia. It was her fault he hadn't left for home when he'd intended to.

"It'll take time to retrieve our weapons at the other end," Chris said. The guns had been checked and would be kept by the plane's pilot. The police got to carry weapons on board, but only in the protective custody of the captain. "As soon as we land, you make a dash for baggage claim and go to the customer service desk. Just in case Sonnie doesn't make it there first. Get that bag of yours and don't let it go."

"Right, I'll do exactly that," she promised.

A phone rang, and Chris turned his on. "Sonnie? Sonnie?" He looked puzzled and said, "Hello."

There was another ring, and he said, "I'm losing it."

Olivia realized it was Aiden's phone demanding attention, and it was in her camera bag on Chris's shoulder. She dug it out and answered.

"Olivia?"

Vanni. She'd recognize his voice anywhere now. "Yes, Vanni. Did you try to call earlier?"

"Only about a hundred times before I had to go on duty. I'm on a break."

She started to explain what had happened, but Chris tapped her and said, "The plane's in. Better save the details for Seattle."

"We're just leaving for Seattle," Olivia said. "I'll tell you all the details when we get there, or Aiden will, I expect."

"Is he okay?"

"Yes. But it's been awful. Ryan Hill and that Fats hurt him. Now we've got to get our hands on my luggage—my grip went on the plane we were supposed to get from New York."

"They're boarding," Chris mouthed.

"I've got to go," Olivia told Vanni.

"I should fly to Seattle," he said. "It's so complicated here with the family, but I want to be with Aiden. What happened to Boss? Olivia, where's Boss?"

There was one big, scruffy dog who was loved by a lot of people. Olivia smiled. "He was shot, but—"

"Damn fools," Vanni said. "Damn them. Ryan never could control himself. He hated that dog."

"Boswell's going to be okay," Olivia said while Chris pulled her toward the gate. "He'll be on his way to Seattle with us. Bye, Vanni."

"Yeah," he said, but didn't sound happy.

Olivia turned off the phone. "He wants to be with Aiden so badly."

"Vanni's a good guy, and a good cop," Chris said, casting another glance over his shoulder. "We also need him where he is. Wake up, Flynn, we're leaving." He kicked the sole of Aiden's boot.

Aiden bounced to his feet, frowning hugely, a fist closed and ready to strike. "Whaddaya do that for, schmuck? My ankles—" He blinked and looked around him. "You could have whispered something nice in my ear instead, dammit."

"Sorry," Chris said. "I forgot the ankles. Our row's already been called."

"Hold on to me," Olivia told Aiden. "Once we're on the plane you can go to sleep again. Vanni called. He'll call again once we're in Seattle. I didn't have time to explain everything that happened. You can do that."

Aiden put an arm around Olivia's shoulders and met Chris's eyes over her head. Chris wasn't just jumping to conclusions, he'd already arrived and was sending "aren't you moving too fast with her?" signals. Aiden looked away. Between trying to figure out ways to escape Ryan and Fats, he'd had time to think about Olivia, about Olivia and himself. He'd contemplated what had already happened between them and questioned what he'd do the next time they were alone. If they were alone. They would be. And he wasn't sure what would happen, but he knew what he'd like it to be.

They checked through and walked slowly down the jetway. Aiden grew anxious again, even more anxious than he'd been before he fell asleep at the gate. He wanted them to be on the plane and pulled back, and sure they hadn't been followed aboard.

Some fuss ahead brought the line to a standstill. He looked over the heads of those in front and saw an oversized bag being carried off. "Move," he muttered. "Move it."

Olivia seemed determined to take some of his weight, which amused Aiden, but also touched him. What was that word? Serendipity. That's what their meeting had been, but who said serendipity couldn't be the start of something really great? It already had been.

A flight attendant at the door to the aircraft gave Olivia a cool glance that went on to include Aiden, but then softened into a smile. He didn't smile back. So she had a couple of biker passengers. They'd gotten through security—admittedly only after the wand had been used on Aiden—so they weren't a threat.

Passengers were stacked in the doorway, waiting to move forward yet again. Aiden looked behind him, expecting to see Chris, but it was several seconds before he caught up.

"You scared me," Olivia said to him. "I thought you were with us."

Chris waved his ticket stub and said, "Dropped the thing."

He got an entirely different kind of look from the attendant, a long, long, interested look.

Their seats were one row from the back. Chris had mentioned going for an upgrade to first class, but they'd decided they ought to be where they'd attract the least attention.

Chris sat on one side of the aisle and Aiden sat on the other with Olivia beside him in the window seat.

Chris leaned toward Aiden and said, "Fish and Moody—and Fats—are out there. You can see the security checkpoint. That's where they are. No Ryan, of course. He's gone back into his hole."

"They're going to make it," Aiden said, careful not to let Olivia hear. "You can bet Ryan told Fats about the bag. We'll have to be damned sure he doesn't get to it first."

"Good job I've got my badge," Chris said. "It'll come in handy if we end up tackling the guy."

"Yeah."

Olivia's fingertips dug into his forearm. "Something's wrong, isn't it?" she said. "Tell me."

Still leaning toward them, Chris said, "Don't worry. Everything's okay."

She grasped the back of the seat in front of her and peered over the top.

Aiden decided he must be hysterical because her stealthy pose made him want to laugh.

"Don't," Chris said to Olivia. "There's nothing, really. Just sit down."

Aiden shook his head. "Fats Lemon was at security. So were Fish and Moody." Olivia wouldn't thank anyone for treating her like a kid.

She plopped into her seat, rolled her eyes, then pushed herself up by the arms to continue watching people coming down the aisle. Aiden eased her down again and said, "Relax. Whatever comes, we'll handle it."

"We most certainly will, but not without very careful planning," Olivia said. "Depending on where they sit, we'll have to make sure we get off first. They absolutely won't want a lot of fuss, will they? Surely—"

"You're right, sweetheart," Aiden said. "And there's nothing we can do yet."

Olivia picked up his right hand and absently traced one of his old scars. She supported his wrist and studied the open welts there. "We'll ask for some dressings for these." She looked directly at him. "We can do that."

This was their first moment of anything close to being together since Ryan had jumped him. The enemy was at the gate and mayhem waited ahead, but Aiden couldn't turn from Olivia.

Her cheeks flushed and her eyes shone. Her lips parted, and she held the tip of her tongue between her teeth.

Nothing like this had ever happened to him before. There were good reasons why it wasn't a good idea to respond to what he felt now. He felt urgent, caught, and he didn't want to escape, wound up so tight inside that his muscles stung. His jaw locked. He absolutely could not look away.

Olivia, moving suddenly, touching his mouth, shocking him. She said, "I'm sorry I've made so much trouble for you, but I'll never be sorry I met you."

She might as well have opened him up and taken away the parts he couldn't live without. For thirty-eight years he'd watched other men fall in love and envied some of them—but he'd never felt a glimmer of the same emotion himself. Most of him had wanted it that way.

Very gently, he took her forefinger into his mouth. He could hardly breathe. She closed her eyes.

Chris tapped his back. "I think they're getting ready to close the doors. Maybe we're safe."

Aiden released Olivia's finger and said to her very quietly, "I'm not safe. I'm in a lot of trouble."

Kitty had her ticket in one hand and her carry-on bag in the other. She stood at a distance, watching the commotion Rupert and Winston were creating.

Fats had said they should all pretend they didn't know each other. Fine with her.

Rupert and Winnie were struggling to be first through the metal detector. So much for giving the impression they didn't know one another. Everyone was staring, and a grumbling line of passengers had piled up behind them.

A waving hand caught her attention. Fats indicated for her to board. Suspicion made her hesitate. Why would he want her to board without him?

At last Rupert managed to shake Winnie off and leap through the gate. He picked his bag up from the conveyer belt, then shouted, "No," when security asked to look inside.

The sensors went off when Winnie passed through the gate. He threw up his hands and repeated the process—including the alarms. Back he went again and took off his watch and rings this time.

Kitty made sure the hood of the furry white anorak Fats had bought her was pulled well forward. That hunky policeman had supposedly been unconscious, but from what Ryan had told Fats when he'd gone back and found him, Detective Flynn might have managed to peek at her.

"Flight 512 to Seattle is closing. This is the last call for flight 512 to Seattle."

Rupert berated a woman at security. The occasional word reached Kitty, "Bloody nerve . . . people like you . . . come *on*, Winston."

Kitty searched the mélée for Fats and finally spotted him. He'd drawn away from the security check point and stood aside, observing Rupert and Winnie.

She turned toward the plane. A United employee was starting to close the door to the jetway.

The sensors blared again.

Kitty stepped backward.

"Let him through, I say," Rupert roared.

Two policemen materialized from the crowd and bore down on the security area.

Fats was walking away.

She held her throat, but that didn't slow her racing heart.

One of the policemen said in a deep, rumbling voice, "Cooperate, sir, and you might make your flight. Let's get this over with."

While Rupert hopped from foot to foot and slapped his hands against his thighs, Winnie glared at the police and reached into his pockets.

His jaw slackened.

He threw himself around and tried to run, but the police stopped him before he'd moved from the spot. The officer with the rumbly voice patted Winnie down before pulling his hand from his coat pocket.

Women screamed and there was a collective gasp.

Winnie held a gun.

The instant before the door would have been completely shut, the flight attendant standing there answered a ringing phone on the bulkhead.

Aiden was a long way from the front, but he had a direct view. When the attendant pushed the door outward again, he gritted his teeth.

"Oh, shit," Chris said.

A woman in a bulky white parka boarded and took a seat in first class.

Final departure preparations were swiftly completed, and the plane pushed back from the gate. Chris ducked his head to see past his two seatmates. He turned back to Aiden and Olivia and said, "They've swung the jetway aside."

Aiden flopped back in his seat, and Olivia rubbed her hands together. "We've won," she said.

Twenty-one

The plane landed in Seattle, and tousled passengers jostled each other to empty overhead bins and pushed up the aisle. Chris carried what baggage they had between them. He also had to reclaim the luggage he'd checked before Olivia had interrupted his plans. Twice he'd tried to reach Sonnie from the plane. She wasn't there, but neither had she checked into the hospital. Despite his comment that he'd take the second item as good news, Olivia felt his anxiety grow.

They allowed the people beside Chris and in the row behind them to go ahead. "The less you crowd the aisles, the faster things move," Aiden said. "A little-known idea that may never gain popularity."

Olivia rubbed his back. A helpful attendant had produced first-aid supplies and helped Olivia clean and dress Aiden's wrists. He'd refused to have his ankles touched, pleading that they were already so swollen he'd never get the boots back on if he once removed them. Olivia thought he felt hot, but he brushed her concerns aside. He "never ran fevers."

Inside the North Satellite, the lights were bright and the pace leisurely in comparison to O'Hare. They moved briskly and took escalators deeper into the building to catch an underground train to the main terminal.

"First thing we do when we get to Chris and Sonnie's is take a magnifying glass to those photos," Aiden said. He wanted, more than almost anything, to know what Ryan Hill either feared or hoped might be in them. "We haven't discussed it, but I take it we've got a reason not to want the other set of prints in enemy hands?"

"We've got a reason," Chris said at once.

Aiden smiled despite his throbbing ankles. "I just wanted to hear that we're all on the same page. If there's nothing incriminating there—"

"We don't want our friends to know it," Chris finished for him and added, "If they discover they don't have to worry about that angle, they could complete their business and go into hiding."

"We could have avoided this angle if I hadn't outsmarted myself," Olivia said.

Aiden looked at Chris and said, "Well, I guess we've all been under a lot of pressure."

"Yes," Chris said neutrally. "And we're almost to baggage claim. Don't worry about it, Olivia. You did what seemed right at the time."

Olivia nodded and averted her face.

The train traveled fast through its black tunnel. Inside the car, more white lights turned faces into masks. Canned instructions were repeated in English, French, Spanish, and Japanese in a woman's sweet, high voice.

"Once more," Chris said, draping an arm around each of them. "Do we have something we want really badly?"

"Yeah," Aiden said, feeling the flush of the chase, "we want to bring the enemy to justice."

"You sound like a character in a comic strip," Olivia said, but she bowed her head and smiled up at him. "You're right. We want them to *suffer*. And we want to clear our names."

"Main terminal," Chris said. "This is where we get off. I hope Sonnie's waiting downstairs."

Olivia glanced at Aiden, and he drew his lips back from his teeth in a grimace. They were both worried that Chris's wife might have needed him when he was out of touch with her.

Baggage claim was more crowded than Chris had expected. "Boss'll be okay for a few more minutes. Over here first," he told Aiden and Olivia, making straight for the customer-service desk. He stood there and searched in every direction. It didn't take an imagination to figure out he was looking for Sonnie. When he didn't see her, he went for his phone and placed a call.

"Look at that," Aiden said to Olivia.

She knew what he meant. "He really loves her. From the way he looks, she's there finally, thank goodness." Chris's face had relaxed, and he smiled with pure pleasure.

"They love each other so much. They've been through a lot together. Mr. and Mrs. Unlikely some people call them, like Chris's brother Roy. He did his best to push them together, then couldn't believe it when it happened. That was in Key West, where Chris and Sonnie met."

"And he helped her with something?"

"They helped each other. They were both heading for the end of the line.

"If Vanni doesn't call fast, I'm calling him and to hell with security. I'll make up a name. I've got to know what's going on in the department. By the way, that terrific Rover we left behind belongs to Roy's partner, Bo. I don't look forward to trying to explain that."

Chris had hung up. He motioned them to the desk, and within minutes his bag was produced. "I don't know where my head's been," he said. "One of Sonnie's friends gave a shower for her, and she took Anna."

"Sorry to interrupt the domestic report," Aiden said, and he was, "but we should get Olivia's bag and get out of here. We can't afford to forget that we could be picked up anywhere if Ryan's done his worst."

"Not unless something's really changed, and Ryan decided to risk making this an official investigation," Chris said. "Last I checked, there hadn't been a bulletin on you."

"Doesn't mean it couldn't happen any time," Aiden said.

"I sent a bag ahead on TWA flight 1207 out of JFK three days ago," Olivia told the customer-service representative. "My name is Olivia FitzDurham. It's a green tartan grip with a shocking pink name tag. That's to help me see it when it arrives on carousels. It really works, you know."

"Yes, ma'am," a heavy-eyed customer-service representative said. She consulted her computer terminal and sighed. "The system's fluctuating. Keeps slowing down. Come on, come on." She punched keys.

Chris was silent, but his impatience to leave showed in his repeated glances at his watch.

"Wouldn't you know it," the rep said. "Now it's frozen. And now it's gone down. I'm sorry. It could be up in five minutes, or an hour or so. We've been through this three times this week."

"Chris should go home," Olivia said. She was inconveniencing too many people. "You go with him, Aiden. I'll come when I get my bag."

"That's one of the more stupid suggestions you've made," Aiden said.

Olivia's cheeks smarted. "Why, thank you, kind sir. Chris, would you please go home to your wife and daughter? I'm embarrassed because I've put you out so much."

"You haven't at all. And I'm in this to the end. But I would like to check on Sonnie in person. I'll get a cab and go on ahead, Aiden. Bring Olivia as soon as you can."

"I should get a room at a hotel out here by the airport," Olivia said. She desperately needed rest.

Chris shook his head. "You're both coming to us. There's a practical as well as a personal reason. Sonnie and I want you with us. And we need to stick together. Don't forget I've got resources at my disposal, too. There are too many unknowns out there."

"You're right, coach," Aiden said. "Take what bags Olivia's got. Now beat it. We'll be there."

Without argument, Chris slung Olivia's two bags over his shoulder, wheeled his own large bag behind him, and set off. He turned back once to wave before hurrying outside. Olivia saw him hail a cab and get in.

"I really like him," she told Aiden.

"You've got great taste. Sonnie had a cesarean with Anna. They're hoping Chris gets to coach through to the end this time. That's why he doesn't want to be out of reach."

The service rep was on the phone, and the answers she was getting weren't pleasing her. "How long?" she asked.

Aiden smoothed Olivia's hair back from her face.

"That's a lot of help. Yes, I'll wait to hear." The representative hung up. "This is going to take a little while. I'm sorry. Might be a good idea to find coffee or something and come back in half an hour."

"Can't we just go through the bags and get it if it's there?" Olivia said.

The blond woman shook her head. "I'm sorry. We've had too much trouble lately with the wrong people taking the wrong bags."

"Come on." Aiden took Olivia's arm. "We'll be back. Let's make sure Boss is okay, then get that coffee."

The baggage area had all but cleared, and the hubbub had faded until the shoes of those who remained clipped noisily on the hard floors. Boss's travel crate was easy to locate. It was huge. The dog lay forlornly inside, his eyes moving from side to side.

"It's okay, old fella, we'll get you out of there as soon as we know we're leaving," Aiden said, sticking his fingers through the front grid to scratch Boss's nose. Boss's response was to get up, present his back to them and flop down again. Aiden shook his head and said, "Looks like we can't get anything right tonight. We'll be back, Boss."

On their way past the service desk, Aiden inquired for the bag again, only to be told the computers were still down. At some level he was tired to his bones, and he knew Olivia must be just as weary. But at another level his awareness snapped and felt every nuance in the atmosphere surrounding him and Olivia. He ought to cool it. Their days together hadn't included a single normal hour. Everything they'd experienced had been extraordinary and played out against a drama most people wouldn't believe if he tried to recount it.

"Let's find somewhere to sit," he said. "Did the coffee idea sound good?"

"No, thank you."

"Tea?"

She gave him a quick smile. "No, thank you."

"Somewhere to sit, then?"

"You sit. You need to be good to your ankles. I'm going out to get some fresh air."

What was he supposed to say to that? He considered a row of black plastic chairs beyond counters that enclosed the silent and empty baggage carousels. At this time of night the airport was a people-spitting machine in sleep mode.

Olivia didn't look back. She walked to doors that opened onto a short-term parking area and went outside.

Aiden didn't want her out there alone.

He didn't want her anywhere alone—ever.

Deliberately keeping his pace slow, he followed and stood on the inside of the doors. To the right, where she'd be out of sight if he'd stayed where he was, she faced the building and balanced her toes on the curb, then jiggled her heels up and down.

Aiden pushed his hands deep into the pockets of his pants. He probably shouldn't let her catch him watching her.

Her arms were crossed, her face turned from him. Her breath sent clouds of vapor into cold, faintly foggy air. A light on the side of the building shone on her head, and he saw beads of moisture glimmer in her hair.

Best just walk away and sit down. She'd be okay.

Olivia wiped a hand over her eyes and kept it there.

Aiden swallowed. They were some pair. People from two different worlds who had collided like magnetized trouble on a collision course.

The leather pants showed what her preferred shapeless skirts didn't; her hips were rounded and very, very nice. But he knew that—he'd seen Olivia FitzDurham in nothing at all and she looked the best then, fabulous then.

She was unique. Everyone was unique, but Olivia was . . . unforgettable.

He turned away and started back toward the chairs. If he could be sure he wouldn't repeat the pattern of selfishness he'd seen in his father, or the man's indifference toward his child if Aiden ever had children of his own, he might be thinking about how it would be to come home to Olivia.

His mother had been a sweet woman, passive but concerned for her one child, her son. His father had provided well for his family, in every way but with his presence. Aiden had never caught a ball thrown by his father, or kicked a ball while his father watched, or heard his father cheering at the edge of the pool when he swam in a meet. The man had sought solitude as if he needed it as much as breath. Hiking mountain trails, hunting, fishing, those had been his passions, but never with his son, and his wife wouldn't have gone anyway. Hilary and Dan Flynn used their son as a messenger between them, not as a symbol of what Aiden had convinced himself had once been love for one another.

But he was okay with all that. Cautious about his own involvements because of it—that was wise—but not hung up on history.

How would it be to come home to Olivia?

He grinned and said, "Crazy."

He really didn't like her being out there alone.

When he got to the doors again, she'd swapped her toes for her heels on the curb and looked over the almost empty parking area.

Olivia was chilled, but she welcomed something to think about other than Aiden Flynn. Not that she wasn't thinking about him, too. She'd rather be inside the building with him, sitting by him even if there was nothing to say—even if he fell asleep again.

The tears that welled in her eyes made her feel angry and sad at once. From the moment she met Aiden, she'd decided she wasn't the kind of woman who would interest him because he was the type of man women stared at and she was the type of woman men did not stare at.

Rubbish. All those preconceived ideas were rubbish. She didn't know for sure that they would have passed each other by if circumstances hadn't brought them together.

Why couldn't she have the courage to find out if they could have more together than an outrageous sexual fling? Each time she thought about it all, her stomach flipped and she saw herself as a stranger, someone she didn't know. How did one go about finding out something like that, anyway?

"Olivia."

She said, "Hello, Aiden," but blinked rapidly rather than look at him. "It's cold. Stay inside."

"You do slip into mother mode, don't you?" he said, but without sounding annoyed.

"I'm not your mother, Aiden, I just care about you." Oh, great, she thought, not that he'd notice what she'd said.

"I care about you, too." He stood beside her, copied her stance by balancing his heels on the curb. "You look pretty cold yourself."

She shook her head.

"Chris and Sonnie love it out here. They say they like the seasons. Every time I come I feel I've walked into one big car wash."

"I like it," Olivia said. "This is the way it feels in London at this time of year."

"Damp and dripping, you mean?"

She smiled a little. "Perhaps. And there's the smell of winter. Fallen leaves."

"Dead and rotting leaves."

"You don't like it here."

He stepped from the curb into the gutter, then walked in a circle around her. "I didn't say that. I like it fine. I'm just not into romanticizing."

Of course he wasn't. "No," she said. "So when I look at droplets of moisture on a cobweb like that"—she pointed—"and see crystal and diamonds by moonlight, or tinsel on a Christmas tree, trembling when the branches move, you see—what?"

He began another turn around her. "You expect me to say moisture on a cobweb. Okay, I see that, but I like looking at it. Little miracles. If I did think about it, I might think that."

"Little miracles," she echoed. "They're everywhere if we ever have time to appreciate them."

"Yeah."

"I wish you'd stop walking around me. You're making me dizzy."

"Good. Maybe you'll fall and I'll have to catch you."

Olivia sighed. "What am I supposed to say to that?"

"Nothing. Put it down to delayed shock. It must just be hitting me and making me say weird stuff." But he stopped his measured pacing. He stood beside her again, but on the street rather than the curb. Still he had inches on her. "It would be a bad idea to get lulled into thinking we're safe."

"Why would we do that?"

"Because apart from Ryan Hill, we're dealing with the most inept bunch of criminals I've ever come across, and I come across them daily. Whenever you've got perps who are repeaters but they've never been caught, they're a bigger problem. They start to think they're above the law. Add stupidity to the mix and anything can happen. You start imagining it's all some sort of elaborate joke, a farce peopled with characters who would be dangerous if they could get their acts together."

Olivia hadn't put it all together like that, but he made sense.

"These people are dangerous because they've got a dangerous machine on their side," he said. "They've got the law. Until we can turn the balance of power we're in deep kimchee."

"If I weren't with you, you could go back and tell them what happened. You might get a slap on the wrist, but they'd probably see how you'd been chivalrous at first, then got dragged in deeper."

Aiden faced her. He didn't feel like smiling. "Good idea. I think I'll take you in and say I hung around because I figured you were into something big and I wanted to hand you to them on a platter. How does that sound?"

Her dark eyes caught the light. The expression there showed she knew he was angry. He disliked himself for that because he could already tell anger scared her.

"Okay," he said. "That wasn't what I wanted to say at all. You bring out the worst in me sometimes."

"I don't want to," she said.

He fastened his right hand firmly over her mouth. "I know. You aren't like any woman I ever met. Maybe there are millions of you in England, but I doubt it. You're irresistible. You don't have the greatest self-image, but you're still irresistible." He slackened his hand on her face, but brushed her moist cheekbone with the pads of his fingers. "Yes, you're irresistible, damn it. I ought to be putting plenty of space between us but instead of that, I'm trying to figure out how to get as close to you as a man ever gets to a woman."

She breathed deeply. He meant physically close. Did men ever understand that women might be every bit as sexual as they were, but that they yearned for intimacy that went much further? She looked directly back into those eyes that shouldn't be so blue that they almost hurt. She'd have liked to ask him if he understood about the kind of intimacy she was thinking about, but she couldn't, not yet—perhaps never.

He framed her face with his fingertips. So light. If she closed her eyes, would she know they were there? She'd know. Her face, then her ears and jaw. The fleeting caress descended the sides of her neck, and his thumbs settled below her collarbones.

With the slightest pressure, he moved her backward from the curb, to a shallow corner where plateglass windows and white concrete blocks came together. She felt the cavernous inside of the airport behind her, but gradually it receded and all she felt or saw was Aiden.

"We could probably check back with customer service now," she said.

Her breathless voice stroked him. "It's too soon," he told her. That kind of stroking excited a man, not always a convenient development.

She looked up at him. "We could get the dressings on your wrists changed."

"We could. They'll wait till we get to Chris and Sonnie's." The tight, semi-transparent top she wore under her mostly unzipped leather jacket gave a sexy peek at her cleavage. Aiden didn't like her in leather and revealing tops, but he liked her cleavage. He liked her heat. "I need to kiss you, Olivia. You don't like public display, but there's no one around."

She stared straight ahead, probably at the jumble of cheap chains against his chest. He wished she'd say something, but didn't expect it.

"You kiss me, Olivia," he said. "That way I'll know you like the idea."

She raised her chin, but not her eyes. "I like the idea of kissing you. I can't believe I've done . . . What I did with you wasn't like me. I don't mean I didn't enjoy it—I did—but I have never behaved like that before. The number of times I've relived every second and come close to . . ."

"And felt aroused enough to climax all on your own?"

"*Don't.*"

"Don't because it embarrasses you, or don't because it's not true?"

She gripped his shoulders, rose to her tiptoes, and kissed him. A desperate kiss, deep and panicky.

"Uh-uh," he managed to say, holding her beneath her arms and enough away from him to part their lips. "You're not going to kiss me to avoid dealing with your own feelings." The heels of his hands pressed into her breasts. He wasn't weary anymore.

"Okay," she said. "Okay, yes. You've changed me. I'm never going to be the same. No woman should walk around *aware*. I mean aware of herself sexually. I can't get it out of my mind—you out of my mind. If I'm guilty of seeing everything that's happening as if it's out there somewhere rather than all around me, it's because I'm too busy wanting to make love with you." She stopped and her mouth remained open.

"So we're even," he said softly. "I may not forget what's happening out there. Business is business and it gets ingrained." He didn't want to talk anymore. Women needed it, the talk, and a wise man learned to give it to them, but hell, he'd like to be covering her, buried in her, in the quiet of a place where they couldn't be found.

She didn't try to interpret the expressions that moved over his face. When he looked at her mouth again, she flattened herself against him, cradled his face, and urged him closer until he kissed her. He was no more leisurely or controlled than she had been. His breath rasped in his throat, and his hands moved over her back, over her bottom. His kiss demanded much more than just a kiss. Just a kiss? The way he used his tongue was more than a parody of what she'd said she'd like them to do. Her body tingled, and the sounds of the night turned to a buzzing in her ears.

Aiden raised his head. "I am so damned aroused, I may explode, sweetheart."

"I'm sorry," she said, jerking her head forward and capturing his bottom lip between her teeth. He might be tall and lithe rather than overtly big, but still she had her arms full to surround his chest and back.

He pressed a thigh between hers and she felt hot and weak. "Hold on," he said. "We're going to have to do something about this."

"Aiden." No, she had to learn when to be quiet.

"What?" he said, kissing her neck, kissing the tops of her breasts through her thin sweater.

"Nothing."

He undid the jacket altogether and stroked her. "I asked you a question," he said. "Finish what you were going to say."

Okay, she would. "You'd never have looked at me if we hadn't met the way we did, would you? I'm not your type."

With his mouth in the hollow of her throat, he grew still. "You believe that?"

"Yes, of course I do."

Aiden pressed the palm of his left hand against her stomach and slid downward until he could fold his fingers over her mound. "Because there's nothing about you that would interest me otherwise?"

"As a person, no. Why would there be? You didn't choose to be with me over someone else."

"No, that's true." He stimulated her through the pants he wished would fly away. "I didn't choose you because I didn't know I had you to choose."

"Oh, don't, Aiden. I can't think with you doing that."

"Don't think. Thinking is definitely bad for you. Return the favor instead. For a man who just happened to meet you, I've developed a real addiction—to you, that is."

"Only . . . Aiden, you don't know me at all, except as a woman who's good in bed with you."

"Seems like a great place to start to me," he said, and kissed her lips again. Anything for silence and a chance to do nothing but feel.

"Men don't like to talk during sex, do they?" she said.

Aiden almost choked. He looked at her. "No," he told her. "I don't think many men like to talk a lot when they're making love. We're pretty goal-oriented. It's a throwback to the days when we hunted the food and dragged it home. We had to be single-minded. Kill or be . . . No, not a good analogy, that."

Her wonderful smile warmed him and made him feel even sexier.

A movement behind her, inside the glass, didn't. A guy with a newspaper wasn't making a good job of pretending to read. "Time out," he said to Olivia. "I say we adjourn until we can lock a door and do whatever we want to do, for as long as we want to do it—without interruption."

She stiffened and turned around sharply.

Aiden wrapped an arm around her shoulders. "Consider that your charitable contribution for the night. You helped a bored guy pass a little time. I bet we helped him forget he was bored at all. Let's see if we can get that bag now."

Walking past the man with the newspaper took more composure than Olivia would have expected to gather. Aiden helped make it easier by holding her close and scarcely looking away from her.

"I want to get out of here," she whispered.

"So do I," he whispered back. "And we're going to."

The same woman was at the customer-service desk. "I didn't write your name down," she told Olivia when she saw her. "The computers are back up. You didn't say your last name was Fitz something, did you?"

"Yes. Olivia FitzDurham."

The clerk had a phone to her ear. She frowned and nodded. "I'm trying to reach the guy who was on duty before me. I hope he remembers."

"Remembers what?" Aiden said, but he didn't get an answer.

The woman turned the monitor so that they could see it. With her pen, she pointed to Olivia's name on the screen.

"Yes, Mark. Sorry to bother you. Right before you got off duty, do you remember the name Olivia FitzDurham?" She looked off into space. "I know, but it isn't an ordinary name."

Olivia leaned across the counter to see the screen more clearly and almost bumped heads with Aiden. Her name was there, but the rest didn't make any sense to her.

"Okay. If you don't, you don't. It's an entry mistake, I guess. Thanks." She hung up. "Your bag shows as having arrived, but then being picked up. Mark doesn't remember that happening. It's going to take time to check and see what did happen. It would be best if you went home, or to your hotel, or whatever. Leave your number and we'll contact you as soon as we track the bag down. It can be delivered to you."

Aiden didn't like the sensation he was getting. "If you don't mind, I think it would be a good idea for us to look through the baggage that's being held."

"We're not supposed to do that without—" She colored and fell silent.

"Yes," Aiden said. "Without the baggage receipt. Olivia has that. And she has identification—including her passport—so there's no reason for her not to look, is there?"

The phone rang and the clerk picked it up. "Customer—oh, hi, Mark. Olivia FitzDurham, yes." She said to Olivia, "What did you say your bag looked like?"

Olivia repeated the description she'd given earlier, and the clerk told her colleague.

"I was afraid of that." She hung up. "Mark says a woman who said she was you picked up your bag right when he saw me coming to relieve him. Apparently she was—well, attractive, with a lot of blond hair."

"Damn it," Aiden said. "Had to be Kitty. She got it with no ID?"

"She gave her name, and he found it here." She tapped her terminal.

"She took out her wallet, then described the bag. He was distracted because ... well, I guess he was distracted. She was really friendly. You know how guys are about that?"

Aiden and Olivia were too sick about what had happened to be nice.

The clerk looked embarrassed. "Evidently the woman said she always uses big pink luggage tags on her baggage."

Twenty-two

Aiden paid off the cab and reached for Olivia's hand. Boss hadn't quit giving them the cold shoulder since they'd sprung him at the airport. He sat at a distance and looked straight ahead.

"Ungrateful hound," Aiden muttered while the cab's rear lights disappeared into the darkness along the winding road above Lake Washington. "We patched him up and probably saved his no-good life. Now he ignores us over something as little as a plane flight."

"In the cold hold of an aeroplane," Olivia said. "Come to Olivia, Boswell. I understand, old fellow."

"You should love it here," Aiden said, deliberately taking his time before leading her down the almost perpendicular driveway to Sonnie and Chris's home on the lake. "It really smells cold, wet, and dead. And added to that, you need to be a cat to see where you're going out here."

"You're in a nasty mood," Olivia said. "It's my bag that's been run off with, but you're the one taking it personally."

"Taking it personally? What makes you think that? At every turn I meet another obstacle. So far I've lost my job, can't go back to my home, I've been knocked unconscious, confined in a motel room, involved in fights while I was handcuffed, chased across the country to get you away to safety only to discover the enemy got here first and made off with your bag—the bag with a set of photos in it. And those photos are what all this is about and could mean Ryan, Fats, and those goons will slip through my fingers altogether.

"Yeah, Olivia, I'm taking it personally."

Olivia decided giggling was out. "This is a brilliant place, Aiden.

It's mystical. Do cheer up. We're too tough, and we've been through too much to fall apart now."

"Who said anything about falling apart?" he thundered. "I do not fall apart. I made a dumb mistake, and I can be hard on myself about things like that. As I should be. How could I stroll off that plane and arrive too late to get your bag—your bag and the woman who stole it? Probably Kitty Fish."

"It had to be her," Olivia said. "She was with the rest of them at O'Hare. We just forgot her."

Aiden let go of her hand and put an arm around her instead. "Which makes me an even bigger idiot than I thought. Boss, quit sulking and fall in here, buster."

They started downhill on a narrow asphalt driveway between huge, dripping fir trees. High above her head Olivia could see a fuzzy sliver of moon behind thin cloud layers. Ribbons of misty fog like old men's beards threaded branches. The scent of fallen, wet needles was unfamiliar and wonderful.

"Do you have to be so damn cheerful?" Aiden said, and wished he could stop his runaway tongue from sounding aggressive.

"How do you know I'm cheerful?" Olivia said, but she put her arm around his waist and squeezed.

Aiden groaned. "See what I mean. Cheerful. You're bubbling, I can feel it, and your feet are *springing* off the ground. You're in pig heaven here. Let me remind you that the end of the world as we know it may be imminent. We are *wanted* people, Olivia."

"Moan, moan, moan. We're innocent people who just have to prove it. And when you don't feel so tired and in pain, you'll buck up again."

"Buck up?" he said and made a scoffing noise he hadn't known was in his repertoire. "That's another problem with you. You're so *British.*"

Knowing when to allow another person to wallow in his misery was important. Aiden could just wallow, but Olivia didn't intend to wallow with him. She whistled and felt grateful when they turned a bend in the steep, slick drive and lighted windows appeared before them. Chris and Sonnie's stucco house was on three levels—the one where people entered, one above that, and one below. The building clung to a bank, and she could see lights on the water beyond.

A bridge over a shallow drop-off led to the front door, which stood open.

Music spilled out, piano music. "I like that," Olivia said. "Popsicle Toes. I love jazz."

"It's Chris," Aiden said. "He plays a lot. Sonnie and Anna like it, and so does he."

"So do I," she said and urged him to hurry to the door. She was a strong woman, but she was running out of steam. "Hello," she called, and tapped lightly on stained-glass panels beside the door.

The music stopped, and Chris appeared with a small, slim woman—slim except for a very pregnant tummy—beside him.

"Hey," Chris said. "We were about to come looking for you. Come on in and get warm. Sorry about your bag, Olivia. Sonnie's rounded up some things for you. Come on in, Boss, old fella. You look awful."

"Hello, Sonnie," Olivia said. "Thank you for helping me. I feel as if I've turned into the freeloader of the century. I've been using borrowed things ever since I got to the States."

Sonnie smiled and offered a thin hand. "I'm pleased to meet Aiden's friend. I've waited a long time for this." She looked from Olivia to Aiden and back again. "A long time for Aiden to bring someone special home to us. Come on in. Anna's in bed, and I hope she stays there. This was a very late night for her—with the shower, and then waiting up for her daddy. And I think she's cutting her two-year molars and having a really hard time with them. If she knew there was a big, beautiful dog here, she'd be down the stairs in a flash." She glanced up a broad staircase that rose from the center of a slate-tiled entry scattered with beautiful Asian carpets.

Aiden hadn't said a word, and Olivia was afraid to look at him after what Sonnie had said. Chris dropped back to walk with Aiden, and Olivia followed Sonnie. The woman's very pronounced limp surprised Olivia. Aiden hadn't mentioned that. Olivia had also noted that Sonnie had scars on her neck but seemed oblivious to them. She was ethereal and charming, and very pretty.

"I've made discreet enquiries," Chris said. "I don't know what happened to Fats in Chicago, but Fish and Moody were taken into custody, then released when it was determined that the gun—I didn't tell you Moody had a gun in his pocket when he tried to get through security—wasn't his, but they don't know who it does belong to. Speculation was that someone dropped it into his pocket."

"Like Fats," Aiden said thoughtfully. "Question is, why would Fats want Fish and Moody stopped from boarding that plane? And why didn't he get on himself? Did Fish and Moody catch the next plane?"

"No record of them doing so. According to O'Hare security, the two men opted to leave the airport."

"How about Kitty Fish?" Aiden asked. "Did you get confirmation she was aboard?"

Chris struck his forehead with the heel of a hand. "It made sense that she was, and that she had taken the bag. Then I didn't give her another thought. I'll check her out to make sure. I did wonder if it was planned for her to be the only one who made the flight."

"This is great." Olivia, half-listening to two conversations, walked backward and said to Chris and Aiden, "So we don't have any idea where Fish and Moody are now. We think Kitty's the one who took off with my bag, but we don't have proof, and we certainly don't know what she's likely to do next. And it doesn't help that we can't even report the theft of my grip."

One long stride and Aiden spun her to face forward again. "We don't need you to fall and injure yourself," he said. "You're right, though. They've got me backed into a corner they must be loving. Vanni should have called by now. He knows how to find out when a plane's landed. I'm giving him a few more minutes, then I'm making contact myself."

"That's not a great idea," Chris said. "I'll do it."

"I'm not calling Vanni. I've got an old friend in New York who will give me the scoop—and tell Vanni to get on it."

"I'm sure Vanni is on it," Olivia said. "Pops has been in the hospital, and it doesn't look good."

"You didn't tell me that," Aiden said. "When—"

"We haven't had a great deal of time," Olivia told him, feeling irritable at his instant attack. "I can't tell you anything more. Maybe your old friend will have more information."

Chris and Aiden looked at each other. Chris shook his head slightly and held Aiden back while the women walked on.

"I suppose you think you're the expert on how to deal with women," Aiden murmured into his old buddy's ear. "Well, you never met another woman like this one."

"And you're in love with her, and she's in love with you."

Aiden took in a breath and let it out through pursed lips. "Drop it," was all he could think of to say.

"Fine," Chris said. "For now. Has it struck you there's something we're missing? Something or someone big?"

"Hell, yes," Aiden said. "I've been kicking it around the whole time, but I'm not coming up with any ideas. Things happened from when Olivia and I left New York. I don't want to waste time on all the details, but Fish and Moody were heard complaining that they hadn't been given the right instructions. That was when they thought they'd been sent to the wrong motel that first night. They assumed we'd never been there. We had. We just got lucky and avoided them. But how would they know exactly where we were anyway? How would anyone know?"

Chris stuck his hands in his pockets. "I think we're on the same wavelength then. They've been getting information on you, and it can't all have come through Ryan. At least, I don't think so."

"It couldn't. Maybe it isn't such a good idea for Olivia and me to be here. If we're magnets for trouble, I don't want you and Sonnie—and little Anna—to suffer."

Chris slapped a hand on Aiden's shoulder. "You've always been quick enough to make my problems your problems. Who was the guy who showed up in Key West when being around me wasn't such a good idea? You, buddy. Come on, Sonnie's going to feed you. All we can do about the big mystery is keep on watching our backs."

A large room overlooking the black lake was warmly lighted by amber-shaded lamps and a snapping wood fire in a huge stone fireplace. Sitting room, dining room, and a kitchen where red tile and stainless steel dominated, were incorporated into the one space. The living-room and dining-room furniture was simple, oak and a mellow brown leather. A scatter of toys reminded Olivia that a small child was in residence.

"We're renovating the lower floor," Sonnie said when Chris and Aiden caught up. "Three extra bedrooms. They're more or less finished, but there's a lot to be done on the rest of the space. The bathrooms are working, though, so you two should be comfortable down there."

Olivia looked curiously from Chris to Aiden and wondered what had kept them talking in the hallway for so long. She didn't say anything. And she'd rather not consider spending the night with Aiden in the Talons' basement. Or maybe the problem was the reverse; she got a thrill at the thought, and that was hardly appropriate.

"Sit down," Sonnie said and walked behind a kitchen island topped with red tile. "I've got some quiche warming. How about hot chocolate?"

"How about booze?" Chris said.

Olivia and Sonnie smiled at each other.

"Scotch," Aiden said.

"Maybe you should make that two," Sonnie said.

Chris laughed. "I'm already planning on it."

"The second one is for Olivia," Sonnie said and pointed to the oven.

Without a word, Chris went to bend down and take out a quiche. He put it on top of the shiny red stove and smiled at his wife.

Olivia wondered what it would be like to communicate without words. "I'll pass on the scotch," she said, "but water would be wonderful."

"We've got to get to those photos," Aiden said.

"First you have to eat," Sonnie said, rubbing Chris's arm. "I know some of what you've been through. Off with those boots, Aiden. We need to see what's going on with your ankles."

Olivia narrowed her eyes at Aiden's obstinate expression. "Off with the boots," she repeated. "Chris, you hold him down and I'll take 'em off."

"We're going to eat," Aiden protested.

Sonnie found a dishpan and began filling it with warm water. "I'll put Epsom salts in this. You can soak and eat at the same time."

Chris muttered something about soaking heads and dodged a poke from Aiden.

Amid muffled moans and pleas from Aiden for the torture to stop, his boots were removed, the legs of his leather pants rolled up, and his feet and injured ankles plunked into the dishpan beneath the round table. Boss took himself off to a corner and arranged himself as if he were settling in to hibernate.

They ate in a glass-enclosed dining room cantilevered from the rest of the house. Quiche and salad, followed by warm apple pie, had never tasted so good to Olivia. From Aiden's quiet concentration, he thought so, too.

Twice Chris got up and left the room. The second time he returned and carried a coffee pot to the table. "Kitty Fish was on the plane. Nothing on her from any hotels or motels near the airport," he said to Aiden. "We're working on downtown hotels, but nothing so far."

"No," Aiden said, holding up a mug for coffee. "But we aren't surprised, are we? She wouldn't use her own name."

"Who is we?" Olivia said. The annoyance she felt was probably out of line.

"We," Aiden said. "Chris and I. We worked together long enough not to have to do a lot of talking about the obvious."

A little, dark-haired girl wearing a red sleeper pattered into the room at a pace that threatened to land her on her nose. She ran straight to Chris, who caught her up and held her, feet pumping, above his head.

Olivia's annoyance melted. "This must be Anna Talon, who is not quite two."

Everyone but Aiden laughed. Aiden appeared bemused.

"Grinch talk," Sonnie told him. "But you soon will be two, won't you, Anna?"

That earned Anna's mom a solemn nod and two raised fingers.

"Okay, madam," Chris said. "Say hello to your Uncle Aiden or you'll hurt his feelings."

Anna looked around, sighted Aiden at once, and gave him a fierce frown. He said, "Hi, Anna. You've grown, and it's only been a few months since I saw you. And you get prettier and prettier."

The child stuck several fingers in her mouth and smiled around them before hiding her face.

"Flattery gets 'em every time," Chris said. "Cuddle with your eyes closed, or back to bed. Which is it to be?"

Anna settled down on her father's lap and closed her eyes.

Aiden studied Chris and his daughter and remembered a hundred times when he and Chris had ridden as partners around New York City. Chris had been as tough as they came, and still was when he had to be. Back then Aiden couldn't have visualized this moment, or the contented way the other man stroked his daughter's curls.

Was Aiden thinking it might be nice to have a child of his own to hold? Olivia wondered.

This calm, quiet domestic scene could lull a person into forgetting her own life was a circus.

"I can't sit here and wait," Aiden said suddenly. "I'm going to hang out at Sea-Tac. If we don't try to stop her, Kitty'll get back out for sure."

"Chris?" Sonnie's voice filled with alarm.

"Don't worry, he's not going. I've got clearance to have flight manifestos checked."

"Checked for Kitty?" Aiden asked. "She isn't going . . . Hell, yes, she's probably going to use her own name because of her needing to produce ID."

"Our friend Ryan will be calling the shots," Chris pointed out. "He could have her take a bus or rent a car to meet up with him."

"If we don't get real lucky, he's going to get everything he wants," Aiden said. "Unless we find something in Olivia's photos, and she doesn't think we will."

"I didn't see anything," Chris said.

Sonnie got up and started clearing the table.

Chris placed the now-sleeping Anna in Aiden's arms and helped his wife. "Let's see them again, Olivia, please. I'll get a magnifying glass."

"I have a good one in my bag," she told him, trying not to stare at Aiden and the little girl.

Olivia got up and collected her bag. She arranged the photographs on the table in the order they were taken and found her magnifying glass. Boswell roused himself and plodded to flop down again at Olivia's feet.

"We need more light." Chris left the room and returned with a halogen desk lamp.

One by one the photographs were studied by each of the four of them. And one by one, they failed to find anything of note.

"These are for one of those home magazines?" Sonnie said, using a second magnifying glass Chris had produced.

Olivia said, "Yes. I don't like most of the artwork either, but you learn to put your own taste aside and make the best of the material you're given."

"I think we're going to lose this one," Aiden said. "But that could turn out to be good news for us, I guess. If Ryan and Fats figure they're in the clear and do a bunk, we're in the clear. If, if, if. If only we knew why they're going to such lengths."

"To protect themselves, of course," Sonnie said.

Aiden decided not to pursue the point. "Even when it's all over, there'll still be some tough explanations to give."

"Like why you snooped around Ryan's computer, you mean?" Chris asked mildly.

"I'm glad he did," Olivia said at once. "That's selfish, but who knows what would have happened to me?"

"Be nice, Chris," Sonnie said.

Aiden looked much too smug but said, "The other photos are more or less duplicates of these?" as if his mind was only on business.

"Not exactly. Penny wanted some different angles. We could make another set if you think it would be worth it."

"Make another set?" Chris narrowed his eyes at her.

Olivia looked from face to face, from stunned face to stunned face. "Yes, make another set. From the negatives. Why not?"

The atmosphere had changed. Aiden turned Anna toward his

shoulder and covered the back of her head while he leaned toward Olivia. "The negatives aren't with the photos in your grip?" he asked.

"I've got all the negatives with me."

Chris leaped to his feet. "There could be something in the other batch. If we could compare the two we might notice a difference."

"Chris," Sonnie said, "there's no need to shout."

"Oh, no," Olivia said, burying her face. "I just assumed all you were worried about was those photos falling into the wrong hands."

"We *were* worried about that," Aiden said. "You weren't to know, but it would have helped if we'd known we had the negatives and could make copies." Anna stirred on his shoulder, rubbed her nose, but fell deeply asleep again.

Chris bowed his head and said, "I'll go get the other set of prints made."

Olivia was past being tired. Punchy came closer to the way she felt. Chris had taken less than an hour to return with very good quality prints made from the negatives she hadn't thought to mention. Each time she thought about it, she screwed up her face and willed the memory from her mind. Not that there had been any revelations since Chris got back.

"We need to try something different," Aiden said. "Break our concentration, then refocus. Let's just shuffle the whole lot up," Aiden said. "Each set is numbered on the back but if we don't know which is which, we might—"

"Okay, okay," Chris said. "You don't need to draw us a map. Mix 'em up, not that I think it'll make any difference. We aren't going to identify anything useful."

Aiden moved the photographs around like a magician hiding a card. "Look for shots of the area, line 'em up, and give it your all."

That bought him some glares but they all went to work again.

The only sound was of breathing.

Boswell snuffled.

"Anna went down okay, then?" Chris said after a while.

Sonnie nodded, but didn't take her eyes away from the magnifying glass she was using.

"Oh, my." Olivia's scalp tightened. She tapped a photo and looked up. "This was taken in that wide corridor. The one leading to a hall at the back. The glass sculpture was at the opening into the hall. Look at this painting."

Sonnie looked first and said, "I don't like it. And it looks just as bad in both photos."

"Let me see," Aiden said. He pored over the images. "I don't think it's *that* bad."

Chris got up and leaned over Aiden's shoulder. "It stinks. In both versions. You're imagining things, Olivia. There's nothing different."

"I am not imagining anything." She pounded the table with a fist and plopped a third shot down. "Same painting."

This time three heads bent over the exhibits, and two of them began to shake slowly from side to side.

"Got it," Sonnie said excitedly. "This had to be in the second batch."

Olivia pressed her hands to her cheeks. "Look on the other side."

"Second batch," Sonnie said, her eyes shining. "How would someone do that?"

"Not sure," Olivia said. "I'm no expert on things like that. But now I remember mentioning a funny smell, and Penny said she thought one of the bathrooms was being worked on."

"Whoa!" Aiden snatched up the three photos. "Would you two mind sharing your little secret?"

"Someone told me you could do that with Goof Off," Sonnie said. "Do you have Goof Off in England?"

"I don't think so. The smell was a bit like turps—turpentine—but not exactly."

"*Olivia?*" Aiden said.

She looked at him, then at Chris, who wasn't smiling either.

"Someone's started removing paint from the canvas," Sonnie said. "What do you see in that one?" She selected a photo.

"Ugly daubs," Aiden said. "A bunch of shapes."

"Colors?" Olivia asked.

This time it was Chris who said, "Red, purple, lavender, different shades of pink."

Sonnie went directly to the third picture. "Now what do you see?"

Both men studied hard and said, "Same," in unison.

"Check out the bottom right corners," Olivia said, bobbing on her toes. "Where you see a signature on one, and all but the first letters missing on the second. And what about the color in that area on the second one?"

"Geez," Aiden said. "I've got to be tired or I wouldn't have missed that. Gray where it should be red."

"Why would anyone do a thing like that?" Olivia asked. "Ruin a painting with some sort of solvent?"

Aiden ran a hand around the back of his neck. "One painting on top of another. Maybe I'll plead that this is so simple, I didn't even consider looking for it. The authentic painting is underneath. The painting on top is done to hide the real thing. The reason for taking some of the outer coat off is to make sure the real thing's there."

"I didn't see it at the time," Olivia murmured. "I wasn't aware of anything but the shots Penny Biggles wanted. The place was really quiet. There was the smell, of course, but it didn't mean anything much at the time."

"This is great," Chris said. "Or it is as long as Ryan sees it, too. If he keeps up the pattern, he won't take a hike without trying to make sure these don't get into official hands. Since the negatives aren't with the photos Kitty lifted, he'll have to assume we have them. He's obviously involved with whatever went on there."

"Art theft, presumably," Aiden said, and was once again aware of a very important missing piece of the puzzle. "You and Penny must have interrupted them, Olivia. But if they took off without the painting, I don't know what they'd be so worried about. We need to find out if there's a case on record now."

Chris hummed and looked over the water, where reflected light rocked on wavelets. "The way Fish and Moody have behaved can only mean there's stolen art work involved. We know there is, otherwise Ryan wouldn't be yelling about it in New York and blaming you and Olivia."

"Ryan isn't working with Fish and Moody," Aiden said. "I listened to Ryan and Fats talking about it. Ryan knows every move the London boys make. They don't know a thing about what he's up to or even that he's involved. Then the really weird thing is that Fats doesn't know everything either. He kept trying to get Ryan to tell him why he didn't want Fish and Moody to find out he was around, but Ryan wouldn't say a thing except that's the way he wanted it. And it's all up for grabs unless we can get our hands on either Ryan and Fats, or the other two—or even Kitty—before they all disappear. Thinking about them rolling in stolen bucks and basking on a beach somewhere drives me nuts."

Olivia put her hand on his. "Don't you think the really bad news is that if Ryan and Fats, or any of them, do see that there's evidence, they'll want to make absolutely sure we don't have it, too? They'll come after us, won't they? I'm not sure we can win whatever happens. We should leave, Aiden. We can't risk drawing in those people here."

Aiden looked to Chris, but rather than say yea or nay, Chris said, "We're safe in hoping we've got a few hours before all hell breaks loose—or not. Darn it, this is a crazy-making case. Anyway, there are beds made up downstairs for the two of you. You'll find some clothes to get along with. You'll make do with some of mine, Aiden. Sleep. I'll wake you up early and we'll see what we've got by then. Go on."

"I'm going to do just one thing first." Aiden got out his cell phone. "I don't want this call traced here." He pressed numbers and covered the mouthpiece. "Don't make a sound."

"It's two in the morning," Chris said. "Who are you calling?"

"The chief's secretary," Aiden told him. "You remember Margy? She often gets in real early."

Chris started to reply, but Aiden shushed him and said, "Good morning, Margy," into the phone. "It's Aiden. I'm okay. I'm glad you're on duty. I was hoping you could give me a rundown on what's happening back there."

Margy didn't say a word.

"Talk to me, Margy," he said gently. "I don't want to put you in a difficult spot, but I need some help. With Vanni at the hospital, and—"

"How could you do this?" Margy said. "How *could* you?" She hung up.

Twenty-three

A clock ticked in Olivia's room. Sonnie had warned that the base-ment of the house wasn't as warm as it should be, but she'd put a down comforter on the bed and Olivia sank deep beneath it, covered her ears, and tried to shut out the relentless sound of the clock.

She wore a borrowed flannel nightie. In the morning she intended to put on an oversized green sweater and khaki cotton pants with a drawstring at the waist. These she had placed on a chair by the bed, ready to grab at a moment's notice. Long woolen socks and someone's pair of discarded tennis shoes would complete the outfit.

Aiden had remained upstairs with Chris for some time after she'd come down, taken a shower, and climbed into bed. Eventually she'd heard his careful footsteps descending the stairs. Obviously he didn't want to wake her up.

The shower had run; he'd gone into the room opposite hers and closed the door.

This was it, the way a heart felt when it was about to break.

They were in an impossible fix, together, but sooner or later it would end, and then what? She hoped, couldn't help hoping, that they wouldn't just walk away from each other, but it wasn't up to her to make the moves.

She turned over and stuck her head out from the comforter to listen. Did anyone still think the moves should only be made by men—anyone other than her mother?

Aiden could really kiss. He did a lot of things just as well.

And thinking about that produced predictable results. Olivia rolled onto her stomach and tried to visualize calming white light flowing through her veins.

What she really visualized wasn't calming. Aiden Flynn naked wasn't likely to calm any woman. The memory of his hands moving over her made certain she couldn't imagine ever sleeping or being calm again.

The clenching around her heart wasn't about sex, it was about meeting a man she already couldn't consider being without.

On the one hand, they were getting a clearer picture of the obstacles they confronted. On the other hand, the clearer the picture became, the more complex and frustrating it also became.

She didn't want to be alone in this room and chasing dead-end thoughts.

The creak she heard could be anything, but she was sure it was Aiden, tossing in bed just as she was.

A door creaked slowly open.

More muffled sounds followed, the kind of sounds feet made when you were trying not to make any noise.

There was a sliding glass door on the lake side of the house. It opened now, and even beneath her quilt, Olivia thought she felt cold air enter the room.

The slider didn't close again. At least, she didn't hear it close.

Aiden had gone outside into the wet night. He was a deeply troubled man who took his responsibilities seriously, and he thought he was responsible for everything bad that had happened while he'd been with her.

Without putting on a light, Olivia threw back the covers and swung her feet over the edge of the bed and into a pair of rubber thongs. The rose-spattered nightie didn't reach her knees, and a pink terrycloth robe Sonnie had left was equally short.

Cinching the robe belt tight, Olivia approached the door and put her ear to a panel to listen. In the distance, water slapped softly at the lake bank.

She opened her door an inch at a time and slipped into an unfinished area with a bare board floor. Puffy, silver-coated insulation showed between open steel studs. The scent there was of fresh wood shavings.

As she'd thought, the sliding door stood open. Spotlights at the back of the house illuminated a long boardwalk leading to the lake and thirty or so feet on either side, but didn't penetrate the deeper darkness.

Rain fell. Not heavy, soaking rain, but fine mist, and the night had grown bone-cold.

Olivia stepped outside and hesitated. He must want to be alone. He was wrong not to include her, to admit that two brains were better than one, but then, he was a man.

Now that was an unfair thought.

She peered in every direction but saw no sign of him.

That sliver of moon still rode in the sky, peering through a hole in the diaphanous clouds. Olivia thought she saw a movement to the left, where the ground sloped off to the water.

What was the worst he could do to her? Ignore her? Be rude and tell her to go away? She was a big girl—she could take it.

With each step she took, her feet squished in the thongs. Moisture coated her skin and turned her clothing cold and damp. She veered away from the boardwalk, tried to pinpoint the spot where she thought she'd seen Aiden.

There was no sign of him now.

She reached the water's edge and searched in either direction. Trees lined the property, forming a black fringe that reached into a padded pewter sky. A boat house and a shed were dimly visible.

Nothing moved but the veil of rain and a breeze through the tall trees, but Olivia felt watched.

Her stomach tightened, and her heart beat too fast to be comfortable. She crossed her arms and turned her back on the house. A few scattered lights showed in the distance, on the opposite side of the lake. The breeze shifted her hair and felt good despite the way the misty rain wetted her neck.

She held her breath, hoping to hear Aiden move, hoping he'd come to her.

He didn't.

The time had passed for worrying about her sodden feet. Olivia began a measured trudge along the edge of the water. Soft ripples bobbled there. She was thousands of miles from home, in a country so very different from her own, and she'd managed the unbelievable feat of meeting a man who had changed her forever.

A figure she knew belonged to Aiden separated from the back of the shed and approached her. His hands were in the pockets of dark pants. If his hair weren't light, she might not have seen him even yet.

There was no doubt that they intended to confront each other in this unlikely place.

Aiden stopped a few feet distant and said, "I don't have a chance, do I? Whether I want to or not, we're going to seek each other out. Maybe I should say I do want to, but I wish I didn't."

"And all I want to do is see you, Aiden, be with you. I know all about the obstacles, but I can't help myself and I'm not going to lie about it."

He started toward her again. "I'm not much for talking a lot. Never have been."

"What man is?" she said.

Aiden stood in front of her now, his hands still in the pockets of his dark sweatpants. The sweatshirt he wore was also a dark color. Even in poor light, it was impossible to avoid seeing a face she couldn't forget if she tried. The profusion of silver jewelry had been discarded. Only the single gold ring in his left ear remained.

Could she even hope to know him long enough to get past the wall of enigma he carried? Did she want to?

"It's true, isn't it?" he said. "Women want to discuss feelings. Men just want to feel. Or maybe I'm being too generous to my side. I don't want complications. I've never had any kind of commitment to a woman, and the thought of starting one now scares me."

Just hearing him talk about it, admit that she was on his mind, gave her hope. "Would it scare you if we weren't in a . . . We're both in jeopardy. Would it make a difference if we weren't?"

"We're going to be soggy as hell shortly. We should go in." He pulled his shoulders up to his ears. "You really want to talk, Olivia?"

"If you do."

"That's not fair."

"Okay, yes, I want to talk."

He wiped a hand across his face. "Let's not go inside and risk waking anyone up. There's a bench in the boathouse. Not too luxurious, but real private."

Olivia took hold of his elbow and steered him in the direction of the boathouse. "It's beautiful here," she said. "One of those parts of the world you don't hear about—or think about where I come from, but golly, is it gorgeous."

"Yeah, it is," he agreed. "I'm a city guy myself, but I can appreciate beauty when I see it. You're beautiful."

She forgot to take her next step and almost stumbled.

Aiden held her arm tightly until she found her balance. "Well, you are. And you don't have any vanity about it."

"Thank you, but we'd better take your temperature. I'm okay to look at, but beautiful is something I'll never be."

"Don't argue with me. Every time I look at you, I . . . I want you."

"Just like that? You want me? So matter-of-fact."

Aiden guided her up the steps to the empty boathouse, to the promised bench near the end that opened to the water. He waited until she sat down, then joined her. "It is a matter of fact. I didn't say I was smooth or glib. What I've said, I mean, and it couldn't be more inconvenient. Even when you first arrived and I didn't know who you were, I felt something."

Olivia wrapped the damp robe more tightly around her.

"You don't have to say anything about that," he said. "We both realize we're caught in a highly dangerous mess we've got to find a way out of—and that it'll take careful planning."

"It smells of tar in here," she said.

"Uh-huh. Reminds me of the docks in New York."

"You like it there, don't you?"

He sat very straight and said, "I like it well enough. Olivia, what I did—what happened that first night on the road—was wrong. It shouldn't have happened, and it was all my fault."

"And you regret it." She would have snatched the words back if she could.

"I—I didn't exactly say that."

Olivia rested her elbows on her knees and her jaw on her fists.

"I didn't say it because it's not true. Do you believe a man and woman can live together and be happy? Not just happy—happier together than if they were apart?"

The question caught her by surprise. "If I didn't believe it, I'd be very sad."

He fell silent. Water swayed, black and glossy, below them.

"I think I know what you're trying to say," she told him. "If you like, I'll make it easy for you."

"How? By second-guessing what I'm thinking?"

"You're prickly."

"I'm caught, dammit. And I don't know if I like being caught and want to stay that way, or if I should run like hell."

As if she could tell him the right answer. She didn't know it, for either of them. "I can't help you, Aiden. I can't help myself." But she did know what she thought she wanted and had at least an inkling of what she'd face without it.

"Okay," he said. "Let's try this another way. Do you think some people are meant to live alone?"

"Yes." How could she say anything else and be honest? Her own father had probably married because it was the thing to do. To Olivia, he had always seemed an irritated man who tolerated domestic life with barely restrained disdain.

Aiden slapped his knees and stood up. "Do you have to be so honest?"

"You wouldn't like it if I weren't."

"Look—" He began pacing back and forth in front of her.

"Be careful," Olivia told him. "You're too close to the edge."

"I'm good on my feet. And I grew up a long time ago."

Olivia pulled her own feet onto the bench beside her and covered them with the nightie and robe. She wasn't going to enter a sniping session about whether or not showing she cared was motherly behavior.

"I'm sorry," Aiden said. "I guess I wanted you to tell me no man or woman can be complete without a partner."

"No, you didn't, Aiden. You want to escape from all this, but at the same time you're afraid you may regret it later. That doesn't make you different from anyone else. A lot of people want everything but don't want anything to have a price. And we're all terrified of missing the best opportunity ever to come our way."

"Okay, okay." He sat down. Olivia was behaving so well, and he was being a creep—and an ass to boot. How did a man learn to follow his heart without messing with his head? He needed his head for his work. But his work was second to Olivia in importance.

Aiden felt cold. Not just the cold from being wet and out in the elements. This was the kind of cold that attacked when you came face-to-face with a truth that could change your life—and you didn't know if the result would be good. He didn't want to want her so damn much.

"Why can't women be satisfied with having a really good affair?" he said, and was only mildly shocked at himself.

She touched the end of her robe belt to her nose and kept her eyes lowered.

"We're not kids. We can cope with thinking about things like that, can't we?" he asked.

"You obviously can. I'm not sure it works for me. I'm in danger here, Aiden. It wouldn't be hard for me to give you enough power to make or break me." She gave a short laugh. "I already have. You know how I feel. Women have affairs just as often as men, don't they? The answer to that is obvious. Some are satisfied, some aren't. Are you asking me to have an affair with you?"

Was he? "I feel like a worm, or maybe something lower."

"Is it what *you* want, Aiden?"

"We're hanging out in the wind. The best thing I can say about what's happened in this case so far is that no one's gotten badly hurt. If we were dealing with normal people—I should say normal criminals—I know the story would be different."

She settled the back of one hand over her mouth.

"Olivia, will you be patient with me? Will you give me a chance to work my way through what I feel and decide if I can even be what you deserve?"

Although he waited, she didn't answer him.

"A man isn't a man until he can take responsibility for the way he is. If he's ever going to be free of the stuff we all carry around, different stuff for different people, he has to forgive anyone who made him second-guess who he is and what he's worth. I'm not going to bore you with old stories, but I am telling you I've still got forgiving and understanding to do."

She tapped her hand against her parted lips.

"Olivia—"

"I understand you better than you know. For what it's worth, for a man who doesn't like to talk about what he's feeling, you do a great job."

"Give me some space, at least until we're out of danger. Let me figure out what's going on all around us, then see how I feel when it's just life as usual?"

"Is it ever life as usual for you?"

"I deserve that," he said. If she wanted him to declare himself now, then she wanted more than he could offer. "It quiets down to a dull drone sometimes. But in the current case, if I'm tied to you, all wound up in you, that could get in the way when I need a clear head to make a decision that could mean life or death."

"And you think it's going to come to that?" Her eyes, when she looked up at him, were black and glittering with tears. "Of course you do. We're outlaws. Ryan Hill never expected you to become involved, but he must be glad you did because you're making it easier for him. If we can't stop him, he's going to walk away like an innocent man."

Aiden didn't like the fury he felt. He stepped closer to Olivia, "Don't make that suggestion to me again. It's not going to happen. I'm going to keep you safe and get us out of this."

"But while you do, you want me anywhere but where you are?"

"No, *dammit*." He took her by the shoulders. Keeping his hands off her any longer wasn't an option. "What I want is exactly what you say people like me want. I want everything, but I don't want to pay for it—not yet. Maybe I want to lease with an option to buy." And maybe he couldn't stop sabotaging himself with his mouth. "No, that's not what I mean. Help me, Olivia. Be my strength and my conscience."

Taking one of his hands from her shoulder, she held it so tightly that the bones rubbed together. "You never told me what the old scars on your hands are from."

The comment distracted him. He shook his head. "Barbed wire. I got hung up on barbed wire."

"In New York?"

"Uh, no, on top of a fence at home. It doesn't matter. I was being an ass—again."

"Your strength and your conscience?" She didn't take her eyes from his. "Just do what you have to do to get us safely through this."

"That's my strength."

She nodded and finally looked away. She looked away and held his hand to her cheek. "I can't be your conscience. Just wait and see, Aiden. And don't worry about me. I'm not ashamed to tell you that I'll take whatever you want to give. Let's go inside. We both need sleep if we're going to be sharp for what's coming."

Not fair, Aiden thought. *Why didn't she get mad and tell him she didn't want him anymore?*

He was tired, so damned tired he didn't want to even remember what had to be dealt with. Swinging a leg over, he sat astride the bench and tried to gather Olivia against him.

She resisted.

"Come on," he murmured. "Let me hold you."

"Because you feel guilty? I don't want you to feel guilty, and I don't want you to throw me crumbs if you do."

"Ouch. Maybe I don't deserve that for being straightforward."

Maybe he didn't. "Forgive me. It's hard to be objective when you've fallen in love at the most inconvenient time imaginable." Let him deal with that, Olivia thought. Sure she was being cruel, but she was hurting, and human.

"Quit fighting me," he said and wouldn't stop pulling her toward him until she gave up. "Yeah, I like your head on my shoulder, sweetheart. I like hearing you say you love me, too. I like it a lot."

She closed her eyes. He liked it, but wasn't ready to return the sentiment. He probably never would be ready.

"Look at me, Olivia. Please."

"No." Wrapping her arms around as much of him as they'd reach, she held on and kept her face buried in his neck.

His big, sensitive hands combed through her damp hair, pushed under the collar of the robe to her back, and smoothed her shoulders. Then, with palms and flattened fingers, he caressed her from collarbone to waist and finally rested his fingertips on her breasts. "Look at me," he repeated.

She did look, and saw intense need and desire in his eyes. The sharply defined angles of his face were set and tensed. He kissed her, and still his eyes didn't completely close. She saw how they lost focus behind slitted lids.

This was power of a kind. She had the power to excite him—something she would never have believed such a short time ago.

Olivia closed her own eyes and gave herself up to feeling, not thinking.

"Stay with me," he said when he paused to let them both breathe. "Don't go. Even if I do things that make you want to leave, don't go. Beat on me, threaten me, make me see I need you."

"You ask too much." Beneath the sweatshirt, his skin felt hot. The texture of the hair on his chest delighted her. The way he sucked air through his teeth when she squeezed his nipples incited and aroused her.

"You've got to promise you won't let me sabotage myself."

His chest hair was both rough and smooth and became a narrow trail to the waist of the sweatpants. "All I can do is ask you to let me be whatever you are, wherever you are," she said. "If you're lonely, I want to be lonely, too—lonely with you until you decide to let me in again. And if you decide to go away, I want to go with you. I want to live inside you and have you live inside me. Now doesn't all that help a man with the jitters? Probably doesn't even make sense to you."

"It makes sense." He spun her around on the bench and sat her facing him, a leg on either side, just like him. His attempts to hike down the robe were futile. "Not very modest," he said.

Olivia smiled at him. She gripped his hard thighs and leaned to nuzzle his neck. "The morning's going to come fast," she whispered, licking his salty skin.

"I don't think I can go in without making love to you."

"Sure you can. And you will if I insist, won't you?"

Aiden raised her knees and smoothed the backs of her calves.

"Not now," she told him, shuddering. "That destroys me."

He smiled. Destroying her in the way she meant had a lot of appeal.

When he played his fingertips on the skin behind her knees, she let him know he'd found a new erogenous zone. She snatched at his wrists when he concentrated on the insides of her thighs.

"Relax," he murmured. "This is all in the name of research. And you've got to sacrifice your bit."

Olivia wasn't cold anymore. Her body burned. It was turn-the-tables time. She thrust her hands between his legs and pulled gently.

"No you don't," Aiden said. He caught her around the waist and lifted her onto his thighs. He undid the robe and lifted the nightie until her breasts were naked. She wore a pair of the panties they'd bought—a red thong that would seem out of character if he didn't already know that his lady was much more than she seemed.

He bent his head and kissed her full flesh. Again and again he kissed until she captured his head and fastened his mouth where she wanted it to be. The sound that escaped her, a softly keening sound, pleased him. It didn't satisfy him.

"Stop," she said suddenly, raising his face and holding it between her hands. "Don't talk. Don't say a thing," she told him.

The sweatpants and thin silk panties might as well not have been there. Aiden raised his hips the slightest fraction, but Olivia gritted her teeth. Her decision was made. She balanced on her toes, and with his willing help, worked his pants down. Seeing him spring free swelled her breasts, dried her mouth, set up an ache where she needed him to be.

She held him, guided him into her, wrapped her legs around him, and crossed her ankles behind him.

Any closer and there'd be no knowing where she ended and he began. He arched his back, let his head hang back, and moved with her.

Vaguely she heard the water caressing the dark confines that welcomed it. A lone gull cried, declared its freedom.

Aiden entered and withdrew from Olivia with restrained strokes that dragged hissing breaths from both of them. He held back his desperation, gave her the time he knew she needed to get as much as he could give her.

Her fingernails, digging into his biceps, brought her his complete— almost complete—attention.

With tears standing in her eyes, she smiled at him, rose over him, and set her own relentless pace. It was Olivia who controlled the pace and orchestrated his climax, and her own. When she had him groaning, it wasn't enough for her. She reached down again to support and squeeze him. He barely held back a shout and released his hold on her to remove her hands before she destroyed him.

"Aiden," she wailed. "Oh, Aiden."

Locked together, still moving, they slid sideways. He did his best to hook a leg around the bench, but failed.

Olivia squealed, and then laughed.

"*Don't* laugh," he ordered. "Do you have any idea what—oh, hell."

The only thing he accomplished as they landed in a heap on rough boards was to make sure he was still beneath Olivia.

They lay there, gasping, chuckling, then trying not to chuckle, and inevitably starting to kiss all over again. Olivia cradled his head, and the kisses grew more urgent, and they rocked together, going deeper and deeper.

She was wonderful, wicked but wonderful, and if he did decide to leave, she could go with him. And if he was lonely, she could be lonely, too—with him.

What did that mean?

The little muscles inside her squeezed him, pulled on him with the throbbing rhythm of her own release, and he could do nothing but empty himself into her.

Twenty-four

Ryan took hold of the small finger on Fats's right hand and said, "You have caused me too much trouble." He held the hand down and forced the finger back until Fats opened his mouth to yell. *"Don't* forget where you are, chickenshit." With a final jerk, he released the finger.

Fats wiped his sweating brow and said, "Like hell, I've caused you trouble." He stuffed both hands quickly under the table. "Someone's finally making some smart moves, and you're pissed off because it's not you."

"Let's get this straight," Ryan said, facing Fats across a yellow, Formica-topped table in a diner near O'Hare. "Fish and Moody got arrested at the airport because you slipped a gun into Moody's pocket."

"I didn't want them in Seattle messing with my plans. And the piece is clean. No way of tracing it to us."

"To you, you mean. And what exactly are *your* plans?" Ryan said, slamming a fist down on top of the bottle of beer Fats had been about to reach for, and smirking when Fats jumped. "Your plans seem to have changed, haven't they? What happened to docile little Kitty, who was going to wait for you in Seattle, holding the bag for you to grab? And while we're on the subject, where did I figure in those plans?"

"I was going to hand it all to you in a fancy package," Fats said, squirming now. "Honest I was. You didn't want to run the risk of Fish and Moody finding out you were around and then putting the extra squeeze on you. That's what the secrecy's all about, right? So all I did was to try to make sure you got what you wanted."

"Crap. I'm the boss. You work for me. I make the decisions, you carry them out. But you decided you wanted to be The Man and you fucked up. Instead of me keeping a back seat and pulling the strings, you've made sure I've got to run the risk of coming out in the open. Did you think I'd like finding out Fish and Moody are back in New York? Unsupervised? How safe do you think it is for them to be running around trying to pull themselves out of trouble with the big shots who paid them big bucks for nothing? And Kitty? Where the fuck is Kitty?"

Ryan had perfected the art of hit-and-run. He hit the opponent hard, then ran before there was any time for recovery. Well, Fats had that number and he wasn't falling for it again. What facts he needed and didn't have, he'd make up.

"Kitty's in Seattle," he said, cursing that fickle piece of tail. "She's holed up in a motel. With the photos. Of course, we know Flynn and the woman must have had a good look before she checked her bag, but they didn't know what they were looking for, and if it's there at all, it's so damn subtle, no one's ever going to pick it up."

Ryan gave a passing waitress the eye. He winked at her, and she smiled right back. Worked every time, Fats thought. Ryan tossed tiny crumbs, and the birds came running.

The waitress came to the table and Ryan said, "I want another beer and some ice cream, a big bowl of vanilla ice cream. Can you arrange that for me, sweetness?"

"One beer and big bowl of vanilla ice cream coming right up." She checked her hair as she walked away.

"Nice ass," Ryan said.

"We don't have to worry about Moody and Fish," Fats said. "They'll probably get themselves killed. If they don't, they'll hightail it back to London and pray they aren't followed."

"And they'll start hatching another plot guaranteed to make my life hell. They'll have to because you don't play games with the kind of people they've been dealing with and hope to get away with it. They're stupid, but they're not that stupid."

Fats rested an arm along the back of his bench seat. One-handed, he tapped a cheroot from a pack, pulled it all the way out with his teeth, and lit up.

"I thought you gave those up," Ryan said.

Fats shook his head "Nah, like 'em too much." They made him feel sick, but he needed any help he could get to look tough. "It would sure help if I knew why you're hiding out from those two guys."

"I'm not hiding out from anyone," Ryan snapped. "So drop that, will you? I don't think you've told me what Kitty's up to, other than waiting in a motel. What's she waiting for?"

"For me to join her," Fats lied, pulling on the cheroot. His palms were so wet, he couldn't risk raising his bottle of beer. "With Flynn and his buddy Talon there, she's afraid they might find her. She's going to move to another motel. But she trusts me to get her out safely."

"Is that a fact? So let's go."

This was what Fats had feared. He couldn't have Ryan finding out that his partner didn't have an idea in hell where Kitty Fish was at this moment. "I'm waiting for her to call with the name of the new motel and a room number. But I don't want that you should put yourself on the line, Ryan. All it would take would be a slip from her, and Fish and Moody would know where to find you. They'd be all over you."

Ryan stared at him. "Kitty knows what she wants, and Rupert Fish isn't it. I say we make a start and get a flight to Seattle. Unless she isn't there anymore. Is that the way it is? She's taken the bag and moved on—because you were damn fool enough to put *all* the winning cards in her hands?"

"No way," Fats protested. "Kitty wouldn't do that. She's too scared. I say we wait for her to contact me here. We don't want to go out there blind."

Ryan looked at his watch. "We'll give it two hours. Then, if there's no word, we go anyway. Her silence will tell us what's in her tiny mind. She'll be planning to take us, Fatsy, and I don't get taken by anyone."

"But we shouldn't leave until we hear from her," Fats said, desperate. "Seattle isn't that small."

"I'm not planning a sightseeing tour. Seattle's waking up, and if you're right she'll be calling before long. I'll be making a couple more calls to the precinct. Clear a few things. Check some stuff to back up my theories. Then it'll be time to surprise Mrs. Fish again. Something tells me she's going to be oh-so cooperative this time."

Fats's gut didn't feel so good. "I gotta take a leak," he lied.

"Beer," the well-built waitress said, sliding the bottle in front of Ryan. "A big bowl of vanilla ice cream, *and,* just in case it isn't quite sweet enough, some extra goodies to choose from." The ice cream was joined by condiment dishes filled with syrups, nuts, and small candies. The waitress, whose nametag revealed she was *Betty*, bent low to Ryan and whispered, "The goodies are on the house."

Ryan gave her the long, serious, I-want-to-know-you look and squeezed her hand briefly.

The woman was fair. She turned pink and said, "You're very welcome."

Once she'd moved away, Ryan ignored the "goodies" and wolfed the ice cream down plain. He used the beer as a chaser, wiped his hands, and said, "Watch this and learn."

All Fats saw was Ryan sitting back in his seat, inclining his head, and looking weird.

Betty arrived beside them at a breathless trot. "You're fast," she said.

"Not unless I want to be," Ryan said in a voice he'd never used around Fats before. "I wish I didn't have to go, but I've got an appointment."

Betty nodded.

Ryan stood up, wiped his hands on a clean napkin, and threw a wad of bills on the table.

"You don't have to do that," she said, moistening her lips.

"I want to." Ryan congratulated himself on being a perfect judge of character. The lady was horny. "What time do you get off?" he said.

Her eyes sparked. "Late."

"The later the better for some things," he told her. "I'll be back, babe."

Fats caught up with him outside. "Are you off your rocker?" he said. "Drawing attention to yourself like that? If someone comes looking, she'll be able to give a perfect description."

"I sure hope so," Ryan said.

Twenty-five

Olivia stood before the Talons' window and looked over Lake Washington. A layer of fog hid the surface of the water, but the sun struggled to appear. Chris had left half an hour earlier promising that the fog would "burn off," and the mountain would "come out." According to Sonnie, he meant Mount Ranier.

"Try and relax a bit," Aiden said very quietly, coming to stand beside her. He put an arm around her waist. "Chris will be getting back to us just as soon as he can."

"Yes." She ought to be thinking of nothing other than clearing her own and Aiden's names—that and getting themselves out of danger. Olivia had much more on her mind.

"I've got bruises," Aiden said. "On my tush and probably in other places, too."

She looked at him sharply, then smiled. "Evidently your balance beam days are over. Better choose another event."

"I was thinking about the trampoline. What d'you think? Could lead to some high-flying experiences."

Olivia scrunched up her face. "Sounds like a good way to break something, and I think it might hurt you—a lot."

"Breakfast," Sonnie said. "C'mon, sit down. I've got to."

Olivia and Aiden gave Sonnie their full attention at once. "You sit down," Aiden said. "You don't have to wait on us. Sit there." He pointed to a chair.

Sonnie sat, sighing as she did so. Promptly, Anna left her quiet game with a hairless doll and climbed on her mother's lap. Sonnie kissed the top of the child's head.

"I love muffins," Olivia said, sitting down, too. Watching Sonnie brought a rush of feelings, warm, sweet, and longing feelings. "Have a muffin, Aiden. This is going to be a busy day. Better top up, as my father says."

They ate, and drank very good coffee. Anna stroked Sonnie's belly and frowned while she pressed an ear there to listen.

Each time Olivia looked up, she found Aiden watching her. No eyes should be that blue, or that capable of disconcerting a woman.

"All those earrings and things you wear," Olivia said, desperate to lighten the mood, "they just clip on really?"

"Sort of," he said.

"Wally Loder, master of disguise," Sonnie said and chuckled. "You should have seen him the first time I met him as Wally in Key West. He came into the bar Chris's brother and his partner own. He was so surly, he scared me. After that Wally Loder was everywhere, getting into all kinds of places in all kinds of disguises."

"You're giving away trade secrets," Aiden said around a mouthful of cinnamon muffin.

"I don't suppose you've had a chance to see all of his cars, have you, Olivia?"

She cleared her throat. "I had the pleasure of riding in a beautiful chartreuse Cadillac."

"Aiden! You did it? You had that thing painted chartreuse?"

He looked pained and reached for Anna, who went willingly into his arms. "It was your husband who said chartreuse would be a good color. He never appreciated my pink Mustang. Vanni always calls it the Pink Panther."

Sonnie held her tummy and laughed. "Maybe Vanni gets muddled up between pink panther and pink pony."

"Oh, sure he does."

Olivia was aware of the history these people shared, a history in which she had played no part. She wanted to be part of the history Aiden would make in future.

The phone rang and Sonnie pushed herself up from her chair. She picked up on the third ring, listened, and said, "Love you, too, honey. Nothing yet. Okay. Aiden, it's Chris for you."

Aiden went to the phone, and Olivia couldn't sit still. She followed and stood a few feet from him, watching the expressions on his face.

"Got it," he said after listening for what seemed to Olivia an eternity. "No, I sure don't have any better ideas. I'll have to be on that plane. Of course you can't come, I know that. You're doing everything you can here. Nothing on Ryan or Fats? Where d'you think Fish and Moody went in New York? No. Vanni can take over there. He's chewing his fingernails down waiting, anyway. Yeah, see you at the airport tonight."

"What plane?" Olivia said as soon as he'd hung up.

"A Kitty Fish is booked on this evening's flight to London. Chris thinks, and I agree, that she intends to run for safety there, then hold up her husband and his partner, and Fats and Ryan. She's grabbed the evidence and taken off—that's obvious."

Olivia touched the scars on the back of his right hand. "Couldn't they all just be allowed to get on with it? Perhaps they've lost interest in us now."

"Dreamer," Aiden said. "Ryan Hill's got the most powerful police force in this country looking for us. Where would we hide? It's my turn to go after them now. I'm going to help Ryan put a noose around his own neck. Then we'll have a chance to clear ourselves. I want my job—and my reputation—back."

He was right and Olivia knew it. "Of course that's what must be done. *Fiddlesticks.* We'd better get reservations on that flight."

"You're not going. Sonnie and Chris will keep you safe here."

When Vanni finally called, Aiden had been playing with Chris's computer in his study, and trying for an hour to get the courage to go downstairs and find Olivia. He knew she was down there because he'd seen her return from a walk.

Olivia was angry with him.

"What made you call Margy?" Vanni said.

"I wanted to get hold of you. She wouldn't listen to a word I said."

Vanni sighed. "It's the pits here, partner. I'm steering a course through an ocean of people who think you're Public Enemy Number One. Ryan's got 'em brainwashed, including Margy. Use your head and don't call the station again. Risk my cell phone, if you want to, but don't give anyone here a clue about where you are."

"I thought Margy would be on my side. I thought she'd believe me."

"She will when we can tell her everything. Listen, Ryan's in the Chicago area. He checked in and didn't even bother to cover up the fact. He reckons Fats has turned rogue on him and he needs to pull him in—only he doesn't know where he is. Evidently Fats didn't tell him you'd left for Seattle because he didn't mention it."

"That's something," Aiden said. Through the study door, he caught sight of a shadow on the wall at the top of the basement stairs. Olivia was listening, and there was nothing he could do about it. He filled Vanni in on Kitty and what he intended to do about her.

"I'm going to join you," Vanni said.

"No," Aiden said, grimacing. "Absolutely not, Vanni. You disappear now, and they're going to figure out it's because of me."

"This is taking too long. It's driving me nuts."

"How's Pops?" Maybe he could shake Vanni out of it, Aiden thought.

Too much silence followed before Vanni said, "Touch and go. If you feel like praying, we can use all the help we can get."

Olivia detached herself from the shadows and moved around to sit on the foot of the stairs.

"Stay put," Aiden said to Vanni, looking at Olivia's profile. It was too late for him; he didn't just want her body anymore, he wanted the woman. "Vanni, you can help me most by staying where you are and letting me know everything you find out. Fish and Moody have headed back to New York. Chris said he was getting the flight details to you."

"I've got them," Vanni said. "I'm not worried about those two. I am worried about you."

"I'm thinking about Pops," Aiden said. He didn't like using the old man to distract Vanni. "Will you tell him that? Tell him I expect to drown in Mama's gravy and his best Chianti when I get back to New York. Got that?"

Vanni didn't sound convincing when he said he'd got it, but he hung up the phone.

This was one of those times when a guy had to wait for the woman to come to him. With very little of his mind on the task, Aiden idly logged back on to his own e-mail account. He'd done so several times that day and found nothing but junk mail.

More junk mail had shown up.

Olivia got up and walked slowly into the study. She leaned on the wall just inside the door. "It's nice outside," she said. "Even if it is cold."

Aiden smiled at her, grateful that she was talking to him again, and more than grateful that she was accepting the wisdom of his going to England without her.

He got up and quietly closed the door.

Olivia put more distance between them.

"D'you think that will stop me?" he asked. Without taking a step, he shot an arm around her and hauled her against him. He bent her backward and kissed her, and his body stiffened. She tried to resist him by refusing to respond. Holding her limp form only whipped him up more. He wrapped her in both arms and kissed her until she gave in, crossed her forearms behind his neck, and kissed him back.

As abruptly as she'd responded, she summoned enough strength to leave him in no doubt that she wanted to stop.

Aiden released her, but couldn't wipe away his smirk. He wasn't alone in this growing obsession. "I'll be back for you, Olivia," he said. "I'm not sure how long I'll be gone. I wouldn't go at all if I didn't have to."

Meaning what? Olivia wondered. "Why are you going?"

"The action's moving that way. I think Ryan and Fats will go to England, too. Sooner or later I'll get my chance to bring them in. Then I'll prove our case."

I, I, I. He was excited now, excited about the chase, but he didn't think she could be of any help to him, even though she had every bit as much to win or lose as he did.

"Is that something you want to read?" Olivia said, indicating Chris's screen.

Aiden saw Vanni's address and moved the cursor to click and open the post. "He's not missing an angle," Vanni wrote. What followed was an excerpt from a post supposedly written by MustangMan, alias Aiden Flynn, and addressed to Ryan Hill: *"Nice of you to send some company along. I hate being lonely. I get bored. Now I can entertain myself, unless you can think of a reason why I shouldn't. You know what I want."*

In a post using his own e-mail address Ryan had written: *"I've got to move fast. I hope I'm not too late."*

And Vanni added a postscript: *"I only wish I was sure what angle he isn't missing this time. The guy is giving me the creeps."*

Aiden looked at Olivia, who said, "Any idea what Ryan's up to?"

"Nope."

"Ryan pretended to be you. He excerpted something you supposedly wrote and sent it to—"

"Yeah, I know." He studied the screen. "He's setting something up. It's important to him to grind down any scrap of credibility I might have left—not that I appear to have any."

Lunchtime came and went. Olivia couldn't bear sitting around, pretending she was going to be a good little girl and do what Aiden had said she must. Chris had called several times to check on Sonnie and to talk with Aiden, who had moved into his own grim space that didn't include room for any extra baggage. He'd closed her out.

Olivia went to the basement again. She'd arrived with very little, and since Kitty Fish had stolen the suitcase, leaving with just as little was guaranteed.

She let herself out onto the boardwalk, and Boswell came around the side of the house to join her. He grinned. Some might argue that dogs couldn't grin, but he definitely did.

"Come along," Olivia told him. "Can you swim?"

He trotted beside her to the water's edge. She freed a stick that protruded from beneath a long piece of driftwood, then hesitated. "It's awfully cold, Boswell."

"That won't bother him," Aiden said, making her jump. "He loves to swim."

She watched his deceptively casual approach. His strides were long, and he covered a great deal of ground very quickly.

Olivia turned back to the water and threw the stick. Boswell waded after it, showing no sign of discomfort.

"You like him, don't you?" Aiden said.

"I'm British," Olivia told him.

He nodded, and chuckled. "And that's all the answer I should need, of course."

Just being near him started a weak feeling in her legs. His long, lean, strong body had an aura that was tangible to Olivia. He didn't have to touch her to make her feel touched. The fragile, exposed sensation crept into her belly and sought out deep places.

But she would not allow him to decide what was best for her. Her seat on the evening's one flight to London was booked. So was the taxi that would wait for her on the street above the Talons' property.

While Aiden watched, Boss swam, snatched the stick between his teeth, and headed toward shore. Aiden shouted, "Attaboy." Olivia might think it the most normal thing in the world for her to be comfortable with the animal, but Boss made most people nervous. She met the dog and wrestled over the stick until Boss decided to let her have it. He started back out and she threw the stick again.

"I'm going to walk a bit," Aiden said. "Will you come?"

She kept her face to the water, but nodded, and eventually joined him. He threaded her hand beneath his arm and held it tight to his side.

"How can you look so well turned out in someone else's sweat-suit?" she asked. "These togs make me into a sack."

"They don't fit you. The sweatsuit does fit me—more or less. And I like the way you look. I like it that you don't fuss over yourself."

"I do sometimes," she told him. "I can quite enjoy dressing up on occasion."

Aiden smiled to himself. In other words, he was not to jump to conclusions about her. "I'm sure you can. I hope you and I can get dressed up and go somewhere special before too long. Like regular human beings."

She didn't answer. Boss's arrival gave her an excuse to shift the attention from herself. "You are a wonderful dog," she told the self-satisfied, wet fifth wheel. "You can do anything. And you are so handsome."

Panting, for all the world as if he was preening himself in the glow of Olivia's praise, Boss pranced ahead. He stopped every few strides to make sure they were following, then ran up the steps to the boathouse.

"The boathouse," Aiden said, taking Olivia's fingers to his lips and nibbling her knuckles. "No fool, my dog. He can probably smell traces of passion."

"Don't," Olivia said.

Aiden ducked to see her bowed face and put an arm around her. "You're embarrassed," he said, swaying her against him. "I keep thinking I've turned you into a woman of the world, but it doesn't stick. I guess you need more lessons."

"*Aiden.*"

"*Aiden,*" he mimicked, observing how Boss ran in and out of the boathouse, showing his teeth all the way to his considerable molars, and panting encouragement. "He wants us to go in there."

"We're not," Olivia said firmly. "Get down here, Boswell. Cover your teeth, they're blinding me."

The dog disappeared inside again. "Now look what you've done," Aiden said. "You've embarrassed him, too. I'll just have to go up and see if I can soothe his feelings. He's not as young as he used to be."

Olivia wanted to go, too. With every step Aiden climbed, she longed to climb with him, but if she did, the outcome was inevitable. They might not actually make love, given the fact that Sonnie was up and about in the house—and because there were serious plans to pull off in the near future—but they wouldn't be able to resist each other completely.

Aiden went inside the boathouse.

For several moments Olivia stood at the bottom of the steps, several moments before she followed him.

He stood at the lake end of the building, looking over the polished steel water. The sun hadn't stuck around, and although the fog had dissipated, a swell rose but never broke the surface, creating a mysterious softness that threatened to become fuzzy again with the already fading light.

Olivia peered around. "Where's Boswell?"

"Swimming," he said. "It's cold. Go on back to the house and get something hot to drink. Sonnie needs company, too."

His abrupt change in mood didn't go unnoticed by Olivia. "Sonnie's resting. I don't feel like going in yet."

He looked into her eyes. "I told you to go inside."

Olivia felt shocked. She also felt annoyed. "What's the matter with you?"

"Probably nothing. Please do as you're told. It's for your own good."

A splashing preceded the appearance of Boswell, who bobbed up from beneath the planking that stretched above the water inside the boathouse. Instantly, Aiden dropped down and stretched out until he could hold the dog's collar and take something from his mouth.

Olivia advanced slowly, step by step. "Is he all right? I'm not a ninny, you know. Let me help with him."

Aiden stared at her with narrowed eyes. "Please, go to the house and call Chris. Ask him to come. Say I could use his help."

A cell phone stuck out of Aiden's back pocket. "Do you know his number by heart?" she asked.

"Yes. But it's beside the phone."

"I'll use your cell phone and you can tell me what number to call."

That earned her another hostile stare. "Okay, have it your way. Sit on that bench and don't move. Don't say a word until I tell you it's okay."

Olivia sat down.

Almost as quickly, she stood up again. What Aiden had taken from Boswell's mouth was a loop of rope. At a command from Aiden, the dog clambered from the water and shook himself mightily, never taking his attention from his master.

Aiden hauled on the rope, making slow progress. He peered beneath the decking, reached underneath, and struggled with something. He hauled again.

Into sight came a sodden, rounded heap. Boswell ran back and forth, setting up a howl that chilled Olivia to the spine. An unearthly howl.

"I want you to get out of here," Aiden said. "For me. Please."

She didn't even let him know she'd heard him. Instead she knelt beside him and reached out to take hold of the rope that encircled the dark, shiny mass. "Two are stronger than one," she said. "I can pull, too."

Aiden's response was to push her aside roughly enough to send her sprawling. He dragged on the line, towed in what it secured, stood up, and braced his legs to heave the burden out of the water.

"Oh," Olivia said. "Oh, Aiden. It's—it's covered with blood." The water that gushed onto the wood spread a rusty stain. The shininess she'd seen was congealed blood spread over a big sack tied at the top.

"There's a body in there," she whispered. "A dead body. I'm sure of it."

"If you get bludgeoned—maybe—stuffed in a bag and submerged in water for however long, I guess you might be dead." He sounded different, cold and calm. "Now are you ready to get away from here?"

"I'm ready to have you stop treating me like an hysterical female. Turn it over. We don't have time to waste here. This is sad, but let's deal with it and move on. It's nothing to do with us."

His next stare held amazement, but he did turn the body over. The sack had been secured over the head, and even though it was sodden, it was evident that whoever was inside had done a lot of bleeding.

Aiden gave Olivia his phone. "I'm tampering with evidence, but I don't know this is a death until I see it, do I?"

"Of course not," Olivia agreed. Her gag reflex was kicking in.

He wrenched the rope from the top of the bag and peeled it down. Olivia couldn't remain standing. She slid to sit on the dock.

Aiden used his hand to carefully wipe mud and blood from the corpse's face and short gray hair.

Fats Lemon's eyes were open.

The phone rang as they entered the house. "Yeah," Aiden said into the mouthpiece.

"It's Vanni. Get to the computer."

"I'm on my way."

He ran up the stairs with Olivia pounding behind him. He'd left

Chris's computer on, and he dashed into the study to refresh the screen.

"You there?" Vanni said.

"Yeah. Bringing it up."

"We've got two choices. Either you get back here to New York, tell the truth, and pray they believe you. Or you keep out of sight until you can get on that plane in a few hours—and pray you aren't stopped. We need breathing room to try to salvage you, friend."

"Is there any talk about knowing where I am or what my plans are?"

"No. They're still looking for you in the Chicago area. See the post?"

"Got it." He opened a piece of mail from Vanni and saw the same setup as before; Ryan quoting MustangMan and adding his own cryptic comments:

"I warned you what would happen if I didn't get what I want, Ryan," Aiden Flynn had supposedly written. *"I didn't, and it has. You'll be working solo now."*

Olivia smothered a cry, and Aiden would have liked to give a good yell himself. "I get it now, partner," he said. "I choose the second option. Wally Loder will be on that plane for London tonight, thanks."

"I think you should come in."

"And face murder charges? I don't think so. I need to be where I can take Ryan Hill down. I'm being framed for killing Fats Lemon."

Twenty-six

"I thought this client was Japanese," Rupert said. "You always said he was." He had waited to see if the coachman in charge of the horse-drawn carriage they'd hired would help them aboard. He hadn't, so Rupert was climbing in.

Winnie gave him a good poke in the rear from behind and said, "Keep your voice down, you twerp."

"How many times do I have to tell you a twerp is a pregnant fish, Winnie? Your powers of recall are failing." Rupert flopped down on a cracked, black-leather seat beneath a telescoping hood that reminded him of the type one saw on British babies' perambulators.

Puffing mightily, Winnie clambered up to join him. His face very red, he leaned over Rupert. "You foolish little man. Do I care if I occasionally give you an opportunity to parade what small, completely insignificant scraps of trivia you manage to retain? This is entirely your fault. If you had done what you should have done in the first place, none of this unpleasantness would have happened and we wouldn't be staring into the jaws of financial ruin—if not of the grave."

Rupert refused to be intimidated. There was no longer a hierarchy between Fish and Moody. They were both heading for disaster. "I thought we were going to meet a *Japanese gentleman* at The Dakota, not take an evil-smelling carriage drawn by an evil-smelling horse presided over by a most probably evil-smelling keeper, or whatever he is. And then go searching for someone who absolutely is not Japanese. And when it's getting *dark*. In Central Park!"

The huge coachman, wearing a bowler hat and long, black coat, heaved himself into a driver's seat intended for someone much smaller. He perched there with his knees jackknifed, like a vast toad. He had long, shiny black hair that flowed over his coat collar, and a glossy green feather looked incongruous tucked into his hatband.

"Imagine," Rupert said, "wearing a feather in a bowler hat."

"Commence, if you please," Winnie said loudly. "Make your way to Tavern on the Green but be prepared to stop if you're told to do so."

Rupert stared at the back of the man's head. "Damndest thing," he murmured. "You'd think he didn't understand a word. Don't tip him, Winnie."

Winston turned up the collar on his jacket, crossed his arms, and tucked his hands into his armpits. "You don't know this man we're meeting isn't Japanese, you know. Damn, it's cold. I hope he shows up quickly."

"When was the last time you met a Japanese called Fanelli?"

Winston flapped a hand. "Doesn't mean a thing. Might think it makes it easier to do business here with a name like that. Or Fanelli may be a go-between for the Japanese."

"Mr. Hasaki wouldn't call himself Fanelli. And he wouldn't send someone with the name of Fanelli without explaining why. I say we get out of this thing now and catch the next flight home."

Winnie clapped a pudgy hand to his brow. "And lose this wonderful opportunity to explain that we do business in good faith and that we're as much the victims of criminal activity as he is? And that we hope to put everything right very soon?"

Sometimes Winnie made remarkably good sense. "There is that, old chap. I say, keep steady up there, will you? You've got the horse wandering all over the place."

The man didn't reply and the horse continued to wander.

"I could *walk* faster than this," Rupert continued. "Say something to him, Winnie. Remind him he hasn't been paid yet."

"Have you looked at the size of him?" Winnie said. "I'm not telling him anything."

They'd caught the carriage on the East Side, at 59th Street, and had already traveled a fair distance into the park. He wanted this over with. "There's a mounted policeman, Winnie," he said through his teeth. "Do you think he's looking for us?"

Winston shook his head slowly and took off his glasses to clean them. "No, I don't think so. I think he's too busy expecting people to be looking at him."

"Bloody great horse," Rupert noted. "Poor devil, being lumbered with that."

"I imagine mounted officers get the animal they're given."

"I was talking about the horse."

"Ah."

"That fellow's enormous and covered with creaking leather. Probably thinks he's a ruddy storm trooper. Boots and all. Oh, my gawd, he's wearing a gun in plain sight, on a horse. An outrage, that's what it is."

"All the police are armed in this country."

"I know that." Rupert shrank as far into the corner of the seat as possible while the horse and rider passed. "Animals are sensitive to these things. They smell fear and danger. Don't tell me a gun doesn't give off an odor of threat."

"Drop it. And stop stuffing those crumbs into your pockets. It's a disgusting habit."

Very deliberately, Rupert bit on the baguette he was carrying. He chewed and while he did so gathered crumbs from his trouser legs and popped them into a jacket pocket.

Winnie sighed, but his nostrils twitched and Rupert took pleasure in the thought that his partner was salivating at the odor of fresh bread.

The carriage made a sharp right turn and set off at a brisker pace.

"Is this the right way?" Winnie said to Rupert. He pulled out a small map of the park and studied it. "No, it is not. I say. You up there. Turn around at once. You're going the wrong way."

The man's response was to hunker down low between his splayed knees and slap the reins against the horse's back to make him break into a trot.

Rupert tried to see ahead, but the horse continued to weave his way, only much faster. The effect was disorienting.

Another abrupt turn, this one to the left, and they were on a narrow track between dense, wintry-looking undergrowth fronting leafless oaks.

The dusk was deepening. Winnie grasped Rupert's hand.

The wheels ground more slowly; the horse mounted a verge and came to a standstill. And a tall, exceedingly thin man stepped from the cover of some bushes. "I'm Fanelli," he said, and got into the carriage. He sat on the same seat with Winston and Rupert, forcing them to huddle together, and said, "You know where to go, Moroni. All the way in, then sit tight till I say."

Rather than set off up the track again, Moroni set a veering course into a gap that didn't look wide enough. It wasn't, but they forced a path and drove away from what civilization they'd left behind until they broke into a clearing. In the center, the trunk of a single massive old oak rose to naked and gnarled branches.

"Out," Fanelli said.

"Out?" Rupert and Winston echoed, looking at each other. They turned to see Fanelli and repeated, "Out?"

Fanelli's response was to raise an evil-looking gun made of a pale metal that resembled stainless steel.

Rupert made to get out of the carriage but was stopped by Winston, who pushed him against the back of the seat, scrambled over him, and fell to the ground. He leaped up with his hands raised.

"You've dropped your specs," Rupert told him.

Fanelli barked out, "Where you're goin' you don't need no specs, fatty. Keep your hands up. Now you, bread man. Out."

Still clutching his baguette, Rupert did as he was told.

"You, too, Moroni." Fanelli followed and circled them slowly. "You don't look like much."

"We're not," Winston said in a rush. "We're not a thing, really. But we're honest, upright business men who—"

"Got took," Fanelli finished for him. "Where did I hear that one before, Moroni? You heard that one before?"

"Sure, boss."

The formerly mute mountain had lumbered from the driver's seat and stood a few feet distant with his feet spread and his gloved hands crossed in front of him. He had a full, red face, bushy brows, and large, eerily soulful dark eyes.

His voice was high-pitched.

Rupert filled his mouth with bread and munched. Fanelli's face looked like a skeleton's with yellowish skin stretched over it. His almost-black eyes protruded, and he rolled a toothpick from one side of his thin-lipped mouth to the other.

"Mr. Fanelli," Winston said, "I am a man under siege. My misfortune is my kind heart. If I had not gone against my better judgment by continuing to champion this ungrateful oaf, we wouldn't be standing here today."

"That a fact?"

"Most certainly. I took him in and gave him a chance when he couldn't get a start anywhere else. But he turned on me. It pains me to say this, but I would understand if you found it necessary to punish him."

Rupert bit and chewed, bit and chewed. Winston couldn't possibly mean what he was suggesting. There had to be an escape plan he was trying to pull off—for both of them.

"What did he do, exactly?" Fanelli asked.

Winston spread his fingers. "I sent him to the woman to . . . buy . . . er, something."

"What woman? What something?"

Winston coughed. He coughed until he choked, and Rupert punched him between the shoulder blades. When he finally collected himself, Fanelli and Moroni were still frowning at him.

"I don't think I ought to give that kind of detail to anyone but Mr. Hasaki. Rupert here was supposed to buy something important so we could feel safe completing our business for Mr. Hasaki—"

"There ain't no Mr. Hasaki no more." Fanelli sniffed and rotated his neck inside his starched shirt collar. "You can think of me as him. So what happened in Notting Hill?"

Winston Moody was cold. Miniature flakes of snow began to fall through the gloom, but he was already as cold as he ever wanted to be. "I shouldn't have listened to you, Fish. Coming here was a mistake."

"It wasn't my idea," Rupert said. "You were the one. And I said we should go to The Dakota, not meet people we don't know in Central Park."

"Don't speak unless I tell you to," Winnie said. "Eat your bread."

Rupert did tear off another mouthful of bread, but a glance at Moroni took his appetite away. The man's big eyes turned a person's stomach. Rupert took the bread from his mouth and shoved it into a pocket.

A bullet zipped past him. "Keep your hands up," Fanelli said.

Winnie slid to his knees and started crying. "He's tidy," he sniffled. "Doesn't like to waste food or make a mess, so he puts the crumbs in his pockets. He doesn't have a gun."

"Okay," Fanelli said. "I just got back from London myself, see. I got friends there. In Notting Hill. How d'you think I knew what I wanted you to get for me in the first place? I just dreamed that piece up? I saw it at my friends' and paid you to get it for me. Paid you two separate checks like you asked. Only you took my money and didn't do your job."

Winston offered up pleading hands. "We meant to call you about it. Honestly we did. But our first responsibility to Mr. Hasaki—to you—was to try to complete our commission."

"You decided you wanted to steal from your friends?" Rupert said to Fanelli, digesting the idea.

"I decided I wanted *yous* to steal from them. You didn't do it."

Winnie stammered, "Give us another chance, please. Something happened and we were interrupted. We had some trouble. You know how that can be. I'll just tell you exactly the problem. We were—er, making sure everything was exactly as it should be before we removed the item, when these people came. A decorator or something, and a photographer. The photographer started clicking all over the place and we couldn't risk sticking around and getting our faces on film, so we ducked out. That wretch"—he hooked a thumb at Rupert— "that wretch was sent to buy the film from the photographer, just in case her camera had caught something inconvenient to us. She wouldn't let him in so, in his wisdom, he decided to conduct business through her letterbox. He pushed in an envelope that was supposed to contain money to pay her and took a packet of negatives from her. Later we found out they weren't the right negatives. And he'd given her our entire bank deposit, including your checks."

Rupert slowly lowered his hands to his sides. If he had a gun, he'd use it to kill Winston.

"I'm going to get the checks back for you," Winston said, getting up from his knees and taking a couple of halting steps toward Fanelli. "I'm closing in on the woman and I'll soon have what you want."

Fanelli spat the toothpick onto the ground. "I don't fucking give a shit about the checks. I made sure they ain't worth the paper they're on no more. What I care about is you jerking me around. You don't jerk me or my people around."

Rupert heard Winnie swallow and didn't blame him.

"You know what I told you to do, Moroni," Fanelli said.

Moroni lumbered closer. "Back up," he said to Winston and Rupert. "Stand against that tree." He now held a gun, an even bigger gun than Fanelli's.

"Oh, no," Winston moaned.

Rupert glanced at him, noted how his legs were pressed together and saw the dark stain spreading down his trousers. Disgusting coward.

"Whatever you say," Rupert told Moroni and began backing up. "Okay if I put my bread in my pockets? You'll see what I'm doing."

Moroni said, "Boss?"

"Let the lamebrain put his bread in his pockets. Maybe he's like them Egyptians and thinks he's gonna need it on the other side." He smirked and snorted at his own joke.

Rupert broke the bread in two and stuffed half in each pocket. It made him feel better to do one, last good thing.

"Feeding his goddamn pockets," Fanelli said, sounding incredulous.

When Rupert and Winston stood with their backs to the oak, Moroni unwound a black scarf from his neck. "Yous can have a blindfold. Take it in turns."

"Thank you," Rupert said.

"You can be last," Moroni told him.

"I'll be last," Winston said. "It's the least I can do."

"I doubt it," Fanelli commented.

"Let him be last," Rupert said. "He never was good at making the best choice. I don't want the blindfold."

"Hands all the way up," Moroni told him. "I gotta see where I'm shootin'. My aim never was so good."

Rupert put his hands up and prayed that at least this once, Moroni would hit the bulls-eye.

"I've changed my mind," Winnie said, "I want to be first."

"Too bad, dickhead," Fanelli said. "Now shut up."

Moroni closed one eye and extended both hands. Rupert looked down the barrel of a gun that wavered in all directions.

"Don't you have a silencer?" Rupert said. "People will hear. They'll be all over you. Swarms of people."

"Sure they will," Fanelli said. "I always interfere with crazies in Central Park. Moroni, one, two, three, shoot!"

"Look at that, boss," Moroni said, slowly letting the gun drop. He took a step back and the gun discharged into the ground. "Look at that!"

Fanelli said, "What, what? Whassamatta with you? Look what you did."

"Rats," Moroni said. "Rats coming out of his pockets. You know I can't stand 'em."

"A rat here, a rat there. Two rats is all I see. Who cares?"

Rupert felt his American friends squirming free, one from each pocket, their tiny claws sinking into his legs as they ran down his trousers.

Moroni screamed.

Fanelli snarled, "Shoot," through clenched teeth.

"Wonder why he doesn't do his own shooting," Rupert muttered.

"Because he's the boss," Winnie said through snuffles. "Bosses don't do their own dirty work."

The rats Rupert had found near a garbage can reached the ground and skittered about eating crumbs. They were adorable.

Fanelli held up a hand and said, "Quiet."

The rustling Rupert heard could be nothing more than wind through the trees—if there was a wind, which there wasn't. Something or someone, or may be several someones, were creeping about under the cover of encroaching darkness, and dense shrubs and trees.

The rhythmic thud of hoofs on hard ground was the next sound. He looked at the carriage, almost expecting to see that the horse had fled. He hadn't.

"It's a Mountie," Winnie shrieked. "A Mountie, a Mountie."

"That's in Canada," Rupert told him. "Here it's a policeman on horseback."

The next thuds were made by Fanelli and Moroni running toward the track as fast as the dense undergrowth would allow.

Rupert elbowed Winnie. "In future, *you* follow *my* instructions. We're going straight back to London."

Twenty-seven

Kitty had planned carefully. Vince at The Fiddle had made it clear for months that he wanted her, and now he'd get his chance—for at least as long as it suited her. Anyway, she quite fancied him, and a girl needed a man around. As soon as she got the money, she'd be off to find a very different sort, one who would understand his place, and his place would be whatever she said it was.

She smiled to herself and made sure the expensive silk head scarf she'd bought completely covered her hair. Courréges sunglasses had been a big splurge when she couldn't use a credit card and her cash was running low, but they'd been worth it. Soon enough she'd have more money than she'd ever go through. Time enough to worry about bills then.

Another thing she'd made up her mind about was that she'd never travel anything but first class in future. She massaged her body into the soft leather seat and sighed. Her ankle-length, cognac-colored leather coat with its luxurious fake mink collar already felt too warm for the plane, but at least she felt safe and rich. Rich could help a girl put up with a lot of things, and she'd have to wear the coat all the way to London, anyway. It was doubtful anyone would have found out she was on this flight, but just in case, she had to be sure she wouldn't be recognized. She pulled a copy of *Lip Service* by Suzanne Simmons from her bag and was deeply involved by the time the plane took off.

Olivia tried repeatedly to make herself comfortable. Everything itched. She'd singled out a woman in first class who was very probably

Kitty Fish. Kitty wore the garb of a flashy woman who capitalized on her appeal to the opposite sex, but Olivia had to admire her—she did it with flair, and if Olivia hadn't seen her several times, she would not have recognized her.

There had been a close call when Olivia boarded the plane. She'd left the Talons' before Aiden, but the cab driver didn't speak English and gave her a tour she might have appreciated if she weren't in a hurry. By the time she checked in for her flight, and her seat toward the back of the plane, most rows had already boarded. Olivia had slung her bags on her back, prayed that their being black would mean they were unremarkable, and bent low under their weight while she walked down the aisle.

Aiden had helped her with a disguise by packing his Wally outfit in an old military duffle bag, which he left in his room. She'd been able to take advantage of his being locked away with the computer to snaffle a handful of earrings—and his trilby. She had punched the trilby inside out and jammed it down to her ears. A black raincoat, so worn that it shone faintly green, covered her sweatshirt and cotton pants, but she'd had to make do with the tennis shoes. She had cut the fingers out of a pair of woolen gloves, and the overall result made her feel smug. Unremarkable. Almost invisible.

A couple of rows into the economy section, she glanced at a man's leg inside dark-gray trousers, and her stomach rolled. She supposed there could be more than one man with thighs shaped just that way—a "touch me" way. But she doubted that.

Then she was at her own seat on an aisle. She put the camera bag overhead, her carry-on under the seat in front of her, grabbed two blankets, and plopped down. Almost at once she managed to bury herself in the blankets and assume a sleeping pose, even though she doubted she'd ever sleep again. How would she ever close out the image of that policeman's mangled face?

Every cliché about women was true, including the one that insisted you "couldn't live with them, and couldn't live without them."

Aiden couldn't think about much of anything but Olivia back at the Talons', sad and lonely—and frightened in case something happened to him. She'd managed to lose herself before he left. He'd gone all around the property but found no sign of her, and then Chris had arrived to run him to the airport and he'd had to leave. The good news was that he felt convinced she wanted to be with him and would do whatever it took to make sure that happened. He still hadn't worked out all his feelings about everything, but he was pretty sure they both wanted the same things.

Kitty Fish had got a good look at him in that motel room. She'd never seen exactly what he looked like when he wasn't in Wally Loder gear, but close enough. He rarely employed a beard and mustache, but they'd seemed the best idea for tonight. They were red, whereas the hair caught in a tail that extended to the middle of his back was pale blond. Sometimes the best place to hide was where you made sure everyone looked at you. The Armani suit Chris had volunteered was the perfect touch.

He knew exactly where Kitty sat. She'd chosen to look like an actress in standard "Yes, I am somebody famous" mode. His hunch that she'd spring for first class had paid off. His own seat was toward the front of economy. He'd considered and discarded business class just in case she'd gone that route instead.

Poor Olivia. She was quite the tiger. Following orders didn't come easily to her, but she'd known when it was time to give in. He missed her already.

Until the moment Aiden had left Chris and Sonnie's, Vanni had kept on making appeals for his partner to go to ground somewhere and not run the risk of being picked up for, in addition to theft and possession, the murder of Fats Lemon. Aiden believed the only way to clear himself was to get his hands on at least one of the principles in the case. He had proof that someone had tampered with a painting in Notting Hill, London. That evidence was useless to him unless he could use it to make someone talk.

By now the local police in Seattle, Chris's boys, would be all over that boathouse. Another good reason to be as far away as he could get and still be doing something constructive.

Maybe he'd give Olivia a call from London.

"No, thank you," Olivia told a porter hovering in the international baggage claim area at Heathrow, "I don't need any help."

All she needed was to keep Aiden in sight—without him seeing her—so that she could follow him and be there if he needed help.

There was a moment, when Kitty Fish hiked the bag that wasn't hers from a carousel—that tempted Olivia to rush at the woman and wrestle her property back. One look at Aiden—or perhaps she should call him Wally—reminded her that she wasn't supposed to be here, and his ego would probably never recover if she upstaged him. Also, making a move too soon could mess everything up.

Looking at him didn't calm her one whit. The suit he wore was dark gray and clearly very expensive. A white shirt and silvery silk tie were the perfect compliment to the red mustache and goatee that had stunned her at first. He wore a wig of long, sleek blond hair tied in a tail.

And every head turned.

She would never have thought of that, of making sure she was noticed, but so different as to be as good as invisible.

He was so lovely. Oh, fiddle, he positively mangled her composure, not that she had any left. He held his head very high and commanded his own space. Passersby stared, but kept a respectful distance.

Oh, good grief, she was going on about him again—even if it was just in her head.

He took off after Kitty.

Olivia took off after Aiden.

Kitty took the green-arrowed "Nothing to Declare" lane and hurried into the frantic melee beyond.

When a ruggedly good-looking man jogged to meet the woman, relieved her of the green tartan bag, and took her by the arm, Olivia followed Aiden's example and studied notices posted on pillars.

The procession continued.

There was an instant when Olivia feared she'd got too close to Aiden. His gaze moved in her direction, and she suffered another shock. Brown eyes. Brown contacts, of course. He hadn't missed a thing.

Allowing a little more space between them, Olivia followed all the way to the taxi rank, where Kitty and her friend commandeered the single waiting vehicle. Aiden walked into the middle of the drive-through, waved down a glistening burgundy taxi, and climbed in.

Panicking, Olivia cast around, but there didn't seem to be another taxi in sight.

A shiny black limousine slid up beside her, and the passenger window lowered. "Where you 'eaded, miss?" the driver asked.

"No, no," she said. "I need a taxi."

"Then this is a taxi," the man said. "I don't see a queue for the limo, and any fare's better than no fare. 'Op in."

Apprehensive, Olivia did get in, and urgency took over from thrift and trepidation. "Do hurry, please. Follow those two taxis that just left."

The limousine shot forward, throwing Olivia to the back of sumptuous black-leather seats. "I'm not sure where they're going and they do have a head start. I'll understand if you can't—"

"Oh, I can, miss, you just see if I can't. 'Ang on to yer 'at."

Twenty-eight

Aiden had never been in London before, and he was traveling too fast to see much of it now. Kitty and her friend's cab was lane-hopping at amazing speed given the heavy traffic.

"Where are we?" Aiden asked.

"East Acton."

So far the guy wasn't verbose.

"How much farther?"

The Indian cabbie looked at him in the mirror and raised his already arched brows.

Aiden colored and felt stupid. "Yeah, right, we don't know where we're going, so we don't know how far it is. It's been a long couple of days."

"We are going northeast, it seems," the gentleman from India said politely. "I am not so certain they are sure of their destination."

Another silence fell, although the noise of vehicles all around them was deafening. Aiden wondered at the absence of car horns but decided not to ask too many questions since they could only add to an impression of ignorance.

"They go directly east now," the driver said eventually. "That was Holland Park. Now we are in Notting Hill."

Aiden shot to the edge of his seat. "Notting Hill?"

"Yes. Trendy now." He rolled the word, *trendy*, over his tongue. "Used to be a war zone, if you know what I mean. Now it's all trendy little shops and the market where people like to be seen buying their hearts of palm, don't you know."

"I know now," Aiden said, trying to reconcile a place he'd heard Olivia mention with this colorful but tiny warren of streets where people seemed determined to outdo each other with the wild colors of their front doors.

"North again," the cabbie announced. "Novice driver, I shouldn't doubt."

They skirted a park on the right. "Kensington Gardens and Hyde Park. Your friends are in a great hurry."

Aiden stopped himself from snapping that the people they followed were pond scum and no friends of his. "Everything seems so small," he said. "Miniature."

The driver laughed and said, "You are probably from Texas, yes?"

Aiden laughed, too. "New York. We've got really big stuff there, too."

Seeing all this with Olivia would be so different. She loved her London, and he'd like to see it through her eyes.

They traveled for what seemed a long time, passing out of the center of London and driving streets lined with cluttered little shops on the ground floors of terraced stone buildings. Minuscule cars and commercial vehicles crammed every inch of road space. Pedestrians scurried along, and Aiden noted that despite many red noses and watery eyes, they seemed jaunty. They kept their coat collars firmly tightened around their necks and talked incessantly to companions.

"Well," his driver said, "this is Hampstead, and that man does not know it at all. He goes everywhere and nowhere, then does it again."

Once more Aiden sat up and took notice. "This is Hampstead?"

"Yes. A quaint place. Very trendy."

Trendy, Aiden decided, was this man's word of the day. "Old-fashioned looking," he replied. "In a nice way." It was also hilly, with ancient deciduous trees spreading their bared branches from behind high garden walls and leggy, leafless geraniums continuing to struggle in window boxes and terra-cotta pots.

Up cobbled way after cobbled way they went, seeing names like Bird In Hand Yard, Flask Walk, Well Walk, then retracing the same route. The other cab made an abrupt right turn onto a steep, narrow, cobbled road called Back Lane and raced upward.

"Better hang back a bit," Aiden said. "I'm not sure they haven't noticed us."

"Who notices anything when they are lost?"

The man was probably right, but nevertheless they slowed down. When they reached the top of the hill, Aiden was grateful they hadn't followed closely. Kitty and her man friend were getting out of the cab. Aiden took in as much as he could without being too obvious.

"Stop here," he said when they began to turn onto a main street.

The cabbie stopped, and Aiden was able to observe his targets going to the front door of 2A, where Kitty took a key from beneath a pot and opened the door.

"There's a limo coming behind us," the driver told Aiden. "I'm afraid I must move."

"Let me out around the corner."

Fortunately, Chris had obtained pounds for Aiden so he was able to pay off the cab. This was going to be sticky. He'd bet a good deal that 2A was Olivia's home. Hanging around outside, or trying to go in through the front door was out of the question.

Where was Wally Loder when he needed him? Or rather, where was Wally Loder's twin when he needed him?

The sight of Kitty Fish taking a man into Theo's house infuriated Olivia. She also wasn't happy that Aiden's cab had passed by and, after a brief pause, carried on.

"Please pull as close into the side of the road as you can and wait, please," Olivia told her driver. "I am right in thinking I can't be seen through these dark windows, aren't I?"

"You got it, miss. You going in there, then? Could be we need to 'ave a signal or something in case you need 'elp."

"I won't need help," Olivia told him, but kindly. "I'll sit here and wait."

" 'Ave it your way." He sounded disappointed.

"I do appreciate your kindness."

His voice brightened when he said, "Think nothing of it. What 'appened to the other lot, then? Was you expecting them to go on?"

"Oh, yes." Where could Aiden be? She needed him, *now*.

Olivia could almost feel the minutes, and her money, ticking away. Not, of course, that limousines had meters. "I really shouldn't keep you any longer," she said to the driver. "To be honest, I'm sure I can't afford to. But thank you."

"I charges a flat fee. Same as what a taxi would run you to get 'ere and we're 'ere now. I'll leave when I'm sure you're well fixed."

There seemed nothing more to say than another "Thank you." And then she saw a tattered fellow shamble from the direction of Heath Street. With the hood of a long, gray rain poncho pulled over his head, he kept his attention on his filthy shoes and the bottoms of trousers that ruckled over them.

The "bum" scuffed into a corner against some railings opposite 2A and slithered down to sit. He assumed an unmoving pose, but Olivia felt lighthearted just knowing Wally Loder was within hailing range.

"Look at that," Olivia's driver said. "Poor old geezer. Cold enough to freeze the . . . It's a cold'un to be out there with nowhere to go. Shouldn't 'appen when some people 'ave so much."

"What's your name?" Olivia asked.

"Nigel Harris. Nigel's highfalutin, but me mum had big plans for me when I was born, I suppose."

"I'm Olivia FitzDurham. That's highfalutin, too, except I think the Fitz bit has something to do with having a bastard for a relative."

Apparently Nigel appreciated that comment enormously. He laughed until he coughed and wiped tears from his eyes. "Hey," he said abruptly. "Where d'you suppose 'e's goin' then?"

"I think I know," Olivia said, watching Aiden make his way slowly across the narrow street and toward the passageway that led to the gardens behind the houses on her side. "It would be a bad idea for him to start wondering about this car."

"Aye, aye," Nigel said. "Leave it to me." He pulled a cloth from beneath his seat and hopped out. Whistling, he began polishing chrome without ever glancing toward Aiden. Aiden had seen him but apparently assumed the car and driver were waiting for one of Olivia's neighbors.

Aiden entered the passage and passed from sight.

For ten minutes—Olivia checked her watch every few seconds—nothing happened other than Nigel's progress around the car. She was getting colder and rubbed her hands together, chafed her thighs and knees. Surely Aiden wouldn't go into that house when he didn't know where Kitty and the man would be.

Another man, this one walking uphill with his hands in his pockets, veered across the road and entered the passage as if he did so every day.

The concept of someone's heart standing still took on new meaning. Olivia got out of the car at once, taking pains to make sure her hat was still pulled well down.

"Let me pay you," she told Nigel, desperate to be off.

"You can pay me when I see you're safe with someone you trust," he said.

"Please, I have to hurry." She had slung the camera case over her shoulder again and she dug into her bag for her purse.

Nigel brought his callused hand down on hers and she looked into his wide, honest face, into his unremarkable but kind eyes. "If there's something you've got to do, do it. I'm not worrying about money."

She nodded, trotted sideways a few steps, turned and ran. She ran after Aiden—and Ryan Hill.

The back gate stood open. Peering at the wedge of garden she could see, Olivia searched for any sign of movement, but saw none. She edged inside and behind the buddleia bushes that had grown into a tangle.

Along the fence she went, holding an arm in front of her face to ward off twigs and branches.

She saw Ryan Hill first. Leaning against the trunk of a big apple tree, and hidden from anyone in the house, he wore a brown leather bomber jacket and khaki trousers and appeared faintly military, particularly with his colorless, close-cropped hair. The most riveting thing about him was the gun he held in his right hand and rested on his left forearm. He looked watchful, but at ease.

A movement near the house had to be made by Aiden. He appeared to be on the ground near green-painted wooden doors that led to a cellar off the basement. She leaned to get a better view and saw him try the padlocked hasp that secured the cellar.

He did intend to go in alone after Kitty and that man.

Another glance at Ryan behind his thick-trunked apple tree brought Olivia close to shouting out a warning to Aiden. Ryan was no longer at ease with the gun resting on his forearm. He'd dropped to a crouch and held his weapon cocked.

Then he started forward, taking advantage of Aiden's concentration on the hasp. A dense clump of pampas grass was his next stop, then a stand of hardy lavatera, its pink blossoms still hanging on.

Darn it, Olivia thought, Ryan Hill was preparing another sneak rear attack on Aiden. This time he wouldn't get away with it.

Olivia would had liked to choke Ryan Hill with lavatera blossoms.

Without taking his eyes from his task, Aiden reached into his pocket.

Ryan lined up his gun, ready to fire.

With a roaring noise in her ears, Olivia pushed out of her hiding place, ran at Ryan's back, and threw herself at him. At the same instant, he heard her coming and started to turn.

On television she'd watched a self-defense program. She straightened her fingers, as she'd seen there, and when she landed on Ryan, knocking him to his back, she brought those locked fingers down and drove them into his eyes.

He screamed and kicked out at her, but he'd dropped the gun.

Olivia brought the side of one hand upward beneath his nose and had the pleasure of hearing him scream again. She'd worry about neighbors coming if she thought they'd ever risk getting involved.

Holding his head, Ryan rolled around on the ground, and Olivia snatched up his gun.

"Get back, Olivia." Aiden had arrived, and he hauled her off Ryan. "The maniac might have killed you."

"He was *going* to kill you," she said, wriggling free in time to face Ryan as he got to his knees.

"Stay where you are," Aiden told him. "It's all over."

"The hell it is," Ryan said. "What are you, clairvoyant? You don't know half of it."

Ryan took a swing at Aiden, a swing Aiden deflected with ease.

"We don't have time for this," Olivia said, glancing repeatedly at the house. "If they hear—and he wants them to hear—if they do, we'll be outnumbered." With that she made a clumsy swing with the hand that held Ryan's gun, and hit him a glancing blow behind an ear.

"Oh," she said, staring at him. "I hardly touched him." But Ryan had fallen as if bludgeoned with a hammer. He lay absolutely still.

Aiden pressed two fingers into the man's neck and looked at Olivia while he concentrated. "Well you managed not to kill him. Congratulations."

She threw down the gun. "Hateful thing," she said. "And don't you sound so judgmental. I was keeping you safe and stopping him from killing you."

Aiden smiled at her and stooped to pocket Ryan's gun. He touched her cheek. "You're right about the time, sweetheart. We've got to move fast."

"Why would they come here?" Olivia asked. "Would they be afraid I might have other copies of the photos tucked away?"

"I think we can bet on it. And Kitty Fish isn't likely to have noticed someone rubbed part of that top coat of paint off, is she? She wants what we've got—something to make comparisons with."

Together they left the garden and rushed out to the street.

"That's Nigel Harris," Olivia told Aiden. "A very nice limousine driver, who brought me here and says he won't leave until he's sure I'm all right. Hello, Nigel!"

"For God's sake, keep it down," Aiden muttered. "If he's willing to keep on waiting, we're probably going to need him."

"Nigel," Olivia said when they reached him. "This so-called bum is my friend." She deliberately omitted Aiden's name. "He's in the same jam I'm in, but I promise you we're completely honest people who have been dragged into something."

Nigel wiped his hands on the rag that was still pristine. "I believe you," he said, but looked disappointed at the arrival of a male interest in Olivia's life.

"Can you keep on hanging around?" Aiden asked. "We're going to need to find a place to stay when we're through here. I'll make it worth your while."

Nigel glowered a bit and said, "I've already told Olivia I'll be staying."

"Thanks," Aiden said, and Olivia sensed he knew he was being seen as a rival. "I've got to go into that house, but I'd like to leave Olivia with you."

"That's fine with me," Nigel said. "You've missed the women, though. One must have been in there already. They both left and took off up to Heath Street. The fella's still inside, though."

Aiden looked inquiringly at Olivia.

"I don't have a clue," she said, then asked Nigel, "What did the other woman look like?"

He polished the glistening bonnet of the car with fresh vigor. "Nothing special. Not like the blond one."

"Okay, I'm going in." Aiden turned his attention on 2A and approached without attempting to be subtle. He rang the doorbell, and the pressure of his finger sent the door swinging inward.

He went in without any hesitation.

Ignoring Nigel's protests, Olivia followed and felt the familiarity of the house settle around her the instant she entered.

The gray afternoon seeped through lace curtains and colored the atmosphere sullen. A musty smell reminded Olivia that the place had been closed up. She looked upward and saw no lights from the higher floors. The back of the house on this floor was in darkness. The door to the basement was open, and the naked yellow bulb that hung from a wire cast its glow inside the entrance to the stairs.

Olivia approached on tiptoe. She didn't want to do anything to handicap Aiden.

There were no sounds coming from below.

She waited, growing more panicky with every breath she took until she couldn't wait any longer.

With great caution, treading softly in the badly fitting tennis shoes, she climbed slowly down the stairs until she could see the scene below.

Drawers had been thrown open and hundreds of photographs and negatives scattered on the concrete floor. Everything that should be on her worktops was on the floor, too, including the heavy guillotine she used for cropping shots, and several cameras. Lenses were tossed into the muddle, and light meters, and rolls of unused film deliberately exposed and left in useless coils. It all appeared to have been stamped on, or swung against walls.

What could she have done to bring about such violent destruction?

"Don't come any nearer."

Aiden's voice startled her with its quiet, almost sad quality. She made him out just inside the darkroom and went resolutely down to join him.

"I told you to stay there," he said.

"And just as you don't need a mother, I don't need a father. I decide what's best for me."

"This isn't best for anyone." He looked away.

On the floor beneath the table that held Olivia's developing trays, in the eerie light that turned everything faintly blue, a man lay curled on his side in a half circle. His head rested in a puddle of fluid that Olivia feared was some of the chemicals she used in her work. There were burns on the back of his neck.

But it wasn't burns that had killed him. Another pool colored the floor, this time a pool of fresh blood. Protruding from the man's stomach were the handles of Olivia's favorite scissors.

"The guy who met Kitty at the airport," Aiden said.

Twenty-nine

"My parents aren't such bad sorts," Olivia said. "You just have to know how to handle them."

Aiden turned on the windshield wipers in her car, only to discover there was no fluid. "The windshield's filthy," he said. "A hazard. I'll get off the freeway at the next gas station."

"Motorway," Olivia told him. "M4. And it's petrol, not gas. The washers don't work, but I carry a shammy. We can wipe the windows, right?"

"Right." He liked the weird little car.

"It sticks a bit in second," Olivia told Aiden of the yellow Mini they'd decided to take rather than involve Nigel and the limousine further.

"It won't by the time I've finished with it. This vehicle is something else. We'll ship it back to the States, and—"

"Half a tick, Aiden. My Mini is headed for the rubbish heap, if you don't mind. Ask my mother. She'll explain."

"Yeah, well, that's a topic for later. A bigger engine will have to go in."

"Where? In the back seat? Aiden, about Mummy and Daddy—"

"We all want to apologize for our folks. I used to. Yours were pretty decent about saying we could go to their place. They didn't even ask a whole lot of questions."

Olivia considered that. "True. I can't say I understand why, since they usually tell me I'm barmy when I call about anything. My brother, Theo, is the smart, successful one. I'm the failure."

"Hey." Aiden glanced at her, and she saw he was furious. "Cut it out. Don't put yourself down that way. Just maybe you're imagining that's what they think about you. They were sure quick enough to welcome you home with a total stranger. We had nowhere to go where we had a chance at being safe until we hear from Vanni. I'm grateful to them."

For a moment she studied his profile, the hard way his mouth turned down. Before they'd left Hampstead, he had picked up his suit and changed out of Wally Loder's tramp uniform. Without the wig, the beard or mustache, and despite the single gold earring Daddy was bound to dislike, he looked—wonderful. Handsome, successful, inscrutable.

She stared out of the passenger window and beneath the bed of a lorry covered with flapping tarpaulin. The Mini was so low-slung that her view was eye-to-wheel with almost everything on the road. "My parents were good about it," she agreed. "I'm surprised. Will we be able to call Chris back again? Or do we have to wait for him to call us?" They had reached Chris, who spoke to them from a delivery room at Seattle's Swedish Hospital. Sonnie was in labor and Chris was coaching. He'd told them to lie low and not to go to the police about the death in Hampstead because he didn't want to risk their being taken into custody.

Aiden had agreed, and so they'd called Mummy and Daddy, who actually sounded thrilled at the prospect of welcoming their errant daughter and her friend into the fold.

"I guess we should be patient and wait for Chris to get back in touch with us," Aiden said. "Sonnie isn't very strong, so I worry about her. I'll tell you their story when we're in a quiet space. Did you notice Chris limps, too—not like Sonnie, but he does?"

"Now you mention it, I did, yes."

"Accident on his Harley down in the Keys. Some woman was trying to kill him, and he got dragged by her car."

Olivia shuddered at the thought.

"I ought to make sure you know you've got company in the weird family department," Aiden told her.

Rain began to fall and the wipers made an even bigger mess of the windshield.

"My dad didn't like being married. He liked my mom, I know that, and me, but he didn't want to be with a wife and a kid. Every minute he wasn't working, he was hunting or hiking or fishing. I thought he was some sort of adventurer and wanted to be like him till I figured out the only thing he gave his family was money. He provided well for us.

"Hell, I liked the guy, but he was a lousy husband and father. Dad was what happened to my hands. One time my mother tried to convince him to stick around more. She said she got scared on her own. Know what that man did? Had a seven-foot brick wall put up all around the property, then started with the barbed wire on top. I was fifteen. I went crazy and tore myself up on the wire. I already had enough explaining to do about the father who was never seen unless you were one of his patients—he was a dentist—and why my mom did everything.

"Anyway, enough of that. It's all in the past."

"But it comes back sometimes. Or it does for me," Olivia said. "It gives you some extra baggage you'd rather not have."

"If you let it." Aiden's own words surprised him. When the time was right, he would tell Olivia that she was the reason he was finally turning his back on memories he couldn't change.

She nodded, but didn't comment on what he'd said. "Eton's nice. Pretty. The famous boy's school is there. You see them in tails and starched collars. It's really rather romantic, I suppose."

Aiden was concentrating on signs and on trying to put together the pieces of everything that had happened since he first horned in on Olivia's e-mail.

"Windsor ahead," she said, and he saw an unreal castle on top of a hill, a vast concoction of crenelated towers and turrets with loopholes. Olivia continued, "We go through the edge of Slough. Eton's not far from the castle. Near the Thames. Mummy and Daddy's house has a back garden that goes right down to the river."

She was jabbering, Aiden thought. He felt her tension. "We're going to be okay," he told her. "Believe that."

Abruptly, she turned sideways in her seat and drew up her knees. She rested her cheek on ripped gray fabric. "Fats Lemon was the first dead person I'd seen that close. Now there's this stranger in my darkroom. Both of them were murdered, and we were probably the first on the scene after each crime. We have to be in even more danger, Aiden, and the danger must still be growing. Someone wants to get us arrested, but it hasn't worked so far. Maybe they'll decide we know too much and decide to kill us, too."

He couldn't argue with her logic. He wouldn't. "We are in danger—we have been from the outset—but you're right, the odds against us have escalated, and it may suit some people to get rid of us. Ryan's bound to be recovered enough from the beating you gave him to be mixing it up for us again."

He smiled at her, but she bent forward until her forehead rested on his shoulder.

"It won't help for us to be scared. That's what they want. Frightened people are easy targets."

"You don't get frightened."

"Sure I do. It just isn't macho for a guy to run around talking about it. Okay, the next exit is Slough, Eton, Windsor." Despite the volume of traffic and the sprawling roads, the countryside was a collage of soft greens that managed to look inviting.

Below the castle, on a road that wound toward Eton, Olivia grew ever more anxious. Aiden had been sweet to share his story about his parents to try to make her feel better, but he wasn't the one about to face those parents in front of someone he cared for.

"Now what are you thinking about?" he asked.

"You see through me. This isn't easy, but it's about Mummy and Daddy. Could you please watch what you say?" She wanted to disappear.

The struggling washers had finally pushed enough rain around to clear some stripes through which Aiden peered. "Would you like to expand on that?"

"I'd hate to, but I will. Do you think you could sound British? English actually?"

"No."

"I knew it," she said, facing forward again and flopping back. "You're going to get shirty. Angry."

"I am not getting angry," he told her. Irritable didn't qualify.

"You mustn't tell Daddy what you do."

"You're going to have to explain what all this is about. Maybe it's a really bad idea for me to come here."

Olivia buried her face in her hands. The odor of petrol that seeped through the bottom of the Mini made her feel sick, and dealing with this type of pressure at the same time was cruel. "It's perfectly fine for you to come to my parents' home. They are a little set in their ways and a bit overly English, which probably doesn't mean anything to you."

"Opinionated and stodgy?" Aiden suggested.

"There's no need to be rude."

"Oh, no, no need at all. You want to know if I can sound English, which I can't, and you want me to pretend I'm not a detective—which I won't."

"It's not what you think. Take this next right turn. If you go farther, we'll be on the bridge. It'll be more a lane than a road, really. Then keep on going until I tell you to make a left turn. It's because Daddy doesn't believe in guns or hunting or anything, and he knows American policemen carry guns. Which brings us to another point."

"Does it?" He should be too tired to think. It might be better if he were. Then he wouldn't be starting, despite the doom that threatened to overtake them, to get a hard-on that didn't intend to be willed away.

Olivia put a hand on his thigh, about two inches from the irrefutable evidence. "The other point is, and this is absolutely not intended as an insult, but Daddy's a bigot."

Aiden shifted in his seat and felt like an out-of-control teenager. He glanced sideways at Olivia, at her soft, wild hair and so-dark eyes, the way she looked at him. Deep into him, deep and intimate. "I'm going to pull over up ahead. We need to get all our facts straight before we go any farther."

She didn't protest. When they were well off the road, he stopped the car and switched off the engine. "Bigoted how?"

"Oh." She pulled up her shoulders. "I don't really know." He liked what that did to her breasts. Their fullness was accentuated, and he enjoyed visualizing how they would be pressed together beneath the unflattering sweatshirt.

"What color bra are you wearing?"

"Aiden!" That got her entire attention. "Why would you ask a thing like that at a moment like this?"

"Why not? You shrugged, and I could visualize your breasts. I just wanted to know what color your bra was. To bring things to living color, huh?" His arousal was no longer under construction.

"My father is bigoted about everything and everyone. He only likes—well, you'd better mumble or something when you talk to him. No, let me hear you sound British—English, actually."

"I'd rather have you answer my question. What are you wearing under there?"

"You're oversexed."

"And you're not?"

"No, absolutely not."

He rested a fingertip on the swell of her left breast and scratched his nail up and down on the thick sweatshirt fabric. "You've got beautiful breasts."

"You're embarrassing me."

"What color."

She turned red, and he brought his face closer to hers.

"I'm not wearing one," she said and blushed an even deeper shade. "I didn't think it would matter with this heavy shirt."

"It matters a lot," Aiden told her. "It's of the utmost importance." With the same fingernail, he gave his attention to a nipple. Olivia gasped and arched her back a little. Aiden smiled.

"We shouldn't be doing this," Olivia said. "This road may look deserted, but someone might come along. And we need to get settled and decide exactly what we're going to do." She looked at his crotch; she didn't know what made her do so, but she had to. Aiden was a big man in every way. What she saw bulging inside his trousers was no exception.

"Doing this, as you put it, even just a little," he said, "will make us think more clearly. Trust me on this. I read it in a very good book."

"What good book?"

"I can't remember. Touch me, Olivia."

The beat of her heart was uncomfortable. Her breathing grew shallow. She kept staring into his lap, wanting to do more than touch his penis through his trousers.

Without even realizing her own intention, Olivia executed a wriggling dive into the back seat. "Come on," she said, wrinkling her nose. "I never did this when I could have been forgiven for acting like a kid. Is it too late to try it now?"

Looking over his shoulder at her, Aiden shook his head and actually turned pink.

"You're embarrassed," she said, and laughed. "Come on, Aiden. Come *on*."

He turned up his palms and shook his head again, but his grin was so wide.

"So I've got to lure you? Is that it?" Wicked she was, but every woman had a right to be wicked now and again. She caught the hem of her sweatshirt with both hands and started to raise it.

Aiden moaned and said, "Don't do that. Please. Or I won't be responsible for my actions."

"Promise?" Olivia pulled up her shirt to show him her breasts.

His smile disappeared, and his pupils dilated.

She drew in a deep breath and leaned against the back of the seat. Her own sexy play turned her on so fiercely, she burned. "Aiden?" she whispered.

Without a word, he got out of the car, threw his seat forward, and climbed into the back, slamming the door shut as he did so. "You . . .

This is natural for you, isn't it? You doing what you're meant to do. I want you, Olivia."

"It was never natural before you."

He reached for her, but she pulled her sweatshirt down and said, "You're the one who asked to be touched first." He didn't resist when she leaned over him, held his shoulder with one hand and undid his belt with the other.

"Oh, sweet lady," he muttered. "I don't think you should do *that*."

"Not even to help us think more clearly?"

"Well." His eyes closed and he gritted his teeth. "Since you put it that way."

Olivia managed to get his trousers unzipped and to reach inside. "There isn't enough room for you in here," she told him and felt wanton but wonderful. "I think I need to let this poor thing out to play. I'll just give it some room and fresh air. It needs tiring out."

"Baby." Aiden let his head settle against the seat back. "Oh, baby, it does need tiring out. I do hope you can figure out a way to get that done here."

The rain beat on the windows all around them. On the inside, steam clouded glass.

Aiden looked down at himself. Olivia had pulled him out from his shorts, and the sight of his straining erection did nothing to calm him.

He rolled his head toward Olivia, placed a hand over her ribs, just beneath the sweatshirt, and felt her grow rigid. She crossed her hands on the back of the seat and rested her forehead on top.

With the very tips of his fingers, he stroked the undersides of her full breasts, and she shuddered uncontrollably. Before he guessed what she intended to do, she crossed her arms and pulled off the shirt. She brought her breasts to his face. When her soft skin met his lips, she moaned and skimmed a nipple back and forth until he opened his mouth and drew it in. She jerked and pressed closer, alternating breasts as if she couldn't bear not to get as much sensation as possible. She mounted his lap and pulled his penis to rest between her legs and against her stomach.

Olivia stroked him, cradled him, managed to slide far enough down to take him into her mouth.

Aiden gripped the edge of the seat.

Her teeth and tongue drove him toward madness.

She didn't release him from her mouth, and he reached down to fill his hands with her breasts. Sensation overtook him, almost overtook reason.

"My God," he said. Cold sweat broke on his brow. He curled over her, caught her beneath the arms and forced her back onto his lap. Then he turned her sideways and held her tightly. She pushed her face under his chin and he heard her crying softly. Women. He would never understand them.

"Did I upset you?" he asked.

"You wouldn't let me finish." She sounded small and broken-hearted.

"Oh, but I wanted to. I still want to. Superhuman willpower isn't one of my goals. I just didn't know how we'd manage afterward. This would have been a one-thing-leading-to-another episode, and we're in the wrong place at the wrong time. Do I get a rain check?"

Olivia looked into his face and said, "As long as you redeem it quickly."

"You've got it."

"Will you stop worrying about how your folks will react to me?"

"I'll try."

"You're all grown up now. You can make your own decisions."

She offered a wan smile. "I've decided I want to make love to you."

"Ditto," he said, but he eased her away. "I say we work as hard and fast as we can to get finished with the enemy, then see what we want when we aren't looking over our shoulders for killers. What do you say?"

"I say move this car. We're wasting time."

Aiden couldn't sit still in his overstuffed, chintz-covered armchair. He nodded at Conrad FitzDurham and popped up to go to leaded, diamond-paned bay windows. "Really something," he murmured. "Really something. You can see the castle from here. Amazing."

"We like it," the man said. "It'll do."

Olivia was in the kitchen with her fluttery mother, making tea, although Aiden could have taken something stronger.

"Lot of chimneys on whatever's on the other side of all the trees," Aiden said. He couldn't see a house but it had to be huge given the number of fireplaces it must have. "Big place, huh?"

"I should say so. Riverside Place. Been in the same family for generations. Etranger's the name. Strangers to me, I can tell you."

FitzDurham's laugh at his own small joke was a mirthless *ha-ha-ha*. "Never seen 'em. Like a splash of something, would you?"

Aiden considered asking exactly what FitzDurham meant, but said, "Great," instead.

"You do the honors, then, there's a good chap."

He should have asked. The room was large and comfortably cluttered with antiques. Aiden ran his gaze over chairs and sofas and tables.

"On the trolley behind the door," his host told him. "Whiskey for me."

Aiden smiled and headed for a glittering silver tray on a mahogany cart. Crystal decanters and glasses sparkled. "Ice?" he asked.

FitzDurham chuckled. "Not unless you want to go and see if there's some in the fridge. Can't abide the stuff myself."

The whiskey delivered, Aiden patted the golden retriever who snored on an obviously very old and expensive carpet and returned to his chair. He took a swallow from his own glass and closed his eyes. "Great," he said.

"Mmm. So, what's all this about?"

Aiden and Olivia had been in the house for half an hour. Aiden guessed he ought to give FitzDurham points for holding back the interrogation that long. "We're in a bind, sir," he said, and swallowed more whiskey.

FitzDurham set his glass aside. "You don't say," he said, but smiled broadly enough to puzzle Aiden. "You and my daughter, I suppose you mean. How long have you known each other?"

"Not long." What seemed a lifetime to Aiden.

"But long enough, what?" A wink from one of FitzDurham's dark eyes seemed more like a tick given his long, spoon-bowl-shaped face. "What did you say you do, my boy?"

"I'm a New York detective," Aiden blurted out. Olivia would just have to make the best of any parental displeasure. She was a big girl, quite a big girl.

FitzDurham frowned and picked up his glass again. "Look more like a successful businessman. I suppose she saw you in your uniform. Women always fall for men in uniforms."

"I don't wear a uniform, sir. And I am successful—just not a businessman."

"Quite. And your people?"

"My people?" He wished he could claim impressive roots, like the Sioux, and say he was actually a chief.

"What does your father do?"

Aiden looked down. "My parents are dead. My dad was a dentist who preferred to ..." He barely stopped himself from saying *hunt.* "He liked the outdoors."

"Dentist, hm? Successful dentist?"

"Very."

"Right."

"Cooee," Millicent FitzDurham caroled, pushing her way backward through the door. "You're lucky I'd already put a bit in, with you arriving on such short notice. We've got a lovely little bakery in Eton. Bath buns, eccles cakes, a nice piece of Madeira, and a Dundee. Olivia made the tea. At least she hasn't forgotten how to do that properly."

"Don't twitter, Millicent," FitzDurham said. "The young people have something to tell us."

"You're not to get worried," Olivia said, walking past her mother to set down a large teapot shrouded with a woolen cover of some kind. "What Aiden and I really need is a safe place to do some planning. You're giving us that, and we're so grateful. Right, Aiden?"

"Right."

Millicent slid her loaded tray onto a round gateleg table and barely stopped a vase filled with red silk peonies from falling off. Her plump, pretty face was very pink, and she repeatedly smoothed down the folds of a brown tweed skirt.

"We'd be more than happy to help with the plans, wouldn't we, Millicent?"

Husband's and wife's gazes locked, and Millicent said, "Oh. Oh, I *see.* Of course we would." She threw her arms around Olivia. "You've always been such a wonderful daughter, so reliable and kind. And you're respectful. You deserve the best at a time like this, and you shall have it. We'll make sure of that."

"Aiden's an American, Millicent. From New York. His father was a very successful dentist."

"New York," Millicent said. "I say. And you're here on business?"

"I guess you could say that." Aiden didn't dare look at Olivia. He wanted to laugh but knew better.

"They haven't known each other long, but we know how it can be, don't we, dear?" FitzDurham gave another of his unlikely winks, this one at his wife. "Sometimes things get out of hand and before you know it, you're in over your head. That can be difficult if the fella's not to be trusted, but obviously Aiden here is going to make sure he does the right thing. Olivia will come out smelling like a rose. Plan away. We couldn't be more happy. And there's no need to feel you have to talk about being—well, you know—in a *bind*, as you said. We're thrilled, aren't we, Millicent?"

"Oh, yes. How many people from your side of the family, then, Aiden? I do think it might be wise to"—Millicent gestured expansively—"to get *on* with it."

"Absolutely," FitzDurham agreed. "Money's no object. Within reason, of course."

"Oh, oh, oh." Millicent opened her mouth wide and danced toward her husband on her toes. "Conrad, do you think—do you? How about Olivia's grandmother's ring? How *perfect* that would be."

When they finally stopped talking and noticed that the objects of their joy weren't saying a word, the FitzDurhams looked puzzled.

"I'm going to let you explain," Olivia said to Aiden. "You'll get through faster."

Olivia knew Aiden hadn't been pleased to be the appointed storyteller, but twenty minutes after he started, he closed with, "So you see how sensitive this is," and she could see that he was satisfied with his efforts, and her parents were eating out of his hand.

"Very sensitive," Daddy said. "But you made the right decision. Coming to me. I was in the Air Force in the War. Know how to think in tight spots, I can tell you."

The phone rang in the hall. Daddy never answered it and didn't like it in the room with him. Mummy trotted out and her raised "hello voice," as Daddy called it, halted other conversation. "Yes," she said. "Yes, a girl. I've got it. I'm very happy for you."

Aiden leaped up. "It's Chris," he said. "He's tracked down the number here instead of using the cell."

Olivia followed him into the hall where Mummy gave him the phone.

"Yo, Chris," he said. "Another girl? Great. How's Sonnie? Great." He said, "Sonnie and a new daughter are fine," to Olivia, who clapped and felt like crying.

Mummy hovered while Aiden listened again. "How do you know?" he said. "Yeah. Next to you, Vanni's the best partner I ever had. So Fish and Moody decided to go to New York instead of coming back to England, and they're holed up in Ryan Hill's place. Wild. I'm glad Vanni had that little brainwave and checked the place out. I'd have hated to walk into the building and see them if I wasn't expecting to."

Daddy joined Mummy.

"Yes, okay. What do *you* think?" Aiden asked Chris.

Olivia put out a hand and he held it, squeezed it.

"Okay, I get it. You and Vanni are both right. We'll get out of here tomorrow. We're both too wiped out to go to Heathrow now. Damn, I hope you *are* right. I do think they're scared. Kitty's probably made sure of that. But I'm not so certain they'll take one look at us, assume we know the truth, and spill everything trying to defend themselves. Yeah. Yeah, okay, it's the best shot we've got. You know I'm not about to keep on running, or have Olivia keep on running. Of course you've got to stay with Sonnie. We'll get out there to visit your new girl as soon as we can. *If* we can."

Olivia didn't care about the caution Aiden issued; he was talking about the two of them as if they might have a future together.

"Tell Vanni I'll call as soon as we get there." Aiden hung up and pulled Olivia close. "Fish and Moody are staying in Ryan Hill's apartment. Vanni remembered how they went directly there after they first got to New York. He figured Fats Lemon might have told them where Ryan's place was—maybe even told them they should go there if they needed somewhere to hide. Vanni found out they'd gone from Chicago to New York and there was no record of them leaving the country. He couldn't find them registered anywhere, so he took a chance and went to Hell's Kitchen. There they were. He told them he was an electrician or something. He thinks they're close to cracking up. He wants us to confront them because he expects them to cave and admit the truth—whatever that turns out to be."

Olivia felt more relief than she knew she ought to yet. "So it's Hell's Kitchen, here we come?"

"Tomorrow," Mummy said, reminding Olivia that she and Aiden weren't alone. "You need a good night's rest first."

"I should say so," Daddy agreed. "And I've got to say, I've never felt more confident of a man's ability to handle a sticky wicket."

Olivia pushed her fingers into Aiden's sides, warning him not to ask about sticky wickets. "Absolutely," she said.

"There'll be plenty of room for the two of you in the blue guest room," Daddy said. "*Won't* there, Millicent?"

"Right, plenty. Why don't the two of you go on up? Conrad will bring your bags."

Swallowing air along with shock, Olivia separated herself from

Aiden, who promptly held her hand again. He said, "Thank you," to her parents and led the way to the stairs.

"One bedroom?" she whispered. "I can't believe it."

"I can," Aiden replied. "They know a good thing when they see it. They don't want you to let me slip through your fingers."

Thirty

Winston Moody observed Kitty Fish with suspicion. "When Rupert telephoned you in London, at that disgusting Fiddle—by the way *I* was the one who thought you must be there—you told Rupert to fuck off, didn't you? Weren't those your exact, charming words, Mrs. Fish? When he suggested you rejoin us here in New York and bring the negatives with you?"

"Can't you see she's tired, Winnie?" Rupert said. "Don't torment her. She's here now, and so are the photographs."

"That's right," Kitty said. She supposed she'd have to get around to explaining that Vince from The Fiddle was dead, but she would not say that was the only reason she'd come here—she'd come because she didn't dare stay in London and get picked up by the coppers.

Someone had to keep a calm head here, Winnie thought, and it would have to be him. "As charmed as I am by your company, and that of . . . what did you say your friend's name is?"

"PJ," Kitty said, careful to smile at her old friend from school. "She's a bit overwrought." True enough. "And tired. But she's been an absolute gem about helping me."

Rupert didn't remember Kitty mentioning this PJ with her over-sized blue eyes behind round, wire-rimmed glasses and long, straight dun-colored hair. He cleared his throat and said, "Right. Well, we'd best take a look at those prints now. The coffee table will do to spread them out." He cleared carefully arranged lines of magazines from the glass top and threw them on the floor beneath.

"I don't like it here, Kitty." PJ's abrupt announcement captured everyone's attention. "You always were the troublemaker. I should have refused to help you. I want to go home now."

"And get picked up for murder?" Kitty said. She had no choice but to intimidate PJ back into her senses. "We had a little problem, Winnie and Rupert. Vince from The Fiddle was supposed to help us, but then he turned greedy and started pushing us around. When we got into the Hampstead house he threatened to take the pictures and run off with them."

"Self-defense," PJ said. "He was coming at me, so I picked up the nearest thing and stabbed him. It was these long shears. I didn't mean to kill anyone. It was his own fault."

Rupert had lost his appetite after Central Park, and now he thought he might vomit.

"What a bloody mess," Winnie said. "And it's *your* fault, Kitty, not hers. You're the one who got greedy and stole our property. I don't know, Rupert, doesn't it seem to you as if we're doomed to be surrounded by devious, dishonest people?"

"It's awful," Rupert said. "There's no honor left in this world, but Kitty never used to be like that."

"I'm not now," Kitty whined. "And I've come to you, haven't I? We'll make a go of it. You two have got plenty of money. We'll get set up here in New York and make a killing. We'll have to be a bit low-key at first, but we'll take on the big time soon enough. It'll be ever so exciting. What do you think?"

"You don't think anything yet, do you, Rupert?" Winnie said quickly. "We have other fish to fry first. Get the photographs."

"Could I have a private word with you, Winnie?" Kitty asked. She didn't like having to smile at the hateful old bastard.

She walked past him and along a corridor leading to the bedrooms. She entered one and waved him inside. This was probably Ryan's bedroom. He must have spent a fortune on a wall covered with audio-visual equipment. A television screen dominated and seemed to Kitty to be as large as a cinema screen.

The anticipation on Winnie's face made her yearn to knee him somewhere very painful. "I don't want to take long over this, but I don't see any other way to approach it. Still a watcher, are you, Winnie?"

He turned a heavy shade of red. "I don't know what you're talking about."

"You know I do. One-way glass anywhere you can put it. Paying off those girls to smuggle you into a shower stall in the locker rooms. Bet you got your eyeful there, even if they were little girls."

"Not so little," Winnie ground out. "And it's none of your god-damn business."

Kitty shrugged and made sure the door was shut firmly. "Then there's the little boys, isn't there?"

"Rupert was so indiscreet. But you gave your word never to men-tion any of this." Winnie's voice became a hiss. "You can't prove a thing against me anyway."

"What if I tell you I can?"

"You're bluffing."

She took a photograph from her pocket and held it out for him to see. Breath escaped him as from a popped balloon. "Where did you get that?"

She put it back into her pocket. "None of your business. And there's plenty more where that came from."

"I won't pay for your blackmail tricks."

"Won't you?"

Kitty unbuttoned the fine wool cardigan she wore over a pink satin camisole.

"Do it up," Winnie said, the flare of panic in his eyes. "Now, you bitch."

"Oh, come on. We know each other better than that. You were quick enough to want to make a fool of Rupert behind his back before, and for a tweedy kind of fella, you were quite good."

Despite his anxiety, Winnie preened a little.

Kitty finished unbuttoning the cardigan and took her arm out of the left sleeve. "Just in case you decide not to be a good boy and help Kitty, I can shout, can't I?" she said. "Oh, come here and give me a cuddle."

Winnie shook his head, but went slowly closer.

"It's about PJ," Kitty said, massaging her left breast beneath the camisole. "She's quiet, but she's passionate, Winnie. And she doesn't meet people easily. She needs a regular lover. She's good, you know. She's studied a lot of weird stuff—sex stuff. PJ's hot and she's ready. I've been with you, remember, so I know what your tastes are like. I think the two of you would make a good pair. Time you settled down a bit." Kitty giggled. Winnie was standing toe-to-toe with her.

"She's a mouse," he said. "Not like you, my girl."

"No, different from me, but a real turn-on. You know what they say about the quiet ones. There are men who would give a lot to find her in their bed every night, but she doesn't like them."

"What makes you think she likes me?"

"I can tell." Kitty pulled one shoulder strap down and clamped Winston's face to her breast. Over his head, she grimaced. Odious, that's what he was. "This is just to tide you over. But go easy with me about everything, will you? And I'll make it worth your while if you do. We could get things sorted out—find a way to get rid of Rupert—and then we could have a party, hm?"

Winnie was noisily inhaling her breast, but he nodded, and she knew he was wavering in her direction.

"Good," she said and gripped his crotch firmly enough to make him squirm and buckle at the knees.

When she'd finished with him, his expression was vague, his little mouth swollen and red. Sweat stood out on his brow. "Tuck yourself all in, there's a good boy," she told him, making sure all was in order with her own clothes. "Then come on out. I've got really good feelings. Working together, we're going to make a great team. With my help, we'll persuade that group at The Dakota that they'd better play the game our way or risk exposure."

She left Winnie mumbling about danger, and returned to the apartment's main room. "Winnie and I do just fine one-on-one," she told Rupert and PJ. "He understands exactly what we were up against in London and how we're going to proceed now. Nothing to worry about."

Rupert showed instant annoyance, which Kitty ignored. She took the photographs from her purse and spread them tidily on the glass coffee table.

A tapping sound started on a conservatory roof on the front side of the apartment. Hail and sleet scudded into the windows. Blue lights shining on a jungle of orchids made the slithering drops sparkle.

PJ rose silently from her soft purple chair and set a large magnifying glass on the table before retreating again.

Winnie appeared, looking calm enough, and went directly to the table. He did glance at PJ and give her a smile that turned Kitty's stomach. PJ seemed nothing other than puzzled, but she smiled back.

"I don't see a thing," Rupert said, sounding relieved. He'd seized the magnifying glass and gone to his knees to pore over the pictures. He moved from one to another, then went back and re-examined a photo here and a photo there.

"Let me look," Winnie demanded. He snatched the glass and bent over the table. He lingered over one picture for a long time and finally said, "There. Damn you, Rupert."

"Kitty, I want the two of you to stay over there," Rupert said. He looked at the photo again and gradually turned cold, then colder. "You're right. It's there and it's clear. I don't know why I didn't see it right off." He raised his face to stare at Winnie. "But don't you try to shove all the blame on me. If we'd been there on time, instead of having to stop so you could look at the Rolls you intended to buy with your take, we'd not only have finished the sampling, we'd have been well away."

"Aren't you forgetting something?" Winnie drew up his lips in a repulsive sneer. "Forgotten the *other*, have we?"

"He who must never be mentioned," Kitty said and giggled. She pointed at the two men. "Why pretend we don't all know it was your friend, Ryan Hill. Is that it? Was he there?"

Winston grew rigid with fury. "One more word on the subject and you can forget sticking around for our lucrative future."

"Really." She slipped a hand into her pocket and started to inch out the photo.

"Stop!" Winnie's jowls trembled. "Just stop it. As it happens, you're right. We were interrupted by Ryan Hill, but it's all right. We made sure he won't bother us again."

"*Winston*," Rupert said, infuriated by his partner's careless tongue.

"Well, these two have told us they've murdered Vince in London."

"Isn't that lovely," Rupert said. "Now we're even. We all know we're murderers. That's not exactly my preferred position in these situations."

Satisfaction warmed Kitty all the way through. "Don't worry, Rupert, you can trust us, just as we can trust you. How did you kill Ryan?"

"I *didn't* kill him. Winnie did. One moment . . . One moment the man was hauling on my collar and demanding the biggest cut of the money. The next Winnie was—"

"*Don't* say it."

"Winnie smashed him over the head with a bronze horse. A bronze horse doorstop, to be precise. Next thing we know, we hear footsteps coming and the best we could do was drag the fellow out of sight and hold our breath."

With a sigh, Winnie said, "Might as well spill all the beans. We heard a man's voice—we think it was the butler—showing people into the gallery. He asked them to repeat their names. One voice was muffled, the other distinct. Olivia FitzDurham. That's how we knew who we had to find afterward. The people who own the house were away. We'd found out they would be and how to get in the back way when the dustmen went into the yard to change the dumpster. Never thought of a butler sabotaging us by letting the others in."

"I don't see anything that would give you away," Kitty said.

"Not the murder," Rupert said, "but the painting we were—er, checking. You can see where we worked on it."

Kitty hurried to him and took the photo in question. After a few seconds, she laughed and said, "Well, you've got better eyes than me. I can't see a thing."

"Anyone who knows the painting would." Rupert bent over the coffee table again. His back ached, but he couldn't bring himself to stop staring through the glass. Then he realized what hadn't crossed his mind. "No—oh, no. Oh, my God, Winnie. Aiden Flynn and the FitzDurham woman must have kept the negatives to these, and they've probably developed them by now. They'll see this photo. When they do, we've had it."

"Now what?" Winnie said.

"Shit," Rupert said quietly. "I told you throwing heavy things around in that house was a bad idea, and not only because you could have missed Hill and hit me. Look at what you did. Might as well have left the body there."

Winnie did look—for a long time before he retreated to a chair and dropped into it like a large bag filled with uncooked dough. "It'll never be noticed. We wouldn't see it if we weren't familiar with the piece."

"The *owners* are familiar. They'll report the damage, you twit. Thank God almost all the bleeding was internal. If there'd been a mass of blood spread around, too, we'd be goners for sure. You mangled the backside of that glass sculpture."

Kitty looked again, too. The photo Winnie and Rupert concentrated on was of a glass-and-mirror sculpture displayed at the end of a corridor. The thing resembled an ugly modern building. She'd had a set of negatives made from the photos. If things went her way. Winnie and Rupert were going to make sure the rest of her life was very, very cushy.

Winston collected himself enough to say, "Well, we didn't leave any blood. And we got rid of him."

Rupert got to his feet, wincing at the pain in his back. "*You* got rid of him, and so I should think."

"I dragged him into that room and told you to keep watch outside. Then you got him into the empty dumpster so all the rubbish would cover him up when it came down the shoot and he'd be hauled away with it. I told you if I didn't come back in five minutes, you were to get on with it."

"Winnie!" Rupert could hardly breathe. "Winnie, I waited five minutes, then I left. You told me how it would be with the dumpster. Then you said you'd be back in five minutes and I was to get on with it. So I did. I went home."

"We left him there." Rupert cringed at the bellow of their two voices.

Aiden and Olivia stood with Vanni in Aiden's apartment. They'd sneaked into the building without incident, and Vanni had made a call to Ryan Hill's place to find out if they'd had any more "electrical problems." Rupert had answered, and the sound of Winston saying something in the background confirmed both men were there.

Olivia looked around the living room and dining room and through the open pass-through to the kitchen. "It's nice," she said. "Big and comfortable."

"It needs time and money spent on it," he told her. "But it's a great place and so close to everything. New furniture—"

"Not all new furniture," Olivia interrupted. "I really like the old pieces. And the wooden floors are splendid."

"Can we save the interior design chat for later?" Vanni said. "When we don't have a pair of crazies upstairs, huh?"

Vanni had behaved strangely since Aiden and Olivia arrived at JFK. His stiff features, the way his nostrils flared, gave away a badly disguised anger and he wasn't sharing his reasons.

Olivia said, "Sorry, Vanni. You're strung out, right?"

He frowned at her. "I've changed my mind," he said. "I'm not sending you up there. In fact, I'm sure it was a mistake having you come back here until we make more headway with the case."

"We couldn't stay in England," Aiden said. "You understood that before. What changed?"

"I don't like any of this. Maybe it would be better to forget the whole thing. Go to ground somewhere until everything blows over."

Aiden had difficulty believing his partner would make such suggestions. "In ten years or whatever? And then only coming back with assumed identities?"

"There are worse things."

"Olivia and I don't have any intention of living like fugitives."

"Look," Vanni said, and for the first time today, Aiden noted how exhausted the man looked. "Fats's murder is being investigated, and your name is at the top of the list of suspects, with Olivia as a probable accomplice. You're 'wanted and dangerous.' It's getting to be a miracle you've dodged a bullet this long."

Aiden refused to be intimidated. "Anything from Ryan?"

"No. But you know that piece of slime. He'll already have popped up like one of those wobbly men, those toys with sand in their bottom. He'll be stirring the pot soon enough."

"Olivia, I'm going up there. The shock value has to be good for something." He decided not to check his weapon in front of her. "Vanni, if I'm gone too long—in your opinion—follow me in."

"Follow us in," Olivia said and, as if to underscore her determination, darted from the apartment ahead of Aiden.

He raised a brow at Vanni, said, "Back me up, partner," and followed Olivia.

By the time he caught up with her, she was turning the handle to Ryan's place. She had guts. He'd always admire that about her.

She threw the door open and marched inside. "Hello all," she said brightly. "Olivia FitzDurham. I think it's time we all had a chat."

By this point, Aiden's Sauer was in his hand. "What the lady wants, she gets," he said. "Hands up. All of you."

He heard Olivia make a choking noise and said, "What's the matter?"

"What are you doing here, Penny?" she said. "I've tried to reach you for weeks, but you were always in France."

Aiden saw the woman she spoke to. A mousy person who wore a navy-blue belted raincoat over her clothes.

"Well, I wasn't really, was I?" this Penny said. "That's just what you needed to think."

"Don't say anything else, PJ," Kitty ordered.

"What a hateful thing to do," Olivia said. "You set me up. Why, Penny? What did I do to you? You sought me out to work with you. We hardly knew each other before."

Penny's mouth pushed out in a stubborn pout. "As long as you were there, I never had a chance with Mark Donnely. He only looked at you—even though you humiliated him."

Olivia felt she'd walked through the looking glass. "Mark and I were friends for years. There was never anything romantic between us. I'm sorry if—"

"Don't be. You're going to get yours. I couldn't believe my luck when Kitty came to me and asked if I could find a photographer who would do a job without asking awkward questions."

"I say," Rupert said, standing as tall as his diminutive frame allowed. "What's all this about you finding a photographer, Kitty?"

"Just listen," Penny said. "It doesn't matter if you know."

"It does," Kitty said, approaching Penny. "Not another word in front of them."

"You don't tell anyone what to do anymore," Penny said. "Kitty found out Rupert and Winnie were planning to knock off some stuff in Notting Hill. So she asked me to pretend to be the interior designer for the renovation there—I'm better than that monstrosity they created, I can tell you—but I was to pretend and get someone to take photographs at just the right time—when Winnie and Rupert were stealing paintings. I went to *London Style* and said I was going to have a piece on this house, and they were interested. I told them there'd be photos. They weren't sure they'd want them because they use staff photographers, but I said it didn't matter as long as Olivia got the experience. It was a good cover for getting her in there.

"Afterward, Kitty was supposed to use the photos to blackmail Winnie and Rupert and we'd be in clover. It was a nuisance, but she got the wrong day, so I had to get Olivia to go back again."

"What were the photos supposed to show?" Aiden asked quietly.

Penny turned up her hands. "I don't know. Kitty just told me what she needed, and I told Olivia. After the second shoot, I did leave for France to be out of the way. Kitty was in charge then. But Rupert and Winnie heard Olivia taking those shots and they were afraid of what she might have caught on film. Rupert got to her before Kitty did. Kitty needed money to pay her off, and that wasn't easy to get. Everything got messed up and we've been running around ever since. And that's not all."

Ignoring Kitty's shouting and loud threats from Fish and Moody, Penny went on to repeat an outlandish story she said she'd heard just before Olivia and Aiden arrived. Outlandish but probably true.

"Damn you, Penny," Kitty said when Penny finished. "Why did you tell them anything?"

"Because I think the best way for us all to win is to go after the people who wanted the paintings stolen. They're all filthy rich, and they should be happy to pay us to look after their reputations."

"That's original," Kitty said. "Blackmail. I think everyone's suggested the same thing."

"You don't know what you're talking about," Winston Moody muttered.

"I just don't believe all this," Olivia whispered. She looked at Ryan Hill's desk, at the fancy computer setup. "Is that where you saw my e-mails?" she asked Aiden.

"Yes," he said. "Thank God."

She couldn't smile at him through the tears in her eyes.

Aiden made sure he didn't look at the door, but he wondered where the hell Vanni was.

"Put the gun away, old chap," Moody said to Aiden. "Makes a fella nervous. And you don't need it here since we all appear to be on the same side. All in trouble."

Aiden didn't want anything in common with these people, but they had a point. He lowered the gun to his thigh.

The door smashed open this time—and bounced off the wall inside. Beretta cocked, Ryan Hill stood in Terminator pose in the doorway. His grin was more mad than evil.

A thud distracted Aiden's attention to the couch, where Winston Moody had collapsed in a jerking heap. Sweat flowed freely down his ashen face. He kneaded the seat with the fingers of both hands, and his chest rose and fell unnaturally rapidly.

"Winnie, he's . . ."

"Keep your mouth shut, Rupert," Moody said in a trembling voice. "We both thought the same thing. Evidently we were wrong."

Olivia moved quietly to Aiden's side and slid an arm around his waist. Even when the world seemed about to swallow them, Aiden found comfort in being near her.

"Listen to you," Ryan said. "Thought I was dead, didn't you? Thought I'd bought it in that house in Notting Hill. You fools. You couldn't even get your stories straight when your lives depended on it, you fools. You *missed* me with the fucking bronze horse, Moody. The only thing you smashed was a lump of glass.

"And why did you try it anyway? The contact at The Dakota was mine. You'd never have known he wanted something you could supposedly get if I hadn't dealt you in. But after all I did for you, you didn't want to share the profits afterwards."

"You wanted a third of everything," Winnie said. "That was preposterous when I was taking all the risks."

"Winnie," Rupert said. "You said you had to get three-quarters because you had extra expenses. I was to have a quarter and maybe more the next time. How could you give him—"

"I never intended to give him a third, did I?" Winston was recovering some of his composure. "I never intended to give him anything. That's why we got rid of him."

Aiden squeezed his eyes shut, but Ryan was still there when he opened them again.

"But you didn't," Rupert wailed. "He's not dead, is he?"

The two of them looked at Ryan and said in unison, "You're supposed to be dead."

Kitty murmured, "Too bad I didn't know that. I knew where he was and could have saved you a lot of trouble."

"I never knew anything about him, period," Penny said.

Rupert scowled. He pulled a packet of crackers from inside his jacket, opened them and crammed several into his mouth. One cracker he crushed in a palm and shoved into his pocket.

Olivia watched scrabbling movements inside the tweed cloth and heard faint squealing—and she backed away. But it was a small gun that Rupert tugged from his coat pocket. "I know I've always said I don't believe in these, but I found this in a drawer in the bedroom. It's loaded. You never know when we might need it."

"Shut *up!*" Ryan yelled. "It's all over now. Drop the Sauer, Flynn. You're finished, too."

"Give up and let you shoot me, you mean?" Aiden said. "So you can say it was in the line of duty and cry, 'hero?' I don't think so."

"You'd have to kill me, too," Olivia announced.

Aiden rolled his eyes but didn't comment.

"No more," Winston said, visibly trembling.

"We can work this out," Rupert said.

Ryan got off a shot so suddenly, everyone in the room exclaimed.

Rupert grabbed a shin and leaped about, crying out, "He shot me in the foot. Why did you do that? He shot me in the foot."

In the confusion, Ryan made a diving plunge into Aiden's legs, and brought him crashing to the floor. Aiden grabbed for the other man's wrist and tried to wrestle the gun loose. A shoe, connecting with his own temple, caught him off-guard. He felt the immediate trickle of blood toward his eye. Another kick slammed into his windpipe, and he looked up at Kitty Fish's wild eyes and giggling mouth.

But that was all for Kitty.

Aiden hung on, willed away the pain the woman had inflicted, and managed to turn Ryan on his back—just in time to see Kitty thump, face-down, on the mauve carpet. A familiar oversized tennis shoe landed between Kitty's shoulder blades, but Olivia needn't have worried that her opponent would continue the battle. Kitty appeared unconscious.

Vanni's voice rang out. "Don't move, any of you. Sorry, Aiden, got hung up on the phone with the narcs. You heard me, creeps. Don't move a muscle."

"Blooming parade," Winston muttered.

Relief was a weak word for what Aiden felt.

"Touch me and he's a dead man," Ryan panted. The muzzle of his Beretta was jammed into Aiden's belly.

As if in slow motion, Aiden saw a wooden chair rise and realized it was in Olivia's hands. He wanted to warn her to back off, but feared Ryan would turn on her instead.

Vanni, moving quietly, pressed his gun to Ryan's head and said, "It might be a good idea for you to let Aiden get up."

The expression in Ryan's eyes turned ever colder, but he didn't remove the painful force he pressed upward into Aiden's diaphragm.

"We're all going to die," Winston Moody moaned. "I can't look, I tell you. Stop them, Rupert."

Rupert sat on the table among the photographs, cradling his profusely bleeding foot. He didn't show any sign of having heard Winston's plea.

Kitty stirred.

Olivia brought down the chair intended for Ryan, and broke it over Kitty instead. She was instantly still again.

Music blared. Trumpet. Winton Marsallis as only he could play the trumpet, but Aiden flinched, and when he strained to locate the source of the noise, he saw Penny fiddling with an amplifier. The woman puzzled him.

Ryan gave a demoniacal grin, and burst into laughter. "Party, party," he yelled. "God. Party, party," and Aiden received a blow to his nose. Blood gushed this time, and he didn't need a doctor to tell him he had a broken bone. "Interfere, Zanetto, and you can blame yourself when your buddy's brain decorates the wall."

"You're disgusting, Mr. Hill," Olivia cried. "Sick. You are an evil man, sir. Evil men must not be allowed to visit their ill tempers on the innocent. Take *that!*" A chair leg made a thwacking sound against the right side of Ryan's head. "And *that!*" The left side got the same treatment. His eyes took on the old deer-in-the-headlights lack of focus, and Aiden didn't waste a second of his advantage. He brought both arms smashing upward beneath Ryan's wrists. This didn't mean the man let go of his gun. And he still managed to stop Aiden from taking aim.

Olivia tried to hold on. Panic swelled, overtaking her control. Most of these people were insane. How did one deal with insane people, insane people armed with deadly weapons? Aiden lay bleeding on the rug with Ryan Hill's stocky body on top of him. She longed to fall on Hill and try to drag him off. She also wanted to yell at Aiden to fight his way from beneath the man.

And what was holding Vanni back? "Vanni," she shouted. "I'll hang on to Hill, you knock him out."

Vanni moved as ordered. Winnie snatched Rupert's little weapon, hid his eyes, and fired in Vanni's direction. Olivia screamed a warning too late. Vanni went down like a big fish thrown on a market stall. Olivia didn't know where he was hit, but he didn't move.

"Aiden," she said in a small voice. "Vanni's been hit. We're all on our own."

He did love this woman, but if they got out of this alive, he was going to have to teach her a few lessons about caution.

"We've got to pull together," she said. "Tell me what to do."

"I'm going to help." From the floor, Kitty amazed Aiden by announcing her intention and rising up with yet another gun, to fire a salvo at Ryan. Actually, at Ryan's rear end.

Screaming, Ryan leaped away from Aiden. He seemed to remember the Beretta and started to shoot, sending everyone else diving for cover. The shots he got off flew wild, embedded in the ceiling and walls before he clapped his hands over his rear and rolled to and fro, helpless in his pain.

Kitty repeated her favorite form of martial art—she kicked Ryan in his bullet-riddled derriere. "You messed everything up, sucker," she said, and burst into tears, which was useful because she was already bawling when a bullet winged her right shoulder.

"I'm on the side of right," Penny said in a wobbly voice. "She's a wicked woman and needs to be stopped. I've stopped her. Did you see that?"

"We sure did," Aiden said, making calming motions with his spare hand as he stood up. He took advantage of Ryan's dull-eyed slump to relieve him of the Beretta. "Thank you, Penny. We can use all the help we can get. I'll have to give you a reference at the police station."

Penny wrung her hands and murmured, "Thank you," over and over again.

Aiden would have liked to smile if his nose weren't burning and throbbing.

"Medic One," Vanni mumbled. He scooted up to lean against the wall. "Get me to an emergency room, for God's sake."

Aiden saved the energy talking would have taken and got to the phone instead. He dialed 911 and gave the address. "Gunshot wounds," he said. "No, no immediate danger to emergency personnel. But advise caution. The situation isn't stable. Four, I think. Four victims. No, that's right, I said *four*. Thank you." He hung up and surveyed the battle scene. Ryan was in more pain than danger. Killy clutched her shoulder and rocked to and fro. There was significant bleeding. Vanni leaned against the wall with his eyes almost closed. Rupert continued to hold his foot, and Aiden could see a hole through the bottom of his shoe, suggesting the bullet had passed all the way through.

With the exception of Olivia and Aiden, and Vanni who also had to be taken to emergency, the entire, disgusting cast was removed by medics and the police. Aiden read disbelief on the men's and women's faces when they first looked the room over, then analyzed the injuries they were faced with—not exactly an abundance of life-threatening situations, but attended by enough noise to suggest something close to a massacre.

"I'm in absolutely great shape," Olivia said to a medic who asked her, yet again, if she was okay.

Despite his throbbing nose and the promise of black eyes and maybe even cracked ribs, Aiden followed Olivia's lead and said he didn't need any help.

When they were finally left alone, the CD player was still repeating trumpet solos over and over again.

Olivia went to turn off the machine.

"Now what?" she said, facing him. "I think we get you to an emergency room, too, and deal with your nose—among other things."

"Not yet," he said. "First I'm going to the precinct house. I'm turning myself in."

Thirty-one

"I'd like to wipe those looks off their faces," Olivia said quietly, trotting to keep up with Aiden when he crossed rain-drenched 51st Street toward the precinct house. "I'm going to give the people you work for a piece of my mind. They ought to know you well enough not to question your loyalty—or your character."

He loved her for her fiery defense of him, but he couldn't face the ribbing she could bring his way—if he didn't get thrown in the tank before he got through the front door.

"Aiden, did you know Ryan was supposed to be dead?"

"That Fish and Moody thought he was, you mean? No. Never crossed my mind." They went into the building, passing a multitude of staring, uniformed officers swathed in rain ponchos on the way. "Those two aren't real. They didn't say another word on the subject afterward. Just kept hammering at each other about who was in charge," Aiden said. "The chairs by the wall are for visitors. Why don't you sit here and wait? It'll be more comfortable than upstairs."

She caught him by the arm and urged him to stop. "Believe in me," she said when he turned to her. "I won't do anything to embarrass you."

"This is getting scary," he said. "I think we're beginning to know each other's minds without even trying. Come on, then. I need you to stand there and look gorgeous. Distract the chief so he gives me a chance to explain before he slams me away."

Olivia made a move to hold his hand, but just saved herself from that mistake. He strode upstairs, taking two at a time, and entered a noisy, crowded squad room where all conversation faded away the moment he was sighted.

"Margy," Aiden said, standing in front of a desk where a middle-aged woman sat. She stared at him and instantly appeared close to tears. "Hey, Margy, it's okay," Aiden told her. "I need to see the chief."

Officers began to move quietly about their business, many of them casting curious stares at Aiden and Olivia. One or two said hi, or clapped Aiden on the back. Everyone else was polite enough, but taciturn.

Rather than use the intercom, Margy had gone to the chief's office, and Aiden's apprehension grew. How did you defend yourself against the kind of case that had been built around him?

"Sit down," he told Olivia quietly. "I will too. Won't help to look as if I'm worried."

Promptly, Olivia took a seat. Wincing at the many sore spots in his body, Aiden followed suit and concentrated on her. He didn't know how he'd moved from being a man determined to protect his bachelor life to a man who approached panic at the thought of continuing his bachelor life. He just had. He had to have Olivia with him, or he wouldn't be interested in anything else that might come his way.

"You need to see a doctor," she said. "You should be there now."

"In time. Not right now."

"Detective Flynn," Margy said, emerging from the chief's office. "He'll see you now. Alone."

Aiden squeezed Olivia's shoulder and made to leave her by Margy's desk.

Olivia had other ideas. She stood up and said in a reasonable voice, "We've shared a great deal in a short time, more than most people will go through in a lifetime. Please could you ask your boss if I may be present for your interview."

Aiden felt himself being watched and swung around to see the chief's head protruding from his open office. "Bring her on in," Chief Friedlander said. "I hope you know I won't tolerate any interruptions from you, ma'am. Speak out of turn, and you'll find yourself downstairs in the lobby."

"Thank you," she said, hoping that sounded submissive and respectful enough. "I appreciate your kindness."

Aiden ushered her ahead of him, meeting Friedlander's eyes as he passed. Colder than any fish. Aiden considered and discarded the notion of smiling himself.

Friedlander closed the door and said, "I'm not being kind. I may never be kind again after the way you've let me down, Flynn." He waved Olivia to a chair beside his desk and indicated where Aiden was to stand before taking his own seat. "You're not going to get far, but you can try to explain yourself."

"Tell him none of it's true," Olivia said, and earned herself glares from both men.

She hunched her shoulders, inclined her head, and pulled her roll-brimmed black felt hat—another Wal-Mart buy—lower over her eyes.

"Flynn?" the chief said. "I guess what I want to hear most is an explanation for your behavior. You screwed up once, and I gave you another chance. This time you've made me look like a fool. A fool who is a bad judge of character."

"Things escalated," Aiden said. "And with every passing day, I had to put more distance between myself and the precinct."

"Really?"

"I was afraid that if I didn't and you got to me, I wouldn't have another chance to straighten things out and present them in the most reasonable and favorable light."

Friedlander pushed his chair away from the old desk and planted his feet, ankles crossed, on top. "And now you think you can waltz back in here with some other fantasy excuse and expect me to try to save you? If that is what you think, then you're in worse emotional condition than I thought you were."

Olivia compressed her lips into a thin, angry line and scooted to the edge of her chair. This was disgusting, outrageous. This man had convicted Aiden without giving him a trial.

"I don't think that. And there isn't going to be any fantasy telling. I can come here now because I'm innocent of any crime, and my job is more important than almost anything else to me." He couldn't allow himself to look at Olivia. She was just unpredictable enough to break into tears.

"Your job is more important than *almost* anything else," Friedlander repeated. "That doesn't make it look good even for what does matter most to you."

"This was all entirely my fault," Olivia said. She popped out of her chair, went to the side of the desk farthest from the door, and sat in another chair, as if putting more distance between herself and the door would make it harder to throw her out. "Aiden is the most honorable, unselfish man I've ever met. He's the most honorable, unselfish man *you've* ever met. If you want to have a group of truly outstanding men and women working for you, show them how much you admire Aiden Flynn and encourage them to try to be like him."

"I think that's enough, Ms. . . . ?"

"FitzDurham. Olivia FitzDurham of Hampstead. And I can tell why Aiden thinks so highly of you. You're a man of courage and insight."

Aiden massaged his temples. She was killing him, but she was wonderful.

"Thank you for the vote of confidence," the chief said.

"I can't do anything less than try to make sure you understand. If Aiden hadn't come to my rescue, I would be dead by now. There. What do you think of that?"

Friedlander swung his feet to the floor, leaned forward, and drummed his fingers on the desk. "Having a little difficulty looking the right way when you crossed the street, were you? Flynn, I'm sure you know what I'm thinking."

Nothing would improve his position here. "I'm afraid I don't," he lied. "Why don't you spell it out?"

"You believed that frightful man Ryan Hill rather than Aiden," Olivia said. Her voice was tight, and she'd lost the color in her face. "You believed him without even giving Aiden a chance. If Ryan Hill could have got his own way, I'd be dead, and I wouldn't be the only one. *Not* that we don't think he's a murderer anyway. We don't know for sure about that man who was murdered in my house in London, but you could bet your baby's bottom it was Ryan who murdered that poor man Fats. Oh, he wasn't nice. He was dreadful really. But he shouldn't have died the way he did."

The two men were very quiet. They stared at her, and Olivia hated herself for her lack of control. No wonder she irritated her parents. They were the souls of discretion, and she must be a complete puzzle to them.

"What," Chief Friedlander said, "is she talking about?"

There was no point in stopping now, especially since Aiden looked incapable of saying his own name, let alone standing up for himself when he was being accused of all manner of heinous crimes. "You don't have to be coy with me," she told the chief. "I've played my part. I've even beaten people up. Well, actually, the same person twice. Ryan Hill kept trying to kill Aiden. I ask you, what would you have done if you were me? You'd have come to his aid."

"Olivia," Aiden said softly. "Thank you, darling, but I can handle this."

"You sit down and catch your breath, Flynn," Friedlander said. "Miss FitzDurham is doing just dandy. Do go on."

Olivia felt flattered. "Thank you. First of all I must congratulate you on the caliber of your people. When I came to this country I didn't know a soul except for Aiden, but Vanni Zanetto and his family welcomed me into their home. I know Chris Talon doesn't work for you anymore, but he helped me in Chicago and in Seattle, and he's been wonderful."

Aiden groaned aloud.

"Are you ill?" she asked, her stomach sinking. "He needs a doctor, you know. After this morning's horrible fight, and all that shooting, he's exhausted and he's hurt, too.

"And, by the way, I have never stolen anything in my life, least of all valuable paintings from someone's walls. And no matter what you've been told, Aiden didn't help me do it, either. He just helped me get away."

Aiden's laughter was the last sound she expected. He made her quite annoyed. Even the wretched chief's mouth twitched.

"I'm British, you know," she told him. "I think I sometimes have a different way of expressing myself."

The man's mouth didn't twitch anymore.

"Aiden Flynn is one of your finest," Olivia told him. "And he shouldn't have to beg to be taken seriously."

"Go on, ma'am."

"I'll take over from here, thanks," Aiden said.

"You'll speak when you're spoken too, Flynn. Go on, Ms. Fitz-Durham."

"I'd be honored if you'd call me Olivia. My parents do."

Another burst of laughter infuriated Olivia.

"Thank you," the chief said, when he'd controlled himself. "Olivia."

"Why were you so ready to believe Ryan Hill and Fats Lemon?" she said, making sure she was all business. "You were so quick to accept Ryan's story, you didn't give Aiden a chance. We had to run or risk not having a chance to clear ourselves. If we hadn't had Vanni Zanetto here and on our side, I don't know what we would have done. We wouldn't have known you had a BAP out for us until we'd already been picked up."

Aiden gave up. Now she'd implicated Vanni for passing on sensitive information. At the very least, he'd be severely reprimanded.

"You know all this?" the chief said.

The old manipulator had her eating out of his hand, and she told every detail of what had happened from the very first time Ryan Hill contacted her online.

Aiden was tired. Tired and hurting. Vanni was still in the hospital for observation. Mama Zanetto, who had broken the news that Pops died the previous week, had taken Aiden and Olivia home before they insisted on leaving for the precinct house. The Zanettos' delight at seeing them had made him both happy and sad. Mama had told how angry Vanni was and how he refused to accept that Pops hadn't wanted further intervention.

"Aiden?"

He met Olivia's eyes. "Yes?"

"If you hadn't looked after me, I couldn't have made it—or not so well. You risked everything for a stranger, for me."

"That must have been hard," the chief said. He'd laced his hands over a flat stomach and was looking off into space.

"But all Ryan Hill had to do was take advantage of Aiden stepping in to help me, and you believed I was an art thief, and Aiden was my accomplice. I know he supposedly had all kinds of proof, but surely Aiden's record should have stood for something."

The chief smiled at her. My, my, a very handsome man he was, too. "I think I'm starting to understand what's happened here. There never was an APB out for you and Aiden. What gave you that idea?"

Aiden's mind did overtime. Buying time, he got up and poured himself a cup of the chief's foul coffee. "You wouldn't want this," he told Olivia.

"And this stuff about you and Olivia being wanted for art theft and whatever else? Where did that come from?"

The coffee was even more bitter than usual.

"Vanni," Olivia said. "Without Vanni, we'd never have known a thing. We wouldn't have known where we should go, or what we should do when we got there—or what we should avoid. He kept tabs on us, knocked himself out for us."

Aiden threw his cup, including the coffee inside, into a wastebasket. He paced to the window and looked down at the activity in the street. "Son-of-a-bitch," he murmured.

"Yeah," Chief Friedlander said. "The way I heard it, you had a thing going with a woman. Sorry, Olivia." He smiled at her. "You had a thing with a woman, and that's why you got him to lie and say you had the flu, and in a few more days, that there were complications. Then, when I had to put you on report and knew you wouldn't have a job when you came back, he broke down. You were the best friend he ever had. His family loved you like another son. He was ready to be disciplined because he'd done wrong, but he'd done it because you meant so much to him. The question is, *why* did he do it?"

"He pulled the strings," Aiden, too numb to completely register what had happened. "He told us exactly what the next move ought to be. And when Ryan got back on the job and I became Public Enemy Number One, Vanni must have wondered what star he was living under. He used that to crank up the pressure."

"Ryan Hill never did come back on the job," the chief said. "We haven't heard a word from him since he went to be with his father upstate. That was weeks ago."

Aiden saw Olivia get up. She walked unsteadily to him and stared into his face. "Vanni set us up?"

"He helped," Aiden told her. "So it seems."

"But he's your friend. He likes you, and so does his family. That's not an act."

"He did it for money," Aiden said. "He did it for a slice of the pie from Fish and Moody—and Ryan Hill. Unfortunately for him, the rest of us didn't oblige him by turning into morons, although we trusted him too much. Or I did. You couldn't have known any different. Kitty Fish's unpredictable moves couldn't have helped him, either."

"Or Penny Biggles's," Olivia said. "Aiden, we didn't trust Vanni too much. We had no reason not to trust him."

A light tap at the door preceded the appearance of Margy's face, complete with evidence of tears shed.

"Hi, Margy," her boss said.

"Why are you so angry with me if no one around here thinks I've done anything wrong?" Aiden asked her.

"Nothing wrong?" Her voice rose to a squeak. "You pretended you were sick and went AWOL. You're going to get fired. We care about you around here—maybe we shouldn't."

"I'll explain this to you later," the chief said. "Aiden's in the clear. He's not going anywhere."

An instant smile transformed Margy's face. She stepped into the office and closed the door. And the smile faded. "Call from St. Philomena's." She swallowed. "Vanni tried to kill himself. It's okay, he didn't pull it off, but they're watching him closely. His mother called to ask if Aiden could go over there."

"On my way," Aiden said. He felt as if he'd lost a brother, but not as if he'd stopped loving him.

"I don't think so," the chief said. "We'll be putting a guard on him. Arrange for that, please, Margy."

She left the room at once.

"We've got to go," Olivia said. "Whatever he's done, there must be a terrible reason, right, Aiden? I don't know him really, but I feel that he's a good man. He must be or you wouldn't like him so."

The chief's expression, the brow he raised at Aiden, sent a clear message that he was impressed by his detective's one-woman cheering squad.

"Permission to go, please, Chief?"

The chief pushed papers around his desk while he considered the request. "I guess it can't hurt anything. Just don't let him talk you into anything. Like helping him escape."

Aiden took hold of Olivia's hand and started for the door. "Thanks," he said. "I just want to hear his excuses for this."

"You're welcome," Friedlander said. "By the way, Flynn, you really look like hell."

When they finally found Vanni, rather than being in bed, he was swathed in warm clothes and walking in the parkland behind the hospital. His mother was at his side, and two plainclothes detectives followed at a pretty tight distance.

Vanni saw Aiden and Olivia and cast wildly about. Aiden felt him deciding where to run, but his mother put both of her arms through one of his and held on tightly. She spoke softly to him, and he slowly faced Aiden and Olivia again, then walked toward them.

He stopped a short distance away, and Aiden saw how much it cost the man to look directly at his partner. "Sorry," he said. Muscles flexed in his jaw. "That's the best I've got."

"They said you'd tried to kill yourself," Aiden said. "You look okay to me."

"They found a scalpel in his pocket," Mama said. "He'd taken it from emergency. He was going to cut his wrists."

"No, I wasn't," Vanni said. "I was going to cut my throat."

His mother cried out and covered her mouth.

"Why?" Aiden asked. "Why would you set me up like that? You didn't give a damn if Olivia and I died. In fact, you were doing your best to make sure that happened."

"I did care, damn you. I didn't want you dead. Things went screwy on me. I made a mistake, got dragged into something, then couldn't get out. And I wanted the money. I wanted to give Pops a chance. I was wrong—he didn't want another chance. If he had, he could have paid for it. I've said I'm sorry. That doesn't make anything better, but it's all I've got. I want to go in now."

"You made sure Boswell was with us," Olivia said, surprising Aiden. "And you asked about him."

"Who cares now," Vanni said "You're something, Olivia. Good enough for Aiden. Not that I'm sure he's good enough for you."

Olivia wasn't to be distracted. "You asked what happened to Boswell before I'd even mentioned he'd been hurt. What was that about?"

Vanni smiled, a ghostly attempt that didn't encourage confidence. "No biggie. I put a homing device in his neck. It helped until it quit sending signals. The dog got shot and the device was destroyed. End of mystery. Is he okay, by the way?"

"Yes. He's with Chris and Sonnie." Even though she supposed she shouldn't, she felt sorry for Vanni.

"How did it start?" Aiden asked.

"Fats was the one who spilled everything," Vanni said. He raised his hands and let them fall, limp, against his legs. "He went on a drunk one night, and I ran into him. Bragged and bragged about how much he and Hill were going to make. Got so chummy, he offered me a part of the action. I accepted. I accepted *after* I knew what they were involved in. But you just stumbled into the middle of things, Aiden. Olivia was set up by Kitty Fish, but *you* didn't have to be any part of it all. If you'd stayed out of it, everything would have worked out fine, and no one would have found out about thieves stealing from thieves. What the hell. Take care of each other." He walked away. Mama peered repeatedly backward past his arm.

The two detectives drew in closer behind them.

Aiden watched them until he couldn't bear to watch anymore, and he turned away.

Olivia's strained face greeted him. She pointed, and he spun around in time to see Vanni heading back toward him. Mama made to follow, but he waved her away, and when the detectives started after him, he yelled, "Get your piece out, Aiden. Tell 'em you'll kill me if I make a run for it."

"It's okay," Aiden called. "I'll take responsibility for him."

The two men looked at each other but stayed where they were.

Vanni came so close, Aiden could see that his eyes were bloodshot and, what he hadn't noticed earlier, his partner had lost weight and his shoulders sagged.

Every rough hour was making itself felt on Aiden. He wanted to pick Olivia up and run with her, run and run until they'd never be found again.

"I don't think I can handle this one," Vanni said. His face shone with a thin film of sweat. "Everything I worked for. Everything I did that made my family proud. It's all turned rotten because I couldn't control my emotions."

Olivia held Aiden's hand so tightly it hurt.

"You loved your grandfather," Aiden said. "Hell, I loved him. I miss him."

Vanni was crying, and Aiden's throat tightened. He murmured, "Get it out if it'll help."

"Nothing will ever help again," Vanni said. From a pocket he slid a hypodermic, shielded by his palm and wrist so that only Aiden and Olivia could see it. "Do this one last thing for me, Aiden. Stand right there as if we're still talking and let me finish it. It'll be fast. You look at the ground, Olivia. I'm so sorry I won't have a chance to know you better."

"What's in the hypo?" Aiden said, frantically searching for a way to divert Vanni.

"Nothing but air," Vanni said. "Nothing but air. Should cause a massive stroke. Gotta try for the artery, but if I miss, the vein will do the trick."

"I can't help you do this," Aiden said. "You're going to pay for what you've done by taking it in your pride. You're going to live with shame until you pay off your debts. But you didn't kill anyone, thank God."

"I'm an accessory to everything that's happened. I owe it to Mama to—"

"To what?" Olivia broke in with such quiet anger, Aiden stared at her. "You owe it to your mother to add to her pain by *killing* yourself? At least she knows you did what you did out of love for your grandfather. You owe it to her to do what takes *real* guts—face up to the crime and pay however you have to pay. Now give me that thing."

Aiden looked at her outstretched hand, then at the alert detectives.

Olivia saw that look and put her hand on Vanni's shoulder. She rested her head on his chest and said, "Please, Vanni, give it to me."

"Time to go inside," one officer announced loudly. "Let's go, Zanetto."

Aiden shifted restlessly, afraid to grab for the hypo in case he caused disaster.

"I can't do it," Vanni said, shaking his head. His left arm was around Olivia. "Understand that I can't do it, both of you." He raised the hypodermic in front of him and rested the side of the needle against his throat.

"Shit," Aiden said. "Give me time and I may learn not to hate you for everything you've put us through. But if you pull this number, I hope you rot in hell."

Olivia cried openly and clung to Vanni.

"You're asking us to help you kill yourself," Aiden said. "I know you aren't into friendship, but shouldn't some shred of decency stop you from that, at least?"

"I'm not ready to give up on you, Vanni," Olivia said. "Give me a chance and I'll be there for you, whatever that means."

Vanni looked at the sky, and Aiden saw when the needle stopped pressing into the flesh of his neck.

"Me, too," Aiden said, although he didn't want to. He'd work on it, but he wasn't ready to forgive and forget yet.

Vanni broke down. He slipped to sit, hunched over, on the grass But he'd dropped the hypodermic.

Thirty-two

The elevator doors slid open, and Aiden waved Olivia ahead of him onto the observation deck. She'd never been to the Empire State Building before. He wasn't about to tell her, but neither had he.

An icy wind whipped against the few hardy souls determined to be able to say they'd been there.

Olivia jammed a green woolen hat well down and tied a brown scarf around it and under her chin. She made straight for the nearest telescope and crowded an eye against the viewfinder. After several minutes, she stepped away. "You get a better view of the lights without that, and you can't see anything else in the darkness anyway."

"It's worth it to come up here for the lights, though," he said, and meant it. The city shimmered beneath low-lying clouds.

"Okay, been here, done that," she told him. "Now I think we should make sure you go home and sleep for several days."

His heart rose. "Sounds like a great idea to me."

Her eyes slid away, and she turned from him. "People need time to get over shocks, and you've had some terrible shocks."

Aiden settled a hand on the back of her neck and said, "So have you."

"I know, and I intend to be smart about it all. We must both be."

"Oh, yes, Olivia. We must."

She stared at colored lights across the city until they blurred and ran together. What a fabulous place. It didn't matter that her nose and face were frozen, or that exhaustion made the inside of her head muzzy.

What mattered was that she was here in this magical, unreal place with Aiden—and the danger was past. She'd have to appear in court as a witness, but not for some time since Aiden had explained that cases like this took a great deal of preparation.

Aiden tried to see the city through her eyes. He'd lived here a very long time, but it still excited him. New York had its own energy. Every day it woke up like a lion, and when it finally quieted down, it was the lion who slept, but with one eye open.

Soon they were the only sightseers left on the deck and they stood, side by side, staring out through the safety wire that surrounded the area.

"Thank you for doing this," she said, "for bringing me up here even though you should be in bed."

"You wanted to come and I'm glad I did. We should both be in bed, and I'm not going there without you."

Olivia averted her face sharply. She would find the words that needed to be said now. Even if she stumbled over them, she would say them.

"Olivia, sweetheart, you keep clamming up on me. It's really cold. Let's go somewhere corny but cute, like the Rainbow Room. I'll buy you something hot and exotic to drink. And get you a meal."

He was making this so difficult, Olivia thought. "I'm packing you off home, Aiden. Thank you for caring so much about me. Your face is a mess. You're all beaten up. You must feel awful, but you're still worrying about making sure I see something of New York before I have to leave. But I'll be back one day, so I'll have another chance."

This was one complex lady. He knew she'd fallen as hard as he had. What he didn't know was just how convoluted a game she was playing in her head right now.

"Ah, I've got my second wind," he said. "I feel like an Irish Coffee and some Tiramisu."

At first Olivia looked aghast, but then she grinned. "Sounds good." The smile drifted away. "Don't you think we've got some talking to do? Serious talking that shouldn't be put off?"

He wanted to scoff and tell her they knew each other's hearts so why talk? "Yes, I suppose we do. I think I know where to go to do that."

"Not your place, Aiden."

"Not my place."

Once down on the street again, Aiden hailed a cab, opened the door for Olivia, and told the driver to take them to the St. Regis Hotel.

On the ride, Olivia concentrated on the scene they passed. It grew very late, and the hardy souls abroad were swathed in layers of clothing, except for those coming and going from fashionable nightspots in their chauffeur-driven cars and limousines.

They arrived at the St. Regis, and Aiden took pleasure in watching Olivia's sharp eyes assess her surrounds. They went to the King Cole Bar with its gorgeous, cherry-oak bar and leather chairs that invited patrons to sink in and stay. The room was crowded with expensively dressed people. Jewels winked and carefully made-up faces showed an animation so many people couldn't all be feeling. Men in evening dress smoked and discussed cigars over cognac.

Olivia leaned close and said, "I will only speak for myself, but I don't want them to think I'm a bag lady and throw me out."

He faced her, untied the scarf from around her hat, and took both off. These he tucked into his overcoat pocket.

"You're wearing a suit," she said, and sounded as if she were accusing him of cheating. "Your collar shines in the dark. You look as if you've got a fashionable couple of days of beard growth. And even if you do have a swollen nose and two black eyes starting every woman in the room is staring at you, dash it all."

He smiled down at her and placed a soft kiss at the corner of her mouth. Then he ran his fingers through her hair, fluffing up her dark curls. "Do you have a lipstick?"

"Yes," she said, but didn't sound happy. "I suppose I have to go and find a washroom and have a bunch of these women sneering at me."

"You're overreacting. Give me the lipstick."

She hesitated, but gave in and handed him a tube from her pocket. He took off the top, used a knuckle to tilt up her chin, and applied lipstick as if he were a makeup artist in his off hours. He made a second, slower pass, this time watching her mouth as if he'd never seen anything as fascinating before. His next kiss landed on the end of her nose. "Mascara."

"Oh, Aiden, we'll draw a crowd."

"You're the loveliest, sexiest woman in the room. Of course we'll draw a crowd. Mascara?"

She worked the much too large black bag from her shoulder and fished around inside until she found her scantily equipped makeup bag. She did have mascara, and this she handed to him.

"Good. Look up. That's a good girl. Now look down slowly. Very slowly, Olivia, to glide your lashes over the brush. I could really get into this. *Voila.* We make a hell of a team. Now the other eye."

"You've done this before," she accused him. "Are you sure you've never been married?"

He chuckled but enjoyed the hint of jealousy he heard. "Never. And I've never put on a woman's makeup, but I've seen it done on one of those makeovers on TV. You are gorgeous. I'm going to tie the scarf under the collar of your coat. You glow, know that?"

A woman in sparkling black and wearing a sable jacket passed by and made a low, purring noise at Aiden. To Olivia, she said, "You make me jealous. He's a dish and he's besotted. You lucky woman." She cast Aiden another look through lowered lashes before she was swallowed in the crowd.

"Why did we come here?" Olivia said.

"Because it's a nice place, and you should only be taken to nice places. And I can afford to take you to nice places. Quick. Two empty chairs."

They sprinted and claimed the chairs, despite a sensation that people were converging on the prize from all over the room. Once seated, Olivia felt unbearably warm and said, "Brace yourself," as she removed her coat, revealing another unlikely collection of borrowed clothing. At least she now had tennis shoes that fitted, even if they were black with silver stripes. And Vanni's sisters had sent over an assortment of clothing. Too bad Olivia had only considered the cold and selected sweats again, these matching. She rather liked herself in yellow, although the nylon fabric swished every time she moved, and the pants hung on her. She hitched them up and pulled the jacket down.

"You're one of a kind," Aiden said. "And I'm so glad. Ordinary women bore me."

"Who's that?" She pointed at a huge painting.

"Keep your voice down," Aiden hissed. "King Cole. That's the name of the bar, remember?"

"Nope. Didn't hear the name."

A waiter approached, apparently on wheels. "Champagne," Aiden said.

The waiter inclined his head and proceeded to make suggestions, finishing with the idea that they might be more comfortable with champagne cocktails.

"We'll be comfortable with a bottle," Aiden said. "You're clearly a man of developed taste. I confess I'm no expert. Please surprise us." He beckoned the man to lend him his ear and when he did so, whispered at length.

Nodding seriously, the waiter left.

Very quickly an array of desserts, some in individual chocolate or china dishes, arrived. They were displayed and described with sub-dued flourish—and the entire tray left on the table.

"We need to discuss some things," Olivia said.

"I know. And this is a good place because everyone is so involved with seeing who's seeing them, they couldn't care less about us. Talk away."

"Yes. Aiden, we came together by accident."

"Yes, and isn't that usually the way it happens?"

She would not let him distract her, not that she thought he was doing so deliberately. "This was different. I was in trouble, and you decided to help me, just as you would have helped anyone. Probably."

He scooped a spoonful of key lime filling from a chocolate shell and said, "But I don't think I'd have fallen in love with just anyone. I never have before. How about you?"

"Of course I haven't. This is the first time." She'd have liked to swallow her tongue.

"Just as I thought. Ah, here comes Lewis."

Lewis displayed a bottle of Dom Perignon with the reverence of the keeper of some sacred place. "I assure you, sir, that this is a masterpiece. I've heard people speak of its smoke, its presence, its unforgettable nose. Phooey, say I. This is a marvel bound to transport even the most spoiled among our clientele. I think you will find it most appropriate." He uncorked the bottle and smiled mysteriously through the faint smoky haze that rose above a thin rim of foam. He offered Aiden a small amount to taste. Aiden did so, and even his uneducated mouth knew it had suffered a taste treat.

"What do you think?" Lewis whispered.

Aiden smiled and said, "A wonder. Thank you."

Beaming broadly, Lewis poured for Olivia, then for Aiden, placed the bottle in a cooler, and backed away.

"Try it," Aiden said, wishing the butterflies attacking his insides would die.

Olivia did try, and she giggled. "Here we are like Fred and Ginger. It's really lovely. Thank you. Aiden, I'm not your type. You're much too full of life and too charismatic for me. Not, I know, that you have any idea of bowling me off my feet or anything like that. But I do think you want to be kind and try to give me a good time when we aren't under duress. It's not necessary. I shall always think of you with affection and—I might as well be honest—I think there will be some longing for me. After all, this staid woman has lived on the edge for a while."

That was when he made up his mind. Longing, huh? It was more than a good start, and he would be riding in after that like the cavalry. "I really like your parents."

"Huh." She appeared bemused.

"Your parents. I liked them, and they liked me. They're hoping you and I are more than a convenient fling. You've got to admit, sex between us is what some might call transporting."

"*Aiden.*"

"Well, it is. Drink more champagne. I don't want it to go flat."

She drank and wrinkled her nose, and drank some more.

"We do things together, in bed and in the shower, and in cars—who knows what possibilities there are—but we do things most people don't even imagine doing. And we're so good at them. Actually, you're the one who's so good at them. I swear you'd probably give me a blow job if I was under the sink fixing pipes."

Olivia appeared aghast. She looked up at two sleek men who were leaning so close, it was a miracle they didn't overbalance. One of them studied Olivia from head to foot, lingering at points in between, and Aiden noted the point when the guy started to get hard.

"You can buzz off," Olivia announced, shocking him. "Both of you."

Making a poor job of nonchalant smirks, the men did leave.

Aiden scooted close to her. "We are wonderful together, you know. And we like each other. Respect each other. We'd fight to the death for each other. I'd take on wild animals for you. But most of all, I'd like to know I'll never have to say good-bye to you because if I do, I don't know what will happen to me."

The tears that rushed into Olivia's eyes were a dratted nuisance. She straightened her shoulders. "Aiden, I'm an alien here. I have to return to England. We should give ourselves time to see if we continue to feel what we think we feel now. If we do, I'll apply for a green card. It might take quite a while for me to get it, but when I do, I could come and get established somewhere, and we could see if we still want to be together."

"You want to be with me now?"

"More than anything."

"I feel the same way."

"But we've been through so much. And anyway, I can't expect to live here without a job, and I can't work without the right papers."

"Looking after me will be a job. Believe me."

Olivia frowned at him. "Looking after you. You mean washing socks and making dinners and so on? I can't cook, Aiden, don't want to. I don't mind doing laundry, but not because someone else wants me to. And I like having my own money, even though I've never had much of it."

"I'll be happy for you to follow your career here," Aiden said. "And that wasn't the kind of looking after me I had in mind. I'm a pretty good cook, and I think men and women should share the load around the house—especially when children come. Of course, you haven't exactly said you'd want to have children."

"Of course I would. I absolutely love children."

"Good. I think we'll make great parents, don't you?"

"Oh, I do . . . you're railroading me, or trying to."

"Not at all," Aiden said. "I'm enthusiastic, that's all."

"There is a lot to think about," she told him. "And we don't know how long it would take to get the work permit."

"More champagne," he said, refilling her glass.

She drank again. "I don't want you to wait for me. Well, in fact I do want you to wait for me, but that wouldn't be fair."

"I love you, Olivia."

Instantly she turned sideways in her chair. "And I love you. I get the feeling that when I breathe out, I'd never breathe in again if you weren't there to make me want to."

"I rest my case." He pulled an odd hexagonal box, covered with worn red silk, from his pocket. "I don't have the faintest idea how you'll feel about this. I have an appointment to . . . Well I've got an appointment for us to see someone tomorrow. Here."

It was a fairly large box and seemed old. Hesitantly, Olivia took it from him, watched his face and the apprehension she saw there, and opened the gold clasp carefully.

That breath she'd mentioned jammed in her lungs, and she doubted it would ever move anywhere again.

"Well?"

"Good heavens. What do you expect me to say? I've never seen anything like it outside a jeweler's window."

"I told you how my father was. He wanted to be free, but he also wanted my mother. The gifts he gave her were amazing."

Olivia looked down at a ring reminiscent of an Egyptian masterpiece. Or perhaps Roman. The deep color of eighteen- or twenty-two-karat gold gleamed warmly. A large, square diamond claimed the center of the ring and was flanked by what she assumed to be pale emerald-cut topaz and green tourmaline.

Aiden took it from the box, raised her left hand and slipped the ring on the appropriate finger. "You've got such beautiful hands. if your fingers were short, it wouldn't look nearly so good. The white diamond is flawless. So are the yellows and greens."

"Yellows and greens?" she said.

"The colored diamonds. They call them fancies. It suits you, Olivia."

"I can't take it. It's too much."

"Who else should have it but my wife?"

Her head felt strange, and she felt pins and needles in her hands. "It's too soon."

"It isn't too soon. It might have been if some of the things that have happened to us hadn't happened, but they have. It's starting to get late. If you leave me, I'll follow you."

"You've got work to do," she pointed out.

He took another box, this one new, from another pocket and opened it. Inside was a simple man's yellow-gold wedding ring. "I like to move things along. This is for me. Like it?"

Now she really was in danger of crying. "It's perfect."

Aiden hailed the waiter and had another whispering episode with him. The man nodded frequently and stood aside while Aiden led Olivia from the bar. But rather than go outside, he went to the registration desk and picked up keys for a reservation that had already been made.

Olivia was too mortified to say a word.

On several floors, they changed elevators for one that required a card to rise all the way to the penthouse. Aiden held the door for her to get off, then opened the only pair of double doors in sight, the only suite in sight.

Sumptuous green-and-gold damask enveloped them, a living room furnished with French antiques, a bedroom with a vast bed draped like a Moorish tent with ribbons of green and gold caught into a coronet overhead.

A knock at the door heralded the arrival of a busboy with the rest of the bottle of champagne. He pushed a trolley from which he unloaded a number of exquisitely wrapped boxes. Vases of roses followed.

When they were finally alone, Olivia knelt by the bed and rested her head and arms on the counterpane.

Aiden poured champagne, piled boxes on the bed, and arranged the roses around the room, all the time keeping an eye on Olivia. She hadn't taken the ring off yet.

"How did you arrange all this?" Olivia asked, her voice muffled.

"Margy helped."

"A bit corny, isn't it?"

Aiden bent over her and said into her ear, "Women love this kind of thing. Don't pretend they don't. And I'm enjoying it, too."

He went into a bathroom large enough to accommodate a football team and ran a bath, pouring in salts that formed mountains of bubbles. A state-of-the-art stereo system occupied an alcove and he took his time selecting the smoky sound of Edith Piaf and a Ricky Martin song or two. Andrea Bocelli wasn't ignored, or the *Notting Hill* soundtrack. He grinned at that. Only appropriate.

"Who needs the bath?" Olivia asked from behind him. "You or me?"

"I don't really know. I just wanted to play with all this."

He looked at her, and his body flushed. She was naked, and so irresistible. She went to the tub, rested her weight on one leg and leaned to scoop up bubbles. These she piled on top of her head and giggled when she caught sight of herself in a mirror. "This woman loves all the fuss," she said.

"The bath's all yours if you like," he told her.

She sighed and studied the huge bath on its clawed feet. "I think I should be lonely in there. I play so much better with others."

All his resolutions to coddle her without giving his own needs a thought were showing signs of disintegrating.

Olivia climbed into the tub, and the pale pink bubbles accentuated the whiteness of her skin. When she sat down, suds adhered to some parts of her, but not others. Her breasts appeared to be supported but not covered. When she began to wash, raising first one, then the other leg from the tub, he feared he was about to fail all his bold promises and turn into an animal.

He stood over the bath and watched her.

"That's not nice," she said. "Peeping Tom."

"Peeping Toms don't peep when the subject can see them doing it. Will you marry me, Olivia?"

She paused and squeezed her eyes shut. "Maybe. Once my official status is in order and we've had a chance to be together under normal circumstances."

"Fair enough," he said. "Once we're married, your status will be official. And we're already together under normal circumstances."

"*Normal?* This?"

"Absolutely. There isn't a soul chasing us around and trying to kill us. And I'm wondering if we should live here for a few months."

Her mouth fell open.

"Maybe not. You should take part in choosing where we settle down. We probably ought to buy a house. After all, when we have children, we'll need the space."

"This is moving too fast for me."

"But you will marry me?"

She frowned and turned her attention to washing herself.

Aiden stripped off his clothes.

"That's not fair," Olivia said. "How am I supposed to think straight?"

"Avoid it, lover. At all costs, do not think straight. Is there room for me?"

She widened her eyes. "It's huge. Ridiculously huge."

Aiden sat on the edge of the tub with his feet in the water. Then he launched himself, landing like a whale and sending a tidal wave of pink-foam-decorated water all over the bathroom.

"You're impossible," Olivia said.

"I know. I like being impossible. Have I told you what talented feet I've got?"

She immediately tried to slide farther back in the tub. Aiden slid farther forward, draped his elbows over the sides, and lifted those talented feet. Smiling angelically, he caught her nipples between two toes on each foot and pinched just enough to make her squirm helplessly. She held the edge of the tub and arched her back. He bent forward from the waist and settled a thumb on her clitoris.

"Aiden Flynn! You are irresponsible and way too forward."

"I'd better stop then."

"Don't you dare."

"Will you marry me?"

"You've made the towels all wet."

Aiden rubbed his thumb back and forth, enjoying the way she sucked air through her teeth and tried to get closer to him. He slid a forefinger inside her and found the place that brought her bottom popping up from the tub.

She ran a foot up the inside of his right thigh and tangled her toes in his pubic hair, and she played with his tensed testicles.

"Now who's being forward and irresponsible."

"Oh, I'll stop at once."

He clasped her foot and helped it explore the whole enchilada.

Without warning, before she could form a complaint, Aiden rose over her, sending a fresh wave over the edge of the tub, and sank down until he could kiss her again and again. Each kiss only made him want to keep on kissing her.

And while they kissed, Olivia guided him into her. He burned. The slippery movement of her breasts against his chest inflamed him more—if that were possible.

He wrapped her close, and with his feet against the end of the tub, set up a rhythm that set them both panting and crying out. She climaxed and clung to him, her fingernails digging into his skin. Aiden was only seconds behind her, and he knew it could not be enough. He would never get enough of her.

"You," he whispered in her ear, "are the love I was waiting for. I didn't know I was, but I do now."

She wriggled from beneath him and climbed, shivering, from the tub. She dried off, then took another dry bath sheet and held it out, gesturing for him to come to her.

Aiden went and let her envelope and rub him down while her own towel fell to the tiled floor. She didn't miss a millimeter of him, and when he was dry, she walked, comfortable with her nakedness, to get him a robe. She helped him into this and didn't complain when he wrapped her inside with him, pulled her to stand on his feet, and walked with her back to the bedroom where he kept hold of her and climbed into bed.

"Sleep?" he asked.

"Uh-huh."

He poked her ribs, and she cried out. "Why did you do that?"

"You can't sleep yet. Just a minute." He turned the lights on and selected a rose. Kneeling beside her, he played the soft rose petals over her face, smiled when her nose wiggled, and applied the tickling strokes to every inch of her. She began to squirm and wiggle and bat at the rose.

"Stop torturing me."

"I will when you stop torturing me."

"I'm not."

He parted her legs and applied rose kisses to the insides of her thighs. "What do you call it?" he asked. "When you admit you love me, that you love being with me, making love to me? You want to have my children? You don't want to be without me? But you won't marry me—now?"

"I call it common sense."

"I call it cruelty. If you leave me, I shall go into a decline and lose my job for sure. By the time you come back, if you come back, I'll be a shadow of my former self and past help."

Olivia pushed him to his back, giggling, and proceeded to take him into her mouth. In a very few minutes, she'd achieved her aim and he was thrashing back and forth until he let go and felt the life flow out of him.

She stretched out on top of him and licked salt from his neck. "Aiden," she said.

"Mm."

"Do you still feel the same?"

He grew quite still. Women. They were such a puzzle. "Feel the same how?"

"You'll go into a decline if I return to Britain?"

"There isn't any doubt. A total decline."

"I see." She opened her legs and clamped his between them, making sure his penis rested against hair. "How many times do you think you could do this—in a short space of time, I mean?"

"Is this a test?"

"It's a question. I'm curious."

"Well, I don't think I'm quite ready to go again now, if that's what you mean."

"That's what I meant. I'm not ready either. So I guess that means we're really compatible."

"Uh-huh." Except he was going to have to teach her not to talk so much.

"Would you marry me, Aiden Flynn?"

"Huh?" He kept completely still.

"I said, marry me. I think I've protested long enough. One mustn't seem too eager about these things."

He clamped her face against his chest and kissed the top of her head. "You're right, over-eagerness puts you in a weak bargaining position. I know the minister at a church near my apartment. A pretty church. Good people there."

"Sounds nice." Yet again the tears flowed, and there wasn't a thing she could do about them.

"Good. The minister has this sliding scale. The sooner the wedding, the higher the fees. Today's Thursday. What do you say to Saturday?"

"Can we afford it?"

"Sure. As long as we throw in season tickets to the Mets, we'll probably still be able to buy dog food for Boss when he gets back."

"Sounds good. Personally, I don't need food."

"Me either. At least until I open the window shades one day and can't stop myself from rolling up inside them."

"Aiden," Olivia said, grimacing, "that's such an old joke."

They didn't marry on Saturday. The minister was out of town, so the ceremony was a week later. Boswell had arrived back, but Olivia wouldn't hear of his being the ring bearer.

Mama Zanetto went to the wedding and cried, as did her daughters. Olivia rather thought the daughters cried because they considered that Aiden should have married a nice Italian girl. Mama cried, she was sure, for her son and the possibility that she'd never dance at his wedding.

Chris was best man. Sonnie stood up for Olivia and looked beautiful in pale mauve silk. She carried a single white rose in one hand, and baby Joan in the other arm. Anna sat on the altar steps and practiced singing her ABCs.

Conrad and Millicent FitzDurham flew over for the festivities, and Olivia's brother, Theo, came with them. Conrad gave Olivia away. Millicent cried. To Olivia, Theo revealed his disappointment at her marrying a man who would always be beneath her. Olivia told him she thought that was often the most comfortable situation between husband and wife, although on occasion experimentation could be good for a couple.